Harry Hall

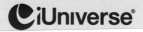

PRIDE AND PASSION

iUniverse books may be ordered through booksellers or by contacting:

iUniverse
1663 Liberty Drive
Bloomington, IN 47403
www.iuniverse.com
1-800-Authors (1-800-288-4677)

ISBN: 978-1-4917-9807-2 (sc)
ISBN: 978-1-4917-9808-9 (e)

Library of Congress Control Number: 2016910440

Print information available on the last page.

iUniverse rev. date: 08/31/2016

To my stepson, Bob, who has been serving our country in the US Navy for ten years. I think he may be the best young man I have ever known. He has always been a supporter and a fan.

To my beautiful wife, Peggy, for making me a better man and helping me deal with my own pride and passion. She has taught me how to love and inspired me to complete *Pride and Passion*.

Contents

Acknowledgments

To Kathi Wittkamper, my editorial consultant. I enjoyed our many long conversations. Your knowledge, understanding, and crazy sense of humor made the task of bringing *Pride and Passion* to fruition a fun ride.

To my niece, Kim, who read the unfinished manuscript and gave me her keen insight.

To Tracie Turner, who typed and read most of the early manuscript and became immersed in it. When she finished her work, she sent me a beautiful card that touched me deeply. I am thankful for her special friendship and honesty.

Prologue

Stratford, West Virginia, May 22, 1959

Penny Kilmer stood in the back of the shoe store and opened the last huge box in a new delivery of shoes. She pulled out a shoebox, opened it to see the style, and admired the shiny patent leather sandal before she began putting boxes of them on the shelves in order of size. When she finished and turned around, Mr. Alan Grant, the store owner, was standing behind her with a big grin on his face.

"I guess it's just the two of us here now," he said. "I've already locked the front door. Would you like a drink?"

"No, thanks," she said, knowing it was inappropriate for him to ask, as she wasn't of drinking age. She glanced at her watch and realized the store had been closed for fifteen minutes.

Mr. Grant retrieved a bottle of vodka from the top drawer of one of the filing cabinets and took several long swallows straight from the bottle.

"I have to go now," Penny said.

"Stay a few minutes," he said. "I want to talk to you. Sit." He pointed to the old blue sofa he had pushed against the back wall.

"You're drinking. We can talk later. Unlock the front door for me," she said as she headed for the doorway to the sales floor.

He followed and pushed her onto an old sofa he kept to the right of the doorway, the one he napped on occasionally while others worked the front. He had a cold look in his eyes that scared her. Penny tried to get up and run, but a large hand reached out and grabbed her hair. She screamed and tried to kick and hit, but he locked one arm around her and held her like a rag doll. Then she sensed him rummaging in his pockets, heard a click, and knew what it was. Mr. Grant kept an old switchblade to cut tape and open shipping boxes, and he was always sharpening and fooling with it like a kid.

He pulled her head back, held the knife in front of her face, and said, "Take your clothes off. We're going to have some fun." He made her strip naked and lie on the sofa. Then he was over her. He kissed, fondled, and sucked her breasts for what seemed like hours. Then he just pulled his pants down and tried to get inside her. He laughed and said she was tight and kept sticking his fingers in her. It hurt, but nothing like when he put his penis in her.

She lay there and focused on a cobweb on the ceiling. He was heavy, and she felt like she couldn't breathe, and he kept mumbling something. When he finally got up, she thought he was finished, but then he made her get on her hands and knees on the sofa, and he took her again from behind.

After he climaxed, he said, "This was all your fault, you little whore, you trashy little slut. You come in here shaking that little ass in front of me, so that's what you get."

Stunned, Penny started to get up, but he stepped back and kicked her. She went over the back of the sofa and ended up on the floor. She could see blood on the inside of her thighs.

Then Mr. Grant came around the sofa. Thinking he was going to kick her or kill her, she curled up to protect herself. He grabbed her by the hair and yanked her to her knees. He showed her the knife again and then put it to her throat and just held it there for a long time. He finally took the knife away and said he knew just what she needed. He stepped up close to her, and she could see the blood on his penis. He slapped her on the side of the head and told her what to do and how to do it.

"If you hurt me," he said, "I'll cut your fucking throat."

Penny began to shake as if an arctic wind were blowing only on her. He put the knife back against her throat with one hand and held her hair in a knot with the other, and then he made her take his penis into her mouth.

When he finally let her go, after threatening to kill someone dear to her if she told, Penny was in a state of shock. Her thoughts were so jumbled, and she believed Mr. Grant would do just what he said if she reported the rape. She thought of her boyfriend, Tyler Harrison, and figured he would kill Mr. Grant if he found out. She'd heard his grandmother tell a story about how he'd killed two roosters that had pecked his legs when he was only five years old, and she could imagine the rage he'd feel if he knew about the rape. She couldn't let him ruin his future on account of scum like Mr. Grant. On top of that, she thought he might not want her if he found out she wasn't a virgin anymore. She knew his pride.

Then a chilling thought hit her: *What if I get pregnant?* The shame she'd face would be overwhelming. If that happened, the only way to hold her life together would be to convince Tyler the baby was his so he'd marry her. Somehow, she'd have to get cleaned up before their date that night and convince him to have sex with her, even though they'd decided to wait until much later, after they were in college. She had to make him think *he* had taken her virginity.

Chapter 1

A Movie Date

Tyler picked Penny up in his dad's car, and they went to see *Pillow Talk* with Rock Hudson and Doris Day at the drive-in theater. Afterward, they had a burger with some friends at the local hangout, and Tyler noticed that Penny was unusually quiet and reserved. They drove around a little and then parked in the gravel parking lot behind a little country church, well off the main road, where they had parked many times before. They would talk, listen to the car radio, and do some heavy kissing, but no more. Well, maybe a little more.

They started kissing, as usual. Tyler had his forearm against Penny's breast and could feel her nipple beneath the fabric. She arched her back and pushed her breast hard against his arm. Suddenly, she took Tyler's hand and slid it onto her breast. He was surprised and a little tentative. He soon realized that she wouldn't have done it if she hadn't wanted it there.

He had been in other relationships and had already had sex with two girls and one older woman, so he knew his way around the female anatomy. Tyler was pleased but still had no desire to rush her.

Her breasts were neither large nor small. They were very firm, and her nipples were like little hard pebbles. Tyler cupped and squeezed her breasts through her blouse.

After a while, he began to alternate that with squeezing just her nipples between his thumb and forefinger. Penny's breathing became faster, and her kissing grew more passionate. She began to undo the buttons on the front of her blouse.

A little startled, Tyler removed his hand and asked, "Penny, what's wrong? You haven't been yourself all evening."

Penny began to cry. "I quit my job at the shoe store."

"When?"

"Just after the store closed today."

He said, "I thought you needed the money for college."

"I do."

"So, why would you quit?"

Penny sniffled and said, "Because Alan Grant is a drunken asshole."

Tyler frowned and asked, "What did he do?"

"Nothing," she said. "I'm just tired of his liquor breath and having to do everything while he sleeps on that sofa in the stockroom." Then she took his hand and put it back on her breast.

Tyler pulled back and asked, "Are you sure about this?"

"What's wrong, Tyler? Don't you like my breasts?"

"Yes, I like them. They feel great! I just don't want you to do anything you're not comfortable with, that's all. Are you sure?"

"Yes, Tyler, I'm very comfortable with it. I love you." She began to undo the rest of her shirt buttons. She pulled the blouse out of her shorts and leaned forward. "Unfasten my bra."

Tyler reached both hands behind her back and quickly unhooked Penny's bra, and she slid it off. When she leaned back against the seat, he began to kiss her again. He started to feel her breasts again. It was the first time he had ever touched her bare breasts. They were perfect, so firm and smooth. Tyler became aware that Penny was making little moaning sounds.

"Take me, Tyler. I want to feel you inside me."

He was so surprised by her new openness that he could hardly believe it. He took his hands away and stammered, "Penny, I ... I can't. We've talked about this before ... waiting till later, when we're in college and all."

"Tyler, how much do you love me?"

"All I can. You know that. We're perfect for each other."

"Then why haven't you tried harder to have sex with me?"

"Sex isn't love. Almost every couple we know is having sex, and they never stay together. I'll tell you another reason. My dad always says most guys walk around with their brains in the end of their penis. I refuse to be like that."

Penny turned toward Tyler and said, "Two years is a long time to wait for sex at our age." She reached out, grasped Tyler's hands, placed them on her breasts, and said, "I'm ready."

"For what?"

"To have sex. Let's do it now."

"What? No way!"

She pressed her breasts more firmly into his hands. "You know you want me."

He pulled his hands back quickly. "No. Not now, and not like this."

"What the hell is wrong with you?" she asked.

"Nothing, Penny! I'm trying to be the reasonable one. You've been upset all night, but you won't tell me why. I don't have a condom. I don't want to be a dad, and I want our first time to be special."

Penny began to cry. She pulled away, turned partly around, and slipped her bra back on. "Fasten it," she said.

She held it in place while Tyler hooked it. She turned and began to button her blouse. Tyler sat back behind the steering wheel and tried to make some sense of the last few minutes.

Finally, after what seemed like hours, Penny asked, "Did you enjoy that?"

"Penny, I love you. Of course, I enjoyed that."

"How stupid do you think I am, Tyler? I know you've dated other girls. Girls are just like guys. We talk too. I know exactly what you did with those other girls. You felt their breasts, and you screwed them. Now I want to try sex, and you stall out on me? I hope to hell you enjoyed these breasts tonight. Try to remember how good they felt, because it will be the last time you ever touch them!"

Tyler leaned forward to touch Penny. He wanted to settle her down and attempt to find out what had upset her. It was a dark night, and with no lights on in the car, he could barely see her.

Suddenly, she slapped him so hard he saw a fireworks display in front of his eyes. The vision in his left eye was blurred, but his immediate concern was his left ear. The ringing was almost unbearable. He wondered if his eardrum had burst or if he had sustained inner ear damage.

His first impulse was to slap her face, but he had no use for men who hit women. His second impulse was to go around the car, drag her out of the car, and leave her ass right there. But he knew that even though he was angry with her, he could not leave her stranded. It was late and dark, and they were eight miles from her home in town.

"Damn it, Penny! That's it. Your ass is going home."

She glared at him as he spoke. "Good! Listen very carefully, Tyler. After two years, I offered you my body. Never again! You're going to regret this for a long time."

After a silent fifteen-minute ride, Tyler stopped the car in front of her house. Penny had cried most of the way. As soon as he stopped the car, Penny grabbed her purse and jumped out. Once out, she turned and leaned back into the car.

"Tyler, don't call me and don't come around. I have nothing else to say to you." Then she backed away and slammed the door.

Tyler put the shift lever into drive and started to mash the accelerator to the floor, but he always hated it when other teenagers did that, so he sat quietly for a few seconds and then slowly drove away.

He went to a little twenty-four-hour diner. Inside, he seated himself in the corner booth and ordered coffee. He was so angry that he was shaking and had to be careful as he drank his coffee. He needed to settle down and think. No matter which mental route he tried, he always ran into a dead end. Penny's actions just made no sense to him. She had acted like a different person. He was convinced that their relationship was over. His assessment was that he had three problems. First, he was too proud to go back or accept her if she wanted to come back. Second, she had hurt him deeply, and he knew the hurt would last for years. Third, though he hated to admit it, he still loved her.

Chapter 2

A Job Offer Falls Through

1963

Tyler Harrison parked his new red-and-white Chevy pickup outside the offices of Nash Builders in Clinton, Maryland. Today, June 3, 1963, would mark the beginning of a new era in Tyler's life, and he was excited. He planned to become a large building contractor in the Washington, DC, area. He felt like a sprinter at the beginning of the race with his foot in the starting block.

He went inside and smiled at Geena, the receptionist, who was on the phone. She smiled and winked. Geena was just as cute as he had remembered. Her hair was dark and cut in a short, curly style. She had a pretty face highlighted by dark, mischievous eyes.

When she finished her call, she said, "Welcome back, stranger. Aren't you a little early?"

"Yes, I am. I wanted time to see if your legs were as nice as I remembered."

Geena laughed. She turned sideways, slipped her foot out of her shoe, pointed her toes, and raised her skirt to a little above the knee. Her toenails were polished, and her legs were tan and smooth.

She looked up and asked, "Well, what do you think?"

He leaned forward and took a long, serious look. He then frowned and said, "I think the legs I remember were thinner. Have you gained weight?"

"I most certainly have not gained any weight. Maybe you need glasses." She raised her skirt a couple of inches more and said, "Come closer and get a better look."

Tyler had forgotten what a great sense of humor Geena had. He came closer until he was only a couple of feet away. When he leaned over, he could smell her. He wasn't sure if it was perfume, hair spray, or shampoo, but it was clean, and he liked it.

"You may be right, Geena. These legs look much better up close. As a matter of fact, they look great!"

"Well now, that's much better." Geena dropped her skirt, slipped her foot back in her shoe, and said, "If you would like to see these legs again, you could invite their owner to dinner. She is currently unattached."

Tyler was surprised but also pleased. He had just assumed that she would be dating someone. "Okay. Why don't we have dinner this evening?"

"That sounds great. Let me give you my phone number and address." She reached for a memo pad and quickly wrote down the information. "Here. I'll be there any time after 5:30 this evening. It's only about two miles from here."

Tyler took the address and said, "I hope you don't mind riding in a pickup truck. It's new, and it's clean."

"Heavens, no. I love pickup trucks. My dad has had one for years. I can drive one too—even if it has a clutch."

"Okay. I'll call you around six, after I get settled in. I just drove in this morning from West Virginia. Now that we have that settled, will you let Mr. Nash know I'm here for our meeting?"

"Well, okay, but I would really rather talk." She dialed the number for Mr. Nash's office and waited for him to pick up. "Mr. Nash, Tyler Harrison has just come in from West Virginia and is ready to see you." Suddenly, her expression changed, and she looked shocked. She said, "But, Mr. Nash, I would rather you tell him." There was a pause while she listened, and then she said, "Yes, sir."

Tyler watched as she broke the connection. "Geena, what's wrong?"

"Mr. Nash wants me to give you a message, and I don't want to do it. He told me if I didn't, I could find another job."

"Look, Geena, I don't want you to lose your job because of me, so what's the message?"

Geena answered, "I still don't understand, but he said to tell you that the superintendent's position has been filled, and there is no job here for you. He also said to tell you he was sorry for any inconvenience and would be happy to recommend you to another employer."

"Is that all he said? He didn't offer any explanation for his sudden change of heart?"

"No, Tyler. I'm sorry. That's all he said."

*　　*　　*

The pickup motor was running. Tyler was sitting in the parking lot, trying to understand what had just happened. He had worked for Nash Builders as a carpenter the past two summers, while he was still attending college. Mr. Nash had liked his work and promised him full-time employment when he had graduated from college. In late March, he had made a five-hour trip to Maryland to talk with Mr. Nash. They had agreed that Tyler would start work in June as a superintendent at a job site in Clinton, Maryland, with a starting salary of $150 per week with full benefits and possible bonuses. That was $7,800 per year! Could he have misunderstood?

He figured he could quickly find another job, because two weeks earlier he had received his degree, with honors, from Winfield College. Tyler was now the proud owner of a bachelor's degree in business with a double major in accounting and economics. Still, the salary Nash had offered would be difficult to match, and he most likely wouldn't start as a superintendent anywhere else. He had liked the idea of starting a little ways up the ladder instead of on the bottom rung. What the hell had he done to cause Mr. Nash to change his mind?

For the umpteenth time, he remembered what his grandpa had often said. "Today is the first day of the rest of your life, so don't waste it and try to do a little good." Tyler had a temper like anyone, but he always tried not to act out when he was angry. He knew it clouded the judgment, and he usually regretted what he said or did when angry. It occurred to him that what he had done to change Mr. Nash's mind was nothing. He had done nothing wrong. For some reason, Mr. Nash had just decided not to hire him, and although that didn't seem right, it was not what made him mad. Not letting him know until he had driven all the way here and threatening to fire Geena if she wouldn't deliver the bad news was part of what made him mad. But what really made him mad was the fact that Mr. Nash would not tell him face to face.

He knew a confrontation with Mr. Nash would not get him the job. That was okay, because he no longer wanted the job. Tyler also knew that if he did not confront Mr. Nash, the anger would eat away at him for years. As his grandpa would say, "It would just stick in your craw."

When he entered the office the second time, Tyler didn't speak to Geena or smile. He just walked past her desk and down the hall. When Tyler reached the door to Mr. Nash's office, he realized that his anger was about out of control. He paused for a few seconds and reminded himself to hold it in check. When he had calmed down some, he pushed open the door and entered. Mr. Nash was seated behind a large, messy desk. When Tyler saw there was no one else in the office except Nash and himself, he closed the door. He then walked to the front of the desk and stopped. He didn't say anything. He just stood there and stared at Nash.

Nash said, "I can see that you're very upset, Tyler. Just settle down some and have a seat."

Tyler never broke eye contact. "I'll stand."

"Okay, suit yourself. What do you want?"

Tyler leaned forward and put both fists on the front edge of the desk. "I want an explanation, and I want it from you, not the receptionist. I want it now, and I don't intend to leave until I get it."

"Okay, okay. I guess you deserve that. Before I offered the superintendent's job to you, I offered it to a thirty-five-year-old man with fifteen years' experience. He turned it down, because he was taking another job. He called me last week and said he didn't like it there and asked if the superintendent's position was still available. Tyler, this is nothing against you, but he has fifteen years' experience as a superintendent, and he is willing to work for the same salary you were going to get. Now, I ask you, if you were me, what would you have done?"

"I've always tried to be a man of my word. You figure it out." He walked to the door, turned back toward Nash, and said, "You know, Nash, I'm only half your age, but I'm already twice the man you are. I feel sorry for you."

When he reached Geena's outer office, he stopped, twisted his head sideways, and took another look at her legs. "I look forward to this evening," he said. "I'll call around six."

Chapter 3

—❦—

A New Place to Live

yler parked his pickup truck at the new McDonald's, which was located just across the road from the main entrance to Andrews Air Force Base. He needed to sit down with a cold Coke, gather his thoughts, and formulate a new plan. He was not in a panic, because he had money and a place to live. After he'd had his Coke, he walked over to a phone booth and looked at the listing of building contractors in the phone book. He tore out the pages and stuffed them in his pocket. Tomorrow, he'd start contacting them.

He thought of his friend Nick who had bought the pizza business he'd owned during his college years and wondered how he was doing. Tyler had borrowed $12,000 to start that business and had sold it for $30,000, which was an excellent deal for Nick. After making about $25,000 per year for three and a half years and selling the place for $30,000, he had taken in $120,000. When he had paid off the balance of his loan, paid all of his taxes, purchased his new pickup, and subtracted all the money he had spent for rent, furniture, and clothes, he still had $75,000 and change in the bank. Tyler smiled and wondered if Mr. Nash had any idea how little his failure to keep his word had affected him.

It was exciting to be in the Washington area again. He loved his hometown and would like to return there some day to live, but it was a thrill to be so near the nation's capital. He liked to read the *Washington Post*. The Redskins had become his favorite football team. Just looking at the main gate of Andrews Air Force Base reminded him that the president's plane, Air Force One, was hangered there.

When Tyler was in the DC area, he felt like he had his finger on the pulse of the nation. He found it impossible to be depressed here. Everywhere he looked there was rapid growth. New homes, more businesses, and new roads were springing up everywhere. The *Washington Post* residential section had predicted that the DC suburbs would be the fastest-growing area in the United States for the next decade. The Washington metro area was like an elixir to Tyler, and he was impatient to drink his fill of success. The opportunities in this area were limitless, and he was sure he would grow his $75,000 nest egg into much more.

Tyler noted the time and thought about all he had to do before dinner. As he prepared to leave, two young, attractive girls parked and headed in for burgers.

Penny Kilmer instantly came to mind. This had been happening for the past four years. Every time he met or was attracted to a new girl, he would compare her to Penny, and the new prospect would fall short. Penny had been gorgeous, smart, honest, and blessed with an abundance of poise and class. Yet, she had still managed a good sense of humor. She had been the love of his life. All this made it more confusing when he tried to understand what had happened. She and Tyler had gone steady during their junior and senior years in high school. He had dated other girls before her, but he had only loved her. Penny was unique and still occupied a rather large space in his confused male brain.

One week after their breakup, Tyler had been waxing a car in the garage at home. He looked up and saw Penny walking up the street. His heart skipped about ten beats. She was wearing a halter top, short white shorts, and sandals. Damn, she looked good! Those long, tanned, perfect legs demanded attention no matter where they were. Tyler had dropped his head and pretended not to see her. She turned and started up the driveway and didn't stop until she was in the shade of the garage.

"Hi, Tyler," she had said.

He'd known that if he kept his mouth shut, he couldn't make a mistake and say the wrong thing. There was no way he would let her know how much he was hurting. Tyler kept his head down and continued to apply wax.

"It won't hurt you to speak to me, Tyler."

He dabbed his pad into the wax and started working on a fresh area. Then Penny began to cry.

"I know how proud you are. Pride is usually a good thing, and it has helped to make you the good person that you are. But sometimes you need to put it aside. Sometimes it gets in the way. You don't have to say you're sorry. What happened between us was all my fault. My behavior that night was wrong, and I'm sorry. Tyler, what we had was special. Please don't throw it away."

Tyler had not responded. For the first time in his life, he was feeling love and hate toward the same person at the same time. He loved her, and he knew it. He also hated her for what she had done to him and their relationship.

Penny slowly walked around the car and came toward him. She lightly placed her hand on his arm and said, "I love you, Tyler, and I want you back. I won't give up until I have you." Then she had turned and walked out of the garage.

When the two girls came back outside with cups in their hands, Tyler glanced at his watch again and realized he'd better get moving.

Tyler was amused at his level of excitement as he approached his new apartment. The sign ahead of him protruded from a large brick planter filled with shrubs and flowers. It read "Keystone Place." Keystone Place was a large garden apartment complex that rambled around through a beautiful wooded area in Camp Springs, Maryland. The complex had a total of 240 apartments. There were twenty-four buildings with ten apartments in each. The buildings were all separate and had their own parking lots. Some buildings had all three-bedroom apartments; some had only two-bedroom units, while most contained only one-bedroom apartments. All the buildings had three floors. The bottom floor had a laundry room, a large storage area for people in that building, and two apartments. The second and third floors had four apartments each. Every apartment had a large sliding glass door and a nice terrace with a railing off the living room.

Last summer, while working as a lead carpenter for Nash Builders, Tyler had seen the soon-to-open signs for Keystone Place. He had checked it out and was very pleased with the location. The price was a little high, but it was the nicest apartment complex in the area. During spring break, when he had come to meet with Mr. Nash, he had picked out his two-bedroom apartment and signed a one-year lease. It was completed and ready for occupancy on the first of May. Tyler had paid rent for May and June in advance, and although he couldn't move in till now, he felt it was worth it to get the apartment he wanted.

Tyler parked in one of the spaces marked for visitors and hurried up the steps to the rental office.

The receptionist said, "Mr. Harrison. Good to see you again."

Tyler was surprised that she had remembered his name.

"Thanks. I'm looking forward to getting settled in."

After some small talk, the receptionist came around the desk. She handed him a thick green envelope. "Everything you need should be in there. Your new keys are in there too. There are two keys to the apartment, which also fit the laundry room; two keys for your mailbox; and two keys that fit your area in the storage room. Welcome to Keystone Place."

His building was located between the pool and tennis courts. Tyler was pleased to see many empty parking spaces in his lot and parked in a wide one at the end. He took the green envelope and one of the two suitcases stacked on the passenger side and headed for his new home. It felt good to have his very own apartment six miles from the nation's capital.

He had rented apartment number 302 for two reasons. First, it was on the top floor, and he wouldn't have to worry about noise from an apartment above. The other reason was his terrace—it faced the trees instead of the parking lot. Poised at his door with key in hand, he mentally crossed his fingers and hoped he would find everything there. He had paid a man his dad had recommended to deliver everything to his apartment. The man had returned late last Saturday night and called to say the job was finished, and all had gone well.

He was pleased with his initial survey. Everything seemed to be there and undamaged. The furniture was in the middle of the living and dining room areas. The boxes had been marked for certain rooms and appeared to all be there. Tyler went to the larger bedroom and opened the door to the walk-in closet. All of his clothes on hangers were there. The mover had even put the mattress, box spring, and bedroom furniture in the correct bedroom. Tyler made a mental note to call and thank him when he was back in Stratford.

Tyler checked the temperature and then turned the air conditioner a couple of degrees cooler. He tried the sliding door and stepped out on the terrace where he could enjoy the sunrise with a cup of coffee in the morning and have the cooler shade in the evening. He tried the phone and was pleased to hear the familiar dial tone. He checked his watch and saw that it would soon be time to call Geena.

He remembered his other suitcase still in the truck and hurried out to get it. With suitcase in hand, he started back up the stairs and noticed the mailboxes. He liked the little brass plate with his name that had been attached to his box. He had his keys with him and decided to make sure they worked. He was surprised to find mail. There were four or five pieces of junk mail and a letter. He smiled when he saw the return address and the familiar script. He hurriedly sat down on the steps and tore open the envelope. What he found were two separate letters—one from his mother, which he expected, and one from his father, which was totally unexpected. He guessed his mom had sent them so he wouldn't be lonely.

Her letter was all on one page. It was sweet and full of don't-forget-to-do advice. The other letter was a first. He had never received a letter from his dad. His eyes got a little moist when he read it. Harold had written two pages that were full on both sides. He had opened his heart and told Tyler how proud he was of him, how much he loved him, and how much he would miss not having him around every day. His father had never been very affectionate and tended to hide his feelings. It was for this reason that Tyler felt all warm inside and was reading the letter for the second time when he noticed two pairs of high-heeled shoes in front of him. He looked up and saw two attractive women—a redhead and a blonde. He guessed they were around forty.

Tyler realized that he was blocking the stairs. He rose quickly and said, "I'm sorry. I didn't see you."

The redhead asked, "Are you moving in here?"

Tyler answered, "Yeah, I'll be in 302."

"Oh, you lucky thing," she said. "We're in 301, so we'll be your neighbors. My name is Alice Newman, and this is Tracy Allen. We both work at the Department of Agriculture."

"Well, hello neighbors, it's nice to meet you both. I'm Tyler Harrison."

Alice, who had done all the talking, was the redhead. She had a beautiful porcelain complexion, and her red hair was long, straight, and shiny and parted in the middle. Alice was maybe an inch over five feet and ten to fifteen pounds heavy. The weight was all in the right places, though, and she was sweet and vivacious. Tyler liked her right away.

Tracy was six or seven inches taller than Alice and very thin. She was wearing a double-breasted light-blue blouse buttoned to the neck, and there was no protrusion where the breasts should have been. Her blonde hair was thin, straight, and chopped off just above the shoulders with a few wispy bangs over the forehead. Her face was pretty with a long, straight nose, but she kept her eyes down. Tyler didn't know if she was shy or if she just couldn't get a word in edgewise when she was with Alice.

Tracy managed to lift her eyes and asked, "Did you get a Dear John letter from your girlfriend? You looked a little wet-eyed when we first saw you."

"No. The letter is from my mom and dad. They mailed it out a few days ago, so I would have mail to open my first day here. I guess they were worried about me being homesick."

"Oh, wow! That is so sweet! You don't have to worry with Tracy and me around. We won't let you get depressed. Will we, Tra?"

Tyler laughed, and they started up the stairs. By the time they got to the third floor, he felt like he had known them his whole life.

Alice asked, "So, Tyler, where are you from?"

"A small town in West Virginia—Stratford."

"Oh shit! Really?" Alice laughed. "We're both from Fairmont, which is, what? About an hour away? We graduated from West Virginia University way back in 1944."

Tyler also laughed with some surprise. "I knew it. I could tell you two were good-ole mountain women right away." Tyler opened his door so Alice and Tracy could see his bachelor pad.

"Wow, what a mess," Alice said. "Hey, Tracy and I are on vacation this week. Let us help you get organized."

Tyler said, "That's really nice, but you don't have to do that."

Tracy laughed. "It's the least we could do for a good-ole West Virginia boy."

Tyler told them about his dinner date and then headed for the shower. Afterward, he hurriedly dressed in oxford loafers, light-gray summer slacks, and one of his burgundy golf shirts. When he returned to call Geena, he found a living and dining room he could barely get through. Alice and Tracy were now barefoot and clad in shorts and baggy T-shirts. They had opened wine, emptied the boxes, and were filling the kitchen cabinets. Tyler joined them, and they spent the next few minutes enjoying the wine and each other. Before Tyler left, he realized that he needed to purchase a number of things for the apartment. They agreed to go shopping together in the morning and then spend most of the day getting the place livable.

Chapter 4

An Evening Out and
the Aftermath

When Tyler arrived at Geena's apartment, she was ready and ran out before he could go in to get her. As he went around to open the passenger door, he was a little dazzled with her appearance. She looked fresh and innocent. Her hair was shiny and bouncy, and her little red sandals flopped loudly as she hurried toward the truck. Tyler especially liked her dress. It was, he thought, what women called a sundress. The hem fell just below her knees. It had two narrow straps over her exposed shoulders, and its skirt flared out in an A-line shape. What he liked most was where the straps ended. The dress was very low-cut. It was white with large red polka dots and made her tan look even darker.

Geena asked, "Are you hungry?"

He patted his stomach and said, "I'm starved. By the way, you look very nice. I like the dress."

She smiled and said, "Me too. I look great in it, don't I?" Before he could respond, she leaned over and kissed him on the cheek. "Hey, you smell good!" she said. She hiked up her skirt, stepped up into the truck, and slid onto the seat. "I like your new truck, Tyler. It matches my dress."

*   *   *

Tyler had observed on more than one occasion that Geena had mischievous eyes. Now, as the candlelight danced across them, he noticed it again. Her eyes were like a harbinger to the real Geena. He guessed that was most likely true of everyone. For an instant, he wondered what opinions she had formed from looking into his eyes.

Geena had selected Winners for their evening of food and drink. Tyler liked it. They served steak and seafood with candlelight and cloth napkins without being too formal. They had just enjoyed filet mignon and lobster tails with an excellent bottle of cabernet sauvignon.

Geena placed her empty wineglass back on the table. "I hate to leave you for even a moment, but every lady must occasionally powder her nose. Will you excuse me?"

Tyler stood and went to pull out her chair. He said, "Take your time. I'll be right here."

As she stood up, most of her small breasts were visible at the top of her red-and-white sundress. When she was walking away, he had a brief mental picture of Penny in the same dress and wondered how she would look. He returned to his seat and made a mental note to stop comparing every female to Penny. It was not fair to Geena to compare her to some mystical female who occupied a pedestal in his mind.

Tyler now found himself in a rather embarrassing situation. As he waited for Geena to return from the restroom, he was falling asleep. He decided to tell her the truth and beg for forgiveness. When she returned, he again held her chair. He then said, "Geena, you're very attractive, and I've enjoyed this evening, but if I don't get to bed soon, I'm going to fall asleep right here."

"I could tell you were tired." She reached across and put her hand on his and squeezed. "What time did you get up this morning?"

"About three o'clock."

"No wonder you're tired. Come on. Let's get out of here."

During the trip home, they made a date to take a drive on Sunday. This seemed to heighten Geena's spirits. She took Tyler's right hand, placed it on the top of her thigh, and held it there with hers. He thought about those super legs and all that lay beneath the fabric his hand was now resting on. To his amazement, he felt only a slight stirring in his groin. *Damn!* He didn't know he could get this tired.

When they arrived at her place, Tyler cut the engine and lights at the end of her walk and started to exit the truck.

Geena said, "No, you stay right there. I'll walk myself to the door, so you can be on your way. I would like a decent good-night kiss though."

Tyler turned to face her and placed his hand carefully on her neck. He kissed her nose, her cheeks, her eyelids, and, finally, her lips. He was not surprised when her tongue slipped between his lips and explored the tip of his.

She pulled away. "I just knew you would be a good kisser. Get plenty of sleep, Tyler Harrison. I want you well-rested on Sunday." She opened the passenger-side door and was quickly gone.

Tyler waited till she got to the door. She inserted the key, opened the door, and looked back at the truck. Then for the second time today, she reached down and lifted her skirt above her knees. She waved good night, dropped the skirt, and stepped inside. Tyler snickered as he drove away.

*   *   *

Tyler entered his apartment and switched on the light so he could make his way through the mess in the living room. For an instant, he thought he might be in the wrong apartment. He recognized his furniture, but there was no mess. The furniture was neatly arranged, and the boxes were gone. It was obvious that his two new friends had put in a long evening. He switched off the light and made for the bedroom. He had decided in the truck that he would just lay the mattress on the floor, sleep on it there, and put the bed together tomorrow. When he reached his bedroom door, the hall light was still on. The door was closed with a large note taped to it: "Hope you like where we put everything. Don't forget our shopping trip tomorrow. Breakfast will be at our place at 9:00 a.m. By the way, we loved the undershorts with the big hearts. Alice and Tra."

Tyler opened the door, and as expected, all was in order. All the furniture was in place, everything had been put away, and the bed was made up. As Tyler undressed, he noticed that the bed was turned down, and his shorts with the big hearts on them were spread on his pillow. He was too sleepy now, but tomorrow he would think of a way to thank his neighbor ladies.

With his head on the pillow, he realized he was still holding the boxer shorts with the hearts. They had been a silly gift from Penny on their first Valentine's Day, along with a card and a small heart-shaped box of candy. As sleep clouded his consciousness, he pictured her on that day and wondered where she was at that instant.

*   *   *

As he slept, Tyler suddenly smelled perfume. It was vaguely familiar. There was a slight rustling sound to his right. When his eyes focused, he could barely make out a female form. She came to the bed and eased herself under the covers. Tyler lay perfectly still, feigned sleep, and waited for her to reveal herself. She said nothing but began to touch his chest and run her fingers through the thick hair she found there. She paused and began to play with one of his nipples. Her lips touched his, and they were familiar, yet somehow foreign. A tongue flicked in and out of his mouth, and her hand began a slow journey downward across his stomach. It made a few lazy circles around his navel and continued south. She wrapped her fingers around his manhood and began stroking ever so slowly. His level of passion was rising quickly.

He started to reach for her, but she backed away. She threw the covers back onto the foot of the bed, climbed over him, and placed a knee on each side of his waist. She then put one hand under his head and leaned forward so her breasts were just above his face. She began to move back and forth, dragging her nipples across his face. He was enjoying the moment but was also anxious to learn her identity. His arms were still at his sides, so he attempted to determine the size of her breasts with his face and mouth.

She crushed the right one against his face with the nipple forced into his mouth. He couldn't tell if the breast was large or small, but he could tell by the sounds she was making that she liked what he was doing to it. She had also reached between his legs and was again stroking him. He forced his right arm up and reached for her. He touched her stomach and began to slowly move his hand downward. He stroked her clitoris lightly. She moaned deeply, and her whole body jumped. She tightened her grip on his penis and shifted her body so she was poised over it.

She whispered, "I want you inside me … now."

She lowered herself and began to enclose his penis. She raised and lowered herself, taking a little more each time, until she had taken it all. She was tight, and he could feel the heat from her vagina. She used her legs and hips to ride him—her hands on his chest, her head thrown back. Tyler had one hand on her right breast and the other on her hip. He felt a tiny bump just at the top of her left buttock. It felt like a mole. It was difficult to think about anything except the climax they were both rushing toward, but her scent, her voice, and now the mole were all familiar.

Then it came clearly in a flashback! He could see her. They'd been at the lake. Penny had pulled the back of her two-piece bathing suit down about an inch and introduced him to her "little beauty mark." She had laughed and said, "If you're a good boy, someday I'll let you kiss it."

He said, "Penny? My God. Penny, is it you?"

She was still moving over him. "Yes, Tyler, it's me. Remember what I told you in the garage when you were waxing the car? I said I would never give up. I know you still love me, Tyler. Tell me. Tell me you love me."

He didn't think he could speak if he tried. He was in shock but was still moving in harmony with her hips. She leaned forward and placed her hands on each side of his face and kissed him deeply.

"Goddamn you, Tyler Harrison, you proud bastard! You're inside of me. Tell me you love me. Tell me!"

"Yes!" He screamed it. He did love her. He had never stopped loving her. He didn't care who heard it. "Yes, Penny, I love you. I love you. I'm so sorry."

Suddenly he was aware of a loud ringing sound. The doorbell? No, not the doorbell. It was the damn phone. Who would be calling in the middle of the night? Penny had stopped moving. He couldn't feel her. As he reached out for her, his eyes opened to a bright bedroom filled with daylight.

He looked down, and his penis was fully erect. It couldn't be. No dream could be that real. He looked to his right, fully expecting Penny's clothes to be there on the floor. They weren't. He could swear there was still the smell of perfume lingering in the air. That scent was permanently etched in his mind. Damn it to hell! She had been so real, and he wanted her back. Now!

He yanked the phone up, glad that he had paid to have an extra one installed in the bedroom. "Hello," he said with a growl.

"Tyler, did I wake you?" Alice asked.

"I was just getting up," he lied.

"Hey, guy, it's after nine, and we have a long list of things to get on our shopping trip. Tracy is waiting to fix your breakfast. She wants to know how you like your eggs."

He was beginning to wake up, and he was hungry. They were both being very sweet and didn't deserve his gruffness. He answered, "Scrambled, and I'll be there in five minutes … And, Alice … thanks!"

He hung up the phone, lay back in bed, and thought about Penny. He wanted her so badly. Penny was right, of course. He'd been too proud to take her back. Jesus, what a fool he was.

Chapter 5

━━━━━◦❦◦━━━━━

An Outing with Geena

t was quarter till eleven on a Sunday morning and already warm. It had rained yesterday, but the forecast today was for a perfect early summer day. It seemed that the rainstorm yesterday had blown away the humidity and cleared the air.

Tyler parked and hurried up the walk to Geena's door. He knew he was anxious, because he was more than ten minutes early and still hurrying. She didn't have a doorbell, but there was a little door knocker with her name on it. As he reached for it, the door opened.

"You're ten minutes early, Harrison. I don't know what they do where you came from, but around here, it's proper to arrive ten minutes after the appointed time. That would make you about twenty minutes early. As you can see, most of me is not ready."

She was wearing a baggy pink robe tied loosely around the waist and old fluffy slippers, and it was obvious she hadn't applied her makeup. He was pleased to see she was very pretty without it. As she stood on tiptoes and reached her arms up to put around his neck, the front of her robe gaped open. She gave him a brief peck on the lips. When she backed away, he glanced down.

"Are you trying to sneak a peek down the front of my robe?" Geena asked.

Tyler felt like a guy who had been caught with his hand in the cookie jar. He smiled, looked down, and answered, "Yes."

"Good. Is that why you came early, so you could catch me before I got dressed?"

"Of course. It's a trick I learned long ago."

Geena laughed and said, "You're a very bad man." She went into the kitchen and returned with a glass of wine. "Drink this and try to be good while I get dressed."

Tyler said, "I'll try, but I can't make any promises."

When Geena came back into the living room, she was carrying an old blanket. She stopped and spun around like a fashion model at the end of the runway. "So, what do you think?"

She wore red shorts with a thin white piping and a white golf shirt with red piping on the sleeves. Her shirt was tucked in, and her waist looked tiny. Her ensemble was completed with red sandals and a wide red bracelet.

Tyler stood up and slowly walked around her. "Wow, I'm a very lucky man."

"Yes, you are. Now grab that basket on the kitchen counter, and let's go."

"Hey, what's in the basket?" he asked.

"Just a few snacks I put together for a very special man, but he couldn't make it. So I decided to eat it with you."

"Lucky me!"

After a forty-five minute drive, they parked in a crowded lot reserved for visitors to George Washington's home on the Potomac. With basket and blanket in hand, they followed the path toward the house. Geena had already been there, but she wanted Tyler to see it. The house was an impressive, huge two-story with a large front porch that had big square columns that were a full two stories high. The front lawn was huge with a gentle slope down to the Potomac River. They found themselves a choice spot under a huge oak tree that looked like it had been there long before George and Martha came along.

Tyler was astonished to see all that Geena was removing from the basket. It reminded him of a Volkswagen commercial he had seen on television that showed about twenty people getting out of a little VW bug, followed by the caption, "And you thought it was small."

She pulled out asparagus spears, sliced roast beef, a macaroni salad, and slices of key lime pie. He started to reach for it, but she said, "Let's have our appetizers first." She then brought out several types of cubed cheese, crackers, and sliced bread.

Tyler realized Geena had a level of savoir faire that he had not previously noticed. He was reminded of his small-town West Virginia background and his own need to become worldlier. She gave him a bottle of wine and a corkscrew. He could not pronounce the name on the bottle, but he loved it. The snacks were delicious, and they ate leisurely as they relaxed and got to know each other. Eventually they talked about their relationship. Tyler was relieved when Geena said she was uncertain about her future but was not husband hunting. She had dated other men and felt she was capable of having a relationship and an occasional affair without losing her heart.

Tyler said he wanted to see some model homes in Silver Spring, and Geena agreed. When they got back to the truck, Geena asked, "Hey, why don't you let me drive?"

Tyler said, "You're a pushy broad, you know that?"

She leaned her head to one side and said, "Yeah, so?"

Tyler shook his head and threw her the keys. She opened the driver's door and got in. Geena reached across, opened his door, and started the truck. Tyler put the blanket behind the seat, and they started toward Silver Spring.

As he glanced at the map, he thought about what he knew about Montgomery County. It also shared a common border with DC but was much more affluent than Prince Georges. It had a high percentage of Jewish residents and was always rated with the top two or three counties in the United States in per capita income. Montgomery County lay to the north of Washington. The wealthiest areas of DC were its north and northwestern sections. As the city had grown and pushed outward, it had naturally pushed its wealth and affluence into Montgomery County. It was where Tyler intended to live in the near future.

They were on I-495, which was part of the new web of the interstate highway system. It was also referred to as the Capital Beltway, or usually just beltway. It was a modern freeway with exit and entrance ramps and cloverleafs. The beltway formed a circle around Washington, DC, and had become a heavily traveled highway. It was usually faster to go around DC than to go through it.

Tyler said, "You're a very good driver, Geena."

She smiled. "Remember, I grew up around here, and I've had lots of practice, but I'm glad you noticed. I think you deserve a reward. You may rest your left hand on the top of my right thigh."

Tyler scooted over toward the middle and put his hand on her thigh. "Oh, yes. That's very nice," he said. "You can drive my truck anytime you want."

She chuckled, leaned over, and gave him a quick peck without taking her eyes off the road.

He slid to the side a little, bent down being careful not to hit the steering wheel with his head, and began to run his tongue very slowly up her thigh. When he reached the bottom of her shorts, he crossed over to the other leg and started slowly down. He soon noticed goose bumps under his tongue.

She stiffened and said, "Excuse me, but what exactly are you doing down there?"

"Just playing," he answered.

"Well, I don't want to seem ungrateful for all this attention, but I do have one question."

Tyler paused and asked, "What's that?"

"Do you want to die?"

Tyler quickly said, "Not today."

"Then you'd better stop. I can't concentrate on driving with that going on."

"Really? Why not?" He started back up the other leg.

"I don't know! I just can't!" She reached for his hair and pulled his head away from her.

When he raised up, he stared at the front of her shirt, and sure enough, there were two distinct little bumps in the fabric. He grinned at her and asked "Do you want me to turn off the air conditioner? You look cold."

She gave him one of her best mischievous looks. "Don't touch it. I can assure you that I'm not cold."

Tyler read the map, and she drove to their first stop. There were five models, all very different. It was going to be a large development with hundreds of houses. They were all brick and expensive, but they looked like boxes. There was very little imagination in the architecture, and the roofs had no overhangs.

After inspecting three models, Tyler went to look at the last two models while Geena went into the office to get brochures and pricing information. When he came back, she took his hand and said, "They have a job opening for a superintendent. I've told them some things about you, so come inside and meet Mr. Cohen. He's going to hire you. Just follow my lead."

Tyler was more than a little confused, but Geena was dragging him across the office. When he got close to the gentleman, he wasn't sure what he was supposed to do, so he introduced himself.

The man took his time, as if he were forming an opinion. Finally, he shook Tyler's hand. "Abe Cohen," he said. Mr. Cohen was expensively dressed in a beautiful gray suit and a gray-and-red silk tie with matching handkerchief. He had gray hair and a gray mustache and looked about sixty.

Geena said, "Mr. Cohen is the builder here. He needs a superintendent, and I told him you've been a superintendent with Nash Builders for two years."

The sales office had become busy. Thanks to the latest arrivals, a young couple with three small loud children, it had also gotten noisy.

Abe gave the couple and their children a disgruntled look. He said, "I have a small office in the back. Follow me."

The office building, if you could call it that, was really a trailer without wheels. Tyler leaned over close to Geena and asked softly, "What was his name?"

Geena gave him a wide-eyed look and answered, "Abe Cohen."

Tyler repeated the name to himself a few times while he wondered how much Mr. Cohen's suit cost. He had never seen one that nice.

Mr. Cohen waited until they were in the office and closed the door. He glanced at the two chairs in front of the desk, both covered with papers. "Just throw those papers on the floor. My main office is downtown. As you can see, I never use this damn place."

Geena picked up the papers from both chairs and stacked them neatly on the corner of the desk. She sat in one chair, holding her huge purse on her lap, and Tyler joined her in the other chair.

Abe sat in a leather swivel chair behind the desk. He turned sideways, crossed his legs with his feet on the desk, and leaned back with his hands behind his head. "Now maybe we can talk. Who is it you work for again?"

Before Tyler could respond, Geena looked at him and calmly said, "It's Nash Builders, and Tyler has been a superintendent there for about two years."

Tyler already knew he couldn't lie for shit and figured Geena knew it as well, but Mr. Cohen didn't know it yet.

"Tell me about this Nash Builders," Cohen said.

Tyler glanced at Geena to see if she was going to answer this one too, but she was looking at Mr. Cohen. He said, "Mr. Nash is a medium-sized builder in Clinton, Maryland. We build about seventy-five single-family homes per year near Andrews Air Force Base."

"Geena said you've finished college?"

"Yes, sir. I have a business degree from Winfield College."

"I've heard of that school," Cohen said. "Supposed to be a damn good school. So, Tyler, tell me. Are you a framing or finish superintendent with Nash?"

Tyler again glanced at Geena for a cue but was again ignored. "Both," he said. *Hell, why not?* he thought. He was on a roll now. "I take the house I'm responsible for from start to finish. I have also worked start to finish on many homes for my father. He builds some homes every summer."

Cohen sat up with his feet on the floor and rested his arms on the desk. "Most of the people in this organization are Jewish. Do you think you could work with them?"

"Mr. Cohen, since the day I learned to drive my first nail, I've wanted to be a builder. I can work with anyone who can teach me or help me gain experience."

Mr. Cohen seemed to be digesting what Tyler had said. He asked, "Lots of people think Jews are pushy and don't really care for us. What do you think about us?"

"Mr. Cohen, I don't know if I'm pushy or determined, but I know it's hard to tell the difference. I also know if I'm not, I will never be successful. I have great respect for Jewish people. I admire their intellect, their work ethic, and their history, but mostly, I admire their spirit. I do think they sort of missed the boat with Jesus, though." *What?* He heard the words, but he couldn't believe they had actually come from his mouth.

Geena looked at him with fire in her eyes. Tyler half expected her to punch him. Mr. Cohen was speechless. His lower jaw had dropped, and he was expressionless. All Tyler could think about was Abe's teeth. They were too perfect. He wondered if they were false and then guessed that they were most likely caps. He wondered how much a mouth like that cost.

Cohen slowly closed his mouth and began to laugh. It turned into a real belly laugh. Geena and Tyler eyed each other with confusion and then joined in.

Abe finally stopped and wiped tears out of his eyes. "Damned if I don't agree with you, Tyler, and I like your honesty. I would give $1,000 if Rabbi Feldon could have heard that. Tyler, can you get away tomorrow for a little while?"

Tyler started to answer, but Geena was too quick. She said, "Yes, he can. Tyler is on vacation this week."

Tyler smiled. He knew he wasn't working, but he didn't know until now that he was on vacation. He was tempted to ask her if it was paid vacation. Abe grabbed one of the many pieces of paper on his desk and tore off a corner. He pulled out a gold fountain pen and started writing. While he was writing, Tyler noticed a diamond ring on his little finger. He made a mental estimate on the price of the ring and the pen.

Mr. Cohen replaced the top of his pen and put it in a breast pocket on the inside of his suit jacket. He stood up and handed the paper to Tyler.

"This is the name of the project manager for this development. I want you to meet with him at ten in the morning. If he likes you, you've got the job. You can talk money with him, but we pay very well, and you'll be expected to earn it."

Geena dumped her purse on Tyler's lap and went around the desk where she gave Abe a big hug and a kiss on the cheek. She said, "Mr. Cohen, that was awfully nice. I think I've figured you out. You pretend to be hard-nosed, but I think you're just a softy."

Abe winked at her and put his index finger up. "She is a very special lady, young man. Make damn sure you're good to her."

Tyler looked at Geena, and her head was going up and down in complete agreement.

"I am, Mr. Cohen, and I agree with you," Tyler said. "Thank you for this opportunity."

On the way to the pickup, it occurred to Tyler that the project manager would call Nash Builders for a reference. How many whoppers had he just agreed to or told?

Once they were in the pickup and ready to go with Geena behind the wheel and the air conditioner running again, Tyler broached the subject. "Geena, why did you do that?"

"Do what?"

"Tell Mr. Cohen that I had been a superintendent for two years."

"I thought it would help you get the job," she replied.

"Then why didn't you tell him I had been a superintendent for twenty years? That would get me the job for sure," laughed Tyler. He saw some of the fire from earlier returning in Geena's eyes.

"Because he wouldn't have believed it. Are you trying to make a point? Look, Tyler, if you have something to say, say it."

"Okay. I don't like lying to get a job."

"Really! You could have fooled me. I thought you were pretty good at it except for the thing about Jesus. That was brilliant."

"Damn it, Geena. I only did that because you started it. I felt like I had to go along with it. I didn't want you to be embarrassed."

"Well, thank you very much for your chivalry, but I'm a big girl. Tyler, I don't want to fight with you. I like you, and this has been a wonderful day, but I'm going to tell you how I feel. I don't consider myself a liar. What we did in there was bullshit. We enhanced your résumé. That's all. Everyone does it, especially around here. Washington, DC, by its very nature is the bullshit capital of the world. So don't come in here with your holier-than-thou values from your little town in West Virginia and preach to me. You know what your problem is? You're too damn proud. You need to loosen up a little. Too much pride makes a person hardheaded and narrow-minded."

Where in the hell had he heard that before? "Okay, Geena. I like you too, and I agree about today. It's been great. I also agree that I can be too proud at times. But I don't think I have to abandon all of my pride and values to be successful."

"I didn't say you did. I said loosen up a little. This is not a discussion group or a Sunday school class. This is the real world, and you have to deal with it realistically. I can tell you're a good person, and that's one of the things that make you special. I don't want you to change, just adapt a little to your surroundings."

"Okay, Miss Know-It-All. Has it occurred to you that Mr. Cohen or the project manager will call Nash tomorrow to verify my experience?"

Geena grinned, and that prankster light returned to her eyes. "Yes, it has. Has it occurred to you who answers the phone and screens all the calls at Nash Builders?"

Tyler laughed and gave a palms up sign that said, "Okay, you win."

Chapter 6

Making Love

The remainder of the afternoon went too quickly. Tyler asked Geena if she knew where the nearest Lord and Taylor was. It was an expensive department store chain that dealt with upper-crust clientele, and he assumed Montgomery County would have one. He was right.

As they headed for the store in Bethesda, they worked on their plan for tomorrow so their stories would agree if someone called for a reference. Maybe it was bullshit, but he still felt a little guilty.

Tyler told Geena about Alice and Tracy and how they had helped him settle into his new apartment. He explained that he wanted to get each of them a nice gift certificate. Geena told him that was really sweet.

Tyler went to the office area on the second floor and purchased two one-hundred-dollar gift certificates while she waited on the sales floor. After that, they spent some time browsing in the ladies' department. Tyler enjoyed watching Geena, and from her comments, he began to realize she had excellent fashion sense.

Tyler was one of those rare men who liked to shop. He had never really analyzed or tried to explain it. He had always enjoyed shopping for his mother and Penny. He had learned that he had a good eye, and his taste in ladies' fashions was excellent. Penny had always loved what he selected for her and thought it was neat that he did the shopping himself. He didn't understand why other men couldn't do the same. He was thinking about that when he spotted it. Geena was sliding hangers as she looked at a rack of summer dresses on sale and went right past it. He stepped forward and pulled it out. It was a size six. The original price was $120. It had been marked down to eighty, and there was an additional 25 percent off sign above the entire rack. Sixty bucks for a $120 dress was a great price.

The fabric was red, black, and white with hundreds of little meaningless designs that made no sense, but altogether, they gave the dress a dramatic look. The dress was very aristocratic, but not every woman could wear this style and look good in it. Tyler knew Geena could. He wanted to see it on her.

He held it up and asked, "Geena, do you like this?"

She took a quick look and said, "I don't think it's me."

Tyler smiled and said, "Don't be so narrow-minded. What size are you?"

"Depends on the brand, but usually six."

"Try it on for me, please."

She took the dress and held it against her. "You really like this?"

"Yes. It was made for you. You'll look so good in this dress that every man in Maryland will want you."

"I know this may come as a surprise, but every man in Maryland wants me now," she mused. "But for you, I'll try it on."

A saleswoman was hovering nearby and quickly appeared and took Geena to the dressing room. Tyler tagged along behind. He made small talk with the saleswoman and waited.

When Geena came out, she asked, "Do you like it?"

"Geena, the dress is perfect, but it only enhances your good looks. What do you think?"

She smiled and said, "I love it. It makes me feel deliciously rich and genteel."

Tyler turned to the saleswoman and said, "We'll take it."

* * *

As they reached her apartment, Geena asked, "Would you like to come inside? We can finish the picnic leftovers."

"Okay, sounds good," Tyler agreed.

After they had finished eating and she was rinsing the last of the dishes, Tyler approached and began rubbing and kissing the back of her neck.

"What are you doing back there?" she asked.

"Rubbing and kissing smooth, pretty stuff."

"Are you having fun?"

"Oh, yes. Much fun."

"Would you like to rub something else?" Geena questioned.

"I'm sure I would if it's part of you."

Geena took his hands and eased them under her top and onto her bare breasts. "These are my A-cups, and I'm proud of them."

Tyler gently cupped her breasts and the nipples and said, "I can see why. They're perfect."

Tyler pushed his erection against her butt, and she reached around and felt it. "I guess we're going to have to do something with this. Would you like to take a shower with me?"

*   *   *

Geena smiled as Tyler slowly and carefully dried every inch of her. He could tell she was proud of her body. Her breasts were very firm and perky. The nipples were dark and rather large. Her tummy was flat, and her skin was dark and flawless. The pubic hair was dark and neatly trimmed. Her back was long and lean like her legs with excellent muscle tone, and her butt was full but still firm and nicely shaped.

Tyler finished his task and hung up the towel. "Geena, you're a lovely woman. You're firm and sleek. You look like a beautiful young gazelle."

She kissed him and said, "Thank you." She turned the bed down and lay on the far side. Then she pulled the cover up over her and patted the spot next to her.

Tyler frowned and asked, "Are you cold?"

"No, not really."

Tyler picked up the edge of the covers and threw them over the foot of the bed. "Good, because I want to look at you. I don't just want to have sex, Geena. I want to make love to you, to all of you." Tyler began stroking, kissing, and nibbling every body part he could find. When he flicked his tongue over her clitoris, he heard her moan. There was a river of wetness between her legs as he fingered her and continued to nibble and lick. Her breath began coming in short gasps. He felt her tense and push her privates up against his mouth as he pushed her over the edge, but he didn't stop. He wanted her to be swept up on a wave and then another and another, each a little higher than the last. When he was sure he'd accomplished this, he quietly moved up her body and began busying himself with her "A-cups."

After a moment, she tried to sit up. Tyler pushed her back down. "Where are you going?"

"Nowhere, I promise. I could stay here till I get bed sores."

"Good, because I'm not finished."

"I know, and I want to help you. I want you to enjoy this too."

"Geena, I don't need any help, and I am enjoying this. Any man who didn't enjoy making love to you should have his head examined. Now just relax. We've only just begun."

He began stroking, kissing, and nibbling each of her parts. After a while, he moved so that he was over her. He placed his left hand under her buttocks, lifted her slightly, and entered her. He began a slow, steady rhythm while kissing her throat and then her breasts. When she was gasping and he felt her hands on his butt, frantically pulling him into her harder, he waited until he was sure she had come, and then he allowed himself to explode inside of her.

He lay there inside her for a few moments. Geena looked at him and said, "That was amazing. I've never had an orgasm before. You were teasing me one minute and deep within me the next. I felt like an orchestra waiting for my maestro."

Tyler kissed her deeply and said, "I can't stop. This is too good. I want you again."

"Take me."

He rolled over, taking her with him while remaining firmly in her. She placed her knees on each side to support her own weight and started to sit up, but Tyler used his hands to force her knees down and moved under her. He had placed her at an angle where she could attain maximum penetration and constant contact with her clitoris. He knew it would allow her to take what she needed, and her need seemed great from the way she started moving. Soon, he tensed, ready to climax again, and she rushed to join him. Tyler eased her onto her side and pulled her back against his front. He adjusted his body to hers so they fit together from head to toe. He placed one arm under his head, and with the other, he reached over her and cupped her breast.

"Tyler?" Geena asked.

"What?"

"Will you stay the night?"

"Geena, a herd of Clydesdales couldn't drag me from this apartment until morning."

Sometime during the night, Geena awoke and missed Tyler. She was relieved when he returned from the bathroom. When he was again under the covers, Geena turned over and threw one of her legs over Tyler and grasped his penis. As she began to stroke him, he responded immediately. She became fully awake when Tyler placed his hand between her legs. She couldn't believe she still felt amorous, but she did.

Geena threw back the covers and straddled him, duplicating the position she had enjoyed earlier. She slowly raised and lowered herself until he was completely within her. Tyler matched her movements as he caressed her nipples.

Geena was moving rapidly, lost in her passion, when Tyler grasped her hips and lifted her off him. Before she could complain, he placed her down on her hands and knees. He quickly repositioned himself and slowly began to penetrate her from behind. He varied the speed and angle but remained shallow. She wanted more and pushed backward so hard Tyler nearly lost his balance.

Geena had only found herself in this position twice before and was not particularly fond of it. But as with everything else with this man, she now found she was enjoying it immensely. So much so that she was again excitingly close to orgasm.

To her complete dismay, he withdrew from her, and she quickly found herself on her back. Again, before she could voice a protest, he had penetrated her and was again teasing her vagina. Willing him to finish it now, she spread her legs till she thought they might separate at the hips. She raised herself toward him and pulled on his butt with her hands. Geena needed to wrap herself around all of him, but still he held back.

All at once she thought she might know what he was doing. She had read somewhere that orgasms that were held back, that were intentionally prolonged, could be much more intense. She wondered for an instant if that was what he was doing. She had no idea. This was the first time she had ever made love with a walking, talking, living, breathing sex manual. Geena quickly decided, though, that if he withdrew from her again before she finished, when she got back her strength, she would kill him.

She was soon approaching her peak again, and just like before, Tyler slowed his movements. Geena tried to lock her legs behind him. "No, Tyler! Not again! Please don't. Oh God, please don't pull out. I want it now. Make me come, Tyler."

He didn't speak a word, but he did answer her. He roughly grasped her butt in one large hand and thrust into her so deeply and savagely that it scared her. It also magnified the moment and gave her the release she needed. She was absolutely stunned at what was happening to her. She was screaming something and had no idea what it was. The orgasm was so intense that she actually felt pain. She wanted to help him, to kiss him, to tell him how wonderful he was. In the end, all she did was enjoy and absorb.

Much later, it dawned on her that she had no idea if Tyler had reached his climax. He was lying beside her now. She didn't know how he got there and wondered if she had passed out for a while. "Tyler, did you finish?" she asked.

"Did I finish? Are you kidding? It was an explosion. I'm sure the top of my head is around here somewhere."

Geena was sure she was too wasted to laugh, but she wasn't. "Shut up, Tyler, and hold me."

"I am holding you," he said.

Oh shit, she thought. There was so much to think about, so much to sort out, so much to analyze. She would just have to … have to do it … tomorrow.

Chapter 7

Breakfast and Another Job Interview

eena wondered if she would look this good in her apron and nothing else. She had to admit that Tyler looked very good in her apron. She was sitting at the kitchen table, waiting to be served breakfast. When the alarm had gone off around six o'clock that morning, she hadn't budged, because she'd been reasonably sure she couldn't walk. Her entire body ached, but she didn't care. After some semiconscious thought, she decided being a paraplegic was a reasonable price to pay for having so many orgasms in the same evening.

Before she could make any other major decisions, Tyler appeared and turned off the alarm. Again, he pulled the covers back until they were on the foot of the bed. She noted this was the second time in a few hours he had uncovered her, and she vowed to have a word with him about that. After the episode with the covers, though, he did a number of nice things that earned her forgiveness. He said good morning, told her how lovely she was, kissed her on the nose, scooped her up in his arms like she was a feather, carried her to the bathroom, and gently deposited her into a tub of warm water. He handed her a washcloth and soap and informed her breakfast would be ready in fifteen minutes.

He did return once to make sure she hadn't drowned. While he was there, he quickly washed her breasts, rinsed her breasts, kissed her breasts, and pronounced them the cutest A-cups this side of the Potomac River. He was off to the kitchen before she could ask if he was familiar with a set of breasts on the other side of the river. She had somehow managed to bathe, wash her hair, brush her teeth, and walk on shaky legs to the kitchen.

She felt very brave but wasn't sure her fellow females around the world would support her. She was having breakfast with her lover after only their first night together with limp wet hair and no makeup. She was afraid Tyler would get a good look at her and think last night had been a mistake, so she opened the top of her robe more so he could glimpse her A-cups. Hopefully, he would look at them during breakfast and not her face.

She looked at the food on her plate, and then she looked at him. He was wolfing his down like a condemned man having his last meal. She didn't have the heart to tell him she normally didn't eat breakfast.

She had to hand it to him, he had been busy. He had run her bath water and made coffee, scrambled eggs, and toasted English muffins with grape jelly. As she ate sparingly, she took time to observe. She guessed a conservative estimate of the number of eggs on her plate would come in at around five or six. She also noticed a little round metal disk with many small holes in it next to the egg carton and wondered what it was. Then she looked at the coffee in front of her and instantly knew what it was. She had a new electric percolator by Corningware. He had put coffee in the basket, but the little round disk was the lid. Without it, all the grounds ended up in the coffee.

Tyler looked up and asked, "Aren't you hungry?"

"I'm not a big breakfast eater," she answered.

"I would think after last night you would be starving. I know I am. I never eat this much for breakfast."

Out of the goodness of her heart, she ate a bit and took a small drink of coffee. The eggs were dry and burnt. The muffins resembled charcoal briquettes. The coffee looked like used motor oil that hadn't been changed for a hundred thousand miles, and every swig provided coffee grounds for no extra charge.

She looked at Tyler again and wondered how he could enjoy this meal when everything was so awful. As if he was reading her mind, he ventured, "I guess the food is not too good. I'm sorry. Cooking is not one of my talents."

Geena smirked. "It's okay. You have enough talent in other areas to make up for it."

"What I can't figure out is why the coffee is so damn bad."

"You used about four times too much, and you left the top off the basket."

"Is that what the little metal disk is for?" Tyler asked.

"Yes," Geena said.

"Let me ask you something else. Do you always eat breakfast with your A-cups showing?"

"Always."

He jumped up so quickly that it startled her. "That calls for a toast." He raised his coffee cup and proclaimed, "Here's to the little breasts so firmly attached to the body of one Geena Morgan. Be it known from this day forth that I like 'em a lot. If ever invited to breakfast here again in this place, not only will I accept, but I will rejoice."

All Geena could do was stare and wonder what he would do next. He sat down grinning and went to work on his eggs and a jelly-covered briquette. She finally picked up her fork again. In spite of the food, she decided it was the best breakfast she had ever eaten.

*   *   *

Isidor Feldman (Issi to his friends) was a smallish man around forty. Tyler guessed he was five foot six in his shoes. He was handsome with sharp features and dark curly hair. Tyler could see he was very neat and fastidious. Mr. Feldman was spit-and-polish and appeared to have no sense of humor. Tyler imagined it would not be easy to work for this man.

They were seated in a small, tidy office in a construction trailer down the street from the sales office where he and Geena had met with Abe

Cohen yesterday. It was the same kind of white aluminum construction trailer that could be found on every job around the DC area. There was a room with a large slanted desk for blueprint reading and racks on the wall for rolled-up prints. The trailer also had three offices, and each had a little air conditioner sticking through the wall. Two were for the superintendents. One for the finish super and one for the framing super, which Tyler would be if he got this job. The third office was Feldman's, and this was where Tyler was now seated.

Feldman began. "Tyler, I got a call from Abe last night. He said you had balls, and I should hire you if I like you. So, make me like you."

Tyler leaned forward a little apprehensively and started. "I don't know how much Mr. Cohen told you, so I'll start at the beginning. My father builds a few houses every summer, and I've worked for him for four years. I've finished a business degree at Winfield College in Stratford, West Virginia, where I managed to make the dean's list every semester. I've also worked a couple of years for Nash Builders in Clinton, Maryland." That was somewhat true. He had worked two summers. "I understand that you need a framing superintendent. I'll need to learn how you work here, but I see no reason that I couldn't do this job. If you're looking for a bright young man who isn't afraid of work, I'm your man."

"You seem like a nice young man, but two years isn't much experience."

"You're right, Mr. Feldman. But you've never met anyone like me. I won't let you down."

Feldman began asking a series of questions regarding what Tyler would do in hypothetical situations if hired. Tyler understood what he should say immediately on most of them, but on two questions, he had no idea. He decided not to try to bullshit Feldman, so on these, he simply said, "I don't know." These were the words that had just come out of his mouth when Feldman glanced at his watch, and Tyler sensed the interview was over. He'd done his best, but he braced himself for an outright rejection or having Feldman tell him he'd call him and let him know.

Feldman sniffed and said, "We start all our supers off at the same salary. You'll get two hundred a week plus bonuses. If you run into a situation where you're not sure what to do, talk to me. Every house you start will be on schedule. There will be a preset date for you to have it framed and roofed and ready to turn over to the finish super. If you're ready on that date, you'll earn a hundred-dollar bonus. We average finishing two houses per week. That could be two hundred extra per week. We'll provide you with excellent hospitalization insurance and a pickup to drive. Abe wants to give you a try, and you're likeable enough. If you want the job, it's yours. You can start next Monday."

On the way home, Tyler thought about the salary and bonuses. Four hundred a week was almost three times what he would have made with Nash. He didn't yet know how difficult it would be to earn those bonuses, but he intended to have them, even if he was the only super in Montgomery County who carried a gun and a whip.

Chapter 8

Working for Abe Cohen

Monday morning when Tyler arrived at work and stepped into his office, he was greeted by a beautiful woman. She was sitting in a frame next to a picture of his folks on the shelf. It was an eight-by-ten, a stunning picture of Geena that had been professionally done at a studio. It was still early, and he knew she hadn't left for work yet. He dialed her number, and she picked up on the first ring.

"I noticed a female right next to my parents this morning, and I wondered if you had any idea how she got there."

"I might know something about that. I hope you don't mind since I didn't ask."

"I don't mind at all. Besides, I can always use a good dartboard. How did you get it in here?"

"On Saturday morning, when we came to clean your office, I wrapped it in a towel and hid it in my purse. Remember when we were leaving and you were locking the door, I said I forgot my purse. I lied. I left it in your office on purpose. So when I ran back to get it, I put my picture on the shelf."

"I can see I'll have to watch you closely. You're a very devious woman. Is the picture mine to keep?"

"If you like."

"I like, and I'll keep it. Do you have any idea how lovely you are?"

Geena sighed and said, "Of course, but why don't you tell me anyway?"

Tyler laughed and said, "Sorry, it's gotten really busy here, and I have to go." As he was hanging up the phone, he was sure he heard something that sounded like, "You rotten shit."

*   *   *

Tyler was lost in thought as he watched the huge spinning drum on the back of the concrete mixer. He had waited two weeks for this contractor. The first week when he had worked with fat, jolly Norm, between donuts, Tyler found out that every house was about three or four weeks behind its schedule. He also found out that Norman had never earned a bonus in the three years he had been with Pride Mark Homes. Tyler intended to change that.

Yesterday morning, he had met with Issi, the project manager, to discuss a rough idea of what he wanted to change. To his delight, Issi had listened carefully and said the plan might have merit. He came to Tyler later that day and told him the company accountant and Abe Cohen would be out for a meeting at two o'clock that afternoon.

Tyler was a little apprehensive about the meeting, but he had gathered all the information he would need and was ready. Leo, the finish superintendent, was the first to show up. He explained that Abe Cohen had a shitload of money and his wife, Valarie, had more. She was a former model and now owned the largest modeling agency in New York. Leo also said that Abe had been building homes for a long time and didn't like change. Tyler pointed out that Abe might be reluctant to change, but he was pretty sure he liked making money, and the plan Tyler had in mind would greatly increase profits.

Abe, Valarie, and Aaron, the company accountant, arrived ten minutes late. Valerie was strikingly attractive.

When Abe introduced his wife, Tyler embarrassed himself by telling her how beautiful she was. Valarie gave him a hug and said, "You're not so bad yourself, Tyler. Would you like to do some modeling?"

Tyler thought for a moment, and answered, "No, but I know someone who would." When Valarie asked who, Tyler showed her the picture of Geena on his shelf, and he could tell she was interested.

Tyler started the meeting. "I've been here a month, and I love it. I'm sure I would love it more if I at least had a chance to earn my hundred-dollar bonus on each house."

He pointed to the chalkboard where he had written money amounts earlier. "This company uses development loans to buy the land and put in the streets and underground utilities. It also uses a separate construction loan to build each house. Because every house and the entire project is behind schedule, the amount of interest being paid is eating away a huge portion of the profit. I'm certain this can be stopped with a couple of easy changes."

Abe asked, "Is the schedule the problem?"

Tyler smiled. "No, sir, Mr. Cohen. The problem is the subcontractors. I already checked with Aaron, and our subs are waiting an average of thirty days for payment after the job is finished.

"Subcontracting for builders is a tough business. Our subs work for many builders. Every Thursday and Friday, they are running from job to job trying to collect enough money to make their payroll. That's why they all start a job and leave before it's finished. Sometimes we have to wait one or two weeks for a sub to come back to finish a job, and that's why every house is three to four weeks behind schedule. I can guarantee you if we pay our subcontractors the same day, or the next day when they have finished, they will stay and complete the job. That will allow us to get this project and every house here on schedule within one month. If we do that, we could save conservatively $85,000 per year on this project. Issi tells me Pride Mark Homes has two other projects about this size. That would be a yearly savings to the company of $225,000."

Abe said, "Damn it, Tyler, that's a hell of a lot of money. It seems too simple. What do you think, Issi?"

Issi said, "I like it, and I believe it'll work."

"What about you, Aaron?" Abe asked.

"It will absolutely work," Aaron answered.

Abe smiled at Tyler. "Well, by God, let's give it a try."

When everyone was leaving and Tyler was erasing the chalkboard, Abe approached Tyler and said, "I take care of my people. If this works, I won't forget you."

"Thank you, Mr. Cohen," Tyler responded.

Valarie joined them. "Tyler, that was very impressive." She handed him a piece of paper. "This is our address in Potomac. I'm having a birthday party for Abe this Saturday evening at six. I would like for you to come and bring Geena, but don't tell her I might be interested in her. I want to observe her in a natural setting,"

"That's very nice, Mrs. Cohen. Thank you, and we'll be there."

When everyone was gone, Tyler sat at his desk. He picked up Geena's picture and studied it. He then pulled out the bottom right-hand desk drawer. He reached all the way in the back and brought out a five-by-seven picture of Penny. He held it next to Geena's and tried to analyze his feelings. He cared for them both, but he felt differently about them also. He caught himself visualizing Penny posed like Geena and then standing in the dress he had bought for Geena and then lying naked in Geena's bed. He wasn't a psych major, but he had a damn good idea what all this meant.

Chapter 9

———— ❤ ————

Breaking Up and Buying Land

eena stopped her old Buick in front of Tyler's apartment and said, "Get out!"

Tyler slammed the door and watched as she sped away. Once inside, he grabbed a beer and sat in his recliner. He was more confused than angry—nothing new when dealing with the fairer sex. He wasn't tired and decided to sit there until he figured out what the hell had gone wrong this evening.

Geena had picked him up, and they had driven to Abe Cohen's home in Potomac, Maryland. The house was huge and beautiful, which was what Tyler had expected. Geena had been nervous about meeting all of Abe's rich friends and relatives. Tyler was looking forward to Abe's sixtieth birthday bash and felt fortunate to be on the guest list.

They were met and ushered to the receiving line, which consisted of Abe, Valarie, and their daughter, Blair. She was a law student at Georgetown University in Washington, DC, and almost as gorgeous as her mother.

Tyler knew that part of Geena's anger was due to Blair. She spent most of the evening flirting with Tyler. He was friendly to her but did not respond to her open advances. She was, after all, Abe's daughter, and he certainly couldn't be rude to her in her own house.

Valarie had pulled Geena and Tyler aside and taken them to the library. She told Geena, after observing her in person, she might be interested in putting her under contract as a model at her agency in New York. She explained that it was the largest and best modeling agency in the country. Valarie went on to interview Geena and answer some of Geena's questions. She also told Geena that she would pay for a portfolio of pictures, and her final decision would be based on those pictures.

On the way back to Tyler's apartment was where the real trouble started. Geena was upset because if she did agree to sign with Valarie, she would have to move to New York. Tyler told her it was a great opportunity, and they could still see each other often. Geena was not happy with that answer.

Next came the Blair situation. Geena asked, "Did Blair ask you about me?"

"Yes, she did."

"What did you tell her?"

"I told her that we were dating, and I liked you."

"That's what you said? That you liked me?"

Tyler could tell this was not going well. "Yes, that's what I said."

"What does that mean?" Geena demanded. "What do you mean when you say you like me?"

"Well, I don't know exactly," Tyler whined. "It means you're beautiful and special, and I like you. It means that I want to be with you and that I choose to be with you instead of someone else."

She turned in her seat toward Tyler and asked, "If I ask you a question, will you tell me the truth?"

"Yes, Geena. I have no reason to lie to you."

"Do you love me, Tyler?"

Damn it! He was right. Women always know the right question to ask. It wasn't fair, because men always gave the wrong answer. Oh sure, men were stronger and louder, but he was convinced they were inferior in every other way. Women were just too smart for men. He guessed his best hope was to continue with the truth.

"No, Geena," he finally answered. "I don't think so."

If a stare could kill, Tyler was sure he would be on his way to the Promised Land.

"What the hell does *I don't think so* mean?" Geena demanded.

"It means exactly that," Tyler replied angrily. "It means that feelings and emotions are difficult to explain. It means that they don't always fit neatly into categories. People themselves don't always know what they're feeling. I don't know what your problem is, but I've done nothing wrong. If I recall correctly, you were the one who said you could easily have a relationship with a man and not fall in love. I agreed, and that is all I've done. What do you want from me?"

Geena started to cry. "What I want is to go to your apartment as quickly as I can and get you the hell out of my car!"

*   *   *

Once back in his apartment, Tyler downed his last sip of beer. Four years ago, he had let Penny slip away because of his pride. He wondered if that was what he was doing now, but he had done nothing wrong with Penny either. He crumpled the beer can and dropped it in the kitchen trash can. On the way to the bedroom, he again wondered if there was one sane young woman out there somewhere.

The following morning was Sunday, and when Tyler was awake, his first thought was of Geena. His second thought was that he was still angry and had no intention of contacting her.

His mood improved when he remembered his afternoon appointment. He had been looking for a large piece of land that he could purchase and subdivide into building lots. The real estate lady had called on Friday, and he would meet the owner today. The parcel was 190 acres, and the location was perfect. But first he had to have breakfast with his surrogate moms next door. He was sure they would ask about the party. He had excitedly told them about his invitation and that he was taking Geena. He had then showed them Geena's picture, and Alice and Tracy had gushed about how gorgeous she was and what a perfect couple they made.

Tracy and Alice were sitting at the dining room table enjoying their first cup of coffee when Tyler came in.

"So, Tyler, how was the party?" Alice asked.

"Not good." Tyler frowned. "I think Geena and I broke up last night."

"Oh, no," Tracy groaned. "What happened?"

Tyler began with the party and the possible offer of a modeling job. He told them about Blair Cohen and how he had tried to tactfully reject her advances. In between their questions, he also told them about the fight in the car on the way home and ended with how Geena had asked if he loved her.

"What did you say when she asked if you loved her?" Alice asked.

"I told her no, I didn't think so."

Tracy, who was pouring coffee for everyone, asked, "What the hell does that mean?"

"Damn it! That's the same thing she asked."

Alice moaned, "The poor thing. She must be crushed."

"Yeah," Tracy agreed.

"Wait a minute here," Tyler observed. "This is not my fault. She and I had a long talk on our second date about how neither one of us was looking for a spouse and how we were both capable of having an affair without falling in love. I don't know what she wants from me."

"I guess she wants you to love her," Alice explained.

"Why?" Tyler asked. "We've only been dating for a month."

Alice sighed and replied, "Because she's in love with you."

"No, I don't think so," Tyler said. "She bragged about how she could make love without being in love."

Tracy said, "But that was a month ago. That doesn't count now."

Tyler sighed heavily. "What the hell is wrong with women? If you sleep with one and you're also nice to her, she falls in love with you."

"Only with some men, Tyler," Alice admitted. "You'll have to be very careful in the future. I think you're one of those men who's just easy to love."

* * *

The 190-acre parcel of land was perfect. It had a rolling terrain, natural drainage, and many trees that would make beautiful wooded lots. It also rested smack-dab in the middle of the most desirable area in Montgomery County. It would not, however, be easy to buy. The real estate agent, Marsha, told Tyler that Ned Stanton, the owner, had already turned down three offers that equaled the appraised value.

Tyler asked, "Does he want more money?"

"No," Marsha answered.

"So, what's the problem?'

Marsha laughed. "The problem is Ned. He doesn't like many people. He's also ill with bone cancer, and I'm sure that doesn't help his mood."

Marsha turned her car into the gravel driveway in front of Mr. Stanton's old farm house. She and Tyler exited the car and headed for the house. Tyler's mind was racing. How could he buy this land when three other bona fide purchasers had failed? No answers came to mind.

"Marsha, do you know how long Mr. Stanton has lived here?"

"Yes, all of his life. He told me he was born in the house, and the land has been owned by the Stanton's for five generations."

Marsha rang the old doorbell, and the door was answered immediately. Tyler was surprised. Ned Stanton had once been a formidable man. He stood more than six feet tall and had large features. He was tan and had a beautiful white mane and mustache. But sadly, most of the meat had left the bones. It was obvious that Ned Stanton's remaining time on this earth would be very short.

"Mr. Stanton," Marsha said, "this is Tyler Harrison. He's the young man I told you about."

"Good afternoon, Mr. Stanton," Tyler ventured.

Ned shook Tyler's hand with a surprisingly strong grip. "How old are you, boy?"

"Twenty-three," Tyler replied, wondering if he was going to be thrown out before he even had a chance.

Ned gave Tyler a cold stare. "You got enough money to buy this land?"

"Well, sir, I have $75,000, and I'm sure I can get the rest."

"Where did a young man like you get that kind of money?"

"I earned it, Mr. Stanton."

Ned didn't seem impressed. "What would you do with my land if you got it?"

Tyler was pleased and thought he might have an opening. "If I got your land, Mr. Stanton, what would you like me to do with it?"

Ned smiled. "If you bought this land, it would be yours to do whatever you wanted, as long as you followed the county zoning rules. Why would you care what I wanted?"

"Marsha told me this land used to be a farm, and it has belonged to the Stantons for five generations. She also told me you were born in this house. I'm sure you're very fond of this place, and I think you should have something to say about what happens to it."

Ned seemed to soften a little. "Come in, and sit down over there," he said, pointing toward an old, worn sofa.

Tyler was shocked. At least he had gotten his foot in the door. Ned followed and dropped heavily into an ancient recliner that looked like it had been purchased twenty years ago at the Salvation Army.

"Let me get this straight," Ned said. "You want to know what I would like to see happen to my land after it's sold?"

"Yes, sir."

"Well, by golly, I never gave it much thought. You can't make much money farming anymore. I think I'd like to see a lot of nice homes built here full of happy families. I guess you know I'm sick and don't have too long. I want to get the sale settled and leave some money to my church for their building fund. The rest would go to my two daughters and my grandchildren."

"Mr. Stanton, that's exactly what I would like to do with your land. If you would sell me this land, I would like for you to help me develop it."

Mr. Stanton leaned forward and asked, "How would that work?"

"I would hope we could work together. We would decide where the streets went and what kind of houses would be built. You could help me come up with a proper name for the development, and we could even name some of the streets after your daughters and your grandchildren."

Ned leaned back in his recliner and thought for a while. "Marsha, can he do what he's talking about?"

"Yes, he can, and I think it's a wonderful idea."

"So why didn't the other three buyers ask me to be part of the decision making for the land development?"

Marsha thought for a moment. "Because they didn't care."

Ned smiled. "I think you may be right."

Tyler waited a little and then asked, "Could you tell me about your church?"

"Not much to tell really. It's a small Baptist church about two miles from here. It's old, and we have outgrown it. We have a building fund, and we need a new, bigger building."

Tyler asked, "Do they have any land to build on yet?"

"We've been looking for two years, but nothing yet."

Tyler smiled. "Mr. Stanton, maybe we could work out something, and your church could be built here."

Ned looked surprised. "You would do that?"

"I can promise I will try."

Ned laughed. "Marsha, draw up a contact for the appraised value. I think Mr. Harrison just bought my land. Tyler, if you and I are going to work together, you need to call me Ned."

"Thank you, Ned. I look forward to it."

*   *   *

When Tyler got back to the apartments, he went straight to Alice and Tracy's. He couldn't wait to share the good news.

"Hey, Mr. Wheeler-dealer," Alice said, "now that you got the land, what are you going to do with it?"

Tyler plopped down on her sofa and said, "I'm going to have it subdivided into nice big lots of about one-half acre each and sell them to builders."

Alice frowned and asked, "You're not going to build the houses yourself?"

"Not this time. I need to know how to buy and develop land, and I'm going to learn all I need to know with this parcel of land."

Her frown deepened. "Can you sell that many lots? How many will there be?"

Tyler leaned over her coffee table as if he were looking at an imaginary map. "Let me answer the last question first. When a piece of land is subdivided for building, about 10 percent is used for roads, sidewalks, and other right-of-ways," he explained, trailing his finger across curving paths on the table. "That would be about twenty acres. So I would be left with approximately 170 acres. If I could get exactly two lots on every acre, that would give me 340 lots to sell, but I won't, so let's say three hundred lots, conservatively.

"Now, you ask me if I can sell them. The answer is yes. I intend to have them all sold within one year. Hardly a day goes by at work that some small or medium-sized builder doesn't come on the job and inquire about buying some lots. Many builders either don't know how or don't have the money to develop their own land, so they're always looking for developed building lots. Because of the wildly rapid growth in this area, there is a huge shortage, and I'm going to help fill it. That's opportunity!"

"Okay, Einstein, how much do you think you can make on each lot?" Tracy demanded.

"That's the part I'm not sure of, but I think I can clear $5,000 on each lot after all development cost."

"My God," Alice exclaimed, "That's $1.5 million."

Tyler laughed. "Yeah, it is. This time next year, I hope to be a millionaire, so I expect you two to treat me with much more respect in the future."

Tracy, who was usually the quiet one said, "Hey, Tyler, go to hell."

Chapter 10

Penny Visits

The air had held the promise of rain all day. It was heavy with moisture, and the million gnats around Penny's rented car were moving so slowly they appeared to be sitting on the air instead of flying. As she mentally ran her plan for the hundredth time, she checked her makeup and ran a comb through her hair. If she hadn't made such a fool of herself on their last date, she could be with him now.

She turned into the parking lot at Keystone Place. As she made her way across the parking lot, Penny did a quick survey. She was wearing pink sandals and white shorts. He had always told her how pretty her feet and legs were. Funny, she had never thought of her feet as pretty until she had dated him. Now, because of him, she noticed other women's feet, and he was right. She tucked her blouse in for the tenth time and hoped it made her waist look small. She checked the neck and made sure the third button was loose. It would give Tyler just a peek at the top of her breasts, and he had seemed fascinated with them.

She reached the vestibule at the bottom of the steps and looked at the mailboxes. His was near the end, and she could see his name above the apartment number. Searching for the nerve to ring the bell, the irony of the situation did not escape her. They had dated. They had been happy. They should still be together. She loved him so much, and she knew she always would. Whoever had said, "You don't appreciate what you have until it's gone," must have been a loser at love.

As she rang the doorbell, her mind raced through what she would do and what she would say. She waited. She rang the bell again and then laughed out loud when she saw the peephole in the door. He most likely wouldn't even bother to open the door, and if he did, he was so damned proud he probably wouldn't speak to her anyway.

The thought that he was inside and wouldn't open the door was really pissing her off. Her first instinct was to kick the door, but she remembered she was wearing sandals. So she used her fists. She was convinced that if she made enough noise, he would open the door.

Her resolve was quickly waning and her hands were hurting when the door to her left opened. A very thin, tall, attractive blonde around forty was staring at her. "Can I help you?"

"If you can open this door, yes. Otherwise, no!"

Then the thin blonde was joined by a short, slightly heavy woman with straight red hair. "What the hell is all the racket?"

"I'm sorry for the noise, but I'm not leaving here until he answers the door."

The redhead said, "Did you stop to think that maybe the reason he isn't opening the door is because he isn't there?"

"Oh, he's in there all right. I saw his red-and-white pickup outside."

The blonde said, "He only drives that on the weekend. During the week, he drives the company truck."

"Do you know Tyler?" Penny asked.

"Yes, we've become very good friends with Tyler since he moved in," the redhead explained. "He called here about six and said he would be home around eight. We often eat dinner or cook out together. Do you mind if I ask who you are and why you're pounding on the door?"

"Penny Kilmer," she said. "Tyler and I are from the same town in West Virginia. I came to DC for an education convention, and I wanted … to see him."

Tracy and Alice gave each other a confused look. Penny turned, started down the stairs, and said, "I'm sorry about the noise. I'll wait in the car."

"Hold on," Alice said. "Why don't you wait in our apartment?"

"No, that's okay. I've bothered you two enough."

Alice stepped forward and put her hand on Penny's arm. "You haven't bothered us at all. Besides, any friend of Tyler's is a friend of ours. Now come on. I insist."

Penny asked, "May I use your bathroom?"

Alice released her and pointed toward the hallway. "Of course you can—first door on the right. Take your time."

They were both laughing when Penny came down the hall from the bathroom. Alice made room for her on the sofa and held out a glass of white wine. "We opened a big jug. Have some," Alice said.

Penny took the glass and sat down. She placed her purse on her lap and took what any lady would have to admit was a hell of a lot more than a sip. "Oh God. That's good. I think I needed that."

Alice laughed and said, "Penny, I don't believe we ever finished the introductions. I'm Alice Newman, and this is Tracy Allen. About twenty years ago, we were from Fairmont and …"

By the time Alice finished explaining how they met Tyler, Penny was into her third glass of wine. She felt so relaxed with these women that she decided to tell them about her experience with Tyler. After a rambling speech, she concluded with, "It was such a stupid thing to do." Penny stopped and looked down at her wineglass. The memory still hurt. She sipped her wine and continued. "I had a very terrible experience at work that day. Instead of trusting Tyler and being honest with him, I provoked a fight. It ended when I slapped him in the car. I thought he was going to punch me, and now I wish he had. Maybe we could have settled it then and there, and we would still be together today."

Penny looked across at the women before her, who appeared to be hanging onto every word she said, and sensed she should shut up. Even so, she wanted to talk about it, so she continued, "I've apologized and told him it was all my fault. I told him I loved him, and I've begged him to give us another chance. Would you believe it? He's never spoken to me since that night. Not one damn word! I've bumped into him either accidently or intentionally maybe thirty times in the past four years, and he still has never said a word. Not one word! I should hate the proud bastard, but I don't."

The doorbell rang. On the way to open the door, Alice said, "That should be Tyler. He promised to stop in after his appointment with the real estate lady."

When the door opened, Tyler said, "I did it." He quickly bent down and picked Alice up. With one arm under her back and the other under her knees, he began swinging her around. "Ned liked my ideas, and we meet tomorrow to sign the papers on a—" At first he thought he was dizzy from spinning Alice in his arms or maybe he was viewing an apparition. But no, it moved, and he realized it was Penny.

Penny asked from across the room, "How are you, Tyler?"

Tyler glared at her with such intensity that Penny took two steps backward and almost fell over the low table in front of the sofa.

He carefully let Alice down and asked, "What the hell is she doing here?"

For once, the talkative Alice was at a loss for words, but the normally quieter Tracy was not. "She came to see you, of course. She was in town for an education convention and stopped by to say hello. You weren't home, so we invited her in. I'll remind you that this is my apartment, and Penny is a guest." Tracy walked around the sofa past Alice and stopped directly in front of Tyler. "I love you like the son I never had, but you'll be a gentleman in my home." She took his large hand in hers and said, "Now sit down and have a glass of wine with us. We're dying to hear what happened with Mr. Stanton."

Tracy led Tyler to one of the upholstered chairs. While she went to get his wine, Alice and Penny sat again on the sofa. Tracy returned with a glass of white wine. She gave it to Tyler and said, "Drink."

He took a rather large drink and glanced around. All three women were smiling at him. He made eye contact with Penny, and she didn't look away. Tyler tried to separate all he was feeling. He had never told her how much he was hurting.

"Well, we're waiting," Alice said smiling. "Are you going to tell us about Mr. Stanton or not?"

Tyler said, "No, Alice, I'm not." He set his wineglass on the table between the chairs and left the apartment.

"More wine anyone?" Tracy finally asked.

"Bring the jug," Alice quickly replied. "My God, remind me never to make him mad. He actually scared me."

Tracy poured and sat. "I think you're wrong, Alice. He was angry, but not that angry. I think he's hurt." She looked at Penny and said, "The wound is still open."

"I think you may be right, Tracy," Penny agreed. "When he was looking at me, I didn't think he was mad. I got the image of a little boy who had just been told his dog was hit by a car. I wanted to walk around this table and hold him." She blinked her eyes to hold back the tears. "But now I know that will never happen."

"Don't be so sure, Penny," Alice said.

"What do you mean?"

"I think it may be time to change tactics. It may be time to play hard to get and see if you can make him jealous."

Penny smiled. "Tell me more."

Chapter 11

A Letter and an Offer

yler had always been a morning person. By six thirty, he had done his thirty minutes of exercise, shaved, showered, and had breakfast. Excited about the land purchase and looking forward to the day, he was moving rapidly when he was stopped by a sheet of paper on the floor just inside the door.

Before he picked it up, he recognized the flowing script and knew it was from Penny. He sat in the nearest living room chair, switched on the lamp, and began to read:

> Tyler, sorry about the surprise visit. I've been hired to teach English at Stratford High, so I was allowed to come to a convention of high school textbook publishers here in Washington. I'm to survey and gather teaching materials for our English department. My trip was paid for by the school. My intent was not to upset you, but to release you. I'm seeing someone now, and it was silly to think we could ever get back together. We will, of course, bump into each other in the future. I'd like to be your friend, but if you choose to continue to give me the silent treatment, that's

okay. I'm sorry for any trouble I've caused. I wish you success and a happy life.

Penny.

He was pissed, but why? He would have to tell Alice and Tracy he was sorry and wasn't angry with them. So if he wasn't angry with them, then he must be angry with Penny. He had been angry enough to hit her on that fateful night a little more than four years ago. Four years was a very long time to stay mad, even for him. He was too quick to get mad sometimes, but he was also quick to forgive and forget. No, he really wasn't angry at Penny anymore.

He read the note again. It came to him in a rather embarrassing revelation. If he wasn't mad at Alice and Tracy or Penny, that only left one person. He was angry with himself. How in the hell was he supposed to get over being angry at himself? He imagined he would have to be honest about his feelings and find the reason for his anger. Well, he certainly didn't have time to do that now.

He quickly folded the note and stuffed it in his pocket. On the way to the truck, his mind was racing. He had thought she was still very much in love with him. The rumor mill and the small-town grapevine back home had always kept him informed, and they said that Penny had never dated anyone since Tyler, even at college.

He stopped at the bottom of the stairs and read the note for the third time. *What does "seeing someone" mean?* he wondered. Maybe the usually reliable Stratford grapevine was wrong. He wondered again what all was included in a relationship titled "seeing someone." Did it include sex?

He had to laugh at his next thought. He wondered if maybe he was jealous. That was stupid. He had to assume she would date sometime, and besides, he had Geena. Well, no. Actually, he didn't have Geena anymore. Damn it! Maybe it would be better to be celibate!

*   *   *

Geena picked up the phone and dialed quickly but replaced it before she entered the last digit. She had been doing this every ten minutes for the past hour. She didn't give in easily. She had really expected him to call. No, that wasn't true. She really didn't expect him to call. He wasn't the one who drank too much champagne, got mad, and acted like a complete bitch.

No, Geena thought, *if anyone is going to call, it will have to be me.* It was Friday night, and it had been two weeks since their fight after Abe Cohen's party. She was not used to calling men and trying to make up. This one was special, though, and she knew it. A partial relationship with Tyler Harrison would be better than none. She loved him, and he liked her, and there was no reason why he couldn't grow to love her. She had to admit selfishly that she missed the sex; it really was incredible. She dialed the seventh digit and waited.

"Hello?" Tyler said.

"How have you been?" Geena asked.

"Busy," he replied.

"Yeah, me too. Listen, can we talk?"

"Sure, why not?"

"I hate the phone. How about I come over?"

"I'll leave the door open," he said.

Geena smiled and said, "Great." She hung up the phone. *More fabulous sex is on the way,* she thought.

* * *

Tyler was staring at the huge wall calendar in the construction trailer on Friday, September 6, 1963. He was sad and happy at the same time. Sad because today would be his last day of work, and he loved his job. Happy because now he could devote all of his time to his plans for land development.

He sat down and looked at Geena's picture. She would be moving to New York next week to begin her modeling career. He had promised to help her pack this weekend. They had made up and had been seeing each other almost every night, so he would miss her. They had already made plans for their first weekend together in New York, and she would be here shortly for their lunch date.

It was astounding how much had happened in his life since he had moved to Camp Springs, Maryland. In three short months, he had lost a job, gotten a better one, dated Geena, became close friends with Alice and Tracy, broken up with Geena, had a disconcerting visit from Penny, committed to buy 190 acres of land, made up with Geena, seen Geena commit to a modeling career, and now he was quitting his job.

He almost felt dizzy. He was still a small-town guy at heart, and everything here seemed to move at an accelerated pace.

He saw a shadow on his desk and looked up. He expected to see Geena, but instead saw Abe Cohen looking back.

"Hey, Tyler, got a minute?" Abe asked.

"Sure, Mr. Cohen," Tyler smiled. "I'm still on your time."

"Yeah, that's what I wanted to talk to you about." Abe frowned and closed the office door.

Tyler liked his outfit and guessed Abe was headed for an afternoon round of golf. He was wearing bright-orange golf slacks and a matching orange and white shirt.

Abe sat in front of the desk and said, "Look, Tyler, I know this is supposed to be your last day, but I don't want to lose you. I spoke with Issi last week, and he tells me that every house in this project is on schedule, and some are actually ahead of schedule. He also said all the men like you, and you're the best superintendent he has seen in twenty years of building."

Tyler smiled. "Those are awfully nice things to say. I'll have to thank him."

"I know when you told me last week that you were leaving, your mind was made up, but I want to make you one final offer." Tyler started to say something, but Abe raised his hand and said, "Just hear me out. I have people working for me whom I don't even know, but I've gotten to know you pretty well. You're bright and very perceptive and mature beyond your years. I like you, Tyler, and I don't say that about many people. I'm going to be honest with you. The years are catching up with me. I can't work the way I used to. I want to slow down and spend more time with Valarie. I need someone to run Pride Mark Homes on a daily basis and into the future. If you will stay on, I'll create a new position. You'll become vice president of operations and answer only to me. I'll give you a very free hand and let you name your own salary package. What do you say?"

Tyler was truly humbled and felt very uncomfortable. Abe Cohen had bared his soul, but more importantly, he was willing to open his checkbook. Tyler hoped he wouldn't spend the rest of his life regretting what he was about to do. "Mr. Cohen, I feel very humble. I could never in my wildest dreams imagine having a job like that. I'm sure you've severely overestimated my abilities. Anyone would be foolish not to accept an offer like this, and that's how I may feel in the future. I can only tell you that from a very early age I've had a huge burning in my gut to be my own boss and be in business for myself. I don't know where it will lead me, but I know I'll never be happy until I find out."

Abe leaned back and slumped in his chair. For a moment, he looked like he was far away. Finally, he looked up and said, "That sounds so familiar. I spoke the same words forty years ago. My father was a poor man, but he worked hard to get me through college and then talked my uncle Mort into offering me a great job."

Abe laughed as he relived his memory. "I turned it down to go out on my own, and my father didn't speak to me for three years. He just passed away in 1960. You know what he said to me shortly before he died?" Abe looked away, and Tyler knew he was fighting back tears.

Tyler waited, and in a moment, Abe swallowed and continued, "He said, you've done well, Abe, but you could have done better with your uncle Mort. So you see, I'm not surprised, but I had to try. I didn't think you would—"

"Hello! Anybody home?" Geena said, opening the door. When she saw Abe, she said, "I'm sorry. I didn't know you were having a meeting."

Abe was up quickly. "Come in here, girl. We were just finishing."

Geena smiled and entered. She was wearing yellow sandals and a simple, inexpensive yellow sundress trimmed in white. On her, it looked like it should carry a designer label.

Abe gave her a fatherly peck on the cheek. "Well, don't you look pretty? My God, Valarie is going to make a fortune with you."

"Oh, I hope you're right, Mr. Cohen," Geena replied.

"Well, let me finish, so I can get out of here." He turned his attention back to Tyler. "I anticipated your answer, and I came prepared." From his shirt pocket, he took out two checks. He handed one to Tyler and said, "This will be your last paycheck here. It includes your regular pay through this week. It also includes an extra month's pay plus all the bonuses you would have earned if you had been here."

Tyler glanced at the check and could see it was written for much more than he had expected. "You didn't have to do that, Mr. Cohen."

Abe waved his hand back and forth to signal that it was nothing. "Tyler, I'm sure you remember our meeting here about six or seven weeks ago. I told you then if this idea of yours worked to get us back on schedule, I wouldn't forget you. I had a meeting this morning with my nephew, Aaron. He's convinced we'll save even more money than your first estimate. I want you to accept this with my gratitude."

Tyler accepted the second check and laid it on the other. He was about to thank Abe when he saw the amount. He was sure he had looked incorrectly. He looked again carefully. The written amount was $10,000. That was more money than many people would earn in two years.

He looked up at Abe, who was grinning widely. An idea quickly began to form. There was something Tyler wanted and needed. It could prove to be worth much more than the amount of this check. Tyler picked up the check and reached it toward Abe. "I can't accept this," he said.

Abe refused to take it. "But I want you to have it."

Tyler stood and leaned over the desk. He slid the check back into Abe's shirt pocket. "There is something you could give me, though, and it would mean much more to me."

"What would that possibly be?"

"Your friendship."

Abe laughed. "By God, that's two times you have blown me away. Ten thousand dollars will buy a lot of friendship."

"I may need a lot sometime. I want to be a builder and developer in this area. I'm young, inexperienced, and have no connections. I'll never ask you to do anything unethical or illegal, but it could be a great help to have a friend like you."

Abe stood up quickly and extended his hand. "I would be happy to be your friend, Tyler. I'll help you in any way I can, and that's a promise. I don't make promises lightly, and don't call me Mr. Cohen. It makes me feel old, and friends should use first names. That goes for you too, Geena."

"Thank you, Abe," Tyler said. "I can't tell you how much this means to me."

Abe turned at the door and said, "Stay in touch, Tyler. It's going to be awfully damned boring around here without you." On the way out, he closed the door.

Tyler stood there in deep thought and remained quiet. He had just turned down a position at twenty-three years of age that 99 percent of all the people in the construction trade anywhere around Washington would be ecstatic to have. What amazed him was that he had no regrets. *If I fail,* he thought, *it certainly won't be from a lack of confidence.*

"Tyler?" Geena asked. "Am I wrong or did you just turn down a $10,000 bonus?"

"No, you're not wrong."

"I know you're very bright, but did it occur to you that you might take the money and ask for his friendship too?"

"Yes, it did, but only for an instant. What I really want is for Abe to feel he owes me, and I think he does now. I think if I call him in the future with a problem he can help me with, that I'll now get more than just lip service."

Chapter 12

Geena Goes to New York

Tyler was at Geena's apartment and was talking about his hunting days in West Virginia. Geena curled her legs up under her and sipped her iced tea. "I didn't know you were a hunter."

"Oh, yeah. I used to be. You know how young guys with guns are. I did all kinds of hunting for a while, but not anymore."

"Why not?"

Tyler looked at her for a little while and then smiled. "I'll tell you if you promise not to laugh."

She said, "I promise."

"My granddad has a 120-acre farm about ten miles out of town. When I was eighteen, our family all went there for Thanksgiving dinner. It was deer season, and I had hunted for a couple of days and had only seen one doe but no bucks. In West Virginia at that time, you could only kill a buck.

"After dinner, I was full and needed a walk. I took granddad's deer rifle and walked to a wooded area on the back part of his farm. I knew there was a herd of deer around there but could never see the buck. As I got closer, I realized the wind was coming out of the east instead of the west. It was also just starting to get dark, and that's when the bucks come out. I hurried to my favorite spot, which was a rock ledge about thirty feet high. At that time of evening, with me downwind, I thought I might just see a buck.

"I had only been there about ten minutes when the does started coming out of the thick brush. They milled around and nibbled some grass, but they acted like they were waiting for something, and then I saw him. A large buck with the biggest rack of antlers I have ever seen slowly came out of the thicket. I was so shocked I almost forgot what I was there for. I was only a hundred feet away, and I couldn't miss. I eased the rifle into place and released the safety. I took a deep breath and let half of it out and was about to squeeze the trigger. Then something scurried past in front of the buck. I eased off the trigger and saw that it was a beautiful fawn. Most are born in the spring, but this one had been born late. It was still fairly small and still had those white spots that they're born with.

"The little one turned and came back to the buck and walked under and between his legs. The buck looked down and used its head to nuzzle it and then licked its face. I stood up and laughed at myself, the great deer hunter. Hell, I couldn't have killed it if I'd been starving to death.

"All the deer looked up when I moved, and they quickly ran back into the thicket, except the buck. He just stood there and looked at me. They're usually the most skittish. He actually walked about twenty feet closer and just looked up at me. I know it's silly, but I almost felt like he was thanking me. I unloaded the gun, put it on my shoulder, and started back to the house. When I turned and glanced back the last time, the buck was standing like a beautiful statue, still watching. I've never been hunting since and have no desire to go."

Tyler leaned back and sighed. "I have never told that to a single soul. Even though I played sports and had my share of fights, I was always afraid people would think I was a wimp."

He glanced over at Geena, who appeared to be fighting back tears. Geena stood up and pulled the yellow sundress over her head. She hadn't been wearing a bra and only had on panties.

"Make love to me, Tyler."

Tyler sat his empty glass on the floor and walked hand in hand with her to the bedroom. They didn't come out till morning.

* * *

Tyler was waving, blowing kisses, and smiling. Geena was waving and crying. She had promised herself not to cry, and she hadn't until she was on the train and he couldn't see her.

He was out of sight now. The train was pulling out of Union Station in Washington, DC, and she would arrive in the Big Apple tonight where she would be met by a car from the Cohen-Berger Agency. But she didn't want to think about that now. It had been such a wonderful day. It would have been perfect if he had said he loved her. He had acted like it, though, and that was a good start. He had taken her to a delicious Sunday brunch at the Mayflower Hotel in Washington. They had then gone for a stroll around the reflecting pool between the Washington Monument and the Lincoln Memorial, and he had bought her a butter pecan ice cream cone with three scoops. He couldn't believe it when she ate the whole thing. They ended up back at his place where they took a bath together, and he made love to her most of the afternoon.

She could smell him now, and she so loved the way he smelled. She was funny about that. She had made love to other men, but she was always in a hurry to wash their scent away afterward. With Tyler, she never wanted to bathe until his scent had worn away. She reveled in it now as she relived the day again and again.

Then she remembered the envelope. He had stuck it in her purse just before she stepped up onto the train, making her promise not to open it until she was on her way. When she opened it, she found a note folded around some money. He had taken his time and written very neatly.

She began to read:

> I'm so excited and happy for you. I know you'll be a
> success. Your personality, like your beauty, is unique. I
> know I'm fortunate to be the one you have chosen to be
> with. I hope you'll still have time for me when you're rich

and famous. I know you have some money, but you can always use a little mad money. It's not a loan, so do with it as you see fit. Can't wait to see you in three weeks. Miss you already. Knock 'em dead!

Tyler

She separated the note from the money. She had sold some things, paid some bills, saved a little, and her dad had given her some. All together, she had put together a bit more than $500, not much to begin a new life in New York City. She counted the money he had enclosed. It was all nice, new, crisp one-hundred-dollar bills. There were twenty. My God, she was rich, and he was so sweet. She spent the rest of the trip rereading the note and dabbing at her eyes.

*   *   *

Tyler was seated at his favorite eating spot. He had stopped at the little Jewish delicatessen located near his apartment. It was a tiny place with a huge menu and four small tables. He was seated in the corner with a very large, very good turkey sandwich and an imported beer. It reminded him of what his mother called a Dagwood sandwich. It had everything on it except the kitchen sink and would keep him busy for a while.

He would take this little interlude for some much-needed reflection. Would he miss Geena? Yes. Did he love her? No. Was he dating her for just sex? No. The sex was great, wild even, easily the best he had ever experienced, but there really was much more. She was funny and sweet and ... She was everything a man could ever want. He cared for her and wanted to protect her, but he didn't love her. Why?

He knew very well why, and it always made him angry to think about it. He didn't know about other men, but he was only capable of truly loving one woman at a time. He was in love with a schoolteacher in West Virginia whom he was either too dumb or too proud to speak with and who was "seeing someone," whatever that meant.

71

He wanted to love Geena. He tried. She was here, and she loved him, and she was so loveable. It came to him now. He had looked for the proof that he loved Penny and not Geena but could never get a handle on it, and now it was so clear and so simple. Geena had been with other men, and it didn't bother him. It wouldn't really bother him if she had an affair while she was in New York. On the other hand, he broke out in a cold sweat whenever he thought about Penny "seeing someone." When he thought that "seeing someone" might include having sex, he became depressed and felt lost.

He had been fine and admittedly smug when Penny was wallowing in her own sorrow and waiting for him to return. Now, however, she was a striking, mature young woman with a life of her own, and she was "seeing someone."

As he looked at his sandwich with only two bites missing, he decided he wasn't hungry. He remembered why he didn't do this soul-searching often. He never liked what he found.

*   *   *

Tyler flopped into his recliner and dropped his mail on the end of the table. It was late October, and he had just returned from his second visit to New York. Geena had been there six weeks, and she loved it.

He glanced at the mail and got excited when he saw an envelope from one of the largest banks in the Washington, DC, area. He hurriedly ripped it open, scanned the letter, and yelled, "Son of a bitch!"

He was holding his fifth rejection letter. He was willing to put up his $75,000 and only needed to borrow the balance of the $228,000 to buy Ned Stanton's land. He only had forty days left on his ninety-day option, and no one would lend him the money. He guessed it was because he was so young, although they never said. The banks just said things like, "We are unable to make this loan at this time."

He had thought of asking Abe Cohen for help, but he had really wanted to do this on his own. He just didn't have a track record yet, and the banks were leery. He had put it off as long as he could. He swallowed a large lump of pride and dialed.

* * *

When Tyler started to enter Abe's office, he saw Abe was on the phone. Tyler hesitated, not wishing to interrupt, but Abe motioned him in with a wave of his hand and pointed to an empty chair across from his desk. The office had a fresh smell of cigars and a very comfortable feeling. Abe ended his phone conversation and came around the desk.

He shouted, "Tyler, how the hell are you?"

Tyler expected a handshake, but instead Abe closed in and gave him a warm hug and several pats on the back.

"It's good to be here, Abe, and thanks for seeing me."

Abe said, "You need to get an answering service where I can leave a message. I've called you twice in the last month and can never reach you."

Tyler nodded and said, "Yeah, I guess you're right. I'll have to look into one. You're not the first one to tell me that. What did you want?"

"The first call was about a little piece of land that I thought you might be interested in, but it was snapped up before I could get in touch with you. The second time was for a golf game. You do play, right?"

"I love to when I have the time," Tyler replied.

"I need to be able to get a hold of you. I've been in business around here for a long time, and I know a lot of people. There are many opportunities or deals that come across my desk that I'm not interested in for one reason or another. If I think they would be right for you, I'd be happy to pass them on to you. I hope you'd do the same for me." Abe settled back in his chair and asked, "Now, what's the problem?"

Tyler swung his portfolio from the floor onto his lap and began to extract papers. He laid the rejection letters on the desk and waited till Abe had scanned them. He then gave him an eight-page copy of the business plan he had submitted to the banks with a brief explanation. The business plan was very thorough. It fully explained all the information one would need to know in order to grant a loan for the purchase and subsequent development of Ned Stanton's land, including all pertinent estimates, cost figures, expected sales, including profits, and a reasonable time frame. Abe studied it and asked a few questions. He then asked, "Why didn't you come to me in the beginning?"

"I guess I didn't want to bother you. I wanted to do this on my own," Tyler admitted.

"First of all, it wouldn't have been a bother. Secondly, I'm going to give you some fatherly advice that it took me years to learn. Now, listen and learn. A little pride is great, but too much can screw up your life."

The words were very familiar, and Tyler had heard them many times before, but they still stung.

Abe leaned forward in his chair and said, "There's no such thing as a self-made man. That's bullshit! We all need some help along the way. The secret is knowing when and where to get it."

"I know you're right, Abe. I'm too hardheaded sometimes, but I'm learning."

"Okay," Abe said and chuckled. "I have one more question. Why didn't you ask this Mr. Stanton to finance this sale himself?"

"I did, and he won't. Mr. Stanton has terminal bone cancer and not much time left. He wants to wrap this all up and give the money to his daughters and some to his church."

"All right, second piece of fatherly advice for today: Most bankers are pricks. Two or three of these banks probably turned you down because they're interested in the land themselves or know someone who is, and the others don't know shit about this business. You need to go to a lending institution that specializes in construction and land development."

Tyler was beginning to feel humble again. He was becoming increasingly aware of how little he knew about this business. "I have to admit that I never thought about that. Do you know a firm that specializes in this kind of financing?"

Abe laughed loudly, tapped the intercom button on his phone, and said, "Grace, would you please get Ben over at Heritage on the phone?"

Abe studied the papers before him and said, "This is a beautiful business plan you have. A bank would be foolish not to lend on this land.

Whoever appraised this land is either a beginner or an idiot. I know that piece of land and its worth well over $1,200 an acre. I would say more like $2,000 an acre."

Tyler said, "I wasn't certain, but I thought that was a good price."

Abe was again glancing over the business plan. "Who helped you with this proposal?"

"No one," Tyler answered. "I even did the typing."

Abe's phone rang, and as he lifted the receiver, he said, "It's a hell of a job. I'm impressed." Abe put the receiver to his ear and said, "Ben, is that you?" He listened for a second. "I'm fine. Listen, if you aren't tied up for the next half hour or so, I've got someone I want you to meet." He smiled and nodded his head. "Great, we'll be right over."

On the way, Abe explained that Benjamin Goldman was president of Heritage Federal Savings and Loan. It was located just across the street. Abe said Heritage had more than 2 billion in deposits, and although it would loan its depositors money for any good reason, it did, indeed, specialize in lending to builders and developers.

In the elevator going up to Goldman's office on the top floor, Tyler asked, "So you think they might be interested in making this loan?"

Abe patted Tyler on the back and said, "I can guarantee it."

"Really?"

"Yes, for three reasons." He raised his hand with the index finger extended and began counting. "One, this is the kind of loans Heritage makes. Two, this is a good loan and deserves to be made. Three, I'm the major shareholder and chairman of the board."

Tyler could not contain his laughter, which was matched by Abe's. "I especially like the third reason," he observed.

Abe winked and said, "I thought you'd like that one."

*   *   *

After giving Goldman some time to review the business plan and ask a few questions, Abe said, "Ben, make no mistake, I want this loan made, and I want you to make it a priority. Tyler only has a few weeks left on his option, and I don't want him to lose this opportunity because we're dragging our feet."

Tyler glanced at the fat gray-haired banker, who was frowning slightly. Goldman said, "Okay, Abe, I'm sure we can handle it."

Abe seemed to relax. "I know you can. If there are any problems, call me. And Ben, I want you to see that Tyler gets our preferred rate."

━●━━━━━━━━━━━━━●━━━━━●━

Chapter 13

Home for Thanksgiving

It was late November and very cold in Stratford, West Virginia. Tyler watched as his father added a couple of split hardwood logs to the fire. He warmed to the hissing and crackling as the blue and orange flames introduced themselves to the fresh fuel. It was good to be home. He had missed the sights and sounds of Stratford, but mostly, he had missed the familiar fragrances of this house and the love he shared with the two people who lived here. This was a special time, and he wanted to savor every minute.

Tomorrow would be Thanksgiving, and he had invited Geena to spend the day with his family in Stratford. They had arrived early that afternoon and were looking forward to a relaxing five days together.

Tyler watched Geena as his mother told one of her favorite stories about Tyler's youth. "We lived in a different house then, and it had a very long concrete front walk. Tyler had a little tricycle that he rode about ten hours a day. He used to hook it to a little red wagon and haul around all sorts of goodies. He was outgrowing it, and we decided to get him a new, larger one on his fifth birthday. He loved it but was having a little trouble getting used to the larger size.

"The front walk sloped down to the road with about eight or ten steps at the end. His dad and I were sitting on the front porch watching, and Harold cautioned him about going slowly down the walk.

"Tyler hooked up his wagon and started down the walk. I guess he was going a little too fast, and his feet just flew off the pedals. I heard Harold say, 'Oh God,' and jump up. When I looked up, I could see Tyler was going too fast and had lost control with his feet off the pedals. I watched helplessly as the new tricycle, wagon, and Tyler went off the end of the walk and tumbled down the steps."

His father interrupted to say, "It really scared me, but I thought Kate here was going to have a stroke."

His mom continued, "Harold was way ahead of me, and I expected the worst. When I got there, Harold was already checking him over, and I was relieved to see he wasn't even crying and only had a bruise on his knee and one elbow. After each one of us hugged and kissed him, he pulled away and started loading all of his goodies back in the wagon. I think we were more scared and upset than he was. A little later, I was changing the sheets in our bedroom when I heard a constant loud banging coming from the backyard. I went to the kitchen and looked out the back window. What I saw concerned me more than a little. Tyler had gotten one of his dad's hammers from the garage and was well on his way to destroying the new trike. Every time he hit the trike, he would say, 'Damn bitch!'"

His mother looked at him and smiled. "He scared me a little, but thank the good Lord he grew up to be a wonderful young man."

His father interrupted her musings to say, "Son, you've quit your job to develop this piece of property. How's that going?"

"Great, Dad. I signed the final papers and paid Mr. Stanton last week. The surveyor provided me with a preliminary plat, and I should have three hundred lots to sell, give, or take a couple. It'll be a very nice community with homes selling above $100,000 and will be named Stanton Farms. We've left room for a park with a pool, tennis courts, a baseball field, and a church."

His dad shifted his weight and said, "It sounds great. I can't wait to see it. When will you be ready to sell some lots?"

"Well, thanks to Abe Cohen and Heritage Federal Savings and Loan, I already have more than twenty builders interested. I hope to have all the heavy work done by next April. That means the streets will be roughed in and graveled. The curb will be finished, and all utilities will be installed. I should have some lots sold and see some houses started by May. If all goes well, by this time next year, I'll have all the lots sold and the streets paved. I'll still have to keep an eye on it and approve the houses, but I hope to have all my money by then too."

"That's pretty fast."

"Yeah, but I'm sitting in the middle of one of the fastest growing areas in the United States. People are begging for new homes, and builders are looking for lots, and I just happen to have three hundred of them."

His father leaned forward slightly and asked, "Do you have any idea what your profit will be?"

"Pretty close, yes. When all the development costs are paid, I will have about $3,000 in each lot. I was going to price them at $10,000, but Abe convinced me to sell them for $13,000 each, and I haven't had any complaints about the price from the builders that are interested. So, if I clear $10,000 per lot, I will take in 3 million. After state and federal taxes, and if I reinvest most of the money, I should clear about 2 million."

It suddenly became very quiet in the Harrison living room. The only sound was that which was coming from the fireplace. It was amazing how some phrases like "$2 million" grabbed people's attention.

His mom broke the silence when she said, "You're kidding!"

Tyler frowned and said, "Mom, you know I never kid about money."

Kate quickly responded, "Tyler Harrison, I want you to know here and now that I expect a very expensive Christmas present."

*   *   *

After breakfast the following day, Tyler took Geena on a tour of his hometown.

"So, this is the famous pizza place," Geena said.

"This is it," Tyler explained. "My first big success, the first of many I hope." Tyler sat quietly for a little while thinking. "I still can't believe that little place made that much money." They were sitting in the Ford he had rented for the week.

Geena turned and asked, "Did you date much during college?"

"I don't know. Quite a bit, I guess."

"Anyone serious?"

"Not in college," Tyler answered and then regretted it.

"How about high school?"

"I dated a girl for a couple of years."

"High school sweethearts are hard to forget. Was she your first love?"

Tyler came very close to saying she was his only love but managed to say, "Yeah, I guess."

He was dismayed when Geena kept pushing and asked, "What was her name?"

He could feel his anger building. He turned to Geena and said, "Penny! Her name was Penny Kilmer." It angered him even more now. Why did he feel like he had betrayed a special trust? They hadn't even spoken for … four and a half years. Well, he hadn't anyway. "We dated through our junior and senior years, and then we broke up after graduation."

"Why are you getting so angry?" she asked.

Tyler had started the car and was driving down College Avenue back toward Main Street. He didn't answer but slowed and turned toward Main Street.

"What's that?" Geena asked, pointing to a huge, old structure.

"Oh, that's Eden West. It's where the president of the college lives. You want to see it?"

"If we could. My God, it's beautiful." As Tyler found a place to turn around so he could come back and drive through the gate for a better look, he gave her a brief history.

"It was built by a coal baron named Fields in the 1890s. He came here from Pittsburg, and people say he owned most of the coal and railroads in central West Virginia at one time. He liked it here and bought this land from the college and then had this monstrosity built. It was home to the Fields family for three generations.

"Finally, in the early fifties, the grandson of the original Mr. Fields died, and his widow donated the place to Winfield College and returned to Pittsburg where she had family. Rumor has it that she never liked it here. I remember seeing her downtown when I was younger, and she was definitely not a friendly woman.

"Anyway, I've heard the college would love to sell it but can't find a buyer. The upkeep alone must cost them a fortune. Anyone with enough money to buy it and then take care of it probably wouldn't want to live in Stratford."

The mansion was two hundred feet long with a large portico on columns that covered the front steps and part of the circular driveway in front of the steps. It was built with gray brick and had black stone around all the floor-to-ceiling windows and the double front doors. The second story was completely enclosed within a very steeply pitched roof broken up with large dormer windows and eight chimneys.

"It looks like a huge doll house," Geena observed. "This is the most beautiful house I've ever seen. My God, it makes Abe and Valarie Cohen's castle in Potomac look like a slum."

Tyler was trying to focus on what Geena was saying, but his attention was drawn to a flood of memories. How many times had he heard Penny babble about this house? He'd been inside four times for receptions or teas. The college always invited local high school students who were college bound to tour the Winfield campus. He had wanted to attend Winfield, and although Penny couldn't afford it, she'd come along for the tour. It ended with an informal gathering at Eden West where everyone got to meet the president and his wife.

Penny had cornered the president's wife later and told her how much she loved the house. When she offered to show Penny around, Penny had grabbed Tyler by the arm and dragged him along. Part of the house was closed off, but what they saw was very impressive. Penny had been absolutely enthralled.

"Tyler!"

He snapped back and asked, "What?"

"I asked you why it's named Eden West."

"I'm not sure," Tyler said, "but people say that the first Mr. Fields had a beautiful flower garden behind the house. Supposedly he called it his Garden of Eden, and it was at the west end of College Avenue, so he named it Eden West. Makes sense I guess."

"It's so lovely," Geena sighed. "It seems like such a shame that the Fields family would ever give it up. I guess everything changes if you wait long enough."

Tyler glanced at his watch. "Tour's over. We've got to go change clothes. The family will do me in if I'm late to Granddad Harrison's."

"You like him, don't you?" Geena asked.

"It's much more than that," Tyler replied, "I love him." Suddenly, Geena leaned over and kissed him on the mouth. "What's that for?" he asked.

"Just to thank you for inviting me to spend Thanksgiving with you and to let you know how special I feel when I'm with you."

*   *   *

Tyler sat at the wheel of the rented Ford with Geena close beside him. His parents were in the backseat, holding the part of the Thanksgiving dinner his mother was bringing. They were all wearing what his mom called their Sunday-go-to-meetin' clothes.

They only had about ten miles to go, and Tyler was taking his time enjoying the drive to Granddad's.

Suddenly, he felt a hand on his groin. Irritated, he lightly smacked Geena's hand and placed it back in her own lap. It was illogical, but he imagined his parents knew what she had done.

"So," Geena asked, apparently trying to get back to her best behavior, "I'm looking forward to meeting Tyler's granddad. What's he like?"

When no one volunteered an answer, his mom said, "Tell her, Tyler. You're his favorite."

"Ah, Mom, that's not true," Tyler replied.

"It most certainly is. He has eight other grandchildren, and he pays very little attention to them. If any one of them would have done some of the things Tyler did, he would have killed them, but in his eyes, Tyler can do no wrong."

Tyler took Geena's hand and said, "Granddad and I have always been on the same wavelength. Some of my cousins think he's weird, and the rest laugh at him. They just don't understand him, and I do. I don't know why. I just do.

"You know, I've argued with him maybe a thousand hours, and I could tell the only argument he really enjoyed was the one I finally won. He was very pleased that day and told me so. Actually, they were more like debates than arguments. He would always prove to me with simple logic how and where my argument was wrong. I've learned much more over the years from being wrong than I ever could from being right. I know Granddad is very intelligent, and although he has very little formal education, he reads a lot, and I bet he could hold his own with any of the great philosophers of the past.

"He taught me that when I agree or disagree with something or when I have made up my mind to do or not to do something, I have to know why. It sounds really simple, but it isn't. But the thing I love most about Granddad is his passion for life. Most older people are very set in their ways and reluctant to change, but he's always willing to listen to new ideas. Somehow he's been able to find the perfect mix between passion and common sense, and because of it, he's the only really truly happy person I think I've ever known."

Tyler slowed and pulled off the narrow two-lane road onto a wide, graveled parking area in front of the house. As they unloaded the car, Tyler glimpsed the house and experienced a little sadness when he realized that being there felt a little strange. He vowed to spend more time in Stratford and more time with his family in the future.

As he held Geena's hand and they made their way up the narrow concrete walk, Tyler thought how small the house looked. It was a simple white clapboard house with a front porch, a swing, and two wooden rocking chairs.

He thought of the inside, where there was a living room with a fireplace that burned coal from early fall to late spring; a big eat-in kitchen with an enormous, old round oak table; three bedrooms; and one bathroom. Tyler knew that everything that didn't fit into these six rooms could be found in the washhouse, cellar, toolshed, corncrib, henhouse, or barn, and if it didn't, a body didn't need it anyway.

The front door opened before they reached the porch, and Granddad greeted them with a very welcome smile. He gave a warm hug to Tyler's mother and received a kiss on the cheek. Tyler and his father shook hands warmly with Granddad but refrained from hugging.

Tyler noted the way Geena towered over Granddad in her heels. He was maybe three of four inches over five foot and thin and wiry. He had just a few long white hairs on his otherwise bald but very tan head. He was wrinkled and had his share of liver spots, but Tyler still thought he looked younger than his seventy-eight years. His movements were quick, and he was not at all stooped like many his age. What made him appear younger were those wonderful gray eyes.

"Ty, I've missed you." Granddad had managed with his stern look and four simple words to make Tyler feel guilty for not paying a short visit on his last quick trip to Stratford.

"I'm sorry, but I'd like to come down and spend the day on Saturday if that's okay?"

"That will be great. Don't forget to tell your grandma."

Tyler ushered Geena forward. She had worn a simple gray suit with a knee-length skirt and jacket over a lighter gray blouse and gray heels. "Grand," Tyler said, "this is Geena Morgan. Geena, I'd like for you to meet Granddad Harrison."

"It's very nice to meet you, sir."

Granddad scanned Geena from head to toe and back up again. It was not in a leering way, but rather like someone appraising a work of art. Then he said, "You sure are a pretty thing, aren't you?"

Geena came back with, "And you're a very attractive gentleman, who obviously knows how to treat a lady."

Granddad gave her a wide smile, turned to Tyler, and jokingly said, "I like her. She can stay." He quickly extended his arm like a cadet escort at the military ball, led her inside, and didn't stop until he had reached the large kitchen on the back of the house. There, Grandma Harrison waited, like a Norman Rockwell grandmother, with her white hair in a tight bun. She was wearing a long, white apron that read, "Try it, you'll like it."

Tyler thought his grandma could have easily been a model in her day. Even now, her skin was just lightly lined. Her blue eyes sparkled and radiated warmth.

"Ruth, this is Tyler's friend," Granddad ventured. "Her name is Geena. Geena, this is my bride of more than fifty years."

"It's so nice to meet you. Can I help you with something?"

"Absolutely not. Guests are not allowed to work."

Tyler watched as his grandfather steered Geena to the living room where a coal fire was burning. Tyler was pleased to see the same familiar arrangement of furniture around the brick fireplace. He and Geena sat on the sofa, while Grandpa took his brown vinyl recliner.

"How long have you known Ty, Geena?" Granddad asked.

"Two and a half years, but we have only been dating for about five months."

"I guess you know him pretty well by now. I've never met a person with his degree of determination in my seventy-eight years." Granddad Harrison laughed and asked, "Want to hear a story about him?"

"Now, Grand, don't bore her with stories about me," Tyler demanded.

Granddad looked slyly at Geena and said, "I certainly wouldn't want to bore you, dear."

"Oh please, Granddad," Geena said dramatically, "I love to hear stories about Tyler."

Tyler sighed with his palms up in a sign of surrender and leaned back to hear the story, wondering which one it would be. "He was about ten, I think," Granddad began, "and he was staying with us for a few days. I remember it was wintertime. He played pretty often with the Ritter boys. We were all in the barn, and I asked the boys to go up to the first loft and throw down a few bales of hay. I always burst a few and kept a pile of loose hay on the floor for the horses and the two milk cows.

"When they finished, I told them they could jump down. It was only six or eight feet, and the hay pile was large and soft. The two Ritter boys jumped, and we waited for Ty. He came to the edge and just stood there. I could see he was turning as white as a corpse. I hadn't known until then that he was afraid of heights. The Ritters were really getting on his case, and I got scared when he began to shake. I was afraid he would fall, so I hurried up the ladder and got him.

"When we came down the ladder, he had a death grip on me. As soon as his feet were on the floor, he ran outside and threw up. I felt so sorry for him, but there was little I could do.

"The oldest brother called Ty a sissy and pushed him. Tyler punched him in the nose, and although the Ritter boy was larger, he went down. Fortunately, it was only a bloody nose, and I made the boys apologize.

"After the Ritter brothers left, we went to the house for lunch. Then I sat down for a little to read. When I finished, I called in the kitchen for Ty, and Grandma said he had gone toward the barn.

"I don't like spying on people, but I was a little worried and curious. I went into one of the stalls and watched him from between the boards. He had climbed the ladder and was in the exact same spot as earlier, white and shaking again, and I was afraid he would faint, fall, and miss the pile of hay. Then he jumped and landed softly on the hay and slid to the floor.

"He turned then and looked up for a long time, as if he were measuring the distance. I was waiting for my chance to slip out when he went back up the ladder. He quickly threw three more bales of hay down and jumped again. That time, when he slid off the pile, he got an old pocketknife I kept stuck in the wall and cut the strings on the bales. Then he got a pitchfork, shook out the bales, and added it to the pile.

"He then did the damndest thing I've ever seen. He quickly scampered up the ladder and disappeared. My heart skipped a beat when I saw him appear at the edge of the second loft. He had gone to the back of the barn and climbed the ladder from the first loft up to the second. It's built up high near the peak, much higher than the first, a good twenty feet above the floor. It must have seemed like a mile to Ty.

"I knew I should stop him, but I have to admit I was caught up in the moment and fascinated with his struggle. He was visibly white again, and he was shaking. He stood there for a very long time, and then I saw him smile. He leaned forward, yelled Geronimo, jumped, and landed square in the middle of the pile. He disappeared for an instant and then bounced up and slid down to the floor. He yelled, 'I did it.' Then quick as a cat, he ran up the ladder, went back to the second loft, and did it again. While he was jumping around and celebrating, I slipped out and hurried back to the house.

"In about ten minutes, he came in and hung up his coat. Then he said, 'Grand, I'm not afraid of heights anymore.' Later that evening, he demonstrated his jumping from both lofts. I waited until he was sixteen until I told him I'd spied on him. Then I asked him why he did it.

"He said, 'I couldn't stand it, Grand, if you thought I was a coward.'"

To Tyler's surprise, both Geena's and his grandfather's eyes became wet with tears. Geena patted Tyler's hand and said, "I always knew you were special."

Tyler looked up and offered, "A little strange, maybe."

His mother suddenly appeared and proclaimed, "Dinner's ready. Come and get it."

Chapter 14

Kate Urges Penny into Action

It was two days after Thanksgiving, and this was the first minute Kate had been alone in the past four days. It was wonderful to have Tyler home, but she would have enjoyed the visit more if Geena had stayed in New York. Tyler was spending Saturday with Granddad Harrison, and Harold had taken Geena downtown for a little Christmas shopping.

As she dialed the number, she hoped she would get lucky and catch Penny at home. Kate wondered why she didn't feel guilty for doing this. She had tried unsuccessfully to dislike Geena and found that she was a very lovely young lady and very much in love with her son. But her decision was quite easy. Tyler and Penny had been perfect together, and they could be again. She was certain that Tyler still loved her and, like most young men, didn't know what was best for him. Kate would just have to nudge him in the right direction; it wouldn't be the first time.

Penny answered, "Hello?"

"Hi, Penny. It's Kate."

"What a nice surprise. How are you?"

"I'm fine, Penny. I guess you know Tyler's home for a week during Thanksgiving, and he brought a friend."

"Yes, I heard yesterday," Penny said.

"Look, Penny, can I be perfectly honest with you?"

"I'd like that, Kate."

"We've talked before about this, and you know I'd like to see you two back together again. You do still want that, don't you?"

"Yes, Kate, more than anything. I've never stopped loving him, and I'm a fool for letting him get away."

Kate dabbed at a spot on her kitchen counter with a dishcloth and said, "We all make mistakes, Penny. He made one too, and if he wasn't so damn hardheaded, he'd see it. You know I'm very fond of you. That's why I called. You need to do something, and soon. This young lady who came with him is a model from New York, and she's very attractive. I think you're much prettier, though. She's trying very hard to sink her hooks into him."

"Kate, I appreciate your effort, but I've done about all I can."

"Well, don't give up, and I won't either. For what it's worth, he and Geena—that's her name—are going to the seven o'clock movie this evening, the one that stars Paul Newman."

"Oh, yeah, I know the one. Maybe I'll go too."

"Why don't you do that," Kate advised.

"Thanks, Kate. I'll let you know what happens."

As soon as they hung up, Penny called Dr. Milton Wesley Randall, thinking he would serve her purpose well. He was a gifted mathematician and professor of advanced mathematics at Winfield College who lived next door to her. He had purchased and remodeled a huge old home next to Penny's rented apartment over a garage. He was handsome in an academic way, tall and thin, with thick, sandy hair. He always dressed Ivy League and was rumored to have come from old Boston money.

When Penny had moved into her apartment, Milton had appeared and pitched in. Since that day, he was always trying to help or borrow something. He had also asked her out a couple of times. She felt guilty for using him in her short-notice ruse, but she was pretty sure he would jump at the chance to take her to the movie. It turned out, she was right.

* * *

The Center Theater had been built just after the war in the late forties and had been recently updated to show the new Technicolor films. Penny persuaded Milton to park at a particular meter near the front of the theater, hoping this would be a good spot to see from but not be seen. It was still a little early, and she and Milton were making small talk in the car when she spotted Tyler. He was too far away, and it was too dark to recognize his face, but she recognized his confident swagger. Unfortunately, Geena was on the other side of Tyler as they passed, and she didn't get a good look at her.

Penny and Milton quickly joined the ticket line behind Tyler and then entered the small lobby and refreshment area, where Penny's knees went weak when she saw Tyler's date. Geena and Tyler were talking in front of the coming attractions billboard. She was striking! The woman was only wearing blue jeans and a sweater, and she was stunning. She looked like she had just stepped off the cover of *Vogue*. Penny just hadn't expected someone this … perfect. Before she could decide what to do, Geena turned and went into the ladies' restroom, and Tyler started toward the refreshment counter.

Penny quickly wrapped her arms affectionately around one of Milton's and said, "Let's get popcorn." Penny used Milton first as a shield so she wouldn't be seen and then as a blocker when Tyler was close. She could only wonder what Milton would think as she pushed him into Tyler.

Milton quickly said, "I'm sorry. Excuse me!"

When Tyler saw her, he looked quickly at Milton and then did a double take—no, maybe a triple take. She saw what she had only hoped for until now. First there had been surprise and then hurt. She was sure of it. Her spirit soared as she realized it hurt him to see her with another man.

"Tyler!" Penny said. "How are you?"

He looked speechless but managed to reply. "Fine."

"I didn't know you were home," she fibbed.

Tyler said, "Yeah, I came in for Thanksgiving."

Penny turned and said, "Milton, I'm sorry." Hanging onto him like he was her man, she announced, "This is Tyler Harrison. Tyler, I would like for you to meet Dr. Milton Randall."

Milton quickly shook hands and said, "Nice to meet you, Tyler."

Tyler said, "Hello, Milton. Excuse me, I need to get some popcorn. Nice to see you again, Penny."

Penny then turned to Milton and said, "Just a small popcorn and a small Coke." She turned and walked away to wait for Milton. She had worn a fall dress and a light coat and heels. Penny walked slowly and tried to flex her calf muscles with each step. She hoped Tyler was looking.

Penny saw Tyler keep glancing back toward her, but she refused to make eye contact. She was thoroughly enjoying herself until Geena came out of the bathroom. She was wearing very little makeup and obviously didn't need it. Penny was sorry to see that the closer she got, the better Tyler's date looked.

When Milton showed up, Penny had him wait while she went to the restroom.

When she and Milton entered the theater, the cartoon had started. Penny spotted Tyler and Geena and steered Milton to the vacant seats three rows behind them. Milton seemed pleased as Bugs made a fool of Elmer Fudd, and Penny watched Tyler and Geena.

Penny really did like Paul Newman, but she was not able to enjoy those eyes this evening. She kept wracking her brain to plan her next move. She wasn't having much luck, when midway through the movie, Tyler got up and went toward the lobby. On a sudden impulse, Penny followed.

When she reached the lobby, it was empty, and she knew he was in the restroom. She waited. When he came out, Penny quickly started across the lobby toward the ladies' restroom. Tyler saw her and cut her off, which was what she had hoped would happen.

"How do you like the movie?" Tyler asked.

"It's pretty good," she said, letting him ask the questions. She was curious where this would lead.

"So, how do you like teaching?" Tyler ventured.

"I like it. If it paid better, I would love it."

"You look really good, Penny. You're even prettier than when we dated."

She wondered what he would do if she threw her arms around him and kissed him. She knew he was trying in his own protracted male way to make a connection with her. She wanted so badly to help and knew she couldn't. She simply said, "Thank you."

He smiled and looked away. He then looked back and forth between her eyes and his shoes. It was the only time she could remember Tyler when he didn't look confident. It was a long silence before he finally spoke again. He stepped forward so quickly she was startled. When he spoke, she could feel his breath.

"Penny … I've done some pretty dumb things in my life. I want you to know that … I'm really … sorry." He was looking directly into her eyes. "I was just wondering … you know, if you would like …"

"Want anything else to munch on?" Milton interrupted. "I decided to get a popcorn."

Penny took a step backward, feeling like she had been caught kissing on the front porch when her dad turned on the light, though Milton had already turned toward the concession stand. She wanted to shout, "If I would like what, Tyler?" but stood helplessly as he turned and walked away.

Chapter 15

———— ❦ ————

A Church Dedication

yler was sitting in the new offices of Harrison Ltd. looking down Georgia Avenue in Silver Spring at a huge advertising billboard with Geena's picture on it. It was mid-April 1964, and spring had sprung in Washington. Everything was new and green with spring flowers everywhere. Tyler had even braved the traffic to view the beautiful and now-famous cherry blossoms around the Tidal Basin and the Jefferson Memorial. The trip had been well worth the time, and it was one he hoped to make often in the future.

As he looked at a twenty-foot-high Geena, he could only venture a guess why he and she were both millionaires. They had both worked hard, but it had come rather easy, it seemed. Tyler had never believed in fate, but he was beginning to wonder. His dad always said that when you work hard and smart, you make your own luck, but Granddad said there was no such thing as luck. He felt that luck was simply when preparedness meets opportunity. There was, of course, much truth in both.

Back in January, Geena had signed a five-year, multimillion-dollar deal to represent Cabrini jeans. Giovanni Cabrini, an Italian designer, was rapidly becoming the most famous in the world. Geena had become an instant millionaire when she signed her name and became the Cabrini girl.

She was also quickly becoming a celebrity. The billboard showed Geena wearing a very tight pair of Cabrini jeans from the rear while looking over her shoulder with a saucy smile. The words across the bottom read: "Geena likes 'em, Cabrini jeans."

Geena also had two television commercials, and almost every magazine featured her in a full-page ad. Geena had flown in for a weekend in late March, and when Tyler had taken her out for dinner, many people recognized her, and a few asked for her autograph.

Valarie had promised that many more companies would want her to represent their products, and she had been right. Valarie had carefully negotiated her contract so that Geena could model and endorse other clothes and products as long as there was no direct conflict with the Cabrini line.

Tyler, still looking at the billboard, thought he should be more pleased. After all, he was the only man sleeping with the woman, while the other men in America could only fantasize about her.

She had been rather angry with him over the Christmas holiday, and for the first time, she had withheld sex from him. She had naturally assumed she would be invited to Stratford for Christmas, but she had been wrong. But they had made up and were now seeing each other as often as their busy schedules would allow.

He had seen Penny twice during his Christmas visit, and both times, she had been with Milton. Tyler didn't like it, but he didn't know what to do about it.

Tyler and Abe Cohen had become very close during the past few months, and when Tyler was ready to open an office, Abe had insisted it be in the building where his offices were. Abe owned the twelve-story building and used the top three floors for his own operation.

Tyler now had an open-ended lease for the entire ninth floor at the ridiculous price of $1,000 a month. Anyone else would have been happy to pay five times that. Abe refused to take more and said he would profit from having Tyler in the building.

The phone interrupted his thoughts, and because the newly formed corporation, Harrison Ltd., only had one employee, and he was it, he answered the phone.

"Could I speak with Tyler Harrison, please?" Tyler recognized the voice instantly. It was Ned Stanton.

"It's me, Ned. How are you feeling?"

"Not bad for an old guy. I had my monthly checkup last week, and my cancer is in remission. It looks like I'm going to live longer."

"Ned, that's great news. I'm very happy for you. I hope you don't regret selling me your farm."

"Not for one minute. I'm real happy with what you've done with the land. Stanton Farms is one of the prettiest developments around, and my church still can't believe their good luck. That's why I called. Just wanted to make sure you would be at the dedication today. It starts at one."

"I wouldn't miss it, Ned, and thanks again for inviting me. I'll see you there."

Tyler replaced the phone on the receiver and thought about the chain of events that had led up to today's dedication. He believed the Lord worked in mysterious ways and wondered again if His subtle hand had anything to do with those recent events.

A couple of months after Tyler had purchased the 190 acres, Ned called. He had decided to move in with one of his daughters, who was now a divorced nurse. He wanted to know if Tyler would buy his house and the ten acres it sat on.

Tyler had originally planned to set aside part of the land he'd already bought from Ned for Ned's church, but then he had another thought. He agreed and told Ned what he intended to do with the land. Ned was very pleased, and they agreed on the appraised price of $60,000.

Tyler quickly divided the ten acres into two five-acre lots and had them rezoned for churches within two weeks with a little help from Abe Cohen. Tyler put up a large sign on one of the five-acre plots and sent letters to every existing church in Montgomery County. Tyler then sold the five acres where the house sat back to Ned for one dollar, and Ned donated the land to his church.

Within one month, three sweetheart land deals were offered to Tyler. He had already optioned two for purchase and was working on the third. Just last week he had signed a contract to sell those remaining five acres to a large Methodist church for $200,000, so he would reap a $140,000 profit.

Then he started thinking about that. He couldn't think of anything else, and it wasn't for lack of trying. He was making money from a church! He tried to rationalize it. They were getting a good price. They were happy with the price, and it was a big church, and they could well afford it. Still, he was making money from a church.

He didn't know if the good Lord was sending him a message or not, but he was pretty sure someone was. He called the church, and at a hastily scheduled meeting, he announced to the minister and trustees that he wanted to lower the price to $60,000, which was what he had invested initially. That way, he explained, he would make nothing, and maybe he could get some sleep.

After a stunned silence, they accepted and did everything but wash his feet. He would never forget, would never try to explain, because he couldn't, the feelings that washed over him after he left that meeting.

Tyler finally decided that the Big Man upstairs did, indeed, work in mysterious ways. It was called "tax breaks." Tyler wouldn't have to pay any taxes for at least a year. Now whenever he thought about it, he had to smile. With God and Abe Cohen on his side, how could he lose? Tyler quickly called his answering service and got his messages. He returned a couple of calls and then headed for the elevator.

When the doors opened, Tyler quickly headed across the marble lobby. On the way, he noticed the large glass case that named all the businesses in the building. There beside the ninth floor was Harrison Ltd. Yes, by God, he was going to make it!

*   *   *

A small stage had been set up on a grassy area behind Ned's old house. It contained a portable pulpit and microphone, which was connected to a number of large speakers spaced evenly throughout the congregation. Behind the temporary stage was a very large sign completely covered with white bedsheets sewn together by some of the good women of the church. Tyler had not expected such a large group for the gathering. There were easily three hundred folding chairs. All were full, and nearly that many people were standing.

The minister finished his invocation, and Tyler raised his head and glanced skyward. Not one cloud could be found on the horizon. The haze and humidity so familiar to the Washington area had been soundly defeated and driven away by a bright sun and a perfect azure sky.

Ned stood and approached the microphone. He did not use notes as he spoke very calmly about the land and the history of the farm. He then turned and pointed out Tyler. He told them how Tyler had sold the land back to him for one dollar so that it would be donated in the name of Ned Stanton and not Tyler Harrison.

"It's him that you need to thank," Ned suggested. "It was his idea to do this, and although I gave a little, he gave much more. He's a very unusual young man, and I would like for him to say a few words if he doesn't mind."

Tyler could feel every eye in the newly mowed field on him, and even though he had prepared nothing, he could not turn Ned down. When Tyler stood up, Ned quickly shook his hand and sat down. Tyler could only marvel at how much healthier Ned looked, as opposed to when they'd first met.

Tyler stood at the microphone, looked out over the congregation, and tried to remember at least one thing he had learned in Public Speaking 101. Absolutely nothing came to mind. Trying to gather his thoughts, he remembered practicing a speech in the kitchen with his mother. It wasn't going well, and his dad had come in to get a cup of coffee. He'd listened for a little while and then said, "Why don't you just say what you feel?"

Tyler smiled and began telling the people what he felt. "Before the end of next week, the five acres that adjoin this property will be owned by the Rockville United Methodist Church. They hope to have their new church completed by next summer. I hope they will make good neighbors. I understand that Baptist and Methodists are allowed to speak to each other."

There was much laughter and some applause. Tyler continued, "During the negotiations to purchase this farm, Ned Stanton and I spent a lot of time working together, and I've come to know him well. Ned is a very good man, and I don't say that lightly. You should all be happy that he's a member of your church, and I am equally happy to call him my friend.

"Since Ned and I signed the papers to give this land to your church, both he and I have been blessed. My business has prospered in ways I couldn't have imagined, and Ned's cancer has miraculously gone into remission. I leave it for each of you to contemplate the meaning of these recent events."

Tyler had to pause, because his voice had crackled and his eyes were a little wet. He suspected his were not the only ones. "I thank each of you, and especially Ned, for the opportunity to share in this dedication. I wish you well in your building endeavor, and I promise you, if I receive an invitation to attend the first service, I'll be there."

The minister thanked Tyler and made a few brief remarks. When he was finished, the architect pulled a cord, and the new sign with a large picture of the future Montgomery Baptist Church was unveiled. Everyone quickly formed a very long line and served themselves to a good, old-fashioned covered-dish dinner.

Chapter 16

Harrison Ltd.

$\mathcal{A}$ week after the land dedication, Tyler, Tracy, and Alice were at Tyler's favorite Jewish deli, and he had even managed to get one of the four tables. Tyler wondered where these people got their food. They had meats and cheeses no one else could get. He would miss this place when he left his apartment at Keystone Place, but he would miss Alice and Tracy more.

Between bites and sips of a foreign beer he had also never heard of, he said, "I feel sorry for you. It must be awful to get up every Monday through Friday and drag yourself to work. Why do you do it?"

"The government pays well," Tracy pointed out, "and they have great benefits."

Alice said, "In case you hadn't noticed, we're both forty-two-year-old divorcees, and we like being employed."

"Yeah, but not by the government, right?" Tyler asked.

"Right," Tracy said. "If I could find a civilian job with decent pay and equal benefits, I'd take it in a minute."

Alice said, "Me too! We both have a little over twenty years in at Agriculture. We could retire at half pay. I'd take it and walk tomorrow if I had somewhere to go."

"Okay, fine." Tyler nodded. "Come to work for me."

They both looked up. "You're serious, aren't you?" Tracy asked.

Tyler ignored her question as rhetorical. "How much do you make?" he asked.

"Give or take a few hundred, we make about $20,000," Alice said.

Tyler looked away and thought for a few moments. Then he turned back to them and said, "I'll pay you each $30,000 per year and match your benefits and retirement. I'll also give you a share of the profits."

"To do what?" Alice asked.

Tyler took the last bite of his sandwich and killed his beer. "To do what you do now."

"I don't understand." Alice shrugged.

"Okay, let me explain," Tyler advised. "I have over $1 million in the bank and will make 2 million or more this year. I have a lease on the ninth floor of a beautiful old office building in Silver Spring, and the remodeling work will be finished in June, so you could put in notices and start in less than two months. I have three great land deals on my desk and don't have time to pursue them. I have other ideas and business avenues I want to enter. I want to expand, but I'm too busy with little details, because I'm the only employee Harrison Ltd. has. Alice, you're an accountant, right?"

"Yes."

"Tracy, you hire people and do personnel, right?"

"Yes."

"Okay. I need someone to help me hire people and properly staff Harrison Ltd. Hell, I don't even know what I need, but I know I need an accountant."

Alice put down her bottle of Coke. "Tyler, we can do accounting and personnel, but we know zilch about land and building."

"Contrary to what you might think, I don't know much either, but I know both of you are bright, and we'll learn together. Listen, you two, I'm going to build a multimillion-dollar company, and I need some key people. I have to have someone I can rely on and trust. We've become like family, and I would trust you with anything, and I respect your opinions. I need help and would rather have you two for employees than anyone else I know."

"Can we think about it for a little while?" Tracy asked.

"Sure," Tyler replied. "Why don't you talk about it tonight and tomorrow and make a list of questions. We'll get together tomorrow night, and I will answer any questions you have."

*   *   *

Tyler opened the door on his truck and could already feel the June heat. It was only seven o'clock in the morning, and already the humidity was in the nineties. As he walked away from his pickup, he could feel the sweat break out and begin to soak into his golf shirt.

When he reached the elevator, he pressed the up button. While he waited, he looked around the underground parking garage. His truck was the only vehicle there so early. Tyler had parked in the space reserved for him, right next to the one that was labeled for Mr. Cohen. When Tyler had agreed to lease the ninth floor from Abe, he had immediately been assigned the privileged space next to Abe's.

When the doors slid open, Tyler stepped into the new home of his business.

He was pleased with what he saw. Most of the ninth floor had been gutted two months earlier, and the remodeling was about finished except for a few finishing touches. Harrison Ltd. was up and running. Alice and Tracy had accepted his offers, and Tracy had already hired a secretary named Liz and some other staff for him.

Tyler placed his portfolio on the edge of the desk and began a detailed reconnaissance of his office. Almost everything was spring green or white. It was amazing how decorators could spend other people's money. She had insisted that his desk could not just be laminated with white Formica like all the others. She had hunted until she found what she wanted. Tyler was now the owner of a desk, credenza, bookcase, shelving unit, and portable bar made in California, and they were oak with beautiful coarse grain. They had all been stained and bleached and were now white. The decorator had explained in great detail why they were so expensive. Each piece was stained repeatedly until the proper shade of white was obtained. Then it received ten-plus coats of hand-rubbed varnish.

Tyler felt decadent when he thought how much he loved the desk. The feeling was almost erotic as he rubbed his fingers over the finish. He was also pleased with the white leather sofa and chairs across the room. The furniture was arranged with tables and rested on a beautiful green and white custom-made rug in an oriental design, which rested on a thick, plush, wall-to-wall spring-green carpet. The white walls were busy with huge prints of famous golf scenes encased in green frames. The large double windows in the corner were covered by custom green shades.

He loved this office and felt good in it. That was good, because he knew he would spend much of his life here. His favorite part of the office was his private bathroom. It was done in white marble and had a sink, tub, shower, toilet, and a dressing area with its own closet. Tyler had been so pleased with the bathroom he had jokingly asked if he could put his desk in it.

Tyler was going over the contracts for some land that he would purchase tomorrow when he heard the light tapping. He looked up and was surprised to see his secretary, Liz, had come in an hour early.

"Hey, Liz, what are you doing here so early?"

"I knew this would be your first day back, and I thought you might need me."

She had worked for him for two weeks, and already he wondered how he had managed without her. Liz was short and slim. Her shiny brown hair was usually up or in a bun. She always wore a dress or suit with heels. In only two weeks, he believed she'd learned his every like and dislike. She seemed actually offended if he did anything in the office for himself.

"What's been going on since I've been gone?"

"The painters and carpet men will be finished tomorrow. Mr. Cohen called about ten times to remind you to come up and see him this morning, and you have a meeting with Alice and Tracy at eight thirty. I took the liberty to order pastries to be delivered at eight o'clock, and I've already started the coffee. I have your other messages when you're ready."

"Okay, sounds good, Liz. Why don't we work our way through the messages before the meeting?"

When she returned, Tyler said, "Oh, by the way, Liz, I would like for you to sit in on the meeting this morning. I want you to know that I value your opinion."

She appeared surprised and smiled. "Thank you, Mr. Harrison. I appreciate that."

When Tracy and Alice stuck their heads in and asked if he was ready for the meeting, he stood up, gave each a warm hug, and said, "Let's do it."

When he and the three ladies were seated on the sofa and chairs, he said, "I want to make a few things clear. I don't wish to be surrounded by yes-men, or, in this case, yes-women. As time goes by, we'll be doing new and different things. I want your honest opinions. It's okay, even good, to disagree with me, but we must all agree to never be disagreeable. I'll listen to any reasonable suggestion or argument, and in the end, I'll decide what's best for Harrison Ltd.

"You need to know how this corporation was set up. In Maryland, every corporation must have three officers and must issue shares of stock. My mother is secretary and owns one share of stock. My dad is vice president and owns one share of stock. I am president and own the other ninety-eight shares. You'll never have to worry about working for someone else. Harrison Ltd. is my company and always will be. It is my hope that we'll be one happy family, and we'll all make a lot of money. Now, tell me what's happening."

Alice opened her folder and began. "All bills and interest are paid except for the final payment on the remodeling. That should be paid by Friday, and after that's paid and payroll for this week is deducted, we'll have a little over $1.6 million in the bank. I hired a new accounting clerk, and he's doing an excellent job."

When Alice was finished, Tracy said, "I've been working on a new personnel guide and will soon finish a company policy manual. I have also hired a new receptionist, and she'll start next Monday."

"Great! Sounds like you two have been busy. Anything to add, Liz?"

"Yes, one thing. I had paging added to our phone system. Anyone can now call anyone else in their office by dialing only two digits. You can reach me by dialing one-zero."

Chapter 17

Tyler's Class Reunion

*I*t was a perfect mid-August evening in Stratford. Tyler was in town for his first class reunion, as the officers in his class had decided to have a get-together every five years. Tyler felt like he was on his way to the prom. His dad had positioned Geena and him in front of the fireplace for pictures with his new Polaroid. On the last one, his mom posed between them.

"Okay, Dad, we'll see that one when we get home. I want to get there a little early."

"What's the hurry?" his mom asked.

"Now that Geena has become a celebrity, and this is my first five-year class reunion, I don't want to look like we're making a grand entrance."

"All right, go on." His dad said. "We'll take some more tomorrow night when you get all dressed up for the formal dinner and dance."

In the car, Tyler explained again that they were going to the Stratford City Park. The Friday night get-together was to be an informal gathering with Cokes, beer, finger food, and cold cut sandwiches. Tyler had asked Geena not to get too gussied up, reminding her that most of his classmates were just small-town folks. She'd found a simple, light-blue sundress with spaghetti straps and cute matching sandals, and Tyler wore white summer slacks and a bright-green golf shirt.

He parked in the new paved lot at Stratford City Park and was surprised to see a new, larger pavilion. It reminded him that now he was only a visitor to Stratford. At a card table just inside the pavilion, Debbie, a former cheerleader, gave out nametags. Despite her great personality, she was obviously starstruck around Geena.

Next was a receiving line with those classmates who still lived in Stratford and had done all the work on the reunion. Everyone seemed to know that Geena was coming, and all seemed impressed. Tyler was very pleased with the casual way Geena handled her elevated status. She was very friendly, and everyone liked her.

Penny and Milton were the last ones in the welcoming line. Milton looked nice in gray pants and a blue short-sleeved shirt that looked like it had been pressed for a military parade. Tyler thought he was a handsome man, but he seemed a little detached. Penny was stunning. Her shoulder-length blonde hair was swept back on one side and loose on the other. She wore a very feminine light-pink summer dress. Her jewelry was simple and white, as were her perfectly manicured nails.

Tyler had looked forward to this event since he had received the invitation back in June. During high school, he had been very popular because of his warm personality, and although he had never really been a member of any particular clique, he was welcomed by all. He found himself laughing about old times and renewing old friendships.

The only discouraging part of the evening for Tyler was Penny and Milton. Every time he observed them she was clinging to him like he was the only man on earth. He couldn't help wondering how much of each other they were seeing. Penny and he had dated for two years without being intimate. How long would she and Milton date before sexual intimacy would become part of their relationship, if it hadn't already?

The evening ended too soon for Tyler, and on the way home, Geena had many questions. "I heard a lot of the guys call you Ace. Were you a good poker player?"

"I was a good baseball pitcher, and they always call the best pitcher their ace. I guess we all had nicknames back then."

"I like your class. They seem like a fun bunch. I don't know what I expected."

"I always liked most of them. Some are a little strange, and they have their own way of doing things, but most of them are damn good people."

"I'll tell you what I didn't expect," she said. "I certainly didn't expect anything like Penny in Stratford. She is lovely and classy."

Tyler thought for a second before he answered. "Yeah, she's always been pretty. We used to date, but that was a long time ago."

*   *   *

Geena and Tyler had dressed, checked each other over, and given their approval. Earlier, Tyler had played golf with three of his classmates and had gotten more sun, and Geena thought he looked like he had just flown in from the islands. Harold was ready with a new fresh pack of Polaroid film.

Geena's antenna had gone up last night when Tyler said he had dated Penny and then abruptly dropped the subject. She had asked Kate about Penny, and Kate had stuttered and stammered that she didn't know her very well and quickly changed the subject, which made Geena's antenna extend another notch.

The reunion was well planned. Tyler and Geena were having a great time and seemed to be the center of attention. Geena could see why he had been popular. She noticed that Tyler went out of his way to meet everyone, including those who were less popular. The Moose Lodge had been rented for the event because it was large and had a bar, a kitchen, and a dance floor. It was decorated with balloons and crepe paper in the school colors, which added nostalgia.

When everyone had finished their desserts, Steve, who had been class president, stood at the head table. He introduced all the class officers who were there and everyone who had worked on the committee. It was then time for every classmate to stand and introduce themselves and their spouse or guest and give a brief history of the past five years.

When Tyler's turn came, he stood and said, "I'm Tyler Harrison, and I'm only here because Geena Morgan couldn't find another escort." Everyone laughed and applauded. "After high school, I went to Winfield College and finished with a degree in business with a double major in accounting and economics. During my freshman year, I started the College Pizza Shop, and then I sold it just before I graduated. For the past year, I've been in the Washington, DC, area, and I recently started a land development company. It's great to see all of you again, and I would like to add my thanks for all the hard work that's been done on this reunion." Geena was smiling but not happy. She had been watching Penny while Tyler was speaking, and Penny had not taken her eyes off him and appeared mesmerized.

Immediately after the introductions, a few prizes were given for things like who had the most children and who had come the farthest. People began to congregate into groups, and Tyler and Geena found themselves surrounded by one. All of a sudden, a very attractive redhead in a low-cut dress stepped in front of Tyler and loudly said, "Hello, Harrison."

Tyler appeared to do a double take and said, "You look great, Joan. I didn't recognize you."

She gave him an affectionate hug and said, "You look great too, Harrison, but then, you always did. I came all the way from Florida to get in your pants, and when I get here, you've been snared by a model."

Geena laughed and said, "Thanks for the warning, Joan."

Joan smirked at her, looked around, and said, "Okay, who wants to hear the best-ever story about Tyler Harrison?" About twenty people said they did and began to crowd around.

"All right, pay attention," Joan said, "because this is a classic. When we were in the first grade, every boy hated girls except Tyler, and he had a crush on me. He damn near drove me crazy. The summer after first grade, my dad built a tree house for me, and one day Tyler and I were up there playing. I told him I would show him mine if he would show me his. Tyler, being the young gentleman, volunteered to go first. He pulled down his pants and proudly said, 'What do you think?' I was shocked. I took a close look and thought it was funny looking, so I laughed and ran into the house."

When everyone realized that was the end of the story, they howled. Tyler joined in and Geena too.

When they finally settled down, Tyler said, "Everything she said is true. I'll never forget it. I stood there for quite a while with my pants down around my ankles before I realized the little bitch wasn't coming back."

Laughter again broke out.

"I did learn a valuable lesson that day," Tyler recalled.

"What's that, Harrison?" Joan asked.

"Never show first!"

Someone in the back yelled, "How 'bout it, Geena, does he show first?"

"Never," Geena replied loudly. "I always show first."

From that point on, if she hadn't been already, Geena felt she was clearly accepted as a welcome member of the group.

*   *   *

The lights dimmed, and the music started. Most headed for the dance floor, and the rest found seats to watch. A few had had too much to drink, but Tyler thought they were all pleasant. After about an hour, the lights came up again, and Nancy Howard, head of the reunion committee, stepped on stage with a microphone.

"We thought it would be fun to bring back the homecoming dance of our senior year. We're going to put on a great old slow song, and I want all those people who attended that dance out here on the dance floor. But there's one catch—you have to dance with the person you went to homecoming with. So if they're here, go find them."

A number of people started yelling and scurrying around. Tyler froze. He hadn't planned on this. Up on stage, Nancy said, "Okay, let's get started. This special dance will be led off by our former homecoming queen and her escort. Penny Kilmer, come on out."

Everyone cheered as Penny emerged from the crowd. She was wearing a low-cut, blue formal dress that ended just below the knees. Her blue heels matched perfectly.

Nancy looked at Tyler and said, "Tyler Harrison, your queen awaits you."

Tyler gave Geena a quick peck on the cheek, and to loud cheers, he stepped forward and gave a very proper bow befitting his queen.

The lights were cut low again, and Nancy said, "Queen Penny, the dance floor is yours."

"Come Softly to Me" by the Fleetwoods started to spin, and Tyler fitted Penny to him, and they began to dance. He remembered how easy she was to dance with and always seemed to anticipate his next step.

"You're on the committee. Did you plan this?" Tyler asked.

"Hell no," she said with a drunken slur. "Are you so pompous to think I would try to sneak a dance with you?"

"No, but I thought you might want to dance with me."

"Okay!" Nancy said over the mic. "You other people with your homecoming date join in."

"Why would I want to dance with you when I have a doctor to dance with?" Penny asked.

Tyler decided to just get through this without causing a scene. "So, how are you and Milton getting along?"

"Famously," she snapped. Penny took his hand, which was on the small of her back, and slid it down until it rested on her buttocks. "He particularly likes this ass. He told me just last night that it was prettier than Geena's."

"It's very nice, Penny." He slid his hand back up and hoped no one had noticed, but she wasn't finished.

"He's also very fond of these," she said, drunkenly rubbing her breasts back and forth over his chest. "Do you remember them?"

Tyler willed himself not to become aroused, but he couldn't help it. "Yes, Penny, I remember." Tyler hoped she was too drunk to notice his arousal, but she wasn't. She pressed her body against the growing lump in the front of his pants. Before he realized exactly what she was doing, she took her hand down from his shoulder and grasped his erection.

"You may be too proud to admit it, but I see part of you still wants me." She released him and said, "I guess it's a little late, you dumb bastard." She stepped back and he could see she was crying. "Now if you'll excuse me, I have to go throw up."

He felt like a dumb bastard as he went looking for Milton to tell him that Penny was sick in the ladies' room.

*   *   *

On the way back to Washington, Geena asked about the dance with Penny, and Tyler almost bit her head off. She was upset and decided not to wait any longer.

"How long did you say you and Penny dated?"

"Two years. Why?"

"Because she is in love with you."

Tyler snorted. "That's ridiculous."

"Take my word for it. Women know! She loves you. Do you love her?"

Tyler sighed and said, "Look, we were only high school kids. We went together for two years. You may not believe this, but we never even had sex."

Geena didn't believe him at first and almost laughed, but after a little reflection, it made perfect sense.

She reached over and placed her hand on his thigh. "Tyler, the next time you're in Stratford, I want you to screw Penny."

"What?"

"Spend the weekend with her. You have my permission. Screw her. Make love to her. Otherwise, I don't stand a chance."

"Why would I want to do that?"

"So I will have an even fight for your love. She is your first love, and because you never had sex with her, she's become some kind of mystery woman. She'll lose some of that mystery when you have sex with her and hopefully becomes just another woman you've had. I can only battle a real woman, not some mystery woman that you've placed on a pedestal."

Chapter 18

———◆◇◆———

Preparing to Enter the World
of the Super Rich

1965

Tyler looked up from his folder, and his eyes slowly and lovingly caressed the fixtures separately. Almost every piece of furniture in this room had been a labor of love. He had decided late last year that it was crazy to battle his way to and from work every day around the Beltway. The trip took nearly an hour every morning and evening, and that time could certainly be put to better use. He made an executive decision; it was time to move to Montgomery County.

Because she was so efficient, Liz, his secretary, spent about seven out of eight hours each day looking for something to do. Tyler had called her in and asked if she would mind helping him with a personal matter. She had said she would love to help, and he had put her to work looking for a new apartment. He hoped it would keep her busy for a few weeks, because he was very specific. It didn't.

She had returned in less than an hour. She had found something she thought might interest him, although not exactly what he had requested.

It was a condominium rather than an apartment, so he would own rather than rent. It was also located about fifteen minutes away in the exclusive neighborhood of Bethesda, Maryland, about one mile outside of Northwest Washington.

Because Liz had been the one to find it, he took her along that afternoon to have a look. It was a five-year-old building with ten floors and three levels below ground. It was located perfectly. The building was set in the center of Bethesda with all of its exclusive shops, restaurants, and department stores and was just one block back from Wisconsin Avenue, which was the main artery where all the traffic and noise would be found.

The building itself was also impressive, and although it had every modern amenity, it looked like it was inhabited by old money rather than the nouveau riche. The lobby was tasteful with marble and Oriental rugs. The building had an excellent security system complete with doormen. The basement had three levels. The lower two levels were for parking, and the third had a salon, a barber shop with a shoeshine boy, and a modern exercise spa with a pool.

Every floor had four condos except the top floor, which had two very large penthouses. It was one of those that was for sale. Tyler understood that, should he want to buy the condo, he would have to be approved by a committee of owners as being worthy to live there.

The penthouse was vacant and huge. It had large rooms with ten-foot ceilings rather than the standard eight-foot. The windows were large and bathed the rooms with natural light. The condo had a foyer, living room, dining room, eat-in kitchen, master bedroom with its own dressing room, walk-in closet, and bathroom. It also had two guest bedrooms, two other bathrooms, a lovely large den with bookcases, and maid's quarters with bath.

In the kitchen the saleslady showed Tyler three appraisals. Two were by independent appraisers, and the other was by Riggs Bank. All three indicated that the condo was currently worth around $300,000, which surprised Tyler. He thought it was worth more.

"What do you think, Mr. Harrison?" the saleslady asked.

"I love it. Tell your clients if they'll sell it for $275,000, I'll take it."

She opened her briefcase and extracted a real estate contract, which she started filling in.

His offer was accepted, and within one week, he had been accepted and welcomed by the other owners. Liz found one of the few decorators in the DC area who spent more time listening than she did talking, and they went to work. He was convinced after a week that the decorator was a mind reader. She seemed to know his taste better than he did. He was so pleased with the outcome that he gave her a $5,000 bonus. Tyler had moved in on the first of December and liked the place more every day. She had used a myriad of carpets, fixtures, accent pieces, fabrics, and colors to create a very warm, comfortable, and inviting home. He had a little over $350,000 invested. That seemed like a fortune to him, but he had more than $3 million in the bank and was expecting that to more than double this year.

*   *   *

It was a cold and rainy day in early February. Tyler was nervous. Today he would decide whether to go ahead with an idea he had been kicking around for years. The phone on Tyler's desk buzzed. He pushed the button for speakerphone and said, "Yes."

"Alice just buzzed from the conference room," Liz said. "They're ready for you."

"Thanks, Liz. I'll be right there."

On the way down the hall, he asked, "How many hours have we spent on this project, Liz?"

"I don't know for sure. We started about six months ago—hundreds, maybe a thousand. Are you going to go ahead with it?"

"I'll let you know after this little meeting. And, Liz, thank you for all your help. I couldn't have done this without you."

"I enjoyed every minute of it." She beamed.

Tyler opened the conference room door and followed Liz in. What he saw was Alice, Tracy, and ten other men and women who each owned a real estate company in DC, Maryland, or Virginia.

Alice said, "If everyone will find a seat, we'll begin."

Everyone quickly found a seat.

Tyler slowly looked at the eight men and two women real estate brokers until he had established friendly eye contact with each one. "Good morning," he said, "and thank you all for giving me this time out of your busy schedules. I'm Tyler Harrison, and I promise not to waste your time. You've already met Alice and Tracy, and this is Liz Winters. We have been working on a project I believe will revolutionize the real estate business. I've asked you all here today because you're leaders in real estate sales in your communities. I need some feedback to make some final decisions. I want to pick your brains and get your honest opinions. In return for your time and effort, I'll treat you to an excellent lunch, but more importantly, I'll invite you to be in on the ground floor of this project."

Tyler began to walk around the conference table as he spoke. "Would each of you take a second and introduce yourself and give your company's name and where it's located?" Tyler glanced at Liz and said, "Would you keep account of their answers?"

After all had introduced themselves, he continued. "You're from Virginia, right?" he asked an attractive, slightly heavy, older woman with salt-and-pepper hair.

"Yes, Arlington," she replied.

"What's the biggest problem you face in your company?" Tyler asked.

She only hesitated an instant before she said, "Contingencies."

"What do you mean exactly?" Tyler asked.

"Well, let's say I show you four houses today, and you really love one. You tell me you want to buy it, and I get excited, and then you say you have one little problem. You have to sell your house first and get the money before you can buy the one I'm selling. So, I have a sale maybe. Many times what I have is a mess."

Tyler went around and asked everyone the same question, and Liz recorded their answers. He allowed them to discuss the issues mentioned and come up with other problems that plagued their businesses. When they had exhausted the list, Tyler retrieved it from Liz. He stood and studied it for a little while before he asked, "How many of you would hire me if I could eliminate most of your contingencies?" Three people raised their hands.

"How many of you would hire me if I eliminated most of your contingencies, got you the best sales people from the other real estate firms in your area, told 80 percent of those people who want you to sell their house that we guarantee it will be sold, and doubled your listings so you have twice as many houses to sell?"

One gruff older gentleman asked, "Can you walk on water too?"

After a certain amount of laughing, coughing, and clearing of throats, Tyler said, "You're Mr. Warner, right?"

"Yeah. Warner Real Estate, Alexandria, Virginia."

"I understand that you're skeptical, Mr. Warner. What I'm talking about is doubling your business or more, and that's hard to believe."

"You're damn right it is, because there isn't that much business to be found in my area," Warner said angrily.

"Mr. Warner," Tyler said, "please don't get mad when I tell you this, but you're wrong. I'm not only talking about new business. I'm talking about taking a lot of the business from your competitors." Tyler paused while that soaked in and until he was sure a pin dropped on the white conference table would have been heard by all. "I know you don't know me very well, and I may look like a young whippersnapper to you, but I can assure you I never kid around when I'm discussing money. I will bet you $100,000 that your sales will more than double in twenty-four months if you join the group I will be putting together."

Mr. Warner's smile disappeared, and he looked around quickly. "I'm not a betting man," he finally said.

"Please let me make myself clear to everyone. I am going to start the first national real estate chain—maybe franchise is a better word—in the United States. The companies that join us are going to be very successful, and the companies that don't may not be around in two or three years. I will be putting $1 million of my own money into this project, and I am deadly serious. Let me give you a hypothetical situation. Your company netted $100,000 last year, and I will guarantee to double your net and put it in a written contract. Now it's a year later, and I have done it. You have an extra $100,000 in your hand. How many of you would pay me $40,000 for making you $60,000 you never dreamed you could make?"

115

It took a little while, but every hand went up.

"Good," Tyler said, because it would only cost you about $20,000." Tyler went to the head of the table. "I promise that each of you will be given the opportunity to be the first to join this project in your area. It will take us a couple of months to get some key people in place and get started. Be sure you take this opportunity seriously."

Tyler turned and opened the door. "I promised each of you a great lunch. Let's go up the street and get it, where I'll also have a chance to get to know you better and answer any questions you may have."

*   *   *

Tyler was seated in the lounge of one of the most prestigious law firms on K Street in Washington, DC. He needed a lawyer for his new real estate chain, and he was there to get one.

"Mr. Harrison, you can go in now," the receptionist said. "It's the third door on the right, and her name is on the door."

Tyler was pleasantly surprised. He had only been sitting in the reception area for two or three minutes, and he didn't have an appointment. He had expected a much longer wait. He didn't have to count doors, because the attorney's office door opened, and she stepped out to meet him.

"Come in, Mr. Harrison," Susan Slater said.

"Thank you, Miss Slater," Tyler said. He was a little taken aback. She was very attractive. She had a pear-shaped face with very high cheekbones, a full mouth, and wide-set deep-brown eyes. All this was surrounded by thick shoulder-length brown hair and set on top of a slim, attractive body that her fashionable business suit failed to hide.

He took a seat and glanced around. There were the usual degrees and awards, but mostly he saw plants and knickknacks. The office had a definite feminine flare. It was also surprisingly neat, which impressed him, because it was unusual for a lawyer.

As they both relaxed, he said, "Please call me Tyler."

"What can I do for you, Tyler?"

Tyler pulled a folder from his portfolio. "I want to ask you a few questions, and then I have something very important to share with you. I want our conversation to be completely private. Nothing we say or any information in this folder is to go any further, and that includes other attorneys in this firm. Will you agree to that?"

She appeared intrigued. "Yes, I will agree until I hear something that would cause me to change my mind."

"You've worked on some franchising here, haven't you?"

"Yes," she said. "We've done some work for McDonald's fast-food chain and four other companies."

"How much do you know about franchising, Susan?"

She thought briefly and then said, "I know it all, Tyler. Whether you believe it or not, I'm a damn good attorney."

"I believe it, Susan, That's why I'm here." He placed the folder on her desk. "In that folder are my ideas, plans, and possible numbers for a chain of nationally franchised real estate firms. I've been toying with this since my sophomore year in college. I want you to study it and make a list of suggestions and questions. Oh, and I need it quickly. Would that be a problem?"

She opened the folder, quickly scanned the contents, and then checked her schedule. "I can take a good look at this tonight and do any research I need to do in the morning. How is 2:00 p.m. tomorrow?"

"Great! And Susan, remember—your eyes only."

"You have my word, Tyler."

*   *   *

When he returned to his office, Tyler went in and sat at his desk. His desk phone buzzed, and Liz said, "Geena on line one."

"Geena, are you all right?"

"Yes, I'm fine. I just wanted to tell you the news."

"Lay it on me."

"I'm going to costar in a movie."

"A movie?! Really?"

"I kept it a secret in case I fell flat on my butt. I flew out here Sunday night and did a screen test on Monday for Alfred Hitchcock, no less. He's already started a new mystery movie and just fired his female costar. He saw me and chose me for some reason I still haven't figured out. He thought I would be perfect for the part. I was scared to death, but he's been really sweet. Guess who the male lead is going to be?"

"It's not Paul Newman, is it?"

"Oh God. I wish it were. It's Tony Curtis."

"I like him. He's great. Not bad for your first movie."

"I still can't believe it," she exclaimed.

"You'll be great, Geena. I can't wait to see it."

"Thanks, love. Can you pick me up at National Airport tomorrow evening at seven thirty, and we'll celebrate?"

"I'll be there." He was happy for her, but not wildly happy like he should be. He wondered if he would ever stop feeling guilty for not loving Geena. She deserved better, and he knew it.

*   *   *

Tyler glanced at this watch. It was some sort of French or Swiss name that he could never pronounce but everyone seemed to recognize immediately. He would never have paid this much for a watch for himself, but it had been a gift from Geena. And it was beautiful.

Geena had arrived last evening and wanted to spend today with him, but he had begged off and promised dinner and a full evening. It was twelve thirty, and he still had to grab a bite and get downtown to Susan's office by two o'clock. Just as he stood up, Geena came through the door of his office. She looked like a movie star in a shiny red raincoat and matching red high heels. She was carrying a white deli bag.

"You were a good boy last night and didn't bother me when I had a headache from that damn bumpy plane ride. You even let me sleep in, so I came to give you a reward."

"Is that what's in the bag?" Tyler asked.

Geena stopped about halfway across the large office and pitched the bag toward Tyler, which he caught. "No. That's only lunch. It's for after." She opened her raincoat and dropped it on the thick carpet. The only thing she was wearing now was the red heels. "This is your reward. You do want it, don't you?"

Tyler quickly walked to the door and opened it slightly. "Liz, call Susan Slater's office and tell her I may be a little late, and then you can go on to lunch. I don't want to be bothered for a while."

She smiled and said, "Sure, Mr. Harrison."

Tyler closed and locked the door. When he turned, Geena had kicked off her shoes and was sitting on the sofa with a wide grin. Tyler walked to the middle of the office and started his own striptease. He slowly dropped clothes on her raincoat until he was naked, and then be pranced around for a while, being sure to include some bumps and grinds.

He abruptly stopped and fell to the soft thick carpet and said, "I'm ready for my reward now."

*   *   *

He almost made it on time. He silently thanked the designer of the new miniskirt as he followed Susan down the hall and into her office. She looked fabulous in hers. He felt a little pang of guilt, since he had just left Geena in the shower in his office, but he was only looking.

When he was seated, he asked, "What did you think?"

"There a couple of things you'll need to change, and one thing you'll need to eliminate so it will be acceptable in all the states. I have some questions for clarification on a few points and a couple of new ideas I think you should include. But overall, I think a national real estate chain will sell like hotcakes at breakfast time, and I think you're going to make a fortune. The idea is both clever and yet simple."

"Good," Tyler said smiling, "Because I respect your opinion. Now, I don't want to do anything wrong or unethical, but can we talk off the record?"

"About what?"

"About your participation in this," Tyler emphasized.

"Okay, go ahead—off the record."

"You agree that it's correct to set up a separate corporation, and Harrison Properties is a good name."

She nodded.

"How would you like to work for me as vice president and help me run Harrison Properties?"

Her mouth sort of gaped open, but she didn't say anything.

He asked, "Do you like it here?"

She thought for a second and said, "No, not really. I work ten to twelve hours six days a week to make a lot of money for the partners."

"What's your chance of making partner?"

She laughed and said, "Piss-poor—off the record. The good-ole-boy system is alive and well here."

"How much money will you make this year?"

"Salary and bonus should come to about $40,000."

Tyler leaned forward and said, "I'll pay you $60,000 a year, and together we can work out a bonus plan that will put you over $100,000 after your first year. I would expect you to be rich after five years."

She started to talk, but he raised his hand. "Hold on one second and hear me out. I want you to do the legal work and help with the management. We can hire other people to help us as they're needed."

He was up moving around in her little office now, and she appeared fascinated.

"There's one other thing I think I need to tell you. You're a very good-looking young lady, and I am very attracted to you. But it will go no further than that. Business and pleasure do not mix. I don't know if that's a problem, but if it is, we need to deal with it now."

"The answer to your question is no, it will not be a problem."

It was almost five o'clock when Tyler left Susan's office. He was very pleased. She was to let him know her decision about working for him within a couple of days. She'd said the legal work for the franchise agreements and setting up the new corporation were fairly simple and could be done quickly. His dream of owning a national real estate chain would soon change from ideas to reality. He was about to leave the world of the rich and enter the world of the super rich.

Chapter 19

Plans for Growth

Tyler was looking forward to the day's staff meeting. He had been in Stratford most of the previous week to celebrate Easter with his family and needed to catch up on what had been happening.

"I think we're ready, Mr. Harrison," Liz said.

Tyler looked up and could see that the pizza boxes had all been cleared away, and everyone was seated around the conference table. He tried to have one of these staff meetings with his key people at least once a month.

"I haven't been able to meet with all of you as often as I would like. I want to thank each one of you for a job well done. When I look at what we've accomplished this year, I still can't believe it. I hired each one of you because you were bright and capable of doing what I needed. I also had a gut instinct, and I liked each one of you. I hope all of you are as glad to be here as I am to have you."

He was welcomed by a lot of smiles and one comment. Chet, the new project manager, said, "I've got to tell you, Tyler. I've worked for quite a few people, and you're the only one I ever liked."

Everyone laughed.

"Thank you, Chet. I know you mean it, and coming from you, I consider it a real compliment. I think all of you know why I hold these meetings. I want you to know everything that's happening. I don't wish to put you on the spot. This is an opportunity for each of you to have some positive input. None of you are shy. Okay, let's get started. Let's go left to right. Alice, why don't you start?"

"Thanks to our fearless leader, we will have a banner year. The profits from our land development efforts are running well ahead of projections. We hope next year to have enough cash on hand to finance our own deals without any borrowing."

Susan Slater was next. "I've been here about two months, and I love it. We started last week signing up real estate firms that want to be part of the Harrison Properties national chain. We have in place now more than ten retired, part-time real estate people ready to begin signing on real estate firms across America. Tyler or I will put in a recruiting appearance at every state real estate convention held in the next year. I don't want to bore you, but I think you need to be aware of how large we plan to be."

She opened a file and took out one sheet of paper. "There are currently 6,500 cities in the United States with 5,000 people or more. In five years, we intend to have a Harrison Properties agency in every one of those and more than one in the larger cities. Our projections indicate that the franchise will have 10,000 members by 1970, which will give us a yearly income of $250 million. That's all I have if there are no questions."

There were none, and Tyler said, "Brad, you're next. I know you've met everyone, but why don't you tell us a little about yourself?"

"My last name is Slater, and I think all of you know that Susan is my younger sister. I'm six foot five, and I played a little basketball at Maryland University a few years ago. I was a pretty successful real estate salesman for one of the firms in the Maryland suburbs. I gave that up and came to work with Tyler to head up a new land-purchasing division. He'll need help in that area as he becomes busier with other projects. For the past thirty days, I've been in Ocean City, Maryland. We're convinced that the growth in that city is going to be phenomenal. With the growing popularity of beach condos, we intend to be the leader. We are quietly buying up beachfront property as fast as we can. We hope to be ready to begin building high rise condominiums next spring. I've already obtained one nice parcel and have options on three others. I also love it here and look forward to working with all of you."

Tracy glanced at Brad to make sure he was finished. She said, "We've hired fourteen new people since the first of the year to deal with Harrison Properties. We're also prepared to handle the new workload when Chet begins those 240 houses at Quail Hollow." Tracy smiled and said, "I love the name of the new subdivision, by the way."

Everyone laughed, because they all knew she had won the contest to name it.

Chet said, "Out at Quail Hollow we've started seven model homes. They'll be finished and ready to show by this fall. I'm excited about them, because they'll be the prettiest, most innovative, and best designed houses in the Washington suburbs. They're going to win us a lot of awards and help us sell out Quail Hollow very quickly."

Tyler said, "Thank you, Chet. Liz, that leaves you."

"Don't be surprised," Liz began, "if you see Mr. Harrison on TV soon. He has agreed to do some commercials for Harrison Properties. The advertising agency we've decided to go with had to twist his arm, but he finally agreed. As you all know, Harrison Ltd. has a lease for the ninth floor, but we're going to outgrow it next year. We hope to get the floor below it soon, so we can expand. But what we really want is our very own building and headquarters out along Interstate 270. I'm working on it. Some other things that Mr. Harrison and I are working on for the future include building condos and townhouses, a shopping mall if someone doesn't beat us to it, and a long-range goal to build a complete city between here and Frederick, Maryland. I think we would all have to agree that Mr. Harrison is a dreamer who makes his dreams come true. I'm just thankful I get to come along for the ride."

The meeting lasted another hour and a half as Tyler asked many questions and got fully updated on what everyone was doing. Everyone left with most of their problems solved and the satisfaction that they could walk into Tyler's office anytime and get the help they needed.

After the meeting, Tyler led Liz to Tracy's office where she was meeting with Alice. Tyler said, "I'm glad you're both here. As head of accounting and personnel, you two need to know what's happening. Liz will no longer have the same job." He then looked at Liz and said, "Liz, you're much too important to me to be a secretary. How would you like to be my new administrative assistant—with a raise, of course?"

Liz beamed. "That sounds great," she said. "But what will I do?"

Tyler said, "First, you'll hire a secretary to do what you have been doing so you can devote full time to working with me. I want you to help me do some of my job and also do some things I don't have time to do. Can you do that, Liz?"

"I'll do my best."

"I know you will. Tracy, you will need to change her job title to administrative assistant and help her hire a new secretary. The secretary will work for her and me."

Tracy smiled at Liz and nodded.

"Liz, what is your salary now?" Tyler asked.

"$12,000 per year."

"Well, I think you're worth about twice that much. Alice, from now on Liz's salary is $24,000 per year, and of course, that will also double the size of her bonus check at the end of the year."

Liz stepped forward and said, "Thank you. Is it okay to hug the boss?"

"Absolutely."

Liz gave him a kiss on the cheek and a warm hug. When she finally stepped away, her eyes looked a little damp.

Changes

1966

*T*yler was seated on the sofa in his office when the three ladies entered. Alice, Tracy, and Liz each found a seat and took it.

"Good morning and thanks for coming so quickly," he said. "As you know, a legal corporation in this state must have three officers. When I set up Harrison Ltd. and later Harrison Properties, I made my dad and mom token officers, because I had to have two other than myself.

"The other day, I was talking with Susan about some other legal matters, and she asked me what would happen to these companies if I got hit by a car and died. I had to tell her I didn't know. Since then, she and I have reorganized these two companies, and you three need to know about it. I love my folks, but they know nothing about what we're doing here in the Washington area, so I have removed them as corporate officers and replaced them with you three.

"Liz, you're now vice president in each corporation. Tracy and Alice, you two are both secretary-treasurers of each corporation. I'm still the president of each corporation. Don't get hung up on these titles, because they're meaningless. No one has any more power because of their title. The power comes from who owns the most stock. I have had Susan reissue the stock in both corporations. Each one of you now owns one share, or 1 percent, of each company, and I own the other ninety-seven. Don't scoff at your one percent. Each of your shares is now worth about $150,000. I estimate that each of your shares will be worth at least $5 million in five years."

All three women sat, apparently stunned and only able to listen.

"Now, for the important part. If I were to die, you three would become the board of directors. I can't run these companies from a grave, but I don't want them to die, so they would become your companies. At the end of each year, you would have to give 10 percent of the net profit to my folks and 10 percent to charity. The rest would be up to you to do with what you want.

"As the national real estate chain grows, you'll have more cash than you can spend. You can diversify or give more money to charity or both. You three would have to make those decisions, but I want these companies to continue and no employees to lose their jobs. If one of you should decide to sell out or retire early, you'll have to select someone in the company to replace you. Choose wisely!"

He walked to his desk where he punched two numbers into his phone.

"Susan, would you bring up all those papers so these three ladies and I can get them signed?"

* * *

When Tyler and Liz's new secretary, her niece Robin, came into the reception area outside his office, Tyler also saw Abe Cohen and his daughter, Blair.

"Where in the hell have you been?" Abe asked.

"Having lunch."

Abe laughed as he gave Tyler one of his now-familiar hugs. After a quick tour of the place and a long approving look at Tyler's office, Blair and Tyler joined Abe at the sofa. Blair would be about twenty-six now and finished at Georgetown Law, and she was all woman. Oh, she was a looker with dark hair and huge brown eyes, and she had a thin desirable body like her model mother. She secreted sex appeal. Blair looked like one of those women you wanted to think twice about making love to because she looked like she might hurt you.

"I wanted you to be the first to know the good news, since it will affect you too," Abe announced. "Blair has agreed to be vice president of Pride Mark Homes, and in a year or two when I step down, she will take over as president."

Tyler leaned forward and shook her hand. "Congratulations, Blair. That's great news. I'm glad you're not going to be a full-time attorney. I don't like many of them."

"Neither do I. That's why I'm taking this job. Also, the money is great, and I like being the boss."

I'll just bet you do, Tyler thought.

*   *   *

When the door to the limo was opened, Tyler got out first. They had been in the limo for more than an hour, and his eyes were used to the low light. He was almost blinded by spotlights, floodlights, and camera flashes. He managed to extend his hand and help Geena from the car.

Someone appeared and told them to follow him. They were led on a red carpet between barriers toward a low platform. Tyler and Geena both tried to smile and not squint. People were yelling out Geena's name, and to Tyler's complete surprise, a few women seemed to be yelling his.

So this is a movie premiere. My God, what a mess, Tyler thought to himself.

He had seen them on television, but this was the first one he had been a part of, and if he could help it, it would be his last. He wondered why all these so-called adoring fans didn't get a life.

On the other hand, he guessed he shouldn't complain. The advertising agency doing his campaign was ecstatic. They knew that he and Geena would appear in most newspapers and morning, noon, and night on the major television networks for a couple of days. He was spending a fortune on advertising and couldn't begin to get that kind of coverage, and it was free.

They had stopped on the platform and were being interviewed by the local Los Angeles CBS affiliate. Geena was wearing a conservative evening dress and seemed to take all this excitement in stride. Geena was a pretty classy lady, and Tyler suspected she might become a permanent fixture out here in La-La Land.

Tyler thought the questions were redundant, but he smiled, looked at Geena, and tried to look extremely interested. The man with the microphone said, "You two have been dating for a long time now."

Geena looked lovingly at Tyler and said, "Yes, almost three years now. He is a very unique man."

Burt, the man with the mic said, "Well, Geena, America wants to know. When are you two going to tie the knot?"

Geena said, "Now, Burt, you have to allow a lady some secrets."

Tyler was relieved and thought Geena had given a super answer when Burt asked, "You do love her, don't you, Tyler?" Burt stuck the mic in front of Tyler, and America waited. Tyler glanced at Geena, and she was smiling at him, but now the smile was more serious, and it occurred to Tyler that she was enjoying this.

Tyler would have preferred to give an honest answer, but there was a problem. He wasn't sure what the answer was. If he said yes, it put him into an area where he wasn't sure he wanted to be. If he said no, it made Geena look bad, and America might think he was a philanderer.

He said, "Tell me, is there any man in America who doesn't love this woman?" *Thank God for my Jewish friends*, Tyler thought. From them, he had learned the age-old technique of answering a question with a question.

But Burt was not easily steered and came back with a follow-up question. "Might there at least be an engagement in the wind?"

Tyler stuck his index finger in his mouth and then held it up as if he were testing the wind. "You never know what the future will bring, but I wouldn't want to give away any secrets."

Later, he was dismayed to learn that it didn't make any difference what he said. What counted was what the media claimed he said, and they claimed there was an engagement in the wind for Tyler and Geena.

* * *

The following evening, Walter Cronkite said, "America has found a new love story to follow." He went on to give Geena and Tyler's names and a brief history of their meteoric rise. He did a voice-over as a number of snapshots and some of the footage from the previous night's premiere showed on the screen. Walter finished with a still of Tyler with his index finger in the air testing the wind. Cronkite said, "Is there an engagement in the air? America thinks so."

Penny switched off the television and said, "You son of a bitch." She hurried into her kitchen where she tore off a paper towel and wiped at her wet eyes and cheeks. She was a little-known English teacher in a small town with seventy-some dollars in the bank and an old, worn-out Plymouth. She didn't deserve Tyler, because she was too damn dumb to get him.

Well, if Tyler Harrison thought that little Miss Penny Kilmer was going to dry up and blow away, he was wrong. She had no intention of quietly going down the path to being an old maid. She threw the tear-soaked paper towel in the kitchen trash and went to the bathroom. She started a bubble bath and took off her clothes. She stared for a long time at her flawless body in the full-length mirror mounted on the bathroom door. She tried to imagine how Geena would look standing next to her. She was convinced Geena's breasts would be tiny, her body a little too skinny, and her feet flat and ugly.

She struck a model's pose and said, "Eat your heart out, you proud bastard."

Penny had a long, soothing bath and felt relaxed as she toweled off. She added a touch of perfume here and there and slipped into a dress. She put a bottle of white wine in the freezer to chill, got out some cheese and crackers, lit a candle in the living room, and without hesitation, she sat down and dialed the familiar number.

"Hi, Milton. What are you doing?"

"Making a math test for one of my classes," he responded.

"Why don't you take a break," she suggested. "Come on over for a while."

"Now?" he asked.

"Yes, now! I have something for you."

"Really?" he said. "What is it?"

Penny laughed seductively. "Something you've wanted for a long time, and I'm sure you'll like it."

"Okay, I'll be there shortly," he promised.

Penny hung up the phone and walked to her bedroom door. The bedroom was neat, and the bed was made. She decided to turn the bed down, and then she saw it. It was staring back at her with the same smug look as the proud bastard that had won it for her at a carnival. She wondered why she had kept the stupid purple stuffed rabbit all these years. She grabbed the hapless, floppy-eared hare none too gently and started for the door. She stopped, looked at her little dressing and makeup table, and picked up an expensive bottle of perfume that Tyler had bought her years ago.

In the kitchen, she stuffed the rabbit into the bottom of the large trash can and poured the perfume down the sink while running the water. She threw the empty bottle in the trash and then regretted it. She should have put a little of it on. Wearing Tyler's perfume while making love to Milton would have been a nice touch.

When Milton arrived, he didn't seem to pick up on any of the obvious hints, including low lights, burning candles, and the fact that the whole place smelled like a French brothel. Evidently, there was still quite a bit of Tyler's gift perfume in the sink drain. Penny was so focused on getting him interested that she completely forgot the wine and cheese.

After ten or twelve minutes of listening to news about his latest math classes, she came close to ripping off her little short dress, jumping up in the middle of the coffee table, and asking, "So do you want to fuck or what?" But she didn't want him to have a stroke, and somehow it just didn't seem appropriate. Instead, she kissed him and put his hand on her thigh. She then had to nudge it upward a little, but when he discovered she was not wearing panties, he was off to the races. He peeled her dress off as she fought to unbuckle his belt and undo his pants. His hands were all over her, but unfortunately, Milton didn't appear to know much about foreplay. He carried her to the bed and climbed on top of her. He was clumsy, and she had to guide his penis into her with her hand. He moaned and started thrusting roughly until his body stiffened, and he literally collapsed on her.

"Milton, I can't breathe," Penny gasped.

"Oh, sorry." He raised a little and slowly withdrew from her and rolled over on his back. "God, that was great. You're so beautiful. I hope it was okay for you."

Somewhere in the back of her brain a little warning bell sounded. It must have been female instinct. She didn't want to destroy poor Milton and render him impotent for life, so she lied. "It was fine, Milton."

Chapter 21

---♥---

Granddad Visits

Granddad Luke Harrison was getting tired of waiting. That woman he'd been living with for more than fifty years had a damn bothersome side to her sometimes.

"Are you coming or not, Ruth?" he growled from the bathroom.

From the bedroom, she hollered, "I told you thirty seconds ago that I'd be there in two minutes."

Yes, by damn, she could be bothersome when she set her mind to it, and she had when he decided to go to Washington, DC, without her.

Tyler had been begging his folks and his grandfolks to come on an "all-expenses paid trip" to Washington. Granddad guessed he was pretty proud of what he had done up there and naturally wanted to show off a little. Well, that was just fine with Luke Harrison. He was eighty-one years old, and thank the good Lord, he still had pretty good health. But if he was going to be doing any serious traveling, he'd better get to it. Ruth, however, refused to go.

Well, every cloud had a silver lining. At least she had agreed to help him pack. She was checking his suitcase now, and he was still waiting in front of the bathroom mirror with his tweezers and electric razor. She had agreed to trim and pluck the hairs on and in his ears. He swore there were more growing there than on his head. He looked at his watch for the tenth time that morning. Harold and Kate would be there shortly to pick him up, and then they would all be on their way to Clarksburg to catch a commuter plane to Washington.

Ruth finally appeared and gave him a real mean look in the mirror. She said, "Luke, don't get yourself in an uproar and your bowels in a downpour, or you might shit yourself."

Soon, with smooth ears and his bag packed, he was ready to go. Harold arrived and put his bag in the car, and then he and Kate hugged and said good-bye to Ruth.

Luke said, "You'd better kiss me good-bye, girl. I may not be back."

Ruth gave him a curious look and asked, "Why not?"

"Well now, I may run across one of those younger Washington women and decide to stay."

"And what would you do with her?" Ruth asked.

Luke thought for a minute and then laughed. "Well, not much, I reckon. On second thought, I guess I'll be home soon." He leaned over, and while he was kissing her cheek, he sneaked a couple of love pats on her backside.

She allowed it and then handed him his hat. "Have a good time," she quipped. "And be careful, you old fool."

He plopped his hat on and stepped lightly across the yard with a big grin. That was what Ruth always called him when she was being sweet.

*　　*　　*

As the plane descended, Granddad could see that real tall monument and what he was sure was the capital with squared structures on each end and the big rotunda in the center. Granddad Harrison was like a kid on his way to summer camp, and he didn't want to miss a thing. He'd been up to Pittsburg once to visit one of his other sons who worked in the steel mill and once to Akron, Ohio, to visit a daughter. In eighty-one years, those were the only two times he had ventured outside the boundaries of West Virginia.

He wasn't afraid of flying, but he was respectful of it, especially since it looked like they were about to land in the water. As he involuntarily lifted his feet and looked down at the water, which was frightfully close, land and tarmac appeared under the plane. An instant later, he felt the rear wheels touch down. He wasn't sure if the fellow up front was a great pilot or just damn lucky, but he was glad to be in Washington and on the ground.

Inside the airport, he saw Tyler right away. He was standing with a small group of other people, and he looked great. Pushing past Kate and Harold, Granddad got to him first.

"You must be Tyler Harrison," he said, pumping his hand.

Before Tyler could answer, Kate grabbed him and hugged him. She looked like she might burst with pride.

"Oh, Tyler, it's good to see you. I've missed you so."

"I've missed you too, Mom. Hello, Granddad."

Harold stood back as always and waited. Finally, after Kate got through straightening his collar and fussing over him, Harold and Tyler shook hands.

"Welcome to DC, Dad."

"It's good to be here, Son. I'm looking forward to it."

When they emerged from the airport, the first thing Granddad saw was a white limousine that looked about as long as a train car.

Kate said, "Wonder who's using that."

All of a sudden, an older Italian gentlemen in a chauffeur's uniform hopped out.

"That was quick, Mr. Harrison," the chauffeur said. He quickly took the bags while Tyler tipped and thanked the porter.

"Is this yours?" Kate asked, obviously dumbfounded.

"Only for a few days. I rented it."

"Where to, Mr. Harrison?" the chauffeur asked.

"The Tidal Basin, Tony. I want to see the cherry blossoms with my family."

"Yes, sir, Mr. Harrison, a good choice."

* * *

"Liz, ask Alice and Tracy to come in," Tyler said. Tyler had brought his mom, dad, and granddad to work with him. They had a full day planned, but first he wanted them to see his offices, and he wanted to give them some information. When Alice and Tracy came in, Tyler made all the introductions and explained how they had become such close friends.

"I wanted you all to see where I work, but that's not why I brought you here. In the past three years, every time I bought one of you something, you always said, 'Can you afford that?' I'm tired of it. I don't want to brag, but you're family, and you need to know what we've accomplished here. Tell them, Alice."

Alice opened a thin folder and took out one sheet of paper. "In the past three years, we've bought ten tracts of land and converted them into building lots. Before the end of the year, we'll have three more parcels of land on the beach at Ocean City, Maryland, where we'll begin high-rise condominiums this fall. We'll start 240 houses soon in our own project called Quail Hollow. We've launched a national real estate chain called Harrison Properties, and we're signing up new firms at the rate of forty per week, or about two thousand per year. In five years, we'll have ten thousand members and an income of $250 million per year."

Tyler noticed that each time she gave more numbers, his family looked a little more shocked.

"We have some very exciting plans for the future," Alice continued. "We have plans to build a large shopping mall and a complete city near here. We have a bit more than $30 million in the bank. As of today, we've had four offers to sell our real estate chain. The latest offer was $50 million. We, of course, will not sell. If Tyler sold all of his holdings and paid off all bills today, he would have about $100 million."

There was a rather long silence.

Kate broke it. "I had no idea. So I guess you really could afford those lavish presents at Christmas."

Granddad laughed and said, "I'd like a new farm tractor." Everyone enjoyed a good laugh.

Harold said, "You know, my car is getting quite a few miles on it."

Kate jumped in with, "And I've always wanted to go to Europe."

Tyler laughed. "That's more like it. There's no use to make all this money if we can't enjoy it."

*   *   *

They were at the elevator when Tyler's secretary, Robin, ran out and said, "It's Geena from New York, and she said it's important."

Tyler said, "I'll be right back."

He followed Robin to her desk and used her phone.

"Geena?"

"Oh, thank God I caught you," she said. "I have an invitation to the mayor's house for dinner, and you must come and take me."

"Geena, my family is here, and I'll be with them for the next five days. You knew they were coming to visit me."

"I know," she said. "But you'll only be gone one night, and I need you here."

"I'm sorry. You'll just have to go without me."

"But I need an escort, Tyler," she complained. "You would come if you loved me."

Tyler ignored the cutting remark, but he was getting mad. "Geena, you are a very bright and beautiful woman. I'm sure you can find an escort for one night."

"You're damn right I can, and maybe I'll spend the whole night with him."

"That would be your decision, wouldn't it?" he said before hanging up the phone.

*   *   *

As the plane with his family aboard taxied away from the gate, Tyler could see Granddad plastered against the window waving frantically. He waved back with broad swinging arms until the plane was out of view. On the way back through the National Airport terminal, pictures of the past few days flashed in his mind. His parents had loved DC and had a great visit, but Granddad had been just like a kid. He had been fascinated by everything and had more fun than anyone.

Chapter 22

━•◦━━━━━◉●◯♥◯●◉━━━━━◦•━

Pride and Passion

*P*enny edged forward in line and smiled at her sister who was seated near her. She checked her robe, hat, and tassel again as she neared the steps. She was very relaxed. After all, this was old hat to her now. She would soon walk across the stage and receive a Masters of English degree from West Virginia University. Her only guest was her older sister who was always her greatest fan. Milton was at an advanced math seminar and couldn't be there, but he had remembered her with a card and a popcorn popper. She loved popcorn.

She was at the top of the steps now, with only four people ahead of her. She glanced at her sister and winked. A couple of rows behind her and to the left, she noticed what looked like part of a familiar face. She leaned back a bit so she could see the whole face, and her heart leaped into her throat. It was Tyler Harrison, and he was grinning.

What? Why? she wondered. *Maybe he's here for another friend or relative. Yeah, that must be it. The University is a big place.*

The lady behind Penny gave her a nudge on the shoulder and said, "Go, Kilmer."

Penny realized they had called her name and hurried across the stage where they were waiting for her. The president of the college shook her hand and gave her the degree. As she started to go to the other side of the stage, another robed gentleman stepped out to shake her hand, and when he did, he gave her an envelope.

When she had returned to her seat, she glanced at her degree to make sure it was hers, and then she looked at the envelope. It was from the English Department. She wondered if it was good news or bad news. She had applied to study for her doctorate, but space was limited. If it was bad news, it would surely ruin her day. On the other hand, not knowing would also ruin her day. She opened it.

What she found was a neatly typed letter from the head of the English Department with three paragraphs. The first one said congratulations and told her she was accepted. The second paragraph also said congratulations and noted that she was the winner of a new scholarship. She read it two more times before it completely sank in. The scholarship would pay all college expenses and provide a $500 per month stipend until she had completed her doctorate.

My God! she thought. *That's as much as my monthly take-home pay from my teaching job.*

Finally, she read paragraph three and found out that the scholarship was totally funded by Harrison Ltd. Fortunately, she was near the end of her row and only had to climb over four people to get out. She got Tyler's attention and mouthed the words: "I want to see you."

They made their way to the lobby.

"I can't accept this," she huffed.

Tyler put his hands up to signify a truce. "Penny, please listen. I have more money than I can spend. I already have funded scholarships to help deserving people further their education, and I will continue to do the same in the future. Why not help someone I know? Also, we need to stop this stupid game we keep playing. We dated. We were young and immature, and it's over. Can't we grow up and be friends?"

Friends? That was a new twist! She had enjoyed being in love with him and very much enjoyed her fantasies of doing some nasty things with him in the buff. Lately, she had even enjoyed being mad at the arrogant bastard, but friends would be a new one.

"Do you think we could be friends?" she asked.

He smiled and extended his hand. "We can try."

She gave him a hug and said, "Thank you. You don't know how poor I am."

"Congratulations on your degree today, and I'm very proud of you," he said a little uncomfortably.

She stepped back as if she didn't trust herself too close to him. "Thank you, friend. I have to get back inside."

"And I'm going to slip out early. Take care."

"Bye, bye," she said softly.

Penny pushed through the door, confused. Did he want to be friends, or did he still love her? Did she still love him?

*　　*　　*

Geena was wet all over with sweat, but she hadn't given up, because she was so close. He had already climaxed, and she was thankful that he was still willing. She had moved to the top, which had become her favorite position. There, she was in control, and she could feel the release coming. She shuttered as the spasms simultaneously took her to the now-familiar heights and depths of her pleasure.

She tried not to think about how special this particular orgasm was. Every climax had to be enjoyed fully, and the meaning could be sorted out later, but her thoughts were clouded with the special significance attached to this one.

Geena was free, not that she wanted to be. She had just made love with her favorite photographer. He had filled in a number of times for Tyler when she needed an escort in New York, and he had literally done an amiable job of filling in for him again. She had become a slave to her libido. She felt the inevitable guilt that reminded her she was the first to have an affair. In a way, though, he had been having an affair for a long time. He loved Penny—of that she was sure.

Geena was fully in love with Tyler, but now she had to wonder how much of that love was attached to the fact that he was, until now, the first and only giver of her precious orgasms. She still wanted him, but it was a relief to know that if she couldn't have him, she could at least find pleasure in another man's arms. It was just so hard to continue to love someone who didn't respond in kind.

*   *   *

It was late November, and Tyler could see his breath when they got out of the truck. He and Granddad had driven to the county dump to make the biweekly trash run. It was located about seven miles from granddad's farm on a narrow paved county road.

"Ty, you're going to ruin me," Granddad explained.

"Oh, I think you're too set in your ways to change now, Grand."

"I'm getting lazy, thanks to you. That new diesel tractor has so much power and does so much work that I have less to do."

"Why don't you let me get you a new pickup?" Tyler asked as he threw the broom in the bed of the old truck and closed the tailgate.

"There are plenty of miles in this old truck yet, and besides, I like working on her."

Tyler looked at the old, faded red Ford pickup truck that was now fifteen years old. "How many times have you and I been here together?" Tyler asked.

Granddad banged his pipe on his boot and thought for a little while. "Over the years, I'd say a couple of hundred."

Tyler could remember the day when this old truck was all new and shiny and Grand had taught him to drive. He had only been ten years old, and Grand had put a flat rock on the seat, so Tyler could see out the windshield. Tyler started the truck and adjusted the defroster.

"Wait a minute," Granddad had said. "Before you take off, let's sit here for a little spell and let the heater run. I want to talk to you real serious."

"Okay, Grand. I'm in no hurry." It was a good thing too, because Granddad took a long time filling and packing his pipe. After he lit it, he took a couple of long puffs and cracked the window so the smoke would suck out.

"I've been thinking about you ever since I got back from Washington. I knew you were doing well up there, but I had no idea you were doing that well. I've lived a long time and seen a lot. Hardly ever does anyone stay on top forever. Life tends to ebb and flow. I guess what I'm trying to say is that I am worried about you."

"I'm okay, Grand. Really. You don't have to worry."

"Aw, but I do. Life has a way of slipping up on you when you least expect it and giving you a swift kick in the seat of your britches. In all my born days, I've never met anyone like you. You have a great capacity. You're the most intense person I have ever seen, and you don't waste it. You seem to be able to direct it into whatever you're doing. That's the reason you've always been grown-up for your age, and it's the reason for your success. But it's also the reason for my worrying about you, because I believe you have an equal capacity to be bad. We all have a dark side, but very few have your intensity to throw into it.

"I have to tell you, your folks, your grandma, and me were very worried about you when you were growing up. We laugh now and tell the stories, but we weren't quite sure what we had on our hands. You have to admit that killing your grandma's roosters and jumping from that upper-level loft weren't natural acts."

"No, I guess not," Tyler said.

"Well, anyway, that's what worries me. Do you ever worry about yourself or scare yourself?"

Tyler thought now about a bully he would have beaten to death if some of his friends hadn't pulled him off … a drunken college boy he had punched in the College Pizza Shop … how badly he had wanted to hurt Mr. Nash when he gave his job to another man … Penny Kilmer and how close he had come to loosening her teeth when she had slapped him.

"Yes, Grand, I do worry about myself. I know I have a problem, and I try very hard to control it."

"It sounds like you're going to be filthy rich and with all that money will come power—the power to do good or evil. You've been blessed with a wonderful gift to do so much good, but God surely has a sense of humor, because he's also equipped you with a hair trigger, and now he's going to sit back and see what you do.

"I'm going to tell you what I nicknamed you, what your folks and I have called you when you weren't around since you were about five or six: Pride and Passion! I want you to always remember pride and passion. I won't always be around to remind you that your cup is running over with both. Either one can be good or very bad. Either one can put you over the top or take you down in an instant.

"Promise me that when your anger starts to come on and you begin to feel yourself losing control, you'll remember this little old man who loves you more than he could ever begin to tell you, and you'll pull back, no matter how hard, that you'll use your pride and your passion for only good. Promise me!"

Tyler found it hard to speak, and his voice cracked and almost failed him, but he said, "I promise, Grand."

"*Pride and passion!*" Granddad emphasized. "You won't forget, Ty—ever. Say it!"

Through tears, Tyler said, "Pride and passion. I won't forget. I promise."

Chapter 23

Flying

1967

From up there, the world below sort of looked like a big quilt. Once in a while there was a triangle or some other odd shape, but mostly there were just squares and rectangles. There didn't seem to be any permanency. While hundreds of little cars and trucks rushed up one side of a highway, there was an equal amount rushing down the other side. In one rectangle, people and machines were hurrying to tear down structures, while in a neighboring plot, others were scurrying to build something new. It all looked like a large ant farm, except ants were maybe smarter and would never waste so much energy.

Tyler smiled as he thought how stupid the human race was at times, but he frowned when he remembered that he was one of its busiest members. Surely the Lord in heaven, when he observed all this with a panoramic view, must constantly vacillate between laughter and tears as he looked at what man had wrought.

"You're a hundred feet low and almost five degrees off your heading," Charles pointed out. "You can sightsee or you can fly, Tyler, but you're not good enough yet to do both."

Tyler knew Charles was right and took immediate action to get the little Cessna 150 trainer back on the correct flight path. Charles Kane—and he preferred Charles, not Charlie or Chuck—was a recently retired airline pilot who owned his own plane and was a part-time flight instructor. He was tall, tan, and handsome for his sixty-one years and, to Tyler's great satisfaction, very laid back.

It was a scenic drive from Washington to Stratford, but Tyler was tired of it. He decided if he could fly, he could get there much quicker and would go more often, which was what he wanted.

"All right, let's turn around and head home," Charles said.

Tyler began to make a slow turn to the left, which took him over Interstate 270. It was all he could do not to look down, because he could see his housing development, Quail Hollow, from here.

"I know you're right, Charles, but I develop land, and when I get up here, all I want to do is see what I've done, or what I can do."

Charles grinned. "You won't have to worry when you take your next lesson. I'm going to put the blinders on you. They're a special pair of glasses and visor that block out everything but the instruments. Someone finally figured out that the best way to teach a person to fly by instruments only was to block out everything else, and they were right."

"Oh, goody. I can hardly wait," Tyler drawled.

"Hey, you're a natural at this. You'll do fine."

Tyler was glad to hear that but still a little apprehensive. Mistakes this high seemed to take on a little added significance.

*   *   *

Tyler couldn't describe it, but he could smell it. It was academia. It was oiled wood floors, paper, old books, new books, chalk, graduation robes, and a certain stuffiness, with an ample helping of pomposity. The wainscoted conference room in the century-old administration building on the campus of Winfield College smelled that way now. It was a pleasant scent and brought back many fond memories.

Like everyone who was an alumni of Winfield College, Tyler had received a letter last week asking for a donation to the building fund for the new gym that was under construction. He had called and offered to help and now found himself in a meeting with President Fairchild, five other college administrators, and three trustees.

What Tyler learned was that the contractor and some material suppliers were owed almost $100,000 and were ready to sue. Also, it would take another hundred thousand to finish because of cost overruns.

Tyler had listened carefully and then asked a few questions. When he was satisfied, he pulled a check and a gold fountain pen from his pocket and began to write. He put the pen away and slid the check across the table.

President Fairchild picked it up and raised his head so he could look through his bifocals. He looked up at Tyler and back at the check with a very broad grin.

"Gentlemen, Tyler has just written us a check for $250,000. Frankly, I don't know what to say."

The vice president of academic affairs said, "How about a simple thank you?"

On the way to his car, Tyler felt about ten feet high. He wondered if helping people and giving away money could be addictive.

After the meeting at the college, Tyler drove around and checked out the changes in his hometown. He ended up back near the college and decided to have a pizza. He parked carefully at the College Pizza Shop. On the way inside, he turned to admire his new car. Everyone kept making fun of his pickup, so he had bought a new Pontiac GTO. It was a four-on-the-floor, and he loved it.

Nick, the owner, was there, and he and Tyler shared a pizza. They finished and were talking about old times when one of the employees came over.

"There's a phone call for you on line three, Mr. Harrison."

"Thank you," Tyler said.

"Come on. You can take it in my office," Nick said. Nick showed him into the office and punched the button for line three. "All you have to do is pick up and talk."

Nick stepped out and shut the door.

"Hello," Tyler said, as he wondered who was calling.

"Oh, thank God I found you," his mother said. "Your Granddad had a stroke, and we're at the hospital. Please hurry."

*   *   *

Tyler actually slid a little as he put the GTO into the parking space. His mother was waiting for him in the lobby of the hospital, and it was obvious she had been crying.

"How is he?" Tyler demanded.

She held him and sobbed. "Not good … He's in intensive care, and he had another stroke after they brought him in. Come on."

There were four beds in the little intensive care unit. An old woman was in one, and two were empty. Harold and Grandma were standing beside the bed holding each other.

Grandma came to Tyler and said, "Granddad has asked for you twice. He's partially paralyzed, and he can barely speak."

Grandma Ruth led Tyler to the bed. Granddad looked so helpless with wires and tubes running to bottles and machines.

She leaned over and put her hand on Granddad's shoulder. "Luke, Tyler's here." She waited but got no response. She shook his shoulder a little and more loudly said, "Tyler's here."

Tyler watched with amazement, knowing what he was seeing would forever be carved in the granite of his memory. Granddad smiled as best he could and struggled until he had his left eye open.

Grandma moved a little so Tyler could lean down close. "I'm here, Grand."

Granddad's lower lip moved a little, and he made a low noise that was inaudible.

Tyler held Granddad's hand. "Take your time, Grand. I'm right here."

Granddad's fingers fluttered in Tyler's hand, and his lower lip began to quiver. Tyler leaned so close he could feel Granddad's breath on his ear. The sound didn't really come from his mouth, but from deep within his throat.

"Pri … ann … pass …"

Tyler wanted to hold him, to hug him, but all he could do was bend close to Granddad's ear and whisper, "Pride and passion. I won't forget ever. I love you, Grand." Tyler felt Granddad Luke's fingers move again, every so lightly. When he raised up, the old man was smiling.

An hour later, while holding his bride's hand, Granddad Luke Harrison went to meet his maker.

*   *   *

At the funeral, Tyler's mind was overflowing as the old Baptist minister tried to explain this thing called death. He spoke admirably to give meaning to Luke Harrison's life, but of course, Granddad had done that while living it.

Tyler sat in a room reserved for family in the huge old house that had been a funeral home ever since he could remember. Across the hall in another room, Tyler could see many of his employees. When Granddad had visited Washington, he had come to the office each morning with Tyler, and everyone had become very fond of him. Many friends, relatives, and loved ones said how peaceful, happy, or just asleep Granddad looked. Tyler had only glanced at the little shell in the casket. He was convinced that Grand, at least the part of him that Tyler had known and loved, had already departed. It also hurt. Just glancing at the casket caused an immense inner weight to press down on Tyler's young, strong heart, and he could only surmise what it was doing to Grandma Ruth.

Tyler usually managed to forget his own celebrity status and tried as best he could to downplay it now. He had phoned Geena and told her about Grand. Then he had asked her not to come because of the attention her appearance would attract. She had been sweet, had agreed, and, of course, had sent a beautiful spray of flowers.

As Tyler stood in Grandma's kitchen later that day, he was bombarded with feelings and emotions that filled the spectrum. There were people crying and remembering and trying to get to family to reassure them. There was the reality that this place and everything in it had belonged to a man who would never see or touch it again.

Contradictory to the emptiness was the gaiety, all subdued, that inevitability could be found anywhere good friends and distant relatives gathered around food. There was enough food to feed an army. It was ironic, as life often is, that all these people would gather here and Granddad Luke had to miss it, because he enjoyed people and they so loved him.

"Tyler, I'm so sorry. I know how you loved your granddad."

Tyler turned and, for an instant, was under the spell of those beautiful deep-green eyes that had mesmerized him on so many occasions. "Thank you, Penny," Tyler replied. "I'm glad you came. Grand asked me many times about you. Back when we were dating, he used to tell me how special you were."

"Really? That sounds so much like him."

Tyler had been talking with a group of people from Granddad's church. Penny addressed the group. "I'm sorry to take him away, but his mother sent me to get him. I'll bring him back." Penny led Tyler through the house and back to Granddad's bedroom.

Kate was standing in the doorway. "Thank you, Penny. Come in, both of you."

When Tyler and Penny were inside, Kate closed the door. Grandma Ruth was sitting on the bed. She looked tired and older as she patted the bed beside her.

When Tyler was seated, Grandma said, "Your granddad had a will, and he also made a little separate list of some of his favorite things and the people he wanted to have them. He wanted you to have this." She placed in Tyler's hand an old, faded tie clasp that was shaped like a farm tractor.

Tyler smiled as he held it close and looked it over. He had given it to Grand sixteen years ago on his sixty-fifth birthday, and Tyler had seen him wear it many times. "Thank you, Grandma. I remember getting this for him."

She touched her eyes with her hanky. "Tyler, your granddad always thought you were very special, and now you've grown up and proved how right he was. Everything we owned together has been willed to me, as it should be, but your granddad took his will uptown to the lawyer's office and made one change a couple of months ago. It comes at the end of the will."

She looked around and then handed the will to Penny. "Penny, would you be a dear and read the paragraph numbered fourteen?"

Grandma took both of Tyler's hands and held them in hers. Penny found the paragraph and began to read, "To Tyler Harrison, my grandson, and son of Harold and Kate Harrison, I bequeath one 1952 red Ford pickup truck, serial number 52T8169BR12. Further, it is my request that he restore this old truck to its original condition and that he drive it and share it often with someone as special to him as he was to me."

The dam broke. The lake of emotions he had been suppressing for the past three days could no longer be held in check. He had succeeded in masking his hurt from the others and had helped Grandma and his folks to be gracious and helpful hosts, but now the facade was slipping. His pride was strong, but just now the passion was stronger. He cried and sobbed openly in the arms of his mom and grandma.

Tyler was aware that he was an attractive man, rich, even famous, but the jury was still out on whether he was fully grown up. Right now, he only knew that somewhere deep inside him, a little boy wanted Granddaddy Luke.

Chapter 24

━━◦●◦━━━◦❦◦━━━◦●◦━━

A Very Bad Day

t was a warm day in April, and Penny was lost in thought. She was thinking about Tyler as she turned her old Plymouth, which didn't have any power steering, into the driveway. She thought about her impression of him at Granddad Luke's funeral and how much she wished she had him back. She excitedly hurried out of the car and looked at the long black limousine next to her driveway. When the door opened, she expected to see Tyler. He was the only person she knew who could afford a limo. But she was wrong on both counts. Geena Morgan got out wearing jeans and a mink jacket. The question now was what did she want?

"I'm sorry to drop in on you, but I was doing some work in Pittsburg, and I figured I'd never get any closer. Can we talk?" Geena asked.

"Sure. Would you like to come up?" Penny inquired. Once inside, Penny asked if she would like a drink.

"No," Geena replied, "but thank you. I won't stay long, and I don't want to inconvenience you." She sat in one of the living room chairs and looked around briefly. "Penny, you win. I give up. He's all yours."

Penny sat heavily in the other chair. "I assume you mean Tyler?"

"Yes, Tyler Harrison," Geena replied. "You know, the man we both love, but neither one of us have."

Penny smelled the strong scent of alcohol and realized her guest had been drinking. She said, "I guess I've been misinformed. I thought you had him."

Geena threw her head back and laughed so loudly that it startled Penny. "Oh, no. I don't have him and never have. I just sleep with him. Oh God, I want him, but he doesn't want me. He wants you!"

Now it was Penny's turn to laugh, and she took it. "I don't think the proud bastard knows what he wants. I slapped him seven years ago next month, and he's still mad."

"Penny, I can't get him for you, but I can get out of the way. I'm just tired of loving someone who can't love me back." She stood up and went to the door. "I hate you, Penny, and I know I shouldn't. It's not your fault, but if he had never known you, I'm sure I could make him love me. I guess that's why I came, because I feel so guilty."

Geena started to cry. "You're a fool if you don't go to him. He's a wonderful man. He's smart, good, kind, honest, romantic, and the best goddamned lover I've ever had."

Geena slammed the door on the way out.

*　　*　　*

April would soon give way to May, and Washington was full of tourists as it experienced its annual rebirth. It was Saturday morning, and Tyler was looking forward to a golf match with Abe Cohen and a couple of bankers that afternoon. He had just finished with the *Washington Post* and was pleased to see that the cherry blossoms downtown were in full bloom. He decided to skip their viewing this year. He remembered that when he had seen them last year, it had been with his folks and Granddad.

He stood and went for the coffee maker. Tyler jumped as his penthouse foyer door slammed. He wasn't expecting anyone, and it had been locked. Tyler started for the kitchen door and yelled, "Who is it?"

"It's only me. I used my key," Geena yelled back from the foyer.

In five seconds, she was at the kitchen door. She didn't look like her usual gorgeous self. She was wearing her familiar jeans and a loose sweatshirt with the sleeves pushed up. It was obvious that she had not applied makeup, and she looked hungover.

Geena marched to the cabinet, took out a mug, and poured coffee. "We need to talk."

Tyler asked, "Did you just get in?"

"No. I got in from Pittsburg last night and spent the night in a hotel downtown."

"Why didn't you come here?"

"Because I knew if I did, I would chicken out and not do what I have to do. You see, I have this problem. I love a man who loves another woman. Oh, that reminds me! I was in Stratford, and I paid your precious Penny a visit. I told her you and I were through, and she was welcome to you. Do you know what she said?"

"No, Geena, what did she say?"

"She said she slapped you seven years ago and you're still mad. She also said, and I quote, 'I don't think the proud bastard knows what he wants.' Well, I know what I want. I just want the man who sleeps with me to love me." She started to cry, and then she was gone.

Tyler caught her in the foyer. "You're right, Geena, and you deserve better. I'm sorry, but you don't have to leave mad. I've tried to love you. I care about you very much, but I'm not in love with you. I wish I were, but I'm not … but we can still be friends."

He stood perfectly still as she reached out and brushed his cheek with her hand. When she dropped her hand, she spat in his face.

*   *   *

It was silly to be scared, but he was, at least a little bit. Millions of people had done this already, but he hadn't. He was sitting at the end of the runway, and he would soon takeoff on his first solo flight. Charles said he was ready, so he must be.

He had done the preflight check twice and had already checked the radio and instruments about ten times. The radio blared with clearance to takeoff, and he acknowledged. He checked the instruments one more time and pulled the throttle full out.

As the light Cessna 150 began to roll, he was sure it would vibrate apart. He was using his feet on the rudder paddles to keep the plane in the center of the runway. The speed was picking up quickly now, and he could feel the little plane getting light as it approached takeoff speed. When it did, he eased back on the wheel, and he was climbing. Tyler remembered to give a little left rudder to counter the right-hand rotation of the engine until the plane quickly achieved level flight on its own.

Yes! He had done it perfectly. A beautiful takeoff. Now all he had to do was accomplish everything on his little flight plan in two hours and land. Landing was about ten times harder than taking off, but he would think about that later. He glanced down and could see he was just over the end of the runway, and already his altitude was two hundred feet. He watched as the low trees rushed by beneath him.

When the altimeter read five hundred feet, he eased the wheel forward a little to lessen his rate of climb and reached for the throttle to slow the engine. When he pushed the throttle back in just a touch, the engine coughed a couple of times and died. Within two seconds, he could see the now-still propeller in front of him, and he could hear the stall buzzer, which meant his airspeed was too slow and the plane would soon start to fall.

He pushed the wheel away from him. The plane began to fly slightly downward, and his airspeed increased, but of course, he was losing altitude quickly with no power to get it back. He quickly looked for somewhere to land. About half a mile away was a fairly flat field just past a stand of trees. He turned toward it.

While all this was going on, he had pushed the throttle back into idle and was turning the key to restart the engine. The propeller was turning with the starter, but the engine would not restart. He looked at the fuel gauge again, and it showed a full tank.

He was down to 250 feet now and barely a hundred feet above the trees, and he knew he wasn't going to make the field. He heard the stall warning again, and then it happened so fast—just the way the manual said it would. The plane stopped flying and started falling out of control, nose first toward the trees. Too late, he realized that he had not radioed anyone.

He had already thought about his folks, Grandma Ruth, the people at work, and Abe Cohen. He knew Alice, Tracy, and Liz would do the right thing. He hoped the good Lord wouldn't mind, but as the leaves hit the windshield, he wondered what Penny Kilmer would be like in bed and was disappointed that he would never know.

*   *   *

Tyler's flight instructor was giving another student a lesson and had taken off right behind Tyler. He observed the whole thing and reached for his radio. Soon, he was circling, directing a rescue squad to the crash scene. Once they found him, Charles landed his plane and ran to his car to drive to the nearest hospital, so he could identify Tyler and maybe call someone. After seeing the Cessna plunge nose first into the trees, he knew the odds of Tyler being alive were very close to zero.

*   *   *

He was there; he was sure. Thank God he had made it. Tyler was so excited, because the light was so bright it had to be heaven. He waited. Someone would tell him where to go or what to do. Maybe he would see Granddad soon. He could hear people talking and yelling—something about how someone might lose his legs. He would just wait his turn. Maybe heaven was busy today. Now that he was here, he didn't want to make anyone angry.

Kate closed her little appointment calendar book and dropped it in her purse. It was such a helpless feeling to just sit and wait for her son to wake up. The prognosis had not changed, and it had never been good.

When she and Harold had arrived, they had been ushered into Dr. Heller's office. He had explained that he was the chief of neurology and

155

would need their permission to operate. Tyler was on life support systems, and his brain waves were almost flat.

During the crash, the dashboard that held all the instruments had been mashed down with such force that it had almost completely severed both of Tyler's legs between the hips and knees. He had come within a drop of bleeding to death, and there had been severe head trauma.

Kate and Harold did what all lay people do in this situation. They gave their permission, signed the papers, and prayed that the good doctor knew what he was doing. The operation to completely restore blood flow and reattach the almost severed legs, took nine hours.

The team of surgeons met with Harold and Kate and tried to explain. When they were finished, Harold and Kate knew precious little. Many questions were unanswered. Would his legs be saved? Would his legs ever work? Would he live?

*   *   *

Kate and Liz had become very close. For more than two weeks, they had lived in a large private room with Tyler, and one of them was always with him. Kate had sent Harold back to Stratford in hopes that working would help his depression. There was nothing to do here.

The swelling in Tyler's brain was down, and it was trying to recover. Although Tyler was still in a coma, they had been able to remove the life support systems, except for the feeding tube.

Sometimes when Kate was gone, Liz talked to Tyler. She had no idea if he heard or not, but she liked to think he did. She knew that Kate had become quite a walker. Kate had told her that she could only stand to sit and look at Tyler for so long, and then the whole room began to close in on her, and she had to get out.

One day, she changed into her old baggy walking shorts and sneakers and said, "I won't be too long, Liz. It looks like rain."

"Take your time, Kate, and enjoy your walk," Liz said.

As soon as Kate was gone, Liz started up her usual one-way conversation with Tyler. That day, she told him about a nice man she had met. "He's

very bright and owns a business. I promised to have lunch with him soon."
Liz stood and rested her arms on the bed so she could see out the window.

"I can't wait for you to meet him. I know you would like him because—"

She screamed and jumped back, but she didn't get far. Tyler had a firm grip with his hand around her slim wrist.

She looked down and saw Tyler staring back at her. All she could say was, "Jesus Christ, Tyler! You almost scared me to death!"

Her scream had worked much better than the call button. Within a few seconds, the room was full of doctors and nurses.

*   *   *

When Kate got off the elevator and started down the corridor, she could see all the people outside of Tyler's room. It was all she could do to will her feet and legs to carry her forward. Just before she got to the door, one of Tyler's regular nurses came out with tears in her eyes.

Kate turned into the room. When she saw the bed, she turned white, and her knees began to give way. Thankfully, a couple of the nurses caught her. What she saw was a wide awake Tyler Harrison, with the head of his bed raised, eating chocolate ice cream as fast as Liz could cram it into his mouth.

"Tyler!" Kate said, laughing through her tears.

Tyler looked over and gave her one of those boyish grins that she had come to love and cherish over the years.

"Hey, Mom. Nice legs."

His voice was a raspy whisper, but oh God, it sounded so good.

She glanced down at her old baggy shorts and laughed. She had received more than a few compliments in her time, but this one had to be the best.

*   *   *

Tyler was propped up in his hospital bed eating dinner and trying to watch the evening news, but he was having trouble concentrating, because his right knee was hurting. Then, like a bolt of lightning, it struck him. It had been two weeks since he had come out of the coma, but he had had no feeling in his legs, and he couldn't move them. He quickly pushed the cart that held his dinner tray to the side and pushed down the covers.

He tried to move his right leg. He watched carefully, looking for the slightest movement or even a muscle twitch. Nothing. His knee still hurt, though, and that was something. He wasn't ready to give up. He reached in the bedside table and took out a large safety pin he had hidden. He opened it and slowly pricked his right knee. He felt nothing. He tried again and again and again.

When the nurse looked in, he was jabbing the pin into his leg around his knee like a madman, and it was bleeding.

"Stop that, Tyler!" she called out. The nurse rushed in and made him give up the safety pin. While she cleaned his knee and applied a bandage, she listened to his explanation. "Did you forget what the doctor told you?" she asked.

"What?" he replied.

"About phantom pain. Even people who have a leg amputated often swear their foot or some part of their missing limb still hurts."

"But it's so real, and it really hurts."

"I'm sorry, Tyler. It's just the garbled message that a damaged nerve is sending to the brain. You may have to learn to live with it."

"That's easy for you to say," Tyler noted. "Your legs work just fine."

"You're right, and I'm sorry, but you'll be happier when you learn to accept your condition."

"Yeah, you're right," Tyler said sarcastically. "I'll try to be a little more thankful that I'm a goddamned cripple."

Chapter 25

<hr/>

Remembering the Promise

It was October, and the trees around Bethesda were at the peak of their color. Tyler had been home in his penthouse condo for four and a half months. His memory was fine, and the severe headaches had all but stopped. Everyone told him he was lucky to be alive, but he didn't feel lucky in a wheelchair with two useless legs. Maybe it was the pride, but he had made up his mind he couldn't live like this. He had thought about suicide but was too proud to bring that shame and feeling of frustration on his family and loved ones, so he did the next best thing. He went into isolation.

Except for Liz, who came once a week, and the nurse she had hired, who was willing to live there and be a part-time maid, he saw no one. He talked to the people at work by phone and memo, but he had not seen an outsider in over five months. Most had finally given up. They no longer called or tried to see him, and that suited him just fine. If he was going to be a cripple, he would do it his way.

As he sat in his wheelchair and looked out the window, he saw no beauty in the perfect fall day. He could only see a never-ending montage of scenes depicting people doing things that he could no longer do.

Tyler also spent part of every day demanding answers from God and not getting them. He had given more than $2 million in land and money to churches, schools, and scholarships. He had also been thinking about setting up a foundation that would spend tens of millions of dollars each year on worthy causes.

Well, two could play this game. If the good Lord wanted him to go through life as a cripple, then He could just find someone else to make money and give it away. From now on, by God, he was going to keep his. A knock on his bedroom door ended today's session with the Big Man upstairs.

"Come in," he said.

It was Liz for her weekly visit. "How are you this morning?" she asked enthusiastically.

"Crippled," he answered.

"Well, I can't help that, but I brought you a surprise."

Tyler looked up and saw Alice and Tracy walking into his bedroom. He glared at Liz. "How in the hell did they get in here?"

Alice, who was never at a loss for words, said, "It's too late to worry about that now, because we're here."

"Well, just turn around and leave!" Tyler shouted.

"Not until I say what I came to say," Alice yelled back. "We miss you, Tyler, and we want you back. You can't sit up here and just wither away. It's just not the same without you. Please come back."

"Are you through, mouthy?" Tyler asked.

Alice flinched visibly, as if she had been struck. "Yes, Tyler. I'm through."

"I'm not," Tracy said. She walked the length of the room to Tyler's wheelchair, knelt in front of him on one knee, and put her hands on his legs.

Tyler looked away as if he were going to be sick.

"Tyler! Look at me," Tracy begged.

He turned and gave her the coldest stare he could invoke. She glanced back through moist eyes. "You've changed my life. When I met you, I was a burned-out, divorced government worker who hated my job and my life. Now I can't wait to get up and face the new day. You did that, Tyler.

"Yesterday I sat and watched Abe Cohen crying in my office because you won't see him. Liz has lost ten pounds and guards your office like a shrine, and every time your name is mentioned, Susan Slater leaves the room.

"When you weren't around, we used to call you Don Quixote at work. You have to admit you're a little different. Alice, Liz, Susan, me, and everyone at work honestly believed there wasn't a windmill anywhere we couldn't kick the hell out of with you as our leader. We don't feel the same way now. It's different. Don't you see, Tyler? We love you, and it will never be the same without you."

Tyler waited to make sure she was finished. "Then why don't you quit?" he asked.

"Oh, no," she said. "I still believe, even if you don't."

Tracy stood, and she and Alice quietly left the room.

When they were gone, Liz said, "I hope you want people to feel sorry for you, because I sure do."

*   *   *

A week later, Tyler's mother came to visit.

"How long are you going to do this to yourself?" she asked.

"Do what to myself," Tyler demanded.

"Be depressed. Refuse to accept your situation. Shut out the ones who love you. Stop living."

"Until I wake up some morning and discover I can walk."

"You know, the doctors want you to do therapy. There is always hope.

"Look, Mom," Tyler said, "I love you, and I don't want to hurt you, but it's my problem."

His mother stood up and went to the door. "You're wrong, Son. You've made it a problem for all of us." She left quickly without closing the door.

*   *   *

In early November, Tyler knew it was a mistake, but he had given in anyway and promised to come home for Thanksgiving after his folks had begged him to on the phone. Liz had found a place that rented vans especially equipped to haul wheelchairs, and he'd gone to Stratford. Thank God, it was about over. Tyler, Liz and his folks would all go down to Grandma Harrison's the next day for the grand feast, and then he would leave on Friday.

Tyler had been in Stratford two days, and he had tried, but everything was different. Conversation with his dad and mom was a strain for them all, and the sooner he was gone, the better off everyone would be. He looked around his old room and hated it. The place looked like a museum. He would tell his mom to get rid of all this crap. Every shelf and furniture surface was strewn with pieces of memorabilia of an overactive youth, and now each piece seemed to laugh at this wheelchair jockey.

"Can I come in?" a voice at the door said.

He knew who it was. "Sure. The more, the merrier. Have a seat, Penny." He indicated the bed and turned his wheelchair to face it.

Penny closed the door and took a seat on the edge of his bed. She was wearing tight jeans and what looked like a man's long-sleeved, plaid shirt, but nothing about her resembled a man. Her long, blonde hair was pulled back with a red band, and with just a hint of makeup, she looked like she was ready to go sledding.

"So, how are you doing, Tyler?" she asked warmly.

"Super, Penny," he snarled. "As a matter of fact, I've had so much goddamned fun the past few months, I can hardly stand it."

"Don't be nasty," she said, frowning.

"I'm sorry. I don't mean to be, really. Every morning I wake up at six in a great mood, and for some reason, at about six thirty, I get this overwhelming urge to be nasty, and I just say piss on it and give in."

She smiled but said nothing.

"Why are you here, Penny?" Tyler asked.

"I wanted to see you."

"You wanted to see me?" He jerked the quilt off his legs and threw it on the bed next to Penny. "There! Take a good look."

He could tell that she tried not to let her surprise show, but she failed. From the bottom of his shorts to his knees was a mass of pink scar tissue, and his legs were only half the size they should be from lack of use.

Penny reached out and traced the scars with her index finger. "I'm so sorry," she said, and a tear splashed on the back of her hand.

"Don't be sorry, Penny. You should be glad."

"Why is that?" she asked as she used a finger to wipe away another tear.

"You always said I was too proud for my own good. Well, I've eaten a shitload of humble pie lately."

"Maybe you'll be a better person for it," she said. "But I never expected you to give up."

"Life is full of surprises."

"Yes, it is," she snapped, "and you have been a big one. I'm not stupid, Tyler. I know you still care about me, although you would rather die than admit it. Why won't you let me love you?"

Tyler dropped his head and sat quietly for a long time. Finally, he said, "Because you're weird. No high school girl in America dates a guy for two years without having sex, but you did. Then for some reason, known only to you, you get all hot and bothered one night and want to have sex, and when I act like a gentleman because I have no condom and I feel we need to talk, you slap my face. Tell me that's not weird."

"Yes, it was, and sometime when you're ready, I'll tell you why I acted that way."

"You missed the whole point, Penny. I don't care." He leaned forward but couldn't reach the quilt. "Now give me the quilt and leave."

She picked it up and stood, but she stepped back one step so he couldn't reach it.

"I'm not ready to go yet!" she shouted. "I have to tell you."

He glared at her and then at the quilt. "I would give $50 million if I could stand up and kick you in the ass."

She laughed. "Everything I own isn't worth $2,000, and I would gladly give it all if you got out of that chair and kicked me in the ass."

He lunged forward to grab for the quilt and realized too late that his upper-body weight was too far forward and his useless legs could not stop him. The chair tipped forward, and he fell at Penny's feet. He had to use his arms and hands to break his fall.

"Oh my God!" Penny exclaimed. "I'm sorry. Are you hurt?"

In a very calm voice, he said, "No. I'm not hurt. Get out." He wondered what he must look like, sprawled on the floor with two ugly sticks protruding from his undershorts.

"Let me help you," Penny pleaded.

This was almost more humble pie than he could stand. He screamed, "Don't touch me! Get out!"

Penny dropped the quilt, yanked the door open, and left.

*　*　*

After Tyler's parents helped him back into his chair, fussed over him, and covered his legs with the quilt, they finally left him in peace. He sat now and tried to cry. He wanted to cry. He deserved it. He was shaking, and he knew he was too angry to cry. He wanted to hit something, to hit someone, to make someone hurt the way he hurt.

He was so mad he felt faint. He was mad at Penny. He was mad at Liz for bringing him here and at his folks for making him come. He was mad at all the people at work, because he'd never asked to be their hero. And yes, he was mad at God for taking away his legs. The tears came then and began to wash the anger away. It hadn't been real anyway. It was a lie, and he knew it. He wasn't really mad at those people or at God. He was mad at the stupid son of a bitch in the wheelchair.

*　*　*

Tyler had just about used up his meager supply of niceness for the day. They had just finished the Thanksgiving feast, but he couldn't find one thing for which he was thankful. Grandma had fretted around him all day like a mother hen.

When she filled his plate for the third time, he explained very patiently that because of the chair he was less active and therefore had to eat less. She said she was sure he was right as she buried his plate with mashed potatoes swimming in butter.

Grandma Harrison had aged ten years in the few months since Granddad's passing. Although she was still sweet, she had lost that quick wit and wonderful sense of humor she always used to fence with Granddad. She seemed to love Liz, but then Grandma loved everyone. She didn't have a hateful bone in her body.

Grandma finally sat down and gave up. "Tyler, with your granddad gone," she said sadly, "I plan to have an auction in the spring. Have you decided what you're going to do with Granddad's truck?"

"No, but I will soon." He didn't say it, but with all that had happened the past seven months, he had forgotten about the old thing. He guessed he would have to do something with it. Later, after changing his shirt and tie for one of his old favorite Winfield College sweatshirts, and against everyone's wishes, he ventured down the new ramp off the front porch onto the lawn. He turned the chair and headed around back toward the old barn. He had less trouble with the simple latch and the large swinging door than he expected and was soon inside.

The truck was dirty and really had turned into a rust bucket the past couple of years. Tyler wheeled the chair around to the driver's door and opened it. He looked in at about twenty spiders, all with their own symmetrical webs, which no doubt supplied them with ample food, as they all looked fat and sassy.

While he was watching the spiders, he realized he too was being watched. A mouse had raised his head wearily and was giving him the once-over from one of four or five holes gnawed in the old seat covers. After a staring contest, the mouse decided Tyler wasn't a threat and casually receded into what had to be a pretty nice pad for a mouse.

The old garage and especially the truck permeated a multitude of familiar odors. While his nose and brain worked as a team to separate and register each smell, one became increasingly stronger. It was Granddad's pipe tobacco. Tyler didn't smoke, but he always loved that old pipe, and now the smell caused a legion of vivid memories.

They were all of a little man who, to Tyler, had always been old but never seemed so, who never said anything bad about anyone, who showed Tyler many of the wonders of nature on and around the farm and was always as excited as Tyler when he viewed them, who could figure out damn near anything, who could usually show him a better way, who would never argue but could discuss for hours and was the perfect devil's advocate, who was blessed with the patience of Job, who more than even his parents taught him that work could be fun and one could always take pride in any job well done, no matter how menial, and who was always fun to be with.

Tyler was certain that if he looked up the word *good* in his old Webster's dictionary, it would simply read: "Granddad Luke Harrison." He was the epitome of good. Surely, as bright as heaven was, it was a little brighter with Granddad there.

Tyler smiled as he remembered their last trash run together, but the smile faded when Granddad's words burst from Tyler's subconscious: Pride and passion!

He had told Tyler he was intense and had a great capacity and was able to direct it where he needed. Tyler wasn't proud of where he had directed his great capacity lately.

Granddad had said either one could put him over the top or take him down in an instant. Tyler wasn't sure if he was at the bottom, but he sure as hell hadn't been on top of anything for the past seven months. It hurt him to think how badly he had treated some people and what an insufferable asshole he had become since the accident. Pride and passion!

Tyler was ashamed now as he heard Granddad say, "Promise me you'll remember this little old man who loves you more than he could ever tell you, and you'll use your pride and passion for only good." Tyler felt now like the insufferable fool he had been. His great capacity to do good lay buried under a thick layer of crystallized self-pity. It was utterly amazing to him now how clear things were and how blind he had been.

"I'm sorry, Granddad," Tyler said to the old red pickup with the pipe tobacco smell. "I forgot my promise, but I won't forget it again. I promise I'll do this for you.

Tyler slammed the door of the old truck and started to wheel himself out, but he suddenly stopped. After all these years, he got it! Tyler finally realized that Granddad had never wanted him to succeed for Granddad's sake, but for his own sake.

On the way back to the house, Tyler felt alive again. What was it Granddad had said so often? Today is the first day of the rest of your life, so don't waste it and try to do a little good.

"I promise, Granddad," he whispered.

Chapter 26

On the Mend Emotionally

1968

Early January started with a nice surprise. Tyler was in his office with Susan Slater going over some contract changes when Liz burst in.

"I'm sorry, Tyler. Can I have a minute?" Liz asked. "This is important."

"Sure. What you got?"

"I just took a call from *Time* magazine. They want to do a feature article about you and put your picture on the cover."

"Are you serious?"

"Of course, I'm serious," Liz replied. "I just got off the phone with the editor!"

Susan said, "You should do this. It would be great advertising and exposure for all you do."

Tyler asked, "What do you think, Liz?"

"Well, you're handsome, smart, rich, and a really good man. I have a feeling most of America would like to know more about you. Yes, I think you should."

Tyler laughed. "Well, my God, if I'm all those things, why not? Call them back and tell them I'll do it."

* * *

Tyler felt like a rag doll lying on the table watching his leg go up and down with no effort from him. It was a strange feeling to see his leg moving and not be able to feel it. It wasn't moving all by itself, because Freeman was providing all the effort. Tyler didn't know if Freeman was his first or last name. When they had met, he had said, "Well, just Freeman. It's nice to meet you."

"I'm Tyler, just Tyler." They had liked each other ever since.

Freeman was a large, muscular black man with long, straight black hair that he always wore in a ponytail. Freeman had explained that his mother was black and his father was an Indian, and that was the reason for the straight hair. Tyler guessed Freeman was about forty.

The doctors at Johns Hopkins said he was the best physical therapist on the East Coast. He had worked for the New York Giants football team until they "pissed him off." Now he worked with some injured Washington Redskins part-time and had sort of a private practice on the side. He wasn't cheap, but he would come to the building where Tyler's condo was as long as Tyler was willing to fit the appointments into Freeman's schedule.

The sessions usually lasted two hours and were done six days a week. The sessions were planned by a team of doctors, and it was Freeman's job to make sure the exercise sessions were done properly. The team had outlined both some short-term and long-term goals. The short-term goals were to stop the muscle deterioration and increase circulation. The longer-term goals were to create more circulation, increase the size of the leg muscles, and hopefully stimulate nerve growth that would make new connections and, maybe someday, restore feeling and movement.

Some of the members of his medical team also put great stock in the powers of self-healing through positive thinking and meditation. They had provided him with a list of people who were all supposedly experts at meditation and getting in touch with one's inner self. In the past six weeks,

Tyler had spent a small fortune and had one or two sessions with a seer from Cleveland, a real witch from Maine, a witch doctor from Africa, a mystic who didn't know where he was from, a monk from Tibet, an oracle who was convinced he was from another planet, a female yoga expert from California with long hair under her arms who believed bathing was a mortal sin, and a guru from India with one very large tooth and killer breath.

None of the sessions had gone well. While listening to ocean waves for two hours with the mystic, Tyler had wet himself. He found out very quickly that he was not good at humming and chanting. He spent sixty minutes in a special yoga position, and during fifty-nine of them, he thought about how uncomfortable he was. He fell asleep watching the monk's candle, and when he and the guru contemplated their navels, all Tyler could think about was the amount of lint in his. After getting rid of all these experts, he learned he was quite good at meditating if he was in a quiet place, if he was comfortable, and if no one was bothering him.

* * *

Tyler had spent Christmas with his folks and had even called Penny and apologized for his behavior at Thanksgiving. The rest of December and all of January were spent in therapy with Freeman and in two one-hour sessions of meditation each day. Well, Tyler wasn't sure it was meditation. He just spent the time looking at a leg or a foot or a toe and willing it to move, and then he'd try to make it move. He would be physically and mentally drained after an hour.

Tyler was starting to mend mentally too. He knew he didn't like the wheelchair and would spend the rest of his life trying to get out of it, but he was finally getting used to it. He could live with being seen in the damn thing, even if he didn't like it, and he had decided he was ready to return to the outside world.

Tyler called the office and told Liz to come over. He instructed her to buy a van with a lift fully equipped to load and handle a wheelchair and then hire someone to drive it.

With her usual efficiency, she showed up two days later for a test run with a new van and Vince Lucci. Although he was born in America and had no real accent, Vince looked like he'd just gotten off the boat from Sicily. He was short, very dark, and wide—not fat, just wide—and had a heavy moustache. Tyler wondered if Liz had checked his background, but of course, she had.

The van was very nice and well equipped. It was white, and Tyler wondered how Liz had gotten the green and white Harrison Ltd. name and logo printed on both sides so quickly. She never ceased to amaze him.

When they met, Vince insisted on calling Tyler "Mr. H." He was very intelligent and had a great sense of humor. He also had a perfect driving record, and Tyler liked him.

The day after the test run, Tyler surprised everyone with a visit to the office. He hadn't been there for eleven months, and it was an emotional reunion, with much hugging, laughing, and crying. The only business he conducted was to set up a meeting for Friday morning, so he could begin to catch up on everything.

When he left his own office, he went up to Pride Mark Homes and got lucky. Abe Cohen and daughter Blair were both there, and the three had a wonderful visit. On the way home, he and Vince went by his favorite Jewish deli for a sandwich. Mr. Edelman, the owner, was so glad to see him, he announced, "It's on the house."

Damn, Tyler thought, *He must really be glad to see me.* Mr. Edelman usually charged extra for lids and napkins.

*   *   *

The meeting on Friday morning was both disappointing and pleasing. Tyler was disappointed that they had done so well without him and pleased that he was surrounded by such competent people. Harrison Ltd. and all its projects, including Harrison Properties, had been running like a well-oiled machine, and Tyler was becoming a very wealthy young man.

The nuts-and-bolts part of the meeting went quickly. Chet Mitchell, the project manager, was proud of his accomplishments. He reported that the 240 homes at Quail Hollow were all finished and sold. He had started the second large subdivision, which would have more than 300 homes, and the third subdivision with 540 homes would have its grand opening in two weeks. With very little direction from Tyler, Chet had put together an excellent team and was now producing two hundred large homes per year with an average profit of $20,000 each and virtually zero complaints. The man was a godsend.

Liz, former secretary, now administrative assistant and proud owner of one share of stock, seemed so happy to have her mentor back she looked to be on the verge of bursting. Along with her general duties, she had taken on the management and supervision of the beach condos in Ocean City, Maryland. She had hired a commercial project manager away from a firm in Virginia, and he headed up the office in Ocean City.

Abe and Blair Cohen had started a commercial building division called Pride Mark Construction, and after some tough negotiating by Liz, approved by Tyler, she had awarded contracts to them to build the first three high-rise condos on the beach. They would be finished and sold out by summer, and five more were slated for the following summer. Liz concluded by telling Tyler that he would be the owner of the penthouse condo in the nicest building.

Tall, easygoing, Brad Slater, Susan's brother, was quickly becoming the preeminent land developer in the DC area. Thanks to Tyler's earlier work, there was a large group of small and medium-sized builders who looked to Harrison Ltd. whenever they needed building lots, and Brad was doing a creditable job of supplying them to the tune of three hundred to four hundred per year.

Along with personnel, Tracy was now the overseer of the national real estate franchise. Her report was brief. There were now 4,200 privately owned real estate firms across America that were members of Harrison Properties, and they were still signing up new firms at the rate of six to eight each working day, or around 2,000 per yrear. The income for 1968 would be a whopping $100 million, and the total expenses, including a $15 million nationwide advertising campaign, would only be about $20 million.

Even Tyler was surprised. Harrison Properties would turn a profit this year of $80 million, and that was only the beginning. It was definitely time to set up a charitable foundation. Harrison Properties alone would make more money than all the other ventures put together, but Tyler loved those other ventures, and he believed in being diversified. He remembered well an old saying attributed to an unknown philosopher: If you put all your eggs in one basket, guard that basket. Alice reported that the estimated net worth of all Harrison holdings was now $190 million, and it was growing rapidly.

Attorney Susan Slater informed everyone that she had settled the lawsuit with the insurance company that represented the airport for $3.5 million. The FAA had completed their investigation. The morning before Tyler's solo flight, an airport mechanic had installed a new fuel tank. Tyler lost the use of his legs, and almost his life, because of a packaging rag. The mechanic never removed it, and when Tyler was airborne, the rag blocked the flow of fuel.

Susan next explained how the new Harrison Foundation would be set up and what its goals would be. She pointed out that those asking for money must be screened and then checked again after they received the funding, but administrative costs needed to be held to a minimum.

Everyone present agreed that they didn't want outsiders telling them how to give away the money. The people in that room had made it, or helped to make it, and they believed they should have something to say about where it went. They also felt Tyler should always have the final say. That pleased him, because he agreed.

Susan assured them that all legal work would be completed and nonprofit status would be gained within two months. They could soon begin to look for worthy recipients. Everyone was pleased and seemed to be anxious to start the do-good business.

*   *   *

Tyler was hard at work going over a set of blueprints for the new headquarters he would build. His two corporations were rapidly outgrowing the two floors they now occupied, and he dreamed about having his very own location along Interstate 270. He had two sites in mind that were perfect.

"Tyler, there are some people here to see you."

When he looked up, he saw that Robin had stuck her head in the door. "Who are they, Robin?"

She frowned and said, "I'm afraid they're a group of people who work here, and they demanded to see you now."

Just then, the door opened wider, and people began to file in to his office. They were all employees, and they didn't look happy. As a matter of fact, they looked like a lynch mob, and they kept coming. *What the hell?* Tyler thought.

When the line finally finished, every employee was jammed in his office, and they were staring at him. Alice stepped around a couple of people until she was in front of his desk.

"Tyler, we have a very serious message for you." Then, almost in perfect unison with her leading, everyone began to sing "For He's a Jolly Good Fellow."

Well, thank God! Tyler thought with a sense of relief. *At least it isn't a strike!*

The group began to separate slowly, and Robin appeared pushing a large cart on wheels. On the cart was a huge cake with one candle and four rather high stacks of magazines.

For an instant, Tyler panicked and thought they had made a mistake and were planning to celebrate his birthday on the wrong day. Then he saw the magazines and smiled. He wheeled around his desk and blew out the one candle.

Alice picked up one of the magazines and held it over her head. "Our leader must have bribed someone. He got a five-page article in *Time* magazine, and his picture is on the cover."

Everyone whooped and hollered and then congratulated him with a handshake or a hug or both. When everyone had gone with a piece of cake and a magazine, he sat back and began to read.

He had been apprehensive a couple of months ago when he gave the two interviews and let them take the pictures, but the more he read, the better it sounded. The article gave some background and history but dealt mainly with the Harrison Properties franchise and the forthcoming Harrison Foundation. It made Tyler sound brighter than he was and offered him up as God's gift to the entrepreneurial world. That embarrassed him a little, but he had to admit that it felt good. What pleased him most was that the writer had been true to his word and ended the article with one of Granddad's often-used quotes: "If you're not willing to do it right, stay the hell away from it."

Chapter 27

◈━━━◦◦♥◦◦━━━◈

Physical Recovery

*P*enny smiled as she read a headline on the front page of Stratford's
newspaper: "Local Boy to Address Winfield Grads." There was a
picture that showed Tyler smiling from his wheelchair. The article chronicled
events in Tyler's life with particular attention paid to his successes and his
recent tragedy. It ended by saying that Tyler had been invited to address the
1968 graduating class at Winfield College, and he had accepted.

She wondered again, as she so often did in her daydreams, if there was
anything he couldn't do. She was happy that he had risen above his deep
depression and decided to go on with his life.

Her life wasn't so bad. Thanks to Tyler's huge scholarship, she planned
to complete her doctorate in two more years. The old Plymouth had died,
and she was the proud new owner of a two-year-old Chevy with power
steering. She had Milton too.

Now all she had to do was decide whether she wanted him. It occurred
to her that she should have firmly made up her mind about that two years
ago when she started sleeping with him. Oh well—spilled milk. He really
could be quite sweet when he wasn't doing a math problem. He was tall
and attractive and had some inherited money. She was starting to become
comfortable with him, like one did with a favorite old pair of slippers, but

somehow she felt there was supposed to be more between a young couple than comfort. He was so damned puritanical when it came to sex.

She would give a month's pay if Milton would take off his clothes and do to her what that dark-haired fellow had done to a redheaded lady in a porn movie she'd seen. Hell, she'd give two months' pay!

*   *   *

The Harrison Foundation was in business. Tyler had just signed a check for $2 million. It was being delivered via courier to Children's Hospital in Washington. They were working on a badly needed new cancer wing, and this would put them over the top.

Tyler Harrison had experienced more than his share of life at the tender age of twenty-seven, and he had amassed a number of memories. His visit to Children's Hospital would assuredly haunt him as one of his most vivid. It was an old brick building with a drab exterior appearance. The inside was worse. The place was dark and dirty and had a distinct odor formed by the combination of antiseptics and dirty diapers.

Most of the younger children had a parent or someone who stayed with them, but some didn't. Those unfortunate children were tied down to prevent them from hurting themselves or wandering around. He saw it all, from day-old babies to teenagers; children who would recover and leave and so many who wouldn't. What he didn't see were smiles; they were few and far between in that place.

One of the last rooms he visited was Holly's. She was a beautiful little seven-year-old black girl who was usually restrained. When he went in, the aide had untied her and was feeding her. Although she would be dead of cancer within a month and she was weak, she was still very cute.

Between bites she asked, "Who are you?"

Tyler wheeled his chair very close. "I'm Tyler. Who are you?"

She gave him a warm smile. "My name's Holly. My mom's a dope addict and don't come to visit no more. I don't know who my dad is. Did you come to visit me?"

Tyler fibbed. "Yes, I did. Is that okay?"

After a sip from a cup, she said, "Sure. Why are you in a wheelchair?"

"Well, I had a little accident, and now my legs don't work."

"Do you have to go live with God?" she asked hesitantly.

Tyler thought for a second. "No, not right now."

"You're lucky," she said. "I have cancer, and I'm going to die real soon, so I have to go live with God."

Tyler just sat there and looked at his hands with a bowling ball–sized lump in his throat. He was very bright and a master at always knowing just the right thing to say, but damned if he could think of a single thing in that moment. Thank goodness he didn't have to.

Holly asked, "Can I hug your neck?"

Tyler's voice had taken a holiday, so he leaned forward, and with the aide's help, Holly was lifted. When she placed those little arms around his neck, he was more helpless than she. She held on very tightly and didn't want to let go. After a while, the aide pried her arms loose and placed her back on the pillow.

The doctor, who was giving him the tour, quickly turned Tyler's chair and pushed him out of the room. The doctor said, "We have to go now, Holly."

Holly said, "Good-bye, Tyler."

From the wheelchair, over his shoulder, he waved. That was all he could manage in the moment. On the way back to the office in Silver Spring, as Vince steered the van through downtown traffic, Tyler made some decisions. Children's Hospital would be the Foundation's first customer. He was truly blessed to be alive and well, and the fact that his legs didn't work seemed very trivial on that day. There was one other thing he couldn't get out of his mind.

Tyler wasn't mad at God and he didn't blame Him, but he promised himself if ever he got to the next world, he had a question for Him. "Why kids?" Grown-ups had all lived long enough to have done some bad things. Some of them even deserved to suffer. But dammit, why children? Tyler could not get Holly out of his mind. Because of the impression she had made, there was a Harrison employee at her bedside every minute until she died. She received toys, and there was someone there to read to her and hug her whenever she wanted.

They worked in eight-hour shifts, and Tyler did his three before she passed away. When the time came, she had a proper funeral, and every employee was there. She did not die alone. People loved her; people cried for her and would remember her. She deserved no less.

*　　*　　*

His eyes were tired, and he rubbed them. Tyler had brought work home and needed to finish it before he went to bed, but his right foot was cold, and he couldn't concentrate. He knew it wasn't real, but it still bugged him. He glanced down at his bare foot and noticed that it rested only a couple of inches from the air vent in the wall.

It had been an unusually hot April in DC, and the air conditioning was already running. The cold air was hitting directly on his right foot. He looked at it and willed it to move. It did! The toes had moved. He tried to wiggle his toes, and they did—not much, but they wiggled. He wheeled the chair to his desk and found a paper clip. He quickly straightened one end, so he could use it like a pin. He held his breath as he slowly bent over and jabbed the top of his foot. Without thinking, he uttered the most beautiful word in the English language: "Ouch!"

*　　*　　*

Tyler had Vince drive him to Stratford, so he could speak at graduation as promised.

After the opening remarks, President Fairchild said, "Please join with me as I welcome to this microphone with much excitement and great expectation, Tyler Harrison."

The wheels were already locked, so the wheelchair couldn't move. Tyler quickly pushed the footrests to the side, and with Vince's help, he stood up. Vince gave him the two canes, and he was on his way. He was wearing a cap and gown, as was everyone on stage, and he guessed that he didn't look too clumsy.

Maybe it was the adrenaline, but he made it to the podium in record time. He estimated maybe fifteen seconds. Freeman, his therapist, would have been proud.

The podium was hollow and served as a perfect closet for his canes. He placed them close so he could retrieve them quickly and easily when he was finished. He leaned against the podium for support and pulled himself to his fullest height. As he slowly panned the crowd, the applause died. He waited quite a while until everyone was settled and their attention was on him.

"I'm sorry about taking so long to get to the microphone. President Fairchild said so many nice things in his introduction that I thought he was talking about someone else."

The laughter came quickly. There was a lot of it, and it was genuine.

"President Fairchild, members of the administration, faculty members, families, friends, and other guests, thank you for the opportunity to share this beautiful day and this great occasion with you. Please join me as I say: Winfield College, Class of 1968, this is your day. I honor you, and I wish each of you Godspeed."

Tyler began to clap his hands and was soon joined by about nine thousand others.

"I stand here today, a very lucky man," he continued. "Some people never get to meet their heroes. I got to grow up with mine, and they're here today. Some of you know them. Their names are Harold, Kate, and Ruth Harrison. For those of you who don't know them, Harold and Kate are my mom and dad, and Ruth is my grandma. Granddad Luke was my hero too. He passed away last year.

"Part of what I want to say here today comes from them, because, like each of you, I am a product of where I've been, what I've done, what I've learned, and who I've known. But most importantly, I'm a product of where I came from, and I came from good stock. I wish that I could share the meaning of life with you, but I can't. You see, I don't know what it is." Tyler paused to let people ponder that, and there was some subtle laughter.

"I do believe, though, that life is a gift from our creator, and we can choose whether we wish to approach it in a positive or negative manner. Class of 1968, when you leave to continue your own trip through life, I ask you to think before you act. It can be easy to lose your direction, to become depressed, to make bad decisions. I speak from experience. Once a deed is done, it can never be changed. You can amend it, try to explain it, and attempt to justify it or apologize for it. You can make the decision to take credit for it, or you can deny it, but you can't change it. No more than you can catch a speeding bullet once you've pulled the trigger.

"When you have lived awhile longer, I hope those who know you will say that you gave more than you took, that you listened more than you spoke, that you always gave more love than you got, and that you took advantage of some opportunities to do good. I challenge each of you to be one of those people who can generate pleasure on the faces of those you know when you come into a room and not when you leave it. If you can live your life in this manner, maybe, just maybe, you can be someone's hero."

Tyler paused again for a long time. He leaned forward now in an attempt to make eye contact with every class member. "If you do these things ... will you change the world? Probably not ... but I'd like to live in your neighborhood."

Again, he paused, both for effect and to let the words he would speak next take shape in his mind. He glanced down at the faculty, who occupied the first five rows of chairs in front of the new grads. What he saw amazed him. A number of faculty members were dabbing at their eyes. He looked more closely now at the grads, to whom he was really speaking, and was met by a number of damp stares.

He was trying to speak from the heart instead of just giving a speech. Evidently, he had. If he could bring forth this kind of emotion from a group of recent college grads who are always cynical at this age, he must have said some pretty good stuff, so he quit.

Tyler reached inside the podium and grasped his canes. He turned and began the return trip. He knew he was tired when the distance back to his chair looked about three times longer than it had earlier. His legs were very shaky and tired, but he was making it. True to his word, Vince was up and watching him like a hawk for any sign that he needed help. When he reached the chair, Vince strong-armed him smoothly into it and took the canes.

Tyler glanced at his watch and smiled. They couldn't complain about his spiel. From start to finish, including the slow walking to and from the podium, it had all taken a shade under eight minutes.

* * *

Tyler was alone on the front porch of his folks' home. Night was winning over day, and the light was rapidly fading. Little did he know when he agreed to give the commencement address, it would be one of his most memorable days. He wanted to reflect on that now and log parts of the day into his long-term memory before the needs of everyday life trampled his recollection into a meaningless blur.

Headlights from a car turning into the driveway brought him back to the present. He didn't recognize the car, but he could tell it was Penny from the light that came on when she opened the door. He used one of his canes to reach out and flick the switch for the porch light. The bulb was yellow, and it cast an alien light that was supposed to not attract bugs.

Penny lightly hopped on the low porch and dropped in the big white swing. "Hi, Tyler," she said.

"How are you, Penny?"

"Amazed!"

"Why is that?"

"Every time you do something unusual, I think I've seen it all. Then you come along with something bigger and better. You surprised me twice today."

"Twice?"

"Yeah," she said. "First when you stood up and walked across the stage, and secondly when you gave the speech. You didn't have any notes, did you?"

"No, I didn't. They all got thrown away yesterday."

"It was beautiful and perfect, Tyler, and very meaningful. You should run for office or start a church. You had everyone there mesmerized."

As she continued to flatter him with remarks about his speech, the light evening breeze shifted, and he smelled her, and it was familiar. It excited him, and he nonchalantly folded his hands over his lap to conceal his excitement. He wondered how much of this sexual attraction could be tallied up to pure animal instinct.

"Thank you, Penny. I did try to speak from the heart."

"Well, you did, and you're the talk of the town. Now tell me about your legs. I'm so happy for you."

"There's not much to tell, really. I started getting some feeling and a little movement about six weeks ago. I have worked really hard with my therapists, and they're coming back very slowly. There are still some places where I don't have any feeling. The doctors are pleased, but very guarded in their prognosis. I guess they don't want me to be disappointed if I don't get back full use, but I can tell you, I plan on running and dancing soon."

"Oh, good," she laughed. "I may need a partner at the class reunion next year."

"Really? Won't Milton be there?"

"No, he won't. I don't think we'll be dating that much longer," Penny admitted.

"Oh? I'm sorry to hear that," Tyler said with a grin.

She laughed, "Shame on you, Tyler Harrison. I can always tell when you're lying."

Tyler laughed too. "Yeah, you always could. I remember when we were dating, I only fibbed to you three times, and you caught me all five times."

Now they laughed together. It occurred to Tyler that it had been a long time since that had happened, and it felt good.

"Since you're not seeing Geena anymore, and I won't be seeing Milton much longer, maybe the next time you're in town, you could come over for dinner."

"Penny, I would like that, but not yet. I don't need another distraction in my life right now. I have to concentrate on my therapy and my exercises. Can I have a rain check?"

"Sure," she said, "but don't wait too long. I'm aging fast." While she was talking, she quickly extracted a little spiral notebook from her purse and a pen. She wrote for a few seconds and tore out the page. When she handed it to him, she asked, "Can you read my writing?"

Tyler held it up to the light. He remembered her writing as he read the note aloud. "This is a rain check, given as an invitation to dinner at the home of Penny Kilmer. It can only be redeemed by one Tyler Harrison, and must be done on or before May 28, 1969, which is one year from today." Tyler folded the little piece of paper and slid it in his pocket.

"Why one year?" he asked.

"Because I'm getting tired of waiting on you, Tyler, and I'm not going to wait all my life. I want you, and if you want me, you have one year to come and get me."

"Okay," he said. "I'll remember that."

"Oh, that reminds me." She got off the swing and came closer. When she was only two or three feet away, she stopped, turned around, and bent over some at the waist with her rear end sticking out, almost in his face. She turned her head so she could see him and said, "Okay, go ahead."

Tyler gave her a bit of a confused look. Then he glanced at her hind side. She was wearing a pair of white slacks. They were drawn tight, and he could see the line of her panties.

"Now go ahead and get it over with," she said.

"What do you want me to do, Penny?"

"Don't you remember?" she continued. "The last time I was here, you said you would give a lot of money to get out of that chair and kick my ass. Well, go ahead. Kick me!"

He laughed. "Maybe later when I can do it without falling on mine."

"Okay, fine. Hey, it's getting late, and I have to work tomorrow." She leaned over and quickly kissed him on the lips. "Don't forget your rain check."

* * *

"Come on, man. That's only eight. I got to have ten!" Freeman yelled.

Tyler was bathed in sweat, and the pain was close to unbearable. As he began the ninth leg raise on the machine that he had grown to hate, he was sure something would tear. The muscle or a tendon or a ligament— something had to give.

Freeman stuck his face about two inches from Tyler's. "You're not even trying, you pussy! Get it up there!"

Unbelievably, the leg straightened, and the weight rose. There was no damn way he could do a tenth one, but with the muscle shaking and Freeman calling him names, he did it.

Before the plane crash, he could have done eighty or ninety pounds ten times easily. It seemed his legs were about as strong as they'd been the day he started kindergarten. But it would happen. He would make it happen.

It was mid-September. At least he had gotten rid of the hated wheelchair. To Vince's great delight, they had sold the van and replaced it with a Cadillac limousine. Tyler had never really wanted a limo. Within a week, he wondered how he had ever managed without one. Vince went through a can of wax about every two weeks. If that was any indication, he liked it too.

*   *   *

As Tyler dried his hands and straightened his tie, he thought about how lucky he was. It was five days before Christmas, and he was walking. Tyler came out of the private bathroom in his office. He walked carefully across to where his folks were. His father had left the sofa and was standing behind it looking at the newest addition to Tyler's office. There, mounted on the wall, were the two canes that had become so symbolic to Tyler. They were mounted horizontally on a piece of green felt. Outside the glass, on a little brass plaque, was the date they were last used. Inside on a long narrow plaque between the canes was a quote. It read: "'Alas, I know if I ever became truly humble, I would be proud of it.' Benjamin Franklin."

"I like your new plaque, Son," his dad said. "It says a lot."

"Yes it does, Dad. I need to remind myself how to be humble. How quickly I became selfish and depressed, how I'm not half as smart as I think

I am, how too much pride can make me do stupid things, but also how I have overcome the need for those canes, how I intend to work until these legs are 100 percent, and how precious every moment of life is."

"You're becoming quite a philosopher," his mom said.

"In that case," Tyler said, "I'll shut up."

Tyler had finally found the perfect spot for the new headquarters of Harrison Ltd. and its subsidiaries. It was not where he had originally intended but now proved to be the best location. For almost three years, Brad Slater had been quietly buying up individual pieces of land to create one huge parcel. When finished in another year or so, it would comprise almost forty-five thousand acres and would be the location of an entire new city, which was now Tyler's number-one goal as a builder.

He had decided the perfect location for his new headquarters would be his dream city. It could be viewed from Interstate 270 and was only fifteen miles north of the Capital Beltway on the way to Frederick, Maryland. That was where the dedication ceremony had been that morning.

His folks had driven up for a long weekend, so they could be here for the dedication and the company Christmas party later that afternoon. The employees had their own dedication. Tyler's folks and every employee had his or her picture taken with Tyler while shoveling dirt. Each would receive a framed picture as a reminder that they were there that day and each was an important part of this company.

He had, in nine short years, amassed an impressive list of phenomenal accomplishments. He was rightly proud of all his entrepreneurial ventures, but as 1968 wound down, it was his philanthropic activities that gave him the most pleasure. The newly founded Harrison Foundation had given $10 million to worthy causes in 1968. Next year, it would double that, and Tyler hoped to reach $100 million per year by 1973.

His last thought before joining the Christmas party with his folks was of two days back in the spring. On April 18 he had signed the $2 million check to Children's Hospital, which was the first foundation gift. One day later, on April 19 in the evening, the feeling began to return to his legs. Coincidence or miracle? God only knew!

Chapter 28

Cashing the Rain Check

Cashing the Rain Check

1969

*T*yler was running harder than he had ever run in his life. He knew without counting that his heart was beating well over two hundred beats per minute, and his breaths, which he could see in this early January freeze, were coming in exhausted gasps. His legs were working as well as they possibly could, but it was not enough, and he felt himself falling. As he went down, he turned his body so he would land on his side and shoulder. He landed softly and unhurt, thanks to two sweatshirts, a jacket, and the rubberized track on which he was running.

"You okay?" Liz asked as she gave him a hand.

"Yeah. With all this padding, I just bounce."

"Well, when you break something, I'm not going to help you."

"Thanks, Liz," Tyler said.

"It hurts me to see you doing this to yourself."

"I don't want to do this, Liz. I have to do it. These legs will only get better if I demand more from them."

He had decided his rehabilitation was going too slow, so on his own, he had begun to run—more like jog, if you could call it that.

Tyler had decided last week to come to this community college track every morning. Liz wouldn't let him come alone, so she came along to harass him.

Tyler began to jog again. The problem was his left leg. Most of the time it was equal to the right one. Although his jogging was contemptuously slow and not pretty to watch, it went okay until his left leg got a late message to move because of the damaged nerves. When that happened, the leg didn't move soon enough to be there to support his weight, and he fell.

He had been secretly counting, and as he finished the day's workout, he smiled. His first day out, it had taken him forever, but he had jogged one mile and fallen nine times. Today at the end of the second week, it still took forever, but he had only fallen six times. It did peeve him a bit that Liz could walk faster than he could jog.

* * *

When Tyler reached the office, he was met by a UPS man. Now sitting at his desk, he began to unwrap the little package. Because there was no return address, he really had no idea what to expect. When the paper had all been removed, what he found was a photo album a little larger than a wallet. As he began to flip the pages, he found pictures on one side and a brief description of that picture next to it on the other side. He began to smile and then to laugh.

On the first page was a picture of a female's rear end in red slacks. To the right where another picture could have been inserted in the plastic holder was a neatly printed card that read, "My butt in red slacks." There was also a date. There were two snapshots taken in jeans, one taken in a tight dress, two taken in shorts, one taken in a two-piece bathing suit, and the last one was taken in a pair of black bikini panties. It was very sexy and showed her tan line.

On the very last page, Penny had written a note. "Just thought that I would let you know I agree. After closer scrutiny, I too have decided that I have a great ass. Hope you enjoy these and that they will serve as a daily reminder for what you've been missing for almost ten years. Enjoy! Penny."

*   *   *

Tyler had done four different commercials for his real estate franchise and could also be seen in almost every magazine published. As a result of a $20 million advertising blitz, Tyler Harrison and Harrison Properties were household names to everyone in America except maybe some hermits and a few cave dwellers.

The demand of his time was never-ending. He no longer had time to work with and visit with the "little people" who so often carried out the work. He had become what all wealthy men become if they are to stay wealthy—an idea man who is good at delegating power. Tyler also hated to admit it, but like all men with money, his taste for expensive things had increased, as had the price and size of his toys.

As Vince turned the long white toy into the regional airport, Tyler could barely contain his excitement. Vince drove through the gate and turned toward the private hangers where a small group of men was assembled.

Along with his devotion to exercising and running, he had restarted his flying lessons. He was now the proud bearer of a private pilot's license for single-engine airplanes, and he had more than five hundred hours logged in the cockpit. Never wanting to be one who would stagnate, Tyler was already working on upgrading his license to two-engine status.

When Vince stopped, Tyler quickly but carefully swung his legs out, and using the door and the seat to push off, he stood and approached the three men. He talked briefly with Charles Kane, his flight instructor and the airport owner. When they were finished, he was introduced to a representative from the Beech Aircraft Corporation from Kansas.

The cowboy boot–wearing young man from Kansas presented Tyler with the keys to his new airplane. It was a single-engine Beechcraft that would comfortably carry four passengers with their luggage and cruise at two hundred miles per hour.

The plane was painted in green and white, and Tyler smiled as he touched the Harrison Ltd. name and logo expertly painted on the side. This was some of Liz's handiwork. She would have the Harrison Ltd. logo stenciled on his underwear if he would let her.

Tyler turned and said, "All right, gentlemen. Let's see what this new Beechcraft will do."

*　*　*

Penny could relax. All she had to do was get a week's worth of groceries the next morning. She sat on one kitchen chair with her feet on another. Because the refrigerator was almost empty, she was eating a bologna sandwich and looking at her toes. She was in dire need of a pedicure, and she could either shave her legs or plat them. She was also sticky and sweaty and had pulled her hair up and wadded it into a rag she often used when she was housecleaning. She decided she couldn't care less. It was the weekend, her place, her life, and she could do what she wanted.

The doorbell startled her. She glanced at her watch on the way and wondered who could be at her door at seven o'clock on a Friday evening. When she opened the door, the sun was low and shining in her eyes. She raised her hand to act as a shield, and she was looking into Tyler Harrison's sensual gray eyes. He was wearing a black tuxedo.

"Are you lost, Tyler?"

"Is this the current residence of one Penny Kilmer?"

She put her hand on her hip and cocked her head to one side. "You know this is where I live," she fretted.

"Good," he said. "Then I'm in the right place." Tyler handed her a little piece of folded paper. She looked at it curiously and then unfolded it.

"Oh my God!" she laughed. "I had almost forgotten."

"It's the rain check you gave me," Tyler prompted. "It entitles me to one dinner at your residence any time within a year from May 28, 1968. Well, this is May 27, 1969, and I'm here to collect. I even dressed up."

She had two thoughts simultaneously: how glad she was to see him and how bad she looked. "It would have been nice if you'd called first," she explained.

"The rain check says anytime in the year. It doesn't say anything about calling or making a reservation."

"Just shut up," she snapped, "and come in."

He bent down and picked up a rather large shopping bag and walked past her and through the doorway.

At least the apartment is clean, Penny thought to herself.

Tyler went to the center of the living room and waited. She closed the door and headed for the bedroom. "Have a seat and make yourself comfortable. I'll just be a minute."

In her bedroom, she quickly shaved her legs with an electric razor and put on an attractive white-and-yellow sundress and a simple pair of yellow flats.

"Sorry," she said as she sat in the other chair, "I think that was a little longer than a minute."

"It was time well spent. You look really great, but you didn't have to change for me."

"That's very easy for you to say," she observed, "since you're sitting there all shaved and showered in a tuxedo."

"The rain check didn't specify dress, and I didn't want to be underdressed," he snickered.

"Well, you don't have to worry about that." She stood and said, "You look very handsome. Now give me your tie and jacket so you can relax."

When he had removed them, she hung them in a small coat closet near the front door. When she was seated again, he said, "I like your apartment. You have good taste."

"Well, I try. Most of this stuff is old or used. You know how some people have French provincial or traditional or early American-styled furniture. Because I've had most of this hodgepodge from the time I moved in here, I have named my style early Kilmer."

While she was laughing, she was smiling on the inside. "So, what brought you here this evening? It must have been those eight snapshots of my rear end."

"No, not really. I did enjoy them, though. They reminded me of what a cute sense of humor you have. Everyone in the office got a kick out of them too."

"What?! You showed the pictures of my butt to people who work for you?"

"Well, not exactly. I thought they were really cute, so I had them framed. Four on the top row with the separate descriptions alongside each photo and four on the bottom row, all mounted and hung on the wall directly across from my desk so I see it every time I look up. I heard a rumor that everyone slips in when I'm not there to take a peek."

"I don't know whether to be flattered or angry," Penny said.

"Well, I don't like you very well when you're angry."

"All right," she said with a smile. "I'll be flattered. So if you didn't come because of the pictures, why did you come?"

Tyler leaned back in the chair and crossed his legs. "I came for a number of reasons. I guess the main one is an experiment. I want to see if you and I have a future. For almost ten years now, you have been the last thing I think about each night before I sleep and the first thing I think about each morning when I wake. You even haunt my dreams. I've allowed you to become an untouchable, almost perfect goddess in my mind who resides on a very special pedestal. Every time I see an attractive female, I compare her to you, and she always falls short. Every time I see any female clothing, I picture you in it. Thanks to ten years of maturity, having to spend time in a wheelchair, learning how to walk again, and never forgetting some things that Granddad Luke said, I have learned to swallow my pride. I don't know if this awestruck feeling is just infatuation or love, but I'm ready to find out."

Penny was speechless. She wished she had recorded what he had just said, so she could replay it every day for the rest of her life. After a while she said, "That was so beautiful I don't know what to say."

"How about, 'Dinner is ready,'" he quipped.

She had to laugh. How could he switch from a gut-wrenching moment to humor so quickly? How did he know that was what she needed?

"You really do want something to eat then?" she asked.

"Yes. I skipped lunch, and it's been a long day. I really am hungry, but not particular."

"I'm very glad to hear that," she admitted. "I was going to the grocery store in the morning, and the fridge is almost empty, but I'll give you a choice. You can have your bologna sandwiches with mayonnaise or mustard."

Now it was his turn to laugh. "I'll take mustard." He quickly slid the large shopping bag out in front of him and brought out two bottles of wine. "I didn't know what we would be eating, so I brought a red and a white."

"The bologna is all beef, so you can open the red."

Tyler brought the bottle of red and the shopping bag and followed her to the kitchen. He placed the shopping bag on the kitchen counter, and she gave him a corkscrew.

While she was getting the bologna and mustard from the fridge, he took a long, narrow box from his bag. "Here, I thought you might need a centerpiece for the table."

She took the box and quickly opened it. She had expected a dozen red roses, but what she found was a dozen of the most beautiful and delicate white rosebuds she had ever seen, some greenery, and a small envelope with her name on the front.

She nervously slid out the card. In his hurried longhand, he had written: "I started to get the standard dozen of red when these caught my eye. I have never seen such lovely roses, but I'm sure they will pale when you hold them."

She willed herself not to cry. When she had recovered some, she stepped close and kissed Tyler briefly on the lips. She stepped back as if he had flipped a switch, and she could feel him go through her whole body like a bolt of current.

"Here, I thought you might need this," Tyler suggested as he handed her a white vase.

"Tyler, the flowers are lovely, but this card is every girl's dream. I will always cherish it. Thank you."

"You're most welcome, madam. Can we eat now?"

"You really are hungry, aren't you? All right, you start the sandwiches, while I put these in the vase with some water."

When she returned, the sandwiches were made, and two glasses of red wine were poured. She put the roses on the table and found a candle. She lit the candle, switched off the light, and said, "Dinner is served."

*   *   *

When Tyler had poured the last of the wine, Penny asked, "Do you have any more wine in your big bag?"

"Oh, I almost forgot. No, I don't have any more wine." He jumped up and reached deep into the bag. "But I do have this." He dropped a small plastic bag of popcorn kernels on the table.

"Why did you bring that?" she asked.

"Well, I wasn't sure you would let me in. I figured if the tuxedo or flowers didn't get me in, I knew the popcorn would. I remembered what you told me once at the drive-in theater when I deviled you about how much you like popcorn. Do you remember what you said?"

"Yes," she laughed. "I said I liked you, but I loved popcorn."

He was still holding the shopping bag, and she wanted to satisfy her curiosity. She said, "So, Mr. Mysterious Man, what else do you have in your shopping bag?"

"That's all," he said innocently.

"I don't believe you," she mused.

"Honest," he said as he turned the bag upside down and shook it. "What did you think I had in here?" Tyler asked, still shaking the bag.

"I was hoping you had brought a change of clothes."

"A change of clothes? Why would I do that?"

She looked down at her hands. She was also in dire need of a manicure. She wondered if he had noticed and then frowned. Of course he had. He never missed anything.

"Well … I thought you would look sort of funny slipping out of here in the morning wearing a tuxedo. I was hoping you were planning to spend the night."

"No, I'm sorry." He sighed and glanced at his watch. He picked up his wineglass and finished what was left. "As a matter of fact, I need to be going," he said as he walked out of the kitchen.

She stood up quickly to follow and had to use the doorway to steady herself. Oh yes, the wine was working.

"What's the hurry?" she ventured.

He was at the closet getting his jacket and tie.

"I have a meeting in the morning with a man who owns a piece of land I have been trying to buy for more than three years. Charles is waiting for me, and we have to fly back tonight."

She had made it to the front door. "Charles?"

"Yeah. Charles Kane—he's my flight instructor. I bought a plane, and we flew it in this evening and landed at the little airport out of town. We made the whole flight in only an hour and ten minutes. I have a pilot's license now, but with the plane being new and us flying at night, I felt better bringing him along. Anyway, he's over with Mom and Dad. I need to get him out of there and fly back."

"Are you saying you flew all the way here just to have dinner with me?" She leaned against the front door, blocking his way.

"Yes, and it was the best dinner date I've ever had."

She tenderly put her hand on his neck and tried her best to look alluring. "It seems like such a shame to go to all that trouble for just bologna sandwiches. You really shouldn't rush off until you've had dessert." She leaned forward and ran her tongue across his lips. "I'm sure you would like it. It's been aging for ten years, and it's just right. I call it, Penny à la bed."

Tyler moved her away from the door like she was a feather. He bent down and kissed her with such passion that she came close to collapsing in his arms. When he released her, she had to concentrate most of her effort on standing and regaining her breath.

"I'm sure it's wonderful," he agreed. "But it'll have to wait. You know, nice girls never do it on the first date."

It was difficult to think fast after two large glasses of wine. "It's been ten years, and I'm not as nice as I used to be."

He had the door open now. "You're still nice to me, Penny."

Back inside, Penny looked at the flowers and then picked up and read the card again. She blew out the candle and took the card to the bedroom.

195

After ten years, he had come. He was being coy, but he was hooked. She smelled something pleasant and knew it was her beautiful white roses.

*   *   *

Tyler looked at the calendar on his desk and found it difficult to believe that it had only been two and a half days since he and Penny had shared bologna sandwiches. It was Monday morning, and he felt exhilarated. Before coming to work, he had run five miles in less than forty minutes, almost without breaking a sweat. Thanks to the exercises and the running, the legs were bigger and stronger than before his accident. Freeman, his exercise guru, had pronounced him whole and had taken his leave.

But the real reason for Tyler's exhilaration was Penny. As he had told her, she had always been in his thoughts. Now, however, she consumed them. He had replayed their Friday night rain check dinner a thousand times. He enjoyed remembering her different expressions, her laugh, her eyes, and the way they hid nothing. She was always a little unpredictable, and he liked that about her.

He had called her Saturday morning to tell her how much he had enjoyed their dinner, and they had laughed and talked for more than an hour. He was elated to see that they were again becoming friends. If they were to build and sustain a long-term relationship, they would need love, and a little lust would add excitement and spice, but friendship would make it endure.

Chapter 29

Chapter 29

Sleeping at Penny's Place

H ere and there a large, puffy white cloud was suspended in the mid-June sky. It was a perfect summer day. There was a wonderful breeze blowing that served as a sufficient deterrent to any haze or humidity. Penny was leaning on her car fender counting her blessings: She was young and healthy and not at all bad to look at. School was out, and it was summer vacation. Her ten-year class reunion was that weekend. She looked especially forward to attending this one, because she would be on the arm of their most phenomenal classmate. She would be spending the weekend with this wealthy and famous guy, and she had every intention of setting the hook and reeling him in; he would be putty in her hands. Besides, he liked her pretty feet.

She looked up and searched the sky. Off to the right, she saw a small plane that appeared to be descending and lining up with the runway. It occurred to her that she had no idea what color or what size Tyler's plane was. She knew it couldn't be too large, or it wouldn't be landing at Stratford. The Stratford airport had been a grass field until six years earlier.

She looked at the buildings that comprised all the airport structures. There was an old two-story farmhouse where the airport owner lived. There was a huge, old Quonset hut-type hanger that actually appeared to be leaning. Next to that was an alien building. It was a new green and white metal building with a gable roof and large sliding doors. On the gable over the doors was a Harrison Ltd. sign.

The little plane had become larger now, and she could see just a wisp of smoke as the two rear wheels touched down, followed shortly by the nose wheel. The little gravel parking lot was close to the narrow asphalt strip, and Penny could clearly see the Harrison Ltd. name and logo on the side of the plane as it rolled by. It turned, taxied back, and stopped near an old gas pump.

A long-haired man wearing coveralls emerged from the old farmhouse eating a sandwich. He rushed toward the plane. Tyler opened the door, stepped out onto the wing, and jumped down. He waved at Penny and quickly retrieved a large and a small piece of luggage from a smaller door near the rear of the plane.

She watched as he shook hands and spoke in his easygoing manner with the other man. Tyler was wearing tennis shorts and a green pullover shirt. He was very tan and fit, and Penny was aware that she enjoyed looking at him. When he picked up the bags and started toward her, she could see the muscles in his forearms and legs. She remembered how those legs had looked like dried sticks when he had fallen out of his wheelchair, and she could not imagine what he had gone through to rebuild them into the stumps that now carried him so easily.

She tried not to look too posed, although she was. She was wearing a pair of short shorts, a shirt with the tail tied under her breasts that exposed her firm midriff, and slinky sandals that exposed as much foot as possible.

"How long you been waiting?" he asked while still approaching.

She glanced at her watch and noted she had been there more than a half hour, but not wanting to appear too eager, she said, "Only about ten minutes."

He stopped a few feet away and just stared up and down at her. "Miss Penny Kilmer, you sure are a sight for sore eyes."

She asked, "In down-home talk, that means you like what you're looking at, right?"

"That's right," he agreed.

The always unpredictable Tyler dropped his bags, came forward, bent to his knees, and kissed the top of each foot. When he was standing, he said, "I've been wanting to do that for ten years."

"Was there anything else you wanted to kiss?" she asked.

He leaned forward and gave her a quick kiss on the lips.

"Yes, there is. Actually, I've written down a rather long list of various places on your body that I intend to get to—soon."

She smiled and looked over each of his shoulders and then up at the sky. "To be honest," she explained, "I was waiting for another guy, but you'll do. Get in the car!"

*　　*　　*

The ten-year reunion of the Class of 1959 was planned around two events. The first was an informal get-together at a local classmate's home just out of town. The second event would be a more formal dinner and dance on Saturday night where everyone would introduce themselves and tell what they had been doing the past ten years.

Penny was on the planning committee and would need to attend both events. Tyler had agreed to attend both events with her. He also had agreed to sit with Penny at the head table on Saturday night, but he would not stand in any receiving line or be part of the welcoming committee for either event. He just simply wanted to downplay his celebrity status as much as possible.

When they arrived and had their nametags on, they were ready to leave the large back porch and walk into the backyard where a couple of early groups were already gathered.

Tyler was holding her hand as they negotiated the steps. "You want a beer?" he asked.

She quickly answered, "No, just a Coke."

"You sure?"

"I'm positive." She leaned over and whispered, "Five years ago at the last class reunion, I got drunk, and I still don't know what the hell I said while we were dancing, and I don't want to. Then three weeks ago you show up, ate all of my bologna, and I got to high on wine to lure you into my bedchamber. That's not going to happen tonight if I have to lock the door and get out my handcuffs."

"Do you have handcuffs?" he asked with a grin.

She winked. "Makes you wonder, doesn't it?" She turned and headed for the nearest group.

Tyler went to get two Cokes. When he joined the group where Penny had settled, Steve, the class president and all-around good guy, asked, "Where is Geena Morgan?"

Tyler laughed. "She got rid of me and moved to Hollywood."

Steve's wife spoke up and said, "We've seen her last two movies, and they were great. I read in some magazine at the beauty parlor that she may get nominated for an Oscar this year. The article also said she's living with some actor who's a real scumbag, and it hinted that Geena has become an alcoholic."

Everyone looked at Tyler as if he knew more.

"I don't know for sure," Tyler said, "but I've also heard the rumors … We don't see each other anymore, but she's a good person and very talented. I hope the rumors aren't true."

"Tyler Harrison! You wealthy hunk, did you miss me the last five years?"

Everyone turned to see Joan Watkins, the nurse from Florida. She still had the bright-red hair, deep tan, nice body, and more-than-ample breasts.

After getting a big hug, Tyler asked, "Are you still nursing those poor old people in Florida?"

"Only the rich ones," she explained. "Are you still searching for the right woman?"

Tyler reached out and pulled Penny close. "I think I may have finally found her."

Joan gave Penny one of those strange looks that women understand perfectly and men never notice. "So," Joan sighed, "you finally hooked him again."

Penny looked up at Tyler and smiled. "I'm not sure that's been decided yet."

* * *

When they reached her apartment that night, Penny asked, "Would you like to come up?"

"Just try to stop me," he chuckled.

On the way up the stairs, Penny asked, "Are your folks expecting you home?"

"I'm a big boy now, and besides, I told Mom I'd probably spend the night with you."

"Oh really?!" she replied. "You sound rather sure of yourself."

"The last time I was here, you tried to convince me that you're not a very nice girl, so I believed you."

"That's just because you tried to get me drunk on your wine. What did your mom say when you told her?" Penny asked.

"She smiled and said, 'Good. It's about time.' She's always liked you."

At the entrance to the kitchen, Penny asked, "Do you want something to drink?"

Tyler went to her and said, "The only thing I want right now is you."

She threw her arms around him. "Oh, Tyler, I've waited so long for you to say that … I … I hope you won't be disappointed."

"Penny, why would I be disappointed?" he questioned.

"Because from the first night we dated, I always wanted you to be the first. I wanted to give you my virginity. I wanted it to be special … like a contract between us."

He took her in his arms and stroked her hair. "Penny, it's okay. I never expected you to wait for me, and I didn't deserve it the way I acted. I always assumed you slept with Milton."

"Yes, I did, eventually, but I never loved him." She started to cry. "You don't understand. Milton, he … he wasn't … wasn't the first. He's not … the one … who stole … my virginity." Her sobbing was racking her body, and she was beyond speech.

Tyler helped her to the sofa and sat holding her. When she had gathered herself a little, he said, "What happened before tonight is in the past. It's not important, and you need to forget it."

She pulled back away from him, and he wiped her tears.

"I can't forget. Believe me, I've tried," Penny said. "I need to talk about it. I have never told anyone about this. Not my mom or any of my best friends. No one!"

"Okay, get it out, Penny. I'm here for you."

"That night when I slapped you, I wasn't myself. I was scared and ashamed and probably in shock. Three hours before our date, I … I was … raped."

When Tyler reached for her, she held up her hand to stave him off. "No, I have to do this! I was at work in the back of the shoe store unpacking and putting up a new delivery of shoes—"

She saw a look of rage on Tyler's face. "You mean that old bastard Mr. Grant?" he asked, as though he couldn't believe it.

Penny nodded, and then she lost it. She sobbed and hit Tyler with her balled up fists. She tried to scratch his face, but he caught her arms and held her tightly until he could feel ten years of pent up rage slowly flow from her body. When she finally relaxed, she pulled her legs up near her chest into a fetal position and rocked back and forth while he held her, and she cried softly.

Tyler was shocked and angry, but mostly he was afraid. How much damage had she sustained? He was sure the physical damage had healed, but the mental damage clearly hadn't. Would this admission help her to heal, or had it put her over the edge? Would he lose her now after all this time? The thought of that began to fill him with anger. Part of it was directed toward the son of a bitch who had done this to her. The rest was turned toward himself.

She had acted strangely that night, and he knew it. He had known there was something wrong, but he didn't care. Dumb-ass Tyler got slapped, and his feelings were hurt, and he'd only cared about himself. He had acted like a complete, flaming asshole and then covered it over by blaming her and being a proud, smug bastard for ten long years.

It hurt him now, as he thought how much she must love him. She had shared her deepest, darkest secret with him—only him. How could he ever make this up to her? God, he was lucky she even spoke to him, much less loved him. He wondered, as she lay against him and whimpered like a beaten animal, if he would ever get the chance.

*   *   *

When his eyes opened, he knew he was in Penny's bed. What he didn't know was where she was. Last night, when she had finished her gruesome story, she had finally exhausted herself. When he was sure she was soundly asleep, Tyler had carried her to the bedroom. He had snuggled close and held her. After another couple of hours of deep thought, he finally fell asleep, fully dressed.

The bedroom door was closed, and that concerned him. What was she doing, or what had she done, that she didn't want him to hear. He was disgusted with himself. He had programmed himself to wake up if she moved or stirred, but somehow he had slept through her getting out of bed and leaving the room.

He found her on the sofa. Her hair hadn't been combed, and she was still wearing the same wrinkled skirt and blouse from the night before. She stood up, and he noticed a coffee mug in her hand.

"You do still drink coffee, don't you?" she asked.

"Yeah. With just a little milk, if you have it."

When she returned with the coffee, he was sitting on one end of the sofa. She gave him his mug and chose to sit at the other end. Tyler was aware that she appeared cool and distant.

"When you've finished your coffee, you can leave," she said.

"Are you telling me I have to go?"

"Yes. I think you should."

"I like to make my own decisions, but why do you want me to go?"

"I would think that was obvious. Your precious Penny is tainted and tarnished," she admitted. "Not only have I slept willingly with another man, but I've been raped."

"You can't help what happened to you, Penny."

"For your information, I've had time to do some research. Almost 80 percent of women who are raped lose the man they're dating, living with, or married to within three years. It seems most men view their women as sexual possessions, and they don't want them after they've been violated."

"I'm not like most men," Tyler protested.

Penny laughed sarcastically. "That's true! You're extra proud, and you want to possess everything."

"I work hard, and I've been very successful. I make no apologies for my possessions, but people are different. They're not things. I have never treated anyone like that."

"I know more about men than you think. After the initial excitement wears off, you'll begin to wonder what it was like with Mr. Grant. Did I resist enough, or did I secretly enjoy it? And why didn't I report it?"

"Why didn't you report it?" he demanded.

"A lot of reasons, I guess. I was in shock and didn't act normal for a while. I went home and locked myself in the bathroom. I got in the tub and scrubbed until my skin was almost raw. I was afraid that if I told, no one would believe me, and I was sure it would ruin my reputation. I guess I was just ashamed and was afraid to let anyone know. Then there was you. I was afraid you wouldn't want me if you knew. I was also afraid you might confront him or even kill him. Then while I was in the tub, it struck me that I might be pregnant. That's why I acted so strangely that night and got so frustrated when you wouldn't have sex with me."

She stood up, took his mug, and started toward the little kitchen. "I really would like for you to go," she said. She set the coffee mug on the counter next to the sink and went to the front door and opened it.

Tyler left the sofa and went to the door, but he didn't go out. He grabbed Penny and held her. She tried to break free, but he pinned her against the wall.

Tyler put his face close to hers and said, "You don't know shit about men. Your dad died before you were old enough to remember him, you don't have any brothers, you never liked your stepfather, and you never had any kind of relationship with him. You've only been with two men—a rapist and a nerd. Don't try to judge me or know what I think from that volume of information."

Tyler stopped talking and kissed her. She resisted him, but he wouldn't relent. He could feel her weaken. Tyler could tell that her desire was increasing. He released her arms, but she clung to him. When their tongues touched, he felt her stiffen and press against him.

Aware of his own rising desire, he broke away. "I stayed with you last night and held you and worried about you. I didn't do that because I felt sorry for you, although I do. I did it because I wanted to hold you, because I get pleasure from just being near you, because I think this is where I belong. So, you see, Miss Cute-Assed Penny Kilmer, you can't get rid of me that easy. I'll be here to pick you up at a quarter till six. Make sure you're ready, because if you're not, I'll kick the damn door in and drag your ass to the reunion in whatever you happen to be wearing." He leaned her against the wall, went out, and slammed the door.

When Tyler reached the bottom of the stairs, he turned to the right to begin the short track to his folks' home. His mind was racing, and he walked for a while until his feet began to hurt. When he looked down, he had to laugh at himself. He had stomped out of Penny's apartment without his shoes and was now trying to walk on a gravel alley in his stocking feet. As he slowed his pace and tried to find a smooth place to set each foot, an idea began to form. He would go home, get clean socks and an old pair of shoes, and then he would go buy a new pair. There was a particular shoe store in town he wanted to visit anyway.

Chapter 30

Penny's Beauty Mark

When he entered Grant's Shoes, it was about noon on Saturday, and they were very busy. It had always been a thriving business.

Alan Grant smiled when he saw Tyler and said, "Welcome, Mr. Harrison. How can we help you today?"

Tyler had been browsing the men's shoes. He turned and looked into the eyes of Alan Grant, straining not to let his emotions show. "I didn't know if you remembered me or not. I haven't been in for a long time."

Alan laughed. "I guarantee there aren't five people in this whole county who wouldn't know you on sight. You're pretty famous around here, Mr. Harrison."

"Well, yeah, I guess so. I keep forgetting that." Tyler glanced back at the shoe display. He picked up a brown penny loafer and handed it to Alan. "Do you have that in a 10E?"

"I'm sure we do. Have a seat, and I'll check."

As Alan returned with a box, Tyler studied him. He was about six foot and well over two hundred pounds. His shoulders were rounded, and his arms were thin. Most of Alan's weight was resting around his middle. When he sat heavily on the stool with his shoehorn, Tyler could see through his thinning hair. He guessed that Alan was about forty, and he wasn't aging well. His complexion was almost milk-white, and Tyler could see the broken veins on his cheeks and nose that were usually the sure sign of a heavy drinker. Tyler slid his feet into the shoes Alan handed him.

"There you go, Mr. Harrison. How do those feel?"

Tyler was finding it hard to concentrate on the shoes. He got up and walked around some and then felt to make sure there was plenty of room at the end for his toes. "These feel fine. I'll take them."

At the cash register, after he had paid, Tyler asked, "Could I talk to you for a minute?"

Alan looked surprised but responded, "Sure, come on in the back." He turned to one of the girls working and said, "I'll be in the back with Mr. Harrison if you need me."

Tyler followed him to the back, which turned out to be a little warehouse with many rows of shoeboxes in tight shelves. He could see there was no formal office. Off to the side there was an old, green metal desk with a swivel armchair and a straight metal chair beside it. There were three old metal filing cabinets and an early American sofa that looked like it might have been delivered by covered wagon.

"I hate to be rude, Mr. Harrison, but we have been really busy this morning and I've been trying to make it to the bathroom for an hour."

"Go right ahead," Tyler said. "I'm in no hurry."

"Thank you," Alan said. "Help yourself to a seat. I won't be long."

As Alan hurried toward the back of the store, Tyler couldn't believe his luck. He had wanted to look around, but now he could have a better look. When he heard what he assumed was a bathroom door close and lock somewhere in the back, he moved quickly to the filing cabinet on the left. He eased the drawer open and was surprised to find what he was looking for in the first one he searched. Way in the back was a nearly empty bottle of vodka sitting next to two full bottles with the seals unbroken.

He closed the drawer and moved quickly to the desk. He listened carefully and then quickly slid out the center drawer on the old metal desk. He decided he was good at this. There, resting next to a rectangular whetstone, was an old, faded green switchblade knife. Tyler picked it up and held it. It was surprisingly heavy. He saw the little recessed button near his thumb and pressed it. Instantly, a polished five-inch blade shot out and distinctively clicked into place.

Tyler noticed that his own hand was shaking and forced himself to relax. He heard a toilet flush but did not panic. He released the blade and pushed it back home until it clicked into place. Then he carefully placed it back exactly where it had been. He closed the center drawer and sat in the chair next to the desk. He only sat for a few seconds before Alan Grant emerged from the rows of shelves.

"All right," Alan said, "what did you want to talk about?" He dropped into the swivel chair and turned so he could see Tyler.

"I was wondering if you've ever considered selling your business," Tyler inquired.

Alan smiled. "Many times, Mr. Harrison. As a matter of fact, I have a standing offer to work as a regional representative for a large shoe distributor. Also, there's a man up in Wheeling who is buying up many of the good shoe stores across West Virginia. He renames them all Mountaineer Shoes. He has made me two offers in the past six months. I have the last one here."

Alan sorted through some papers on his desk, found the envelope, and handed it to Tyler. Tyler skimmed the letter. It offered to buy the complete business, including the building and all fixtures, for $125,000. He also noted that the offer had been made less than two months ago.

Tyler placed the letter and envelope back on the desk. "Are you going to sell to him?"

"Not for that price." As Alan went on to explain why not and how much the business was really worth, Tyler glanced at the sofa.

It was a cream-colored fabric with brownish trees here and there. He tried to imagine what the person would be like who had thought the fabric had been attractive at some time. Then on the right cushion something caught his eye. It looked like four or five little brownish red circles on the light fabric. Tyler was almost certain that he was looking at Penny's blood that had been left there ten years earlier.

Tyler noticed that Alan had paused.

"Do you have a figure in mind that you would sell for?" Tyler asked.

"Yes, and it's not unreasonable. I'll sell everything for $140,000."

"I'll take it," Tyler said decisively and stood up. "I'll send someone around next week to make the arrangements."

"That will be great! You won't be sorry, Mr. Harrison. This is a good, solid business."

Tyler was already moving toward the doorway that led to the front of the store. He turned suddenly, and when he had eye contact with Alan, he asked, "Do you remember Penny Kilmer?"

Tyler was watching the eyes carefully, and he saw the reaction he was expecting. For an instant, they registered shock and surprise. Alan then suddenly looked away and too quickly asked, "Who?"

"Penny Kilmer. She teaches up at the high school now. Real pretty blonde. She used to work here."

Alan nervously said, "Oh, Penny. Yeah, I remember her. Why do you ask?"

"Oh, no special reason, I just remember her working here part-time when we were dating, but that was a long time ago." Tyler paused until Alan looked at him. "I'll be in touch," Tyler said.

* * *

Penny was ready and waiting at five o'clock. She remembered Tyler saying he would pick her up at a quarter till six, and if she wasn't ready, he would kick the damn door down and drag her ass to the reunion in whatever she was wearing. Penny wasn't sure if he was serious, but knowing Tyler, she wasn't going to take any chances.

He showed up at exactly fifteen minutes till six in his white limo with Vince driving. Penny was more excited than a high school girl. As she locked her door and started down the steps, Tyler was out and around the car. He looked very dapper in a light-gray pinstriped suit.

She was wearing a light-pink dress with only one strap over her left shoulder. Her jewelry was simple but dramatic. There was a wide gold bracelet on one forearm and large gold earrings on each ear.

Tyler stepped up on the last step and blocked her way. When she stopped, he leaned forward and kissed the end of her nose.

"I feel sorry for the other women there tonight," he said.

"Oh? Why is that?" she asked, fishing for the compliment.

"Because they won't be with me," he mused seriously.

She made a face and punched him lightly in the gut. "You think you look that good, do you?"

He said shyly, "I know I do, because my mommy said so when I left."

She laughed. "Did you know you left your loafers here this morning?"

"Yes. I noticed that when I started down the gravel alley."

"Why didn't you come back and get them?"

"I'm going through a phase where I need to suffer, and I can tell you, by the time I got to the end of that damned alley, I was suffering." Tyler reached into the inside pocket of his suit jacket and produced a long, thin, red velvet case. "This is for a very special lady."

"Tyler Harrison, you are always full or surprises." She looked at the case and could see that it was from Tiffany's in New York. Inside, she found a delicate gold bracelet with "Penny" inscribed on the nameplate. There were two very large diamonds, one on either side of her name.

"I hope you like it," he ventured.

"I love it. Thank you."

"I'm glad. I had it custom-made for you." Tyler took it out of the case and held it up so she could see the back. "Read it," he said.

She looked closely at the back of the nameplate and read: "June 1969, together again." She blinked a few times and said, "You make me feel like a princess."

Tyler took the bracelet, and Penny held out her wrist.

"Oh, no. This was designed with a special ankle in mind."

When he knelt down, she slipped her bare foot out of her heel and placed it on his knee. He fastened the clip and stood up. They both looked at it.

"What do you think?" she asked.

"I think it looks much better there than it did in the case."

*　　*　　*

Tyler and Penny made it to the reunion dinner dance five minutes early. The evening went pretty smoothly for the most part. Once though, while they were slow dancing, Tyler began to get excited. When Penny noticed, she took every opportunity to rub against him where his excitement was most prominent. When she wouldn't stop, Tyler said, "You know, I think I may have been wrong. You *are* a bad girl."

"Oh really, Tyler?" She giggled and reached around and squeezed one of his buttocks. "What would make you think that?"

Near the end of the evening, a slightly overweight female classmate approached Tyler and said she'd had a crush on him in junior English class. Her name was Tina, and she informed everyone that she had just gotten her second divorce. She said she had never known a famous person like Tyler and asked if she could have his autograph. He was a little embarrassed but said he'd be glad to. She handed him a felt-tip pen and stepped in close. Her dress was fairly low cut, and she promptly reached in and extracted one of her breasts.

"Here. Sign this," she said.

Tyler swallowed and quickly scribbled his name on the ample space above the nipple. She thanked him with a kiss on the cheek and went off to show anyone who wanted to see, which turned out to be a rather large crowd.

Penny took the pen from his hand and laughed.

"What's so funny?" he demanded.

"That's the first time I've ever seen you embarrassed," she noted.

Everyone in the group agreed and began to laugh, which only served to embarrass him more.

Tyler and Penny were still laughing and talking about their classmates when they stepped inside her apartment, and she locked the door. She threw her purse in one of the chairs. She pushed Tyler against the door and started to take off his jacket.

"Well, let's see now. You know I'm not a virgin and that I was raped. I haven't had any alcohol, so I won't make a fool of myself." She had his jacket off now and was almost finished with the tie. "I must have missed something. Can you think of any reason we can't make love tonight?"

He kissed her then. In the beginning, it was a soft, warm kiss, but it quickly grew into something more. Her hands alternated between trying to get his clothes off and exploring his body. With her help, he was soon down to his undershorts and socks.

He ended the kiss and picked her up. On the way to the bedroom, she kicked off her heels.

Tyler softly let Penny down to stand beside the bed. He went behind her, and while touching and kissing, he loosened the catch on her dress and slowly slid the zipper southward. When he came around to be in front of her, she stepped back and pushed the strap off her shoulder. She stood proudly as the dress fell away.

"Penny, for years I have made you beautiful and perfect in my mind, but you're even lovelier in person."

She smiled and placed a finger on his lips. "Everything you see is for you, Tyler. It always has been. Please, love me now."

*   *   *

When they had each reached the climax that Tyler had obviously prolonged as long as possible, Penny cried.

"Why are you crying?" he whispered.

She looked into his eyes and spoke very slowly. "I've always felt that sex could be wonderful with the right person. Ever since I met you, I've known instinctively that you are that person, but never in my most intimate dreams did I imagine it could be this beautiful. I know that whatever happens to me in the future, this will always be the most unforgettable night of my life."

"I feel the same way, Penny. I don't ever want it to end." He kissed her and said, "I've got to tell you that as great as it was, I held back some. I was intentionally gentle with you. I'm a very active and passionate lover, but I didn't want to frighten you the first time."

She giggled and snuggled closer. "Me too," she explained.

"Me too, what?" Tyler inquired.

"I held back too, but I won't this time." She pushed him onto his back and was quickly over him. "You haven't cornered the market on passion, you know. Don't ever hold anything back from me, Tyler. I'm not fragile, and I won't break. I may even scratch or bite or scream."

Tyler feigned surprise. "Dear me, Miss Kilmer. What would your English students think?"

She gave him a roguish look. "I would hope that they would think that Miss Kilmer is a great lay. Now," she pointed out as she slowly enclosed herself around his manhood, "all I have to do is prove it."

*   *   *

Tyler kept hearing his name over and over, and he was becoming very annoyed. If he could only find the culprit, he would gladly choke him or her. In an attempt to do just that, he opened his eyes and saw Penny sitting on the edge of the bed at his side.

Actually at the angle he was looking when he opened his eyes, all he saw were two magnificent breasts. "You don't have any clothes on," he noted.

"Neither do you!" She got up and pranced back and forth a couple of times. "Besides, I've been trying to get you to notice me for ten years. I may never wear clothes in your presence again. Oh, that reminds me," she said as she bent over and backed up until her flawless rear end was literally in his face. "See my little beauty mark?"

At that distance, it was hard to miss. He looked at the tiny dark mole just above her buttock. He couldn't resist. "Yes, I see the big, ugly, hairy thing."

She reached back and smacked him on the shoulder. "Stop that now, and be good. You know it's cute, and you love it."

"So," he said.

"Well, kiss it," she ordered.

He did as he was told.

She stood up and said, "A long time ago I showed it to you, and I said someday, if you were a good boy, I might let you kiss it." She leaned over, kissed his cheek, and whispered in his ear. "You were a very, very, very good boy last night, and that was your reward."

"Can I have another reward?" Tyler inquired.

"Maybe," she replied.

"Go away and let me sleep for at least two more hours."

"Sorry! It's my place, and I make the rules here. We have to get up, take a shower together, and eat some eggs. Then, I'm going to give you the chance to be a good boy again."

"Must be my lucky day," he observed as he wondered if he were capable of walking to the shower.

Chapter 31

·|•———————————•ᗒ♡ᗕ•———————————•|·

Tyler Confronts Mr. Grant

"Are you with me on this? Do you understand why I'm doing this?" Tyler had asked Penny.

She had pressed her lips together and nodded, and he appreciated that, knowing it wouldn't be easy for her to go back to that shoe store.

It was just after five o'clock on Friday evening, one week from the night he had found out that Alan Grant had raped Penny. Tyler and Alan were walking up Main Street toward the shoe store that Tyler now owned. They had just left a simple settlement where the deal was consummated at the law offices of a local attorney who handled all the affairs for Tyler's dad.

Last Sunday, before Tyler had left to fly back to Maryland, he had told Penny about his plans to buy the shoe store and get Alan Grant out of town as soon as possible. He asked Penny to wait at her apartment while he went to the settlement, so she wouldn't have to see the son of a bitch again.

When Tyler and Alan reached the store, Penny's older sister, Brenda, was there to meet them. Brenda looked like a slightly smaller, slightly older version of Penny, which she was. She was ten years older and had two small children. She was also slim and blonde.

It turned out that Brenda was the perfect person to manage the new shoe store. She had worked in shoe stores since she was a teenager and had managed one of the other two shoe stores in Stratford for seven years. Tyler had hired her to run his new store at a considerable increase in salary, and she had seemed thrilled.

Together, Brenda, Penny, and Tyler had decided to close the store for three weeks and remodel. There were already large paper signs inside the display windows that announced the grand reopening of Classic Shoes in three short weeks.

"You're right on time," Brenda observed.

As Alan unlocked the door, Tyler said, "The papers were all in order, so all we really had to do was sign our names a few times."

When they were inside, Brenda went off with Alan to familiarize herself with the store she would now be managing. It had already been agreed that Alan and Brenda would meet tomorrow afternoon, so he could remove personal things and any other items not included in the sale. Tyler browsed around until they were finished and then asked Brenda if she would mind waiting a few minutes in the car while he spoke to Alan.

When Alan let Brenda out, he started to relock the front door, but Tyler said, "Just leave it unlocked. We won't be long." Tyler turned and walked to the rear of the store where the desk was. He sat in the same straight metal chair beside the desk that he had occupied last Saturday and indicated that Alan should sit at the desk in his old swivel chair.

Alan hesitated and looked nervous. He moved instead to the filing cabinet. "How 'bout a drink, Mr. Harrison?" he suggested.

Tyler replied, "No, thanks. I have a date later this evening with Penny Kilmer, but you go right ahead."

Alan opened the drawer and lifted out a nearly full bottle of vodka and a paper cup. He quickly poured an ample amount into the cup and drank it like water. Alan then filled the cup a second time before walking over and slowly easing into the old swivel chair.

"You seem nervous this evening," Tyler observed.

Alan looked away. "No, not really. It's just that this business has been in my family for a long time." He glanced quickly at Tyler. "What was it you wanted, Mr. Harrison?"

"I want you to look at me, Alan," Tyler said.

Alan took a large gulp from the cup and turned a little so he was facing Tyler.

Tyler stared coldly into his eyes and said, "I know, Alan."

To his credit or the vodka's, Alan didn't look away, but his eyes looked like they might explode from their sockets. "I don't know what you're talking about."

"Don't make matters worse by lying to me. I've known for a week now. That's why I bought the store. I'm not sure I agree with her, but Penny doesn't want to pursue it. It would be difficult to prove after all these years, and she doesn't want to have to relive it all over again. So, you're getting off lucky. I know your new job is going to be out of town. What I want you to do is sell your house and get out of town quickly. I don't want Penny to ever have to look at you again."

Alan started sweating, and he took another large swig from the cup. It must have bolstered his courage. "I'm not admitting anything, and this isn't Washington, DC, or Maryland. You can't come here and order me around."

"Alan, I can have you done away with anytime and anyplace I choose. Fortunately, I'm not that kind of person, but don't push your luck."

"You're a big feeling son of a bitch, aren't you?" Alan whined. "You think you can just go around and threaten anyone. You don't know every damn thing. What did she tell you?"

Tyler thanked the good Lord for his calmness. "She told me what happened."

"Wrong, Harrison! She told you her version. Want to hear mine?"

"No, Alan. I don't."

Alan laughed and leaned forward with a sneer on his face. "Well, Mr. High-and-Mighty, you can kiss my ass. What would you say if I told you the bitch enjoyed it?"

He got his answer very quickly. Tyler hit him with his fist. Alan's reflex reaction was too slow. Tyler threw a straight punch as hard as he could, and he leaned into it with his full body weight. He aimed it for the veined nose on the front of Alan's face and was fully satisfied when he felt the bone and cartilage collapse.

Two things immediately surprised Tyler. The first was that he had hit Alan hard enough to knock him backward and completely out of the overturned chair. The second was that his hand didn't hurt at all and appeared to have sustained no damage.

Alan had landed on his side and was mumbling incoherently. Tyler stood up and pulled the center desk drawer open. For a moment, he realized that he was out of control and tried to stop himself, but he was incapable of coherent thought. His leg was against the overturned swivel chair. Tyler bent down and picked it up. He swung it around and threw it toward the far wall. When it hit the concrete block wall, the chair snapped from its base and fell into two pieces. Tyler stared at the two separate pieces for a while and then smiled. It had been a pretty damned good throw, and he was proud of it.

He reached into the drawer, took out the green switchblade, and walked toward Alan. When Tyler bent down, he was amazed how much blood was flowing out of Alan's nose. Tyler slapped him a couple of times, reached under his head, and grabbed a fist full of longish hair before yanking him up into a sitting position. The movement helped Alan to come around, and when he opened his eyes, he leaned back in fear and whimpered. He quickly touched his nose, which was resting at an odd angle and beginning to swell. He let out a yelp and removed his hand.

"You broke it! You broke my goddamn nose."

Tyler smiled back like a wild man. "I think you're right." He raised the switchblade very close in front of Alan's face and pushed the button. When the blade snapped into place, Alan began to cry.

"Oh God. I'm sorry. Please don't kill me."

Tyler smiled and stuck the knife against Alan's neck. "How do you think Penny felt when you did this to her?"

"Scared," Alan moaned. "Please don't kill me. I beg you. I ... I didn't mean to do it. I had too much to drink, and I wanted her ... please ... I'm sorry."

"Did she beg you to stop?"

"Yes. Oh God, yes, but I couldn't stop. I wanted to, but she was so beautiful. I'm so sorry. Please believe me. I didn't mean to rape her. Please ... don't kill me."

Tyler smiled and said, "I'm not going to kill you, Alan. Stand up!"

When he was standing, Tyler carefully led him to the sofa and turned him so he faced it. "Don't move, Alan. I don't want to cut your fucking throat, but I will."

Tyler stepped back so he was behind Alan and hooked the knife under Alan's belt and cut it. He smiled when he saw how sharp the knife was.

"Pull your pants down Alan!" Tyler ordered.

Alan was sobbing and shaking, but he didn't reach for his pants. Tyler reached around and grabbed his head and bent it back. "Your pants or your throat!"

"Okay! Okay!" Alan whined.

Tyler released him, and Alan quickly lowered his pants to his ankles. "Now your shorts."

Alan was weeping softly now and trembling with fear, but he slid his undershorts down. "Please don't hurt me! I'll do whatever you say."

"Bend over, put your hands on the sofa, and spread your feet as much as you can."

When Alan hesitated, Tyler kicked him on the ass. "Now, you son of a bitch."

Alan quickly bent at the waist and placed his hands on the sofa cushion. "What … what are you going to do?"

"I'm going to give you a quiz, Alan, and there's good news and bad news. The good news is that the quiz will be very easy. The bad news is that if you answer one of the questions wrong, I'm going to cut your balls off. All you have to do to keep your nuts is tell the truth. Now the first question is—"

"Tyler! Stop this!" Penny screamed from the door.

"I told you to stay at home," Tyler barked.

"I couldn't," she said. "I was afraid you would do something like this."

He turned, looked at Penny, and smiled. "Well, you were right. I'm glad you're here, Penny. Now we'll know if he's telling the truth."

She started to speak, but he put up his hand and gave her a halt sign like a policeman directing traffic. He then brought the hand to his face and placed the index finger on his lips.

"Alan. Did you enjoy raping Penny?" Tyler asked.

Alan began to sob and gasp for his breath. "Yes, I'm so sorry. Please forgive me, but yes."

"I believe you, Alan. That's why you still have your balls."

Penny was crying now, and she moved toward Tyler. When she was next to him, he reached out and put his arm around her shoulder.

"Was she tight, Alan? Was she? Was her pussy tight?" he screamed.

"Yes," Alan sobbed.

"I can't hear you, Alan!"

"Yes! Yes, she was tight!"

"Did you know she was a virgin?"

"Oh dear God. No! Please forgive me, Penny. I didn't know. Please … I'm so sorry."

Penny raised her hand and touched his cheek. "That's enough, Tyler. Please stop this. If you go on, you won't be any better than he is."

Tyler gave her a little squeeze. He turned to Alan and said, "Stand up and pull your pants up."

While Alan pulled his shorts and pants up and slowly turned around, Tyler released the blade on the knife and dropped it into his pocket.

"My God! He's going to bleed to death," Penny shouted.

Tyler reached over on the desk, took a box of Kleenex, and gave it to Alan. "Stick some of these up your nose."

Alan took some and wiped under his nose and carefully began to push one up each side of his nose. When he was finished and the blood flow had diminished, he said, "Please try to forgive me, Penny. I was drunk … and you were so pretty. I never meant to go through with it … but I couldn't stop. Please … I'm sorry." When he finished, he hung his head.

"Alan," Tyler said as he moved close, "look at me."

When Alan raised his head, Tyler continued. "What you did caused Penny and I to be separated for ten long years. I can never forgive you for that, but you have your life and you still have your balls, so things could be worse. Do you have good hospitalization, Alan?"

"Yes, very good," Alan replied.

"Good," Tyler said, and then he punched him again. This one was also on the nose, but only with about three-quarter power. He didn't want to kill him; he just wanted to hurt him.

Alan stumbled backward and fell onto the sofa. He grabbed his nose and howled like a stuck pig.

Tyler leaned down and yelled, "Shut up and listen! Penny and I are leaving town tomorrow. We'll be gone for a week. Don't ever let me see you in Stratford again. If I do, Alan, I'll kill you! I swear to God, I'll kill you!"

Tyler turned and lifted the phone from the desk. The cord was long enough, and he set it beside Alan on the sofa. He lifted the receiver and handed it to Alan. "If I were you, when the emergency squad gets here, I'd tell them I fell."

Chapter 32

Tyler Declares His Love

Everything had to come to an end, including their unbelievable week together. Penny felt like Cinderella watching the clock as it moved ever nearer to midnight. It seemed like only minutes since the episode on Saturday evening with Alan Grant at the shoe store. On Sunday morning, she had flown with Tyler in his plane to Maryland. She wanted to know everything about his life there, so he spent the whole day showing her around in his limo. They started at Nash Builders in Prince George's County where he'd been fired before he'd started. He showed her with pride the houses he had built, the land he had bought and developed, the building where his offices were located, the place where his new headquarters and a complete new city would be built, and ended with his penthouse in Bethesda.

Monday morning was a little different, and Penny would remember it for years. Long before any self-respecting rooster would make a peep, Tyler dragged her kicking and screaming out of her warm bed. After he forced her to dress, Tyler put socks and tennis shoes on her feet, while Penny made threats that she promised she would carry out as soon as she was awake.

Penny was seriously concerned about the sanity of Tyler when he took her to a high school track and expected her to jog with him. She gave it the old college try for a few laps, and then she sat on the bleachers and announced that she was on strike. He finally took her home and let her have juice, an English muffin, and a shower.

When she was dressed in sandals, slacks, and a summer top, they headed for the office. When they entered the outer office, Alice and Tracy were there to meet her. They were very sweet, and Penny remembered how nice they had been to her when she'd come to Washington to surprise Tyler. They introduced her to Liz, while Tyler rushed off to talk with Susan Slater about some important legal matter.

Tyler returned and in forty-five minutes, gave Penny a whirlwind tour of his office, and then took her around both floors and introduced her to everyone who worked for him. Next, she sat in on a two-hour staff meeting and was awed by the number of decisions he made and the amount of work he accomplished.

On the way to his favorite deli in the limo, Penny said, "They love you, you know."

"Who?" Tyler questioned.

"All those people who work for you. I watched them react to you. You know their names and what they're doing, and you're so warm and friendly with them. Even at the staff meeting, you really don't tell people what to do. You ask them."

"I love them too. They're all very good at what they do. It's because of them and the great job they do that I can spend all this time with you."

"In that case, I love them too," she agreed.

When they arrived at the deli, Tyler informed Penny she could only have one-fourth of a sub, because she was going to spend the rest of the afternoon trying on clothes. They started at Saks Fifth Avenue.

On the way home that evening, Tyler pulled out the receipts from the five locations where they had shopped. "According to all these receipts, you're a perfect size six. If you gain weight and can't get your cute butt in all this new stuff, you owe me a little over $16,000."

Penny looked in the mirror and was satisfied Vince couldn't see her. She pulled up her blouse and exposed her bra. "Kiss," she ordered.

Tyler dutifully kissed each point and also kissed the smooth, tan skin just above and between her breasts.

She pushed him away, dropped her blouse, and said, "Consider yourself paid."

"Wow! I knew they were great, but I had no idea they were that great."

She gave him one of those wide-eyed looks that only she could do. "Well, now you do."

*   *   *

On Tuesday, they went to the beach at Ocean City, Maryland. For four days, they had sunbathed, made love, walked on the beach, made love, went boating, made love, shopped, made love, played miniature golf, made love, and talked for hours. They had made a lot of decisions.

Penny wanted to teach at the college level. She was also a small-town girl at heart and really liked Stratford. Tyler was tied to the Washington area for many reasons. He surprised Penny by telling her he wouldn't mind living in Stratford, but it was impossible now. He also wanted her to finish her PhD and told her he liked the idea of being able to sleep with a doctor. In the end, they decided to leave things as they were for a while. He would come to Stratford as often as he could, and she would spend time in Washington on long weekends, holidays, and for part of the summer.

*   *   *

When Penny had toweled off and dried her hair, she came out of the bathroom and crossed the bedroom. Tyler was lying on the bed with the *Washington Post*. When he saw her bouncing across the room naked, he threw the newspaper on the bed and quickly spread out a big beach towel.

This was rapidly becoming one of her favorite daily rituals. For the next twenty minutes or so, Tyler rubbed and massaged every part of her body with some kind of fabulous smelling, extremely expensive lotion with a name neither one of them could pronounce.

When he had finished, he kissed her and said, "I wonder which one of us enjoys that the most."

She pointed to the enlarged lump in the front of his shorts and said, "I think you do."

Before he could catch her, she ran and locked the bathroom door. When he pounded on it, she said, "Stop! We have to dress for dinner."

When she emerged from the bathroom wearing a slinky, strapless, little dress with no bra, Tyler just stared for a while. "I'm sure that's what the designer had in mind when he made this dress. Funny, you don't look like a small-town girl."

"Good, because I'm not in Stratford now," Penny noted.

When they reached the restaurant, they were a little early and the waiting area was full, so they had a seat at the bar. Penny knew she wasn't much of a drinker but decided to have a champagne cocktail. Thankfully, they were called to their table soon, and she took the remainder with her. Tyler ordered seafood for her, steak for him, and a bottle of good white wine, because she was having seafood and she always preferred white. When they had finished their salads, Tyler reached across the table and held her hand.

"Penny, I have some things I want to say."

She put down her fork and gave him all of her attention.

"We lost ten years, and it was mostly my fault. Please forgive me for that. I was young, dumb, and a bit too proud. I would give everything I have to go back and recapture those years, but of course, we can't. I plan to try to love you twice as much in the coming ten years to make up for it. This week has been the happiest of my life. I own many things, but you bring me more joy than all those things combined. I love my folks and Grandma, and I loved Granddad Luke. I dated and cared for Geena. I like the people at work, and some of those who are closest to me, I love. But next to what I feel for you, all these other feelings are minuscule. You consume me. You have become the center of my life."

At that point, Penny had to find a tissue to dab away her tears of joy.

Tyler continued, "I haven't yet said that I love you. It's so easy to say when we're having fun or when we're making love. I wanted to be sure, and now I am. I've never said these words to another woman. Penny, I love you. I know now that I've always loved you, and I'm sure I always will. When

I think about my future with you, I get goose bumps. So if you don't love me, you better get up and run out of here as fast as you can, because I'm going to be real hard to get rid of after tonight."

Penny tried as best she could to smile through her tears but found she wasn't very good at it. She knew she couldn't speak without sobbing, so she finished her salad and champagne cocktail and wiped at her eyes between sniffles.

During the main course, after she had recovered, she said, "I was beginning to wonder if I would ever get to hear those three words. I was afraid you were one of those men who seems incapable of saying I love you. Not only did you say it, but you said it so beautifully."

Tyler smiled. "I'm so thankful to finally have you back. From the day we started dating in high school, you've never been out of my mind. I think you have affected every decision I've ever made."

Penny smiled and said, "Promise me that you won't stop loving me and that you won't stop telling me."

The restaurant they were in was very nice and rather expensive. Like many nicer restaurants, it had a number of smaller rooms with a few people in each rather than one huge room like a dining hall or cafeteria. The room they were seated in was one of the smaller and only held eight tables.

"I promise," he replied and immediately stood up. "Excuse me! Could I have your attention please?"

Everyone, including the waiters, stopped what they were doing to listen.

Penny was startled and dropped her fork.

"Please forgive me for being rude and interrupting your dinner. I won't take long. My name is Tyler Harrison, and this lovely creature is Penny Kilmer."

One woman interrupted loudly. "See, Frank. I told you it was him!"

"I would like for you all to witness this." He turned and looked at Penny. "I love you, Penny Kilmer ... I love you."

Someone said, "Oh, that is so beautiful."

Someone began to applaud, and soon everyone in the room was clapping.

Tyler raised his hands to ask for silence. "So now you know. If anyone ever asks you who Tyler loves, be sure and tell them Penny."

As he was sitting back down, Penny said to the now-captive audience, "That won't really be necessary, everyone, because as soon as I get him out of here, I'm going to kill him."

Everyone laughed, and most stopped by to meet them or offer their best wishes as they left. Tyler was absolutely crazy, but it was Penny he was crazy about, and that was okay with her.

Penny knew she shouldn't drink, but somehow in all the excitement, she had consumed a champagne cocktail and two large glasses of wine. She could usually get a decent buzz from one glass of wine. In another ten minutes, she wouldn't be able to find her ass with both hands. For some reason, the thought seemed funny, and she giggled.

"Tyler, do you have any idea what I'd like to do to you right now?" she asked.

When he shook his head, she indicated with her index finger that he should come closer and listen. He leaned over the table, and she explicitly explained what she wanted to do to him when they returned to the condo.

He grinned. "Really? Do you think you can do all that?"

"You bet your ass I can," Penny said too loudly, and when she realized she had, she followed it with another giggle.

"Waiter!" Tyler called out. "Check!"

*　　*　　*

When Tyler and Penny entered the condo, Penny dropped her purse, kicked off her heels, and ran to the bedroom. She jumped in the middle of the huge bed and stood up. She let her dress fall to her feet, revealing she had been wearing no underwear. She kicked the dress onto the floor and asked, "Are these great boobs, or what?"

"They're the greatest!" Tyler replied.

"Do you love 'em?"

"I love 'em!"

"Would you like to kiss 'em?" she slurred and giggled.

"I would love to kiss 'em."

She did a not too graceful half turn and bent some at the waist, so her rear end protruded more than normal. She looked seductively and said, "Tell me this isn't a fabulous ass!"

"It is one of the great asses of all time," Tyler agreed. "It should be photographed and mounted on a wall."

Penny laughed and then surprised herself with a very unladylike burp, followed by more laughter. "I agree." She kicked her feet out and landed on her back. "Well, hurry up and get naked, Tyler. I have a special treat for you."

"I can hardly wait." Tyler laughed.

When he started undressing, Penny suddenly became very aware that the room was spinning before everything went black.

Chapter 33

❦

Giving

As Penny sat and surveyed the mess in the living room, she knew she was the happiest woman east of the Mississippi. She was seated with Tyler in Harold and Kate Harrison's living room, and the mess was enough wrapping paper to fill the local garbage truck.

Except for her sister Brenda and her mother, Penny was not very close to the rest of her family. It was good to be here with these people, all in their pajamas. She felt loved and accepted as a member of the family.

Penny and Tyler had loved Christmas shopping for everyone. Penny was learning it was fun to shop when you could afford the whole damn store. They had split up and shopped for each other too.

Penny had bought Tyler lots of clothes and a watch. She had admired the watch he wore a few weeks before, and he had casually mentioned that it had been a gift from Geena Morgan. She decided it had to go.

When he unwrapped the new one and put it on, he held the old one in his hand and asked, "What am I going to do with this one?"

Penny took it and pitched it over to Tyler's dad. "Merry Christmas, Harold. Enjoy!"

Everyone laughed.

When all the packages were unwrapped, everyone relaxed with eggnog or a cup of coffee. Tyler came in offering refills on coffee and said, "I noticed a very large package that hasn't been opened behind the chair in the corner."

Kate asked, "Really? Who's it for?"

Tyler looked at the little tag and said, "To Penny Kilmer. From Santa."

Penny said, "Well, I must have been a good girl. Bring it over here, and I'll open it."

"Oh, no," Tyler said. "You have to come and get it."

Penny made her way through the spent wrapping paper to the large box. When she bent to pick it up, she found it was very heavy. She awkwardly carried it back and sat it in front of her chair. When she had removed the paper and opened the top, she found another box. When she opened that one, she found another box. When she opened that one, she found another shoe-sized box and about six bricks.

She took one brick out and held it up for everyone to see. "Now I know why it was so heavy. It seems that Santa is being very mysterious. Would you know anything about this, Tyler?"

"No way! My name's not Santa."

Penny took out the shoe-sized box and began to unwrap. Again, she found a wrapped box, within a wrapped box, within a wrapped box. Finally, as she was opening a very small box, which she was sure was the last box, she knew what it was. A ring! He was going to make if official. It would be just like him to do this with his family present. She lifted the top of the last box and found it full of white tissue paper. When she removed and separated the tissue paper, she found a key. She even looked under it for a ring. No ring, just a key.

"It's a key," she said, holding it up so everyone could see.

"A key!" Tyler said.

"I wonder what it fits," Kate said.

Harold laughed. "You know, I was the last one to go to bed last night, and I bumped into Santa. I remember he did mention leaving something out front."

Everyone followed as Penny moved over to the front window. She parted the blind and looked. "Oh my God! It's a Corvette! It's a red Corvette with a big red and white bow on it." She jumped up and down, screeched, and hugged Tyler. "Can I drive it?"

"I don't see why not," Tyler replied. "It has a full tank of gas, and it's yours."

"Is it a stick or an automatic?" Penny asked.

"It's a stick," Tyler replied.

Penny ran to the closet to get her coat and gloves. She remembered her first car. It was on old, used Plymouth two-door that looked like it had been through the war and lost. Still, she had liked everything about it because it was her first, except it was always so damn hard to steer.

"Tyler, it does have power steering, doesn't it?"

"It does have power steering," he replied.

She felt a little guilty. "You already got me so much. You shouldn't have. Why did you do this?"

"Because I'm head over heels crazy in love with you."

Penny looked at Kate who was wearing a full smile. "You know, Kate, I had to wait for ten years for him to come to his senses, but I think it was worth it."

Everyone laughed at Tyler and then piled out the door to go for a ride in Penny's new Vette. The fact that it was cold and they were all still wearing their jammies didn't seem important.

*   *   *

1970

Vanguard. Tyler liked the sound of it, and Penny loved it, because she had originally thought of it. According to Webster's, it meant the leaders of thought, taste, and opinion. If Tyler could pull it off—and everyone believed he could—Vanguard, Maryland, would be the cutting edge of new city development in America.

He had been planning this city for years in his mind and for at least four years on paper. It would be located near Interstate 270 between Washington, DC, and Frederick, Maryland. The site was huge and mostly wooded, and would be the home to about 150,000 people within twenty years. Most of the people who lived in Vanguard would also work there.

Those who had seen the plans said it was the answer for planned development and would be a model for years to come. Vanguard would have its own ZIP code, as well as a town square, office buildings, and retail areas, not to mention a mall, homes, condos, apartments, schools, a hospital, a local bus system, two golf courses, three lakes, tennis courts, ball fields, soccer fields, a concert center, a playhouse theater, biking trails, walking and jogging paths, and two parks. It would also house the soon-to-open headquarters of Harrison Ltd., Harrison Properties, and the Harrison Foundation.

As Vince steered the green and white Harrison limo toward the National Institute of Health in Bethesda, Maryland, Tyler and Penny finally had time to talk. Tyler had scheduled the Vanguard grand opening, complete with ribbon cutting and ceremonial shovels, during Penny's spring break so she could attend. The ceremony was finished now, and she was becoming a full-fledged celebrity. She must have been photographed a thousand times during the day. The media was clamoring for more information about her and she found it both exciting and disconcerting. These days, Tyler rarely granted an interview, which only seemed to heighten his mystique. He wasn't a recluse; he just valued his private life and his family and friends. Tyler used the press when it benefited him or his cause and ignored them the rest of the time. This frustrated them, as well as most of the people around the country. They couldn't seem to understand why a soon-to-be twenty-nine-year-old with a few hundred million dollars just wanted to be a regular guy.

Also, everyone was enamored with Tyler and Penny's story. They were in love and back together after ten years, and they had been high school sweethearts. It was a classic rich handsome prince and beautiful princess love story, and America wanted to know more.

"Tell me again. Where is it we're going?" Penny queried.

"To see Abe Cohen. You know, I told you about him. He was diagnosed with cancer last week, and he's being treated at the National Institute of Health. It's a huge research center in Bethesda near where I live. I want to see him, and I want him to meet you. He and I have become very good friends."

"Here we are, Mr. H," Vince announced from the front seat. He was out quickly to open the door for Penny.

Once inside, Tyler and Penny were quickly ushered to Abe's room. Tyler expected to see a sickly old man in a hospital bed. What he saw was a handsome man of sixty-seven years sitting in a leather chair, wearing silk pajamas, reading the *Washington Post*, and looking rather feisty.

"Abe?" Tyler ventured.

Abe threw the paper on the floor and was up immediately. As he and Tyler hugged warmly, Abe said, "Damn, you move fast. I just saw you on the noon news about an hour ago."

"Really? What did they say?" Tyler questioned.

Abe gave one of his hearty laughs that always seemed like it should come from a larger body. "Oh, you know how the media is. They always get everything wrong." He glanced at Penny and gave her a devilish wink. "They said something stupid about what a great place Vanguard would be and how you were God's gift to the Washington, DC, area."

Tyler laughed and said, "Well, it all sounds right to me."

Abe ignored him and moved in front of Penny. She was wearing a tight spring dress with matching heels.

"You have to be Penny," Abe observed. "He has babbled about you and showed me about a hundred pictures. I'm glad to see the rest of you is as cute as your butt."

She grinned and hit Tyler on the arm. "Have you seen those pictures, Mr. Cohen?" she asked.

"We're all friends here, so you call me Abe. Yes, I've seen them. Hell, everyone in Washington has seen them. You should be glad they're only in his office. Tyler usually does things in a big way. I'm surprised he didn't put them on billboards all across America."

"Oh my God," she laughed. "Don't give him any ideas."

It was obvious to Tyler that they were going to get along just fine. He decided to be still and let them get to know each other—not that he could have gotten a word in edgewise anyway.

There were four leather chairs in the room, and they all got comfortable. After a while, Abe told them about his cancer. Tyler was relieved to hear that it was only two small tumors on one lung and was operable. They would soon remove that section of lung and would follow up with radiation and chemotherapy. Abe was lucky that he had regular checkups and his doctor had insisted on a chest X-ray.

*   *   *

Tyler decided he wanted a larger and faster plane, but if he bought one, he couldn't take off or land it on Stratford's little paved strip. So, in typical Harrison fashion, he bought the airport, hired the previous owner to run it, built a new wider and much longer runway, and installed runway lights for night landings.

It was this new runway Penny was walking along now. She had arrived early and decided to have a look at the new runway. She hadn't seen Tyler for two weeks. He had called last night from some little town in Maine and promised to arrive there today around five. Tyler had been on a whirlwind tour to take a look at and meet some of those who had applied for grants from the Harrison Foundation. It was Friday evening, and he would stay until Monday morning when Penny went off to school.

Penny had planned a little weekend trip, and she smiled when she thought about the two days they would have together. Her smile widened even more when she thought about the three nights they would be together.

She could feel a shiver pass through her body. Penny wondered if she was becoming a sex addict or had always been oversexed and just didn't know it. She could not conceive of ever getting tired of making love or of getting bored with Tyler as her lover.

She heard the plane before she saw it. When it landed, it had two propellers and no Harrison name or logo. She thought maybe it wasn't him, but she saw him waving when he taxied near the hanger.

When the door opened, he hit the asphalt running. She found that she was soon in the air going around and around and receiving lots of hugs and kisses as Tyler repeatedly told her how much he had missed her. When he finally put her down and went back to get his travel bag, she noticed his lawyer, Susan Slater.

"Susan, how are you?" Penny asked.

"Fine, Penny. It's nice to see you."

The ride into town was crowded, but they managed. During the short ride, Tyler caught her up to speed on what was happening. The plane was only leased, and he would use it until the new one was delivered. Charles Kane, his flight instructor, part-time pilot, and close friend would wait and fly Susan back home that evening. He would then return early Monday so Tyler could fly back to Maryland.

Tyler instructed Penny to go to the shoe store he now owned. Penny found a parking place near the store on Main Street. She was convinced her fear of parallel parking was gone when she stuck her Vette within three inches of the curb on the first try.

The store was open until nine o'clock on Friday evenings. When they went in, Tyler was glad to see the place was busy with customers. Brenda soon finished checking someone out at the cash register, and Tyler asked if he could see her in the back. The whole store had a fresh, new look.

After introducing Brenda and Susan, Tyler asked, "Brenda, do you have a dollar?"

She looked confused. "Not on me. Want me to get one out of the register?"

"No," Tyler replied. "It needs to be your own money."

Still confused, Brenda nodded her head and went to one of the new filing cabinets where she kept her purse. She returned and handed a one-dollar bill to Tyler. "There you go, Tyler," she said.

Tyler took the dollar, put it in his pocket, and handed her a little sheet of paper. "This is a receipt for the dollar you just gave me."

Brenda looked at Penny as if to say, "What the hell is going on?"

Penny stared back, shrugged her shoulders, and gave her an I-don't-know look. Brenda took the receipt and hoped an explanation would follow.

"Congratulations, Brenda. When you sign the rest of the papers that Susan has here, you'll be the proud new owner of Classic Shoes."

Now, Brenda was even more confused. "What … what did you say? I can't buy this store."

Tyler laughed. "You just did, and I'd say you got it for a pretty damn good price."

Some of Brenda's color had faded, and she looked somewhat unsteady. After a pause, she asked, "Why on earth would you do this?"

Tyler leaned forward and placed a hand on each shoulder. "Brenda, believe me I can always use a tax write-off. Penny made an excellent suggestion a few weeks ago. I spend a lot of time running around giving away money through the foundation. She said I should help Stratford some, because the economy around here is slow. I thought about what she said, and I agreed. I decided to start with you. I love your baby sister, and you're one of my favorite people, so don't thank me. It's something I wanted to do."

Brenda gave him a huge hug. "All right, Tyler, it's your money, but if you ever need a good price on shoes, come see me."

"Okay, it's a deal. And, Brenda. I want to give you some good advice. The store, everything in it, and all the money in the business bank account is yours now. You can do anything with it you want, but if I were you, I would keep it. I know a secret about the economy around here, and it's going to increase dramatically very soon. I think this store may well double its sales next year."

Penny asked, "What's going to happen, Tyler?"

"It's a secret," he said with a snicker, "but be sure to read Monday's local paper."

After the papers were signed, Penny dropped Tyler off, so he could visit with his folks while she drove Susan back to the little airport.

—◦❤◦—

Chapter 34

Plumbing Problems

I t was just getting dark as Penny turned off the powerful engine. That was another reason she loved this man. Most men would insist on driving and being in charge, but Tyler never did that when he was with her. He always just seemed happy to be along, and whatever she wanted was fine with him.

This little weekend trip had been her idea. She had rented a cabin at one of the state parks a couple of hours from Stratford. She was looking forward to a whole weekend with nothing to do at a cabin in the mountains with her man and no telephone.

When they were inside, he reached for her and held her. "I didn't know two weeks could be so long," he said. "Damn, I missed you."

As he began to kiss her, it was evident that he wanted her now. She pushed him away. "Oh, no you don't! I need a shower."

Two minutes later, she heard a knock on the bathroom door. "Do you need some help in there?" Tyler asked.

"I'm doing fine, thank you. Besides, I know from past experience that you can't be trusted. You start out washing the merchandise, and then you want it."

"But I like the merchandise," he pointed out. "It's very nice."

"You're right, and it's well worth waiting for."

At last, she pulled the curtain aside, stepped out onto the bath mat, and opened the door for him. She found him naked.

"I left the water on for you. In you go," she directed.

"But you have wet parts that need to be dried, and I want to help, especially with these," he said as he started to dry her breasts.

She pushed him into the shower and said, "You're incorrigible."

From the shower, he said, "And you're cruel."

"I am not!"

"Yes, you are," he said laughingly.

"Well, maybe a little," she said as she reached in and turned off the hot water.

He let out a rather loud shout and said a couple of very, very bad words. After that, he was quiet for the rest of his shower.

When he finished, she was ready with a towel to help him. Her towel was now a wrapped turban around her hair.

He looked at her and said, "I thought you were supposed to wrap the towel around your body instead of your hair."

She put her arms up to loosen the towel. "I can change it if you want."

He pushed her arms down quickly. "No, no, that's fine. I need to check and make sure you got these good and dry. I wouldn't want you to get a chill." He bent down and began looking very closely at her breasts.

She waited, she thought patiently, for quite a while. "Well, what do you see?" she finally asked.

"Boobies."

She put her hands on her hips. "I know that!"

"I see something else," he chuckled.

"What?"

"I think the little dark tips are growing."

She could feel his breath on her chest. "They'll grow much faster if you kiss them."

"Really?" he said with feigned surprise. "Are you sure?"

"Just shut up and kiss them! Two weeks was a long time. I want you now, Tyler!"

Tyler was standing, and she was trying to climb and pull herself higher. With his help, she was soon pleasantly impaled.

She wrapped her long legs around Tyler and found that she liked it very much. He placed his hands under her upper thighs for support. For having never done it this way before, she thought she was quite good at it. She was matching the rhythm of his movement perfectly and could already feel herself building toward a climax.

Oh, yes, she decided. *This is heavenly.*

After she climaxed, Tyler took one of the remaining towels from the bar with one hand and spread over the cold front edge of the sink. Penny sensed his movement, and with her arms around his neck, she made an effort to support more of her own weight. With the towel in place and using both arms again, he turned and eased her down until most of her weight was supported by the sink.

Tyler let go of her thighs, and the sink pulled loose about two inches from the wall, breaking the hot water pipe, which leaked in a forceful spray. He yelled and grabbed two towels together and held them in the spray to divert it, then he grabbed the valve and turned it. The spray stopped instantly.

He stood, turned to look at Penny, and when their eyes met, they both started to giggle like a couple of teenagers who had pulled off a prank without getting caught.

"No dinner for you later," Tyler explained.

"Why not?" she asked.

"Because your butt must be getting bigger," he laughed. "It ripped the sink right out of the wall."

She grinned and then hit him, but not too hard. He wrapped his arms around her so she wasn't a threat.

"God, I love a feisty woman," he said with a smirk. He then swept her up, carried her to the bed, and did a truly fabulous job of finishing what they had started.

Almost every time she and Tyler made love, Penny felt a little sorry for most other women. She knew that few would ever reach her satisfaction level. Most were unaware that it even existed, and sadly, some only viewed sex as an obligatory drudgery to keep their mates. Again, she thanked her lucky stars that Tyler was a skilled and considerate lover.

After a while, Tyler said, "It's getting late, and we'll want to use that sink in the morning. I'll use the towels to soak up the water on the floor, while you go down to the front desk and tell them we need a plumber."

They had been snuggling, and she was very comfy. "I have an idea," she said.

"What's that?"

"You do them both, and I'll lie here and keep the bed warm."

He spun her around like a feather, and before she knew it, she was lying on top of him. He raised his head and lightly kissed and teased each nipple. At just about the point when she was deciding she didn't want him to stop, he quit and lowered his head.

"I will never kiss these buds again if you don't go," he announced.

"I'll go! I'll go! I'll go! But you should know that I intend to call you nasty names all the way."

Tyler leaped off the bed and threw her a pair of jeans. "Fine," he said.

It was dark but not cold, so she walked. It was only about a quarter of a mile to the big lodge where Tyler had checked in earlier. When she reached the front desk, she was met by a woman with a puckered face who looked like she spent her spare time sucking lemons.

"Yes?" the sour-looking lady ventured.

"Hi," Penny said. "Could we get a plumber to fix our bathroom sink? We're in one of the cabins."

"What's wrong with it?"

Penny wondered if this woman's face would crack if she smiled. "It pulled loose from the wall, and it's leaking."

"And how exactly did this happen?" she asked.

Penny was sorely tempted to say, "Oh, well, you see, I had my legs wrapped around Tyler Harrison while he was standing up screwing me, but he got tired and rested my cute little ass on the sink, and the damn thing ripped out of the wall. Can you imagine that!"

Instead, she lied and said, "Tyler was leaning on it while he was shaving, and it pulled out of the wall."

The lemon sucker didn't smile, but she did perk up. "You said *Tyler*. Is this Tyler Harrison's cabin?"

"Well, yes. It's our cabin. I'm staying with him."

"I didn't know it was his cabin. We'll get the emergency plumber out there right away."

Feeling like the great Tyler Harrison's concubine, Penny said, "Thank you. I'm sure he'll appreciate it."

On the return walk, she realized that he knew they would ask how and what had happened and had sent her to dream up the answers. He was probably sitting in the cabin right now laughing. He would pay for that.

Chapter 35

Granddad's Truck

It was Monday morning, and Penny felt like she had popped a few uppers. It was the usual euphoria she felt during and just after being with her man. But she was at school now and needed to tone it down a notch or two. Most people who were going through a regular Monday morning work routine were suspicious of or just plain didn't like anyone who was too effervescent.

Someone handed her the local paper, and she remembered that Tyler had said to be sure and check Monday's paper. The entire front page was covered with a huge headline and story. The headline read: "Harrison to Locate Factory Here."

The article said that the writer had been treated to a personal phone interview with Tyler Harrison. It went on to say that he had hired some new people who would help him build a huge factory near Stratford and start a completely new company. The factory would manufacture a new line of tennis shoes and sneakers. Tyler said the original idea had come from his sweetheart, Penny Kilmer. She had told him that he should use some of his money to help the economy in his hometown. Tyler went on to say that people who wanted a job should be able to find one without having to leave Stratford. The tennis shoe market was almost unlimited and should provide excellent employment for those in and around Stratford for decades to come.

*   *   *

Penny was about to enjoy a bowl of fresh popcorn when the phone rang. She started toward the phone but backed up so she could take the popcorn with her.

"Hello?"

"Hi, babe. What are you doing?" Tyler asked.

"Getting ready to eat some popcorn."

"Oh my God, I'm sorry. I didn't know. Want me to call back later?" he asked laughingly.

"No, smart-ass," she quipped. "I'll have you know that I'm being awarded a PhD in English this Saturday, and I'm very bright, so I have no trouble doing two things at once, like eating popcorn and talking."

"I think I love you more when you're angry."

"I'm not angry. If I were, you would be talking to a dial tone."

"Okay, good point," he admitted. "You will never believe who called me just now."

"Who?" she asked through a mouthful of popcorn.

"The president!"

"What's wrong at Winfield College now?"

"No." He laughed. "Not President Fairchild. President Nixon."

"Really?! You mean him, not an aide or a secretary?"

"Yeah. I thought he was someone jerking my chain for a minute or so when he introduced himself as Dick Nixon. He asked about Vanguard, Maryland, and the Harrison Foundation, and he seemed to know quite a bit about both. He told me about an independent economic council he is forming to advise him and Congress on economic affairs. Then he asked me to serve as one of its members."

"Oh, Tyler, sweetheart. That's great. I'm so proud of you. You did say yes, didn't you?"

"Yes, I did, but there's a problem."

"A problem? What did you do? Tell him what you usually say about the government."

"What?" he demanded.

"That people who work for the government couldn't find their asses with both hands, and let's see … oh yeah, and the government doesn't know its ass from a hole in the ground."

Tyler chuckled. "Well, it's true! That's why I'm going to go help them out."

"You said there was a problem?" Penny asked.

"Yeah, our first meeting is this Saturday at the White House. It lasts most of the day, and President Nixon will be there and have lunch with us. So if I go, I can't come to see you get your doctorate."

"Hey, I'm a big girl. You go to your meeting, and I'll have Brenda take lots of pictures."

"I'll fly in as soon as the meeting is over on Saturday night," Tyler promised. "At least we can spend the rest of the weekend together. I'll call to let you know what time I'm arriving."

"All right. Have a nice meeting, and don't be too outspoken."

*   *   *

Penny glanced at Brenda, her mother, and the few other friends who had come to see her walk across the stage to receive her doctorate degree. She smiled and gave a little wave. This one was special, and she was going to enjoy it. It said she was more than just Tyler Harrison's woman—she was Dr. Penny Kilmer.

The line moved forward, and then it was her turn. She stood and basked in the limelight while her name and her degree were announced. Suddenly, she felt two new emotions, and she had promised herself earlier that she would not do this. She was going to cry, and she missed Tyler. She made her way to the table, received her degree, turned and raised it for her family and friends to see, and headed for the down ramp. When she reached the bottom of the ramp, a photographer stepped almost right in front of her and snapped three or four pictures, which completely blinded her. Some photographer had noticed her name on the program or recognized her earlier and had been bugging her ever since. She knew it was him, and she was tempted to give him a piece of her mind.

She pushed past him, and after a couple of steps when she could focus again, she turned and saw that the photographer was Tyler.

"What are you doing here?" she asked, surprised to see him.

He pulled her out of the aisle so others could pass. "When I woke up this morning, I was miserable and felt guilty. I called the White House and left a message, and here I am—right where I should be."

"Do you have any idea how much I love you?" she asked.

Tyler held her and said, "Yeah, about half as much as I love you. Now go sit down before we disrupt this place anymore, and take this with you." He handed her a small package and left to return to his seat.

She quickly returned to her place among the other graduates.

When she had removed the paper and opened the jewelry box, she found a beautiful cameo on a chain with an exquisite raised profile. It was very feminine, and she loved it. As she looked closely at it, she noticed something familiar about it. Then she saw it! The raised profile on the front was her. It had been custom-made, and the lady on the front was definitely her. *Damn it!* She was going to cry, and she was sure everyone in the whole place knew who she was now, and they were all watching her. Through her tears, she saw the tiny button on the right side and realized the cameo opened. When she depressed it slightly, the front swung open on its little hidden hinges. On the inside of the back, etched into the gold, in a delicate script were five words that read, "Want to play doctor, Doctor?"

It was so like him, and so unexpected, that a very loud, unladylike belly laugh erupted, and she was sure that everyone was looking at her. She put on her new cameo and didn't hear a word of the remainder of the ceremony.

On the outside, in the warm sunlight, there was much picture-taking and gaiety. Everyone wanted to give her a hug and congratulate her. When the reception ended and the festivities were winding down, Penny decided to ride back with Tyler. On the way through the parking lot, Penny asked, "Did you rent a car?"

"No."

"So you came in the limo?"

Tyler stopped and pointed. "No. I came in this."

Penny looked and saw an old red pickup truck. But it didn't look old. The style was old, but the truck looked like it had just come off the showroom floor. Then she remembered reading part of the will the day of Granddad Luke's funeral.

"It's your granddad's old truck, isn't it?"

"Yeah," he beamed. "I had it restored."

While he showed her around it, she watched how proud and excited he was. She was certain he loved this old truck almost as much as he loved her, and she was glad. It was one of the many things that made him special. Under that tough exterior lurked a very soft and sentimental core that gave him meaning and substance.

"Oh, sweetheart, it's beautiful," Penny exclaimed. "I wish your granddad could see it."

Tyler grinned and looked up. "I like to think he can."

She smiled and said, "Yeah, maybe you're right."

He held the door for her, and when she was seated on the passenger side, he leaned in and kissed her. "Granddad wanted me to have this old truck restored so I would always remember him, but he also wanted me to use and enjoy it. He said to go for a ride with someone special and enjoy it the way he and I did. I can't wait to take Grandma and Mom and Dad for a ride. They will love it. But … I wanted you to be the first."

* * *

"Tyler Harrison, is that what I think it is?" shouted Grandma Ruth from the front porch.

"I don't know, Grandma," Tyler answered. "What do you think it is?"

"Well, from here, it looks like your granddad's truck on the day he bought it."

"I tried, Grandma. It's been fully restored with all original parts. I'm sorry it took so long."

"Nothing to be sorry about, Tyler," Grandma said. "I know you stay pretty busy. Now, give me the keys, and let's go."

Tyler gave her a rather surprised look and threw her the keys, which she caught. Ruth walked slowly around the pickup, as if she were the final inspector at the end of the assembly line. At last, she said, "It's perfect, Tyler. I love it. Now, promise me you'll drive it often."

"I promise, Grandma."

Ruth gave him a special grandma hug and said, "Come on, Penny. I need to show my grandson the proper way to drive an antique Ford pickup."

"Thanks, Grandma Ruth, but Tyler has been looking forward to this for months. I'll wait in one of these comfy rocking chairs on your front porch. Your first ride needs to be just you and Tyler."

"Thank you, Penny," Ruth said. "That's very sweet. We won't be long." She turned to Tyler and proclaimed, "You'd better latch onto her while she's still available. She just may be too good for you, boy."

"Oh, you think so?" Tyler ventured. "You know, Grandma, that's not the first time I've been told that."

◆•━━◦❤◦━━•◆

Chapter 36

Grandma's Ring

*P*enny pushed back from the table and began to gather up the dishes, and Grandma helped. When they finished the dishes, Grandma said, "Tyler, I have something for you." She went to her room, returned, and took her seat at the table. Then she placed a beautiful, ornate silver jewelry box on the table. "Before I give you this, you have to hear the story behind it.

"Your grandpa Luke was a little crazy sometimes, but that's one of the things I loved about him. You remember about twenty years ago when he had the two gas wells drilled on the farm?"

"I sure do," Tyler answered. "Grand and I used to ride down there and watch while they were drilling. I still remember the chugging sound the drill made."

Grandma laughed. "Yes, and the whole farm smelled like gas until they were finished and got both wells capped. Well, it turned out they were really good wells, and they're still producing today. We ended up making more than twice as much money as we had hoped. Your grandpa was tickled pink, and I guess all that money was burning a hole in his pocket. He came in here one Friday evening and told me he was taking me out to dinner, and I should go in there and get all gussied up.

"Never being one to turn down a dinner invitation, especially one I didn't have to cook, I was ready in ten minutes. Well, he took me way over to Clarksburg. We ate at a really fancy new Italian restaurant. It had red linen napkins and tablecloths, and they served wine. I remember, because we ordered a bottle, and we drank the whole thing. Then we had a nice dessert with coffee, and that's when he did it. He pulled this tissue out of his pocket and placed it in my hand. Then proceeded to tell me for a good five minutes how much he loved me."

Penny asked, "What was in the tissue, Grandma?"

Ruth opened the silver box and pulled out a stunningly delicate gold wedding band with diamonds placed all the way around. "There are almost three carats of perfect, clear-cut diamonds set all around it."

"Oh, Grandma, it's gorgeous," Penny gushed. "It's so unique. I've never seen a ring like it."

Grandma handed it to Penny and said, "It's beautiful, isn't it?"

Penny carefully handed the ring to Tyler, who handled it like it was the Holy Grail. He said, "Grandma, Penny's right. This is the prettiest ring I've ever seen."

"I'm glad you like it, Tyler, because from now on, it's yours."

"No, Grandma. I couldn't take this."

"Don't you tell your grandma no, Tyler Harrison. You listen to me. Your grandpa and I decided long ago that we wanted it to go to you. Besides, I have arthritis in my fingers, and I can't wear it. And no, I don't want you to get it when I'm gone. I want you to have it now. You do what you want with it. Let it be a keepsake, or give it to your wife someday, if you ever find some woman who will have you."

Tyler chuckled. "Well, it sure will be easier to find one with a ring like this. Thank you, Grandma. I can never tell you how much this means to me."

"Oh, I don't know. I think I have a pretty good idea," she said with a gleam in her eye.

Ruth took the ring back from Tyler and stared at it lovingly. "Penny, you have beautiful, feminine hands and nails, just like I did when I was younger. Here, try it on."

"No, no, I couldn't, Grandma," Penny replied, pulling her hands back.
"Oh hush, girl. Just put it on."

Penny smiled and carefully slipped it on her ring finger and just looked
at it for a while. She finally said, "Grandma, it's a perfect fit."

"I thought it might be," Ruth said. "What do you think, Tyler?"

"Well," Tyler said, although he looked like he had lost some color. "Yes,
it … ah … looks good, I guess."

When Tyler looked away, Grandma winked at Penny, and Penny just
grinned.

Chapter 37

Surprises

It was three weeks before Christmas, and Penny hadn't seen Tyler for two weeks. He was planning to come in this weekend but had just called and said he couldn't make it. He seldom got angry, but he seemed pissed on the phone. He said there had been some huge screw up by some contractor at the Vanguard project, and he would have to stay and iron it out.

When Penny hung up the phone, she thought for a minute and quickly made her decision. It was a few minutes after four o'clock on Thursday afternoon. Within fifteen minutes, she had called the vice principal, gotten a substitute teacher for Friday, called the commuter airline out of Clarksburg, booked a seat on the six o'clock flight, and headed for the airport.

She would surprise him. She would not bug him or get in his way, because he was busy, but she would be there. Maybe she could do some Christmas shopping. Penny was itching to put her thirtieth birthday present to good use. When she had opened the present from Tyler, it was a new Visa credit card in her name. She had never had a credit card before and asked how it worked. After Tyler explained, she asked, "What's the spending limit?"

"There is none," he informed her.

"What do you mean, there is none?"

"Your card has no spending limit. You can spend all you want, and they send me the bill once a month. It's a special card. Very few people in the world have one."

She wanted to make sure she understood. "You mean I could go spend $50,000 this month?"

"Yes," he said with a smile. "You could spend a million."

She looked down at the card with added respect. "My God! Are you sure you trust me with this?"

"Don't be silly, babe. I would trust you with anything. You're almost living with one of the wealthiest men in America. You should look and act like it. If you see something you want, buy it."

So she was flying to DC to surprise her man. Simple enough—just put it on the card. She often felt a little funny and sometimes a little guilty for having access to so much money, but it sure did make life simple.

*   *   *

The cab stopped, and she realized she had arrived. She told the driver to go around to the back of Tyler's building. She read the meter and gave him a sizeable tip. Penny saw the guard working the garage approaching her.

"Good evening, Miss Kilmer," he said.

She felt bad, because she didn't remember his name, but he was a very nice young man who was always pleasant. "How are you?" she asked with a smile.

"Fine, thank you."

"Do you know if Tyler is at home?" Penny asked.

"Yes, ma'am. He came in about an hour ago. Would you like for me to call him?"

"No, no, I just flew in, and I want to surprise him."

When she stepped off the elevator, she hoped it wouldn't make any noise. She was relieved when the doors closed noiselessly, and it began its trip back to the ground floor. She placed her overnight bag on the thick plush carpet, so she could use both hands to unlock and open the door. She did it as quietly as possible and set her bag inside on the foyer's marble floor. She stood and listened, but the only sound was the pendulum on the huge grandfather clock.

She tiptoed across the foyer and down the hall. She could see a soft light coming out of the den. She eased one eye around the door frame and peered in. She saw Tyler sitting on the big sofa looking across the room, and there was a woman, lying with her head on a pillow on his lap. He was softly stroking her hair.

While she stood there and waited for her heart to start again, she knew she would view this every day for the rest of her life. The woman was only wearing a bra and panties, but Penny couldn't see her face. It was difficult to make out any details. The only light was a small lamp on Tyler's desk, but that was across the large room, and they were facing the other way.

Penny knew she was going to be sick, and she had to get out. There was nothing to be gained by confronting them. As she started to leave, the woman murmured something and sat up. She then turned toward Tyler, and the light poured over the features of her face. Penny was too numb to be shocked anymore. It was Geena Morgan. Geena nestled against Tyler and leaned her head on his shoulder.

Penny watched and listened as Tyler put his arm around Geena and said, "I'll always be here for you, Geena."

Somehow Penny made her way to the front door and got out without slamming it. She ran the few steps to the fire door, which opened to the stairwell and threw up on the landing. She found a tissue in her shoulder purse and wiped at her mouth and nose. She had to get out … to get away from here.

*   *   *

Tyler had always loved Christmas until now. Holidays without Penny were no fun. His mom and dad had invited Grandma Ruth up for the day. They all knew Tyler was hurting and were very careful not to mention Penny. At the end of day, Tyler drove Grandma home.

"Tyler, I'm sorry. I really like Penny, and I'd like to know what's going on."

"I'm not sure, Grandma," he replied. He, of course, knew what was happening, but it was a little difficult to explain. "I did a dumb thing, and now she won't speak to me."

Grandma asked. "Well, you still love her, don't you?"

"Yes, very much."

"Well, get your hind parts over there and fix it."

Tyler smiled. "I'm working on it, Grandma."

*   *   *

1971

Vince turned into the lane that led up a small rise through the trees to the new headquarters. Tyler thought it was impressive. The architecture was colonial with lots of dormer windows set in the steep roofs, white columns, large windows, shutters on doors and windows, and multicolored used brick. There were a number of buildings placed strategically among the huge old trees. None were taller than three stories. There were office buildings; a large cafeteria; a credit union for employees; a huge recreation building with a gymnasium, pool, indoor tennis courts, running track, racquetball courts, exercise machines, a ton of weights, and locker rooms with showers; three parking garages; and maintenance and storage buildings. All were connected underground with bright, wide tunnels. Of course, one could use the walks outside if the weather was pleasant.

The whole place was beautiful and functional in an understated way. It didn't look like a business or workplace, but that had been one of the goals. If someone had strung some Spanish moss through the trees, the new headquarters would look like a beautiful old college campus that might have been plucked from Charleston, South Carolina, or Savannah, Georgia.

Vince stopped under the large, columned portico.

"You straight on what to do?" Tyler asked him.

"Yeah, Mr. H. You want me to go back to your place and pick up Geena Morgan and take her wherever she wants to go. Right?"

"That's right, Vince, but she is not to leave your sight. You go up and get her in the penthouse and ride the elevator down with her. Wherever she goes, you go with her. Understand?"

"Okay, Mr. H. I'll stick with her like glue."

Tyler made a quick trip through the main lobby and reception area, up a rather grand marble staircase, through another private reception area, which included Robin's desk, past Liz's office, and into his private sanctum. It couldn't be called an office. It was more like a suite or an apartment—a home away from home.

It was more than twice the size of his old office, which had been huge. He had let the architect and the decorator talk him into it. Now that he had used it a couple of days, he liked it. The dominant colors were still spring green and white. The carpet was custom-made, a light-gray plush with the Harrison Ltd. logo included in the design. He still had a huge bathroom and walk-in closet, but he had added a full kitchen and bedroom. He could camp out here for quite a while if he needed to.

At the far end of his office, which had been the decorator's idea, were a number of parallel partitions, which provided a large amount of extra wall space. She had turned it into a little gallery, a private display area, for all the photographs, plaques, and awards that Tyler had and would amass over the years.

*   *   *

Tyler looked up from his desk. He glanced at those eight snapshots of Penny's ass and wondered if Penny would ever speak to him again. He picked up the phone. It had become a ritual he performed every morning since the night Penny had come to his apartment and seen Geena there. If she hadn't forgotten her bag, Tyler wouldn't even know why she was angry with him. While Tyler was getting ready for bed that night, he had walked into the foyer to make sure the door was locked and saw a bag with Penny's monogram sitting near the front door.

He had called her every morning and evening for a month. She seldom answered the phone, and when she did answer and heard his voice, she hung up immediately.

He hung up the phone, and again, his mind went back to that night. Geena had showed up unexpectedly, and they had spent the evening together. She'd said she needed his help, and she did. As it stood, Geena was still staying at his place.

* * *

Penny sat at her little kitchen table and thanked God for the four inches of snow that had fallen the previous night. School had been cancelled, and because it was Friday morning, she would have a much-needed three-day weekend. She stood and poured another cup of freshly brewed coffee and looked down at the white lump on the driveway with snow drifted up against one side and wondered what she would do with her Corvette. She had loved it so much. It had become a symbol to her, much like the old red truck was to Tyler. The Vette said that she was still young, independent, intelligent, and successful.

It was late February, and it had been two and a half months since her eye-opening visit to Tyler's penthouse. She had vacillated almost hourly since then on what to do with her car. She could keep it, give it to Brenda, sell it, or send it back to Tyler, but most of the time, she just wanted to torch it.

Of course the Corvette wasn't the only reminder of a failed romance. Everywhere she looked, she found something they had bought together or something he had given her, including her entire wardrobe. She had wrapped the ankle bracelet and the cameo and put them away where she couldn't see them. It would be a long time before she was ready to deal with them.

She was comparing her feelings of anger and depression when the phone rang. It was early, and she assumed it was Tyler calling again, so she ignored it.

Oh! How she wanted to hurt him … to get back at him … to tell him …

Suddenly, she set her cup in the sink and walked to the bedroom. She was punching in the number from memory before she was seated.

"Harrison Companies," a crisp, clear female voice announced. "How can I help you?"

"This is Penny Kilmer. I want to speak with Tyler Harrison—now."

"Hold on please."

She didn't have to wait long.

"Penny! Babe, is that you?" Tyler asked.

"There's no babe here, but yes, this is Dr. Kilmer."

"I'm so glad you called. How are you?"

"Pissed. And you?"

"Awful."

"Really?" Penny asked. "I'm so sorry to hear that. Why don't you have Geena come over when she's in town so you can screw her? Maybe that will perk you up."

"Penny, please listen to me. It's not what you think. I'm only trying to help her. I don't feel that way about Geena."

"Of course you don't, you pompous bastard! You can't care about anybody but yourself. You say you don't want Geena. Give your lawyer, Susan Slater, a call. She always looks at you like she wants to eat you. I'll bet she would be a great fuck."

"Penny! Stop it! Listen to yourself. You're hurt and angry for no reason. I love you so much. Please don't do this."

"Oh, wow! Does that sound familiar? You know, Tyler, what goes around comes around. I seem to remember walking up your driveway a few years ago when you were waxing the hood of a car in your folks' garage. I begged and pleaded and professed my love while you continued to wax the hood. You wouldn't even speak to me. I stood there and cried, and you wouldn't even look at me. You were a proud, cruel son of a bitch then, and you still are. You didn't utter a word to me for five years. So, please do the same again. Don't come around or call me. I will welcome the silent treatment."

"Penny, I can't do that. You're assuming that I did something I didn't."

"You go to hell! And stop lying! I know what I saw. What you did to me is worse than what … Alan Grant did to me … in the back of that shoe store." She began to shake with sobs. "At least he was ashamed of what he did!" she screamed. "He couldn't … look me in the eyes … when he fucked me."

She slammed the phone down. Then she did it again and again. She stood and yanked with all her strength, and the cord ripped out of the wall. She threw the phone down the hallway, and it bounced and rolled all the way into the living room.

Damn, that felt good!

Penny stood and stared at the phone. The anger slowly retreated, and the overwhelming weight of her loss began to press down on her as she threw herself across the unmade bed. She relived that night and the events that followed, and she couldn't stop it until the complete reel had passed before her mind's eye.

She saw herself tiptoeing down the hall, being shocked to the point that she couldn't breathe, getting out the door, throwing up on the landing, coming out of the stairs, and that nice young man getting her a taxi. She again felt the same confusion and frustration that she'd felt then. When the taxi driver asked her where to go, she had no idea. It was too late to go back to the airport. She asked him to take her to a nice hotel.

As she walked across the lobby of the Washington Hilton on Connecticut Avenue, she realized that her overnight bag was sitting on the marble floor in Tyler's foyer. Thank God she still had her purse. She presented the Visa card and started to ask for a room but changed it to a suite. He could afford it.

She used the credit card again when she signed for breakfast. When the waiter returned with her card and a receipt on a tray, she signed the receipt, and he gave her back the card. When the waiter left, she idly studied the card. It had been issued by a large bank in Washington. An idea began to take shape in her mind, and she had smiled.

A short taxi ride dropped her at the bank. Penny had approached the first available teller, presented the credit card, and told her what she wanted. Within a minute, she was seated in a huge, old, ornate office across from a Mr. Plummer.

"Now, Miss Kilmer, what can we do for you?" he asked as he held her Visa card.

"I want to use my credit card for a cash advance. Is that a problem?"

"No, ma'am. What amount would you like?"

"One million dollars." It took a little doing, but when she left the bank an hour later, she had a cashier's check for $1 million.

While she waited for her commuter flight back home, she pulled out her little calculator, notebook, and pen. She quickly figured that in the seventeen months they had been together, they had made love about 125 times. When she divided that into a million, she got $8,000. So it had cost him eight grand every time he'd bedded her. She was sure it wasn't a record, but still it wasn't bad. She was sure she was worth it.

As she boarded the plane, she wondered how much it had cost him every time he screwed Geena. She realized that she was thinking like a whore, and she didn't like it, but she felt that was the way he had treated her. She wasn't proud of it, but she hoped Geena had cost him a lot less. For some stupid reason that she couldn't grasp, Penny wanted to be the most expensive.

When she arrived back at her apartment that evening, she cut the Visa card into little strips and dropped it in the mail to Tyler. She didn't need it any more. Penny decided she could live very nicely on her salary and the interest from $1 million, which she planned to invest soon.

Rehashing those events always drained her, and she curled up under the covers for a little nap. Before sleep came, she realized that she felt better. Calling Tyler and telling him what she thought was just what the doctor had ordered.

Chapter 38

New Opportunities

o you think you and Penny will get back together again?" Geena asked.

Tyler smiled and thought it was a good sign that Geena cared. "Oh, yes. I'm sure we will." He had never told Geena that she was the reason he and Penny were now split up, because Geena had enough guilt and problems to handle without him adding any.

"You sound awfully sure," she observed.

"Yeah, I am. We're both too damn proud and stubborn, but we're hopelessly in love, and eventually, love conquers all."

They were standing in the foyer of Tyler's penthouse. Vince went by with her two pieces of luggage. "Geena, your bags will be in the car, and I'll be out front when you're ready to go. Don't wait too long if you want to make your plane," Vince pointed out.

"I'll be right there, Vince. Keep the motor running."

"Are you sure you don't want me to go to the airport with you?" Tyler asked.

"Yes, I'm sure. I hate good-byes, and I want to get this one over. I'm a big girl now, and I have to get out there on my own again. Let's see. This is early May, right? My God, I've been living here and bugging you for five months."

"You haven't bugged me, and it's been a pleasure," Tyler said.

"I don't believe you, but it's kind of you to say so. Maybe now you can get back to a normal life around here." She took his large, strong hands in hers. She had always loved his hands and the way he used them. "You told me one time that you wished you loved me, but you didn't. It hurt me at the time, but I'm a little wiser now, and thanks to you, I understand what you tried to tell me. How will I ever repay you for everything you've done?"

"Very easily," he began. "Go out to Hollywood and knock 'em dead. You're a great talent, and I still want you to win an Oscar. This role is perfect for you, and it should get you a nomination. Just choose your friends a little more carefully, and stay in touch."

"I will. I promise." She kissed his cheek and then embraced him warmly for a long time. When she pulled away, she said, "I love you, Tyler." Then she turned and hurried out the door.

* * *

Tyler loved this new Learjet so much that he was almost at the point of creating places to go just so he could fly it. A perfect landing like he had just performed was so exhilarating. It was like a 280-yard drive on the first tee; a smash or an ace performed on the tennis court; a large business deal completed after months of work; and yes, like making love to Penny, but nothing in his life could ever compare to that.

He had flown in that afternoon to spend a long, quiet weekend with his folks and Grandma Ruth. They had some sort of outing to a state park planned, and he was looking forward to it. He needed to take care of two pieces of business that afternoon, and then he would relax and enjoy his family.

When his new toy was safely put away in the hanger, Tyler came out and waved to his mother.

"I don't know much about it," she admitted, "but that looked like another perfect landing to me."

"It was," he replied. "What can I say, Mom. I'm just phenomenal. But of course, you already know that since you're the one who had me."

She laughed. "Yeah, I guess you're pretty phenomenal. Of course, you get it from my side of the family."

"Shame on you, Mom. I'm going to tell Dad what you said."

"You do, and your favorite dinner will go in the trash."

"Really? Well, he didn't need to know anyway."

She laughed. "That's my boy. Now, where to?"

"The factory site first and then the college."

*　　*　　*

Tyler and Kate walked around the side of the factory which would soon be ready to make tennis shoes. The July sun was hot, and he took off his shirt as they looked over the construction. Tyler talked with many of the workers as he inspected the site. He met with the project manager and superintendent and was pleased to learn everything was on schedule.

Later, Kate dropped him off at the college, and he said he would walk home when he was finished. With only summer school in session, things were very relaxed at Winfield, and he was shown into President Fairchild's office immediately. After handshakes and some brief small talk, the old gentleman got down to business.

"I have two matters I need to discuss with you," the president informed Tyler. "At the last trustee's meeting, I put your name into nomination to join our board as a trustee, and you were confirmed immediately by a unanimous voice vote."

Tyler was shocked. Everyone on the Board of Trustees was older than fifty, and most were from the education field. "I have to tell you that's quite a surprise," Tyler noted.

"Well, it shouldn't be," Fairchild suggested. "What I want to know is, will you accept?"

"Yes, of course. I'd be honored, and it would be a pleasure to work with the gentlemen on the board. I'm just not sure why they would want me."

"Managing a college is going to be more and more like running a business, and I think most people would agree that you're highly adept at managing a business." Fairchild chuckled. "We also felt if you were good enough to sit on President Nixon's Economic Council, you might be good enough for us."

Tyler laughed and said, "Thank you. I look forward to it. You said there were two matters?"

"Yes, yes, I did. The other matter involves Penny Kilmer."

"Penny?" Tyler asked, wondering what she had to do with any of this.

"Yes. Professor Fleming, who was one of our professors of English, has taken a position with another school. This has created an unexpected opening in our English department, and Penny has applied for it, along with some forty others."

Tyler thought for a moment and asked, "What are her chances?"

"She has her doctorate now, and everyone here at the school knows and likes her. She interviewed very well. There are some people with more experience, but we always like to work with people from the community when we can." Fairchild paused and leaned back in his old leather high-backed chair. He put his fingertips together like a spider doing push-ups on a mirror. "To be perfectly honest, we know that you and she are not an item anymore, and we were concerned about how you might feel."

Tyler didn't hesitate. "That's true. We're not seeing each other right now, but I'm pretty sure we will in the future. But whether we do or not, I would like to see her teach at the college level. I know that's what she wants, and she's worked very hard for her PhD."

"Okay, thanks for your honesty. She has the position, and I'll see that a letter of notification goes out today. And, Tyler, I'd appreciate it if this conversation was to go no further than this office. These matters dealing with personnel can be a little sticky sometimes."

Tyler knew the meeting was over when the old gentleman stood and came around the desk. Tyler stood and said, "Yes, I agree. I'm sure she'll do a fine job."

When they were at the door to the office, they shared a perfunctory handshake, and then Tyler was surprised when President Fairchild embraced him.

The president stepped back and ventured, "I hope you don't mind, Tyler, but as you know, Mrs. Fairchild and I only have one child, and our daughter could never have children. I like to think of you as the grandson we never had."

Tyler smiled. "Thank you very much, President Fairchild. That's twice you have honored me today."

*   *   *

It was a beautiful July afternoon, and Tyler enjoyed the lazy small town as he walked toward his parents' house. A number of people beeped their horns or yelled a hello from their cars or from their porches as he passed by. Although he hadn't planned it, when Tyler reached the alley that led to Penny's garage apartment, he turned in.

Before he reached the apartment, he saw her. She was sunbathing in the backyard, or as she always said, "catching some rays." She had her trusty old folding lounge chair, beach towel, spray bottle, and portable radio. She was lying on her back with her head nearest him in a bathing suit that he didn't recognize. It was orange and made her look even darker than she was. It was cut somewhere between a conservative two-piece and a skimpy bikini.

Tyler felt like a voyeur as he stood at the corner of the garage and stared. He hoped no one was watching him watch her. He could see her breasts rise and fall with her breathing, and he felt like a silly teenager as he became aware that he was getting excited.

She didn't hear his approach. The radio was on, and her pretty foot was tapping at the still air as it beat out the rhythm to a golden oldie.

"If you have some lotion, I'd volunteer to rub it on," he ventured.

She sat up suddenly and asked, "What the hell are you doing here? I thought I asked you to leave me alone." She quickly draped a large beach towel around her body.

"Yes, you did," Tyler replied. "As I recall, you asked me to give you the silent treatment. Well, I was wrong when I did that before, and it caused us to be separated for many years. You're making the same mistake now, and I love you too much to let that happen."

She grabbed the radio and stood up. "You don't have a choice, asshole." She pushed against him and started to go around him.

"Wait a minute!" he ordered.

Over her shoulder, she advised, "You go to hell!"

Tyler grabbed her by the upper arm and spun her around so fast that her head looked like it was on a rag doll. The radio fell from her hand, hit his shin, and bounced on the grass at his feet. He kicked it so hard that pieces flew off and landed silently in the neighbor's shrubbery some fifty feet away.

"Tyler! You're hurting me!"

He eased his grip on her arm and said, "I'm sorry. I don't want to hurt you. Geena and I are nothing more than friends. I don't know what you saw or what you thought you saw, but you're wrong. I understand that you were hurt and angry. It's time to get over it now, so we can be together. I know you're also a silly romantic, and I love that about you too. I'm even willing to win you back."

He leaned forward and grasped her shoulders and felt her tense. "Penny, you're the dominant color on my palette. I can't paint the rest of my life without you. Do you understand? I'm miserable without you. Even my successes are no fun, because you aren't there to share them with me. I'm not going to live this way much longer, Goddamn it! Do you hear me?"

She refused to reply, so he released her and stomped out of the yard.

* * *

Penny heard the lid drop on her mailbox at the bottom of the stairs and knew the mail had just been delivered. On the way down the stairs to get the mail, it occurred to her that she had her little routine down pat. Without Tyler in her life, she was close to becoming an old maid schoolteacher at the ripe old age of thirty.

She lifted the lid, retrieved the mail, and started back up the stairs. The telephone bill was on top, followed by two pieces of junk mail and a letter from Winfield College. In the kitchen, she sat down and opened the letter from Winfield. She knew before she started reading what it would say: Thanks, but no thanks. Don't call us, we'll call you. She didn't have enough experience, and she wasn't published.

After hastily scanning the letter, it struck her that it didn't say that at all. It said if she wished to take the position and join the faculty as Associate Professor of English at Winfield College, she should contact the personnel office immediately.

She yelled! She jumped around! She yelled some more while jumping around! Penny ran to the bedroom and dialed the number of the high school to put in her notice. When she finished with the principal, she held the button down for a second and released it. When she had a dial tone, Penny quickly punched in the numbers and waited.

"Harrison Companies, how may I help you?"

Penny had Tyler's name on her lips when she realized what she had done. She had wanted to tell Tyler the good news; she wanted to share it with him. She quickly hung up the phone and could feel the tears as she realized she wasn't supposed to love him anymore. How could she have done that? Damn it! It was like a reflex. What a ninny she was. She looked at the phone and almost before she knew it, she saw it bouncing and rolling down the hallway into the living room with part of the cord still attached. *Let's see now, that's the second phone this year. Well, it felt wonderful!* And thanks to the bastard she almost called, she could afford it.

On the short walk across the lawn to the landlord's house to use their phone to call the phone company and tell them her phone was out of order again, she wondered if Tyler had anything to do with her getting the position at Winfield.

Chapter 39

❦

Wooing Penny

It was Friday, and the most exciting Labor Day Weekend of Penny's life lay ahead, but she was unable to savor it the way she should. She would begin lecturing students on Tuesday morning. She had just read in Friday's local paper on the front page that Tyler Harrison had been elected as the youngest member ever to the Winfield College Board of Trustees.

She was getting dressed now to attend a meeting where the trustees would meet and mingle with the faculty. He would be there, of course. She had already heard the pretentious bastard land his new jet plane a couple of hours ago.

As she went carefully down her stairs toward the trusty ole Vette, which she had decided to keep, she wondered if he might show up with another woman. Penny decided not to think about that, because it hurt.

She saw him right away as she entered the little hall for the reception, or mixer, or whatever it was. He was standing with the other trustees, next to President Fairchild in the trustee receiving line. When her turn came she stepped forward and coldly shook his hand without looking into his eyes.

"Hello, Tyler," she said.

"Hello, Dr. Kilmer, and congratulations, Professor."

What he said sort of caught her off guard, and she glanced up, still not into his eyes, but rather just barely off to one side where she saw the most amazing thing—a few gray hairs at his temple. She quickly looked at the other side and saw the matching ones.

Without thinking, she blurted out, "My God, Tyler, you're getting gray."

He smiled. "Yes, I've noticed those, and I suspect you're the cause." He leaned over so no one could hear. "You look stunning, Penny, and I intend to get you back very soon."

She gave him her best contemptible look. "Don't waste your time."

*　　*　　*

After the reception with the trustees, Penny went to her office and worked on a syllabus for one of her classes. She got home late, quickly changed clothes, and decided to have a sandwich for dinner. She was sitting down to get wrapped around a huge sandwich when she heard something like one of those air horns on a train or a big truck. It sounded close, and she went to the window to investigate. A huge truck was backing into her alley. It looked new and very clean.

She wondered if her landlord had decided to add some gravel to the driveway, or maybe he was getting some dirt. The truck stopped a good distance from her car and near the edge of the lawn. Penny watched as the bed began to lift up into the dumping position. She could see into the bed, and it looked like white gravel. The tailgate opened, and the load began to pour out. Penny wasn't sure, but it looked like too much gravel for the driveway. When the bed was all the way up, the truck moved forward until all the load had poured out. As the bed began to descend, the driver stepped down with something in his hands.

Penny almost choked on her sandwich when she realized it was Tyler. She moved back quickly so he couldn't see her, but her curiosity soon won, and she peered around the edge of the curtains. He had driven a stake into the ground, and it looked like a little sign was attached. He looked up at the window, blew a kiss, jumped up into the truck, and drove away.

She waited a while, fearing that he would return and wondering what the hell he was doing delivering gravel. When she couldn't stand it any longer, she went down to get a closer look. She hurried by to see what was on the sign. It read: "I know you used to like me and love popcorn. Maybe if I keep you in popcorn, you'll like me again."

Penny glanced again at the huge pile. She went a little closer and looked. Popcorn! The whole damn pile was popcorn. She reached out, scooped up a handful, and tasted it. *Not bad*, she mused, and then she laughed. *Talk about unpredictable. This crazy man had brought her an entire dump truck load of popcorn. Well, he could be really silly and sweet … Oh, no! He wouldn't!*

Penny realized this must be part of his trying to win her back. Did the sneaky bastard really think he could weasel his way back into her good graces with a load of popcorn? Well, he could go to hell! On the way back to the apartment, with two handfuls of popcorn, she wondered if he had anything else planned.

* * *

It was a glorious Saturday afternoon for a college football game, and Penny was having a good time. For her, the game provided an opportunity to people watch. The administration wanted a friendly campus. To that end, all faculty members were expected to attend the first home football game and, of course, the one during homecoming weekend.

While dressing for the game in a beautiful fall dress with a matching scarf thrown around her neck and over one shoulder, Penny had gotten a phone call from Dr. Vera Richardson. Penny had been a substitute in a bridge group at Vera's home a few times and knew her quite well. She was a very attractive lady in her midforties who had recently divorced. She didn't want to attend the game alone and knew that Penny wouldn't either. Dr. Richardson had been the registrar at Winfield College for seven years. She was very personable and liked by all. She also had a talkative nature and was always up for a little fun. Penny knew she would make an enjoyable game companion.

The game had started, but they were much too busy talking and watching the latecomers to notice. Vera was in the process of telling Penny what a boring shit her former husband had been when she said, "Jesus, will you look at that. What a man."

Penny looked down and saw Tyler, dressed to kill in gray slacks and a double-breasted blue blazer with a gray and red striped silk tie. He was moving slowly along the aisle in front of the first row of seats. It seemed that everyone from local townspeople, students, faculty, and Winfield administrators knew him and wanted to shake hands or say hello.

Vera nudged Penny with her arm. "Look at them, every one of them."

"Who?" Penny asked.

"The women silly. Just look at them. Every one of them has her eyes glued on Mr. Harrison."

Penny glanced around from side to side. She couldn't find one woman who wasn't looking intently at Tyler, and she felt a tinge of jealousy until she remembered he was no longer her man.

"I'm sorry you two aren't together anymore," Vera ventured. "Do you still love him?"

"Sometimes, I guess. When I'm not hating him."

"I'm sorry. I always thought you were perfect for each other. I hope you can get together again, but I've got to tell you, I'd give anything for one night between the sheets with him."

"Vera!" Penny interrupted. "Shame on you."

"Oh bullshit, Penny! You're too young and beautiful to be a prude. Don't ever get like that. I lived with the most prudish man in the world for more than twenty years. Listen, Penny, I know we nice educated women have always been held to a higher sexual standard. Well, that's ridiculous! Every woman needs a really good screwing now and then, and I haven't had one since I was back in college. I'll just bet that Mr. Tyler Harrison is a wild man in bed. Did you hear the speech he gave in this stadium a couple of years ago to the graduating class?"

"Yes, I did," Penny recalled. "I was here with one of his scholarship winners."

"I never knew any man was capable of such emotion. He just stood up there and talked without notes, and you knew it was from the heart.

I was so touched by what he said, I cried. If he can open up like that and share with a group, I can only imagine what he's like one-on-one. He must be a great lover."

Penny hesitated, but only for a moment. "He's totally awesome."

"Penny, don't get mad at me and feel free to tell me to shut up, but I'm going to tell you something. Under this hair coloring is a lot of gray, so I'm supposed to be very wise and all knowing. The man is worth a few hundred million, great-looking, wonderful personality, and an awesome lover. I don't know what the hell happened between you two, but maybe a guy like that is worth forgiving. I mean, Jesus. No one is perfect."

Penny said, "I don't know what I feel. Tyler has very strong feelings, and he evokes strong feelings. One minute I want to hold him, and the next minute I want to slap him. I ache to have him touch me, and then I just want to kill him. I want him, and I don't want him. I hate the rotten bastard, and I love him. I don't know what I want!"

Penny glanced up when a small plane appeared over the stadium. She was quite surprised to see something like this in her part of the country. It was a little single-engine plane flying very slowly and trailing a large banner. It reminded her of the beach where the planes would fly up the beach pulling banners that advertised everything from restaurants to concerts.

"Penny, look at this. Is that cute, or what? Some college boy has gone all out to impress some girl."

Penny looked more closely at the plane and the banner making its lazy circle around the field, and her heart did a few leaps and ended up in her throat. The banner read: "Love You, Babe."

Babe had become Tyler's private pet name for her. She immediately attempted to hide her surprise, but she had to smile. It really was sweet and romantic. Mr. Unpredictable. She quickly wiped away the smile and replaced it with a frown when she realized that he might be watching her. Penny glanced down where Tyler was seated, and sure enough, he was looking back. He discreetly pointed with his index finger toward the sky, grinned, and blew her a kiss. Penny wished she could raise her hand and extend her long, lovely middle finger at him, but she couldn't risk her job for that.

Chapter 40

Geena's Visit

When the doorbell rang, it annoyed Penny. She quickly turned off her portable electric typewriter, gathered her comfy granny gown around her, and headed for the door. She had recently put up new sheer curtains over the upper half of the door that was glass and could only make out a vague shape.

What she saw when she opened the door was a tall, thin woman wearing huge sunglasses and a scarf. Before she could react, the woman ducked quickly by her and was inside. Penny recognized her as she brushed past and was almost bowled over by surprise and anger. Geena Morgan, dressed in sneakers, jeans, and a leather jacket, turned and removed her starlet sunglasses and scarf.

"Do you have any idea how hard it is to fly from Los Angeles, California, to Clarksburg, West Virginia, and then sleep on a bench in the terminal until someone turns in a damn car so you can rent it?"

Penny, who could not have cared less about Geena's travel woes, finally found her voice. "What do you think you're doing here?"

"We have to talk," Geena ordered.

"Wrong, Geena!" Penny stepped forward and grabbed the leather fabric of Geena's jacket and began to propel her toward the door. "Now get your skinny ass out!"

Geena stiffened her legs and resisted. "Not till we talk! Liz told me what happened, and you have to know the truth!"

Penny pulled harder until Geena was again moving toward the door. "I was there! I saw what happened, you goddamned whore."

Geena spun around and slapped Penny across the face. Penny released her hold and fell back a step. Her hand came up to her face, and for an instant, Penny saw bright flashes of light. She punched Geena somewhere in the face and felt a couple of her nails break while the other two dug deep into her palm.

Geena fell back a couple of steps and screamed. Now it was her turn for her hand to come up to her face. Penny watched as Geena stared in shock at her bloody hand. Blood was dripping from her mouth.

Again, Penny grabbed her jacket. "Get in the kitchen before you bleed to death."

Most of her anger spent, Penny made an ice pack for Geena. While Geena bitched and moaned in the kitchen, Penny clipped her two broken nails, inspected the punctures in her palm, and applied some antiseptic cream. Her hand was throbbing, and she could feel her heartbeat in two fingers that were now too stiff and swollen to move without great pain.

When Penny came back into the kitchen, Geena was busy studying herself in a compact mirror from her purse. She turned and scowled at Penny. "I wish you'd look at my lip."

"This may be hard for you to grasp, but I really don't give a damn." She almost smiled as she saw that it was at least twice its normal size and was turning a nice, deep purple. "If it's any consolation," Penny continued, "I have about eight hours of typing to do between now and Tuesday morning with this." She held up her stiff swollen hand for Geena to see.

"Does it hurt?" Geena asked, with slurred speech.

"I can feel every heartbeat in it."

"Oh, good. I'm so glad. How about your shiner? Does it hurt too?"

"What shiner?" Penny asked.

"Your shiner! You're going to have a black eye very soon," Geena noted.

Penny looked at her for a second, and then with her good hand, she grabbed up Geena's compact from the kitchen counter. The first thing that she noticed was a little swelling, but she also noticed that the coloring beside and under her eye was surprisingly close to that of Geena's lip.

Penny rudely pushed by Geena on her way to the fridge for another tray of ice. "Damn you. I should punch you again."

Geena turned around and glared. "We can fight or talk, but I'm not leaving here until we talk."

"Five minutes, Geena. That's how long you have to talk. Then your ass is leaving here, one way or another."

Geena said, "I came here today, because Liz called me from Maryland and begged me to come and because Tyler is the best friend I have in this world. Liz said he's tried to explain what happened, but you wouldn't listen. I'm not sure what all had happened or what you saw, but you seem to think he and I were having an affair."

"What the hell would *you* think? I show up to surprise the man I love and find you in your underwear sprawled across his lap."

Geena stopped talking for a moment and looked down at her sneakers. Finally, she spoke. "When Tyler refused to love me and I quit seeing him, I started seeing men I thought wanted me. They did, but for the wrong reasons. Before I even knew it, I was an alcoholic and addicted to pills."

She paused and looked up. Penny could see that Geena was either a great actress, or there was more hurting her than her lip. "But I was handling the pills and the booze, or I thought I was. Then I found out I was pregnant, and ... I didn't even know who the father was ..."

Geena started to cry, and Penny began to slightly feel the ice melt around the part of her heart that housed her feelings toward Geena Morgan.

"I'm sorry I slapped you, Penny. I guess when you called me a whore, it sort of hit home. I'd lost complete control of my life. When I found out that I was pregnant, it shocked me into being straight for a couple of weeks, but I couldn't stay straight. I was so strung out that I started having blackout periods, and I couldn't work. The last one was when I woke up in a motel in Maryland. I was bleeding and thought I was having my period until I realized I'd had an illegal abortion. I ... I ... killed my baby."

She stopped speaking and cried softly for a while. Penny gave her a tissue and waited.

"When I realized that I could no longer help myself, I knew I had to get help, or I would soon be dead. I saw the name and address of the motel on a book of matches in the room and knew I was close to Tyler. I called him at the office, and he wanted to come get me, but I promised to meet him at his penthouse in Bethesda. In order to get up enough courage to go, I got drunk and passed out in the cab. The driver, thank God, took me to the right place and notified the doorman. Tyler came down and carried me up. I had thrown up on myself, and that's why I wasn't wearing a dress. When I finally told him the whole truth the next day, he took over in typical Harrison whirlwind fashion. He had doctors and psychologists in right away. It was like a private treatment facility. I had three nurses who worked eight-hour shifts and also served as guards. He removed all booze and medication, even aspirin. He kept me there for a few months, and he and Liz spent as much time with me as humanly possible. When I was able, he would slip me out so I didn't go crazy, and he took me every week to see my dad."

Geena wiped her eyes dry and looked directly at Penny. "Penny, he did for me what no one else would. Not even my father! He loved me, not romantically, because he only feels that way about you. Jesus Christ, one of the reasons I left when I did was because I got sick of hearing about you. The man is absolutely consumed with you.

"You see, he's the only one who loved me enough to help me and enough to forgive me. He's my friend. Thanks to him, I've recovered and can now go on with my life. I'm not cured, and I never will be. I will always be an alcoholic and a recovering addict, but I know I'll never use again, because I couldn't let him down.

"He doesn't know I found out, but the assistant director on the film I'm shooting now let it slip that Tyler agreed to finance the whole film so I could get another start, but only if I got the starring role. Would you believe that he calls almost every day to see how I'm doing?"

Penny smiled. "Yes, I could believe that."

"I swear to you, Penny, I didn't know why you and Tyler were no longer together until Liz told me. I guess he didn't want me to know; maybe he was afraid it would upset me again. You have to take him back. You're

275

killing him inch by inch. Everyone at work says he doesn't care anymore. When I talk to him, he tries to cover, but he's so depressed he can't hide it. Penny, you don't have to forgive Tyler, because he hasn't done anything. Promise me you'll take him back and make him happy again. And please forgive me for interfering in your life and making such a mess of things!"

Penny reached over and squeezed Geena's hand. She didn't hate anymore, and she was sorry that she had. Hate always consumed so much energy. It didn't leave room to see the light of reason. She had always respected Geena, even when she didn't like her. Her respect had grown a hundredfold. It took courage to overcome all that she had and boundless courage to come and share it all with her after she had taken Tyler away from Geena.

Penny smiled and said, "You know, I'm sorry I punched you. Do you think we could ever be friends?"

Without hesitation, Geena answered, "Yes. I'm sure we could. I think it would make Tyler very happy."

They spent the next hour talking about Tyler over soup and sandwiches. Penny told Geena about the popcorn and the banner. When she told her about wanting to give him the finger, Geena laughed so hard her lip started to bleed again.

When Geena finally left, they agreed that Tyler would never know about their little meeting. They also agreed that Penny couldn't go running to Tyler immediately or give in too easily. He had to think he had won her back, or he might get suspicious. When Geena left, Penny tried to type, but spent most of the time wondering what would happen next.

Chapter 41

Another Breakup

Penny parked the Vette, snatched her briefcase, collected her mail, bounded past the pile of popcorn, and headed up the stairs to her apartment. Life was good, and it was about to get even better. She was quite pleased with her fine, beautiful self. It was Tuesday afternoon after the long Labor Day weekend and the first day of college classes for the academic year. If her two classes today were any indication of what teaching at the college level would be, bring it on. The students were bright, attentive, and actually interested in what she had to say.

She deposited her briefcase and her mail on the armchair nearest the door and headed for the bedroom. She needed baggy shorts and a T-shirt. She would then hurry to the kitchen for fresh lemonade and some serious contemplation. Now, thanks to Geena's surprise visit, there was no more panic.

Penny knew she would certainly have to apologize for the accusations and for not believing a man who she knew in her heart would never lie to her. Now, as she reminisced about the countless number of crazy things this wonderful man had done for her and with her, she laughed. She could hardly wait until their next meeting or phone call.

She finished her lemonade and headed for the living room to check her mail. The second envelope in the pile had no stamp. It was plain and only had her name on the front. She opened it and felt her heart rate quicken when she recognized Tyler's handwriting.

> Penny, Mother and I just finished a long talk, and she's very upset with me and my decision. I guess I will never understand women. Anyway, my mind is made up. Our relationship throughout the years has always been stormy—too many ups and downs. We are obviously too independent and too headstrong to ever have a lasting relationship. I've had a few relationships with very different women, and all have been dismal failures.
>
> I now understand that the popcorn and banner were overly romantic silliness. Tell your landlord I'll have someone coming to clean up the stupid popcorn tomorrow. Everyone in Stratford is laughing at me. My businesses and charity foundation are suffering, and my employees and friends think I've gone over the edge.
>
> It's done, Penny. I'm through. Don't try to contact me. I promise to do the same, and no, I never had sex with Geena when she was at my place. I was only trying to help an old friend.
>
> Oscar Wilde once made what I always thought was a very sexist comment about men and women. He said: "A man can be happy with any woman, as long as he doesn't love her." It took a while, but I now understand the wisdom of his words.

How long had she been sitting there in a daze? She had read the letter three more times. Panic was starting to set in again. *Please, no!* And then, like a ton of bricks—no, ten tons—it hit her. She grabbed the letter and scanned it. Yes, there it was: "Everyone in Stratford is laughing at me. My businesses and foundation are suffering, and my employees and friends think I've gone over the edge."

Bingo! She was sure. It was his pride. She had hurt and shamed him, just like the night when she had slapped him. It was over. She knew she had lost him. He was so explicit in his message about their relationship having no future.

* * *

Kate was still upset when the phone rang. She and Tyler had argued loudly, and Tyler had left without saying good-bye. She was already bewailing what she had said.

"Hello?" Kate queried.

"Kate. Thank God you picked up. I got a terrible letter from Tyler, and he said we were through."

"Yes, I know about the letter. He told me he didn't need this shit any longer. He said he was damn sick and tired of women trying to control his life, and he stomped out."

"Oh dear God," Penny said. "I've been a fool, Kate. He's tried to get me back, and I've laughed at him and hurt his pride."

Kate gave a disgruntled laugh. "Well, I certainly didn't help matters. I told him Granddad Luke would be ashamed of him. I think we're both at the top of his shit list right about now."

"Kate, you said he left. Do you know where he went?"

"Yes, he was on his way to the airport, so he could get the hell out of Stratford." Kate waited for the expected reply but heard only a dull click followed by a dial tone.

* * *

Tyler's mind was on fast-forward. Penny would not listen to reason. He'd be damned if he would grovel at Penny Kilmer's feet any longer, no matter how pretty they were. He checked the sky to make sure no one was trying to land as he applied the left brake and began his turn onto the runway. He could feel that old familiar tension that he always felt just before a flight. He loved this plane and loved flying it.

He was reaching for his sunglasses when movement off to his right caught his eye. Someone was waving from the little parking lot. He adjusted his sunglasses and focused on the person who was more than a quarter mile away. He couldn't make out who the frantic waver was, but he recognized the car. A red Corvette!

What in the hell does she want? She obviously wants me to stop. I should have mailed the letter. Whatever, he thought as he began to add power.

As the plane began to roll, he glanced at the parking lot and didn't see her. He was at about twenty miles per hour and gaining speed when his peripheral vision picked up some odd movement. *What the?!* The red Corvette was no longer in the parking lot. It was moving fast and bouncing as it made its way across the mowed field toward the runway.

Tyler couldn't believe his eyes! He wasn't sure what she intended. Her present angle appeared to be on a collision course with his airplane. He needed to make an immediate decision, so he slowed down. The runway was a little wet from rain, and it appeared that she too was trying to slow, but she lost control. He could see her wheels sliding across the wet grass. She was too close. He let off the brakes, hoping to get past the point where he had estimated she would be, and then he glanced to the right and saw the Corvette disappear as the cockpit passed.

Then he felt the shudder and heard the dull thud. The Learjet, now out of control, lurched to the right while leaning to the left. Tyler waited for the left wing to slam onto the runway. His extensive flight training had never covered this. Somehow, the plane righted itself, and the left wing never hit. The Learjet shot off the runway into the grass field to the right. The jet came to a stop quickly, as the wheels on the landing gear settled into the soft, wet field.

The first thing Tyler saw when he dropped the steps was a red Corvette with the top mashed in. He was angry and concerned about the damage to his plane but decided that could wait. He headed for the car to confront Penny. She was slumped over toward the passenger side and mumbling.

"I'm … sorry … Tyler."

"Are you okay?" Tyler asked.

"Sorry … love … you."

Tyler reached in and carefully pulled her to an upright position in the driver's seat. When he pulled his right hand from behind her, it was covered with blood. He leaned her forward for a closer look and found a large gash on the back of her skull. Her scalp was open and lying back in a flap.

Tyler quickly opened the door and lifted her out. As he rounded the car to put her in the passenger seat, she was limp and unconscious. He drove like a madman to get her to the hospital.

* * *

Tyler could barely see Penny in emergency room three. Her gurney was surrounded with medical personnel. Like anyone in this situation, he felt small and helpless. Well, he could do something. He quickly told the lady at the desk that if he was needed, he would be in the small hospital chapel.

As he tried to compose a proper prayer, the old feeling of inadequacy returned. Tyler was a true believer and felt certain in his faith. But he always felt so small when he spoke with his maker. He made up his mind to offer the best prayer he could muster on such short notice. He knew God's grace was real.

He was praying when he heard someone say, "Mr. Harrison."

He turned and said, "Yes."

A rather heavy, young, unattractive nurse said, "If you come with me, you can talk to the doctor now."

They soon reached what he guessed was the emergency room doctor's office. The heavy nurse said, "Dr. Andrews, this is Tyler Harrison."

The doctor was small with light-colored, thinning hair. His complexion was very light, and Tyler guessed he was in his late thirties.

"I'm afraid the prognosis is not good," the doctor blurted out.

"Where is Penny now?" Tyler asked.

"She's in X-ray now. Should be out of there in about thirty minutes and then on her way to Morgantown. If she's going to make it, she'll need specialized care."

Tyler was very familiar with Morgantown, West Virginia. It was the home of West Virginia University and the medical school. They had received a rather large grant from the Harrison Foundation just last year.

Dr. Andrews continued, "I placed a call earlier to the trauma unit, and a special ambulance is en route. I estimate it should arrive about the time Penny comes out of X-ray."

"Excuse me, Doctor." It was the nurse again. "I have Penny's sister here."

Brenda rushed in and hugged Tyler. She looked frantic. "Tyler, my God, what happened?"

"I'll give you the details later, but Dr. Andrews has ordered a special ambulance to transport Penny to Morgantown. He was about to tell me about her condition."

"Morgantown? My God, it must be bad."

"I'm sorry we have to meet like this. I'm Dr. Andrews. May I be honest with you?"

"Yes, please," Brenda agreed. "I need to know."

"Your sister has a severe head injury. She appears to have sustained no other injuries. When Tyler brought her in, her heart and breathing had stopped. We were able to start her heart but not her breathing. We're using a respirator and a mask to breathe for her now. While I was working with her in the emergency room, she flatlined."

"Flatlined? What's that?" Brenda demanded.

"It means her heart stopped again. In reality, she has already died twice today. What concerns me the most is that the part of her brain that controls the heart and breathing appears to have been damaged. The neurology department at the university is excellent, but honestly, it doesn't look good."

Tyler squeezed Brenda's hand, feeling dumbstruck. Brenda began to sob, and Tyler was in shock. The anger that felt so real when he'd left the letter earlier that day seemed tawdry and petty now.

Chapter 42

A Time for Waiting

*S*he felt so special. Every morning when she woke, she pinched herself to make sure the past eight years hadn't been a dream. No, it was real. She was a corporate officer and Tyler's right-hand woman. He had hired her to be his administrative assistant. He was the boss, but also a close associate and good friend. The boss needed her now, and it was such a pleasure to be there for him.

"You must get more rest," Liz ordered.

"Have you been talking with Mother?" Tyler asked.

"Not about that."

"Well, she's always trying to get me to go back to my room and get some sleep."

He looked away, and Liz knew how much he was hurting.

"I couldn't stand it if I wasn't here." He paused and waited till he could speak again. "What would I do if she ... you know, if she doesn't wake up? Or if she does? Do you understand, Liz? I have to be here."

"Yes, Tyler," Liz lamented. "I understand. But please, at least take time to shower and change your clothes."

* * *

Tyler had finally given in to his fatigue. After his shave and shower, he had taken a short nap. He was now awake, lying on his back and looking at the ceiling. If the Lord above ever played baseball, he had to be a pitcher. What a huge curveball life could throw your way when you least expected it. Four days ago, he had left that stupid letter, and now Penny was in a coma.

He was sure he was all right now, but it occurred to him that he too might have been in shock part of the time since the accident. The guilt that all this was directly or indirectly his fault was heavy. He was hopeful when he arrived at the university hospital that the level of frustration would decrease. It had literally worsened by a multiple of ten.

Dr. Meyers, the chief neurologist, always had the same answer: "We'll have to wait and see."

Penny's heart had stopped twice on the ambulance ride to Morgantown. It was quickly determined that Penny had sustained a concussion and a cracked skull, and her brain was swelling due to the trauma. The brain stem at the top of the neck and the bottom of the brain was damaged and not functioning properly. Because that portion of the brain was in total control of breathing, blood pressure, and heartbeat, she could die at any moment.

Tyler had arrived in Morgantown about thirty minutes after the ambulance with his mother and Penny's mother, Martha. She was attractive for a lady of nearly sixty and looked very much like an older version of her daughters. They were immediately besieged with the news that Penny's brain swelling would most likely be her demise. Dr. Meyers and the other doctors on his team felt if there was any chance for survival, the pressure on her brain must be relieved.

Permission was given, papers were signed, and she was rushed to an operating room where a small hole would be drilled into her skull. This would hopefully reduce the pressure and allow her brain to heal. There were, of course, no guarantees, but instead, there were additional warnings. The anesthesia used during the operation might also stop Penny's heart.

*   *   *

The past four days had seemed like forty. Penny had survived the operation but remained in a coma. The hospital staff had provided great care, and Tyler knew it was partly because of the celebrity status he enjoyed.

Within hours after the operation, Liz had arrived with Vince in the Harrison limo. She had booked ten rooms in the new Holiday Inn two blocks away. Everyone who needed or wanted to be there had a free room and first-class transportation.

Tyler sat up on the edge of the bed and smiled when he thought about Vince. Tyler had invited him up to see Penny and her room. He had timidly stood at the foot of the bed with his rosary and lamented what a great lady she was. Tyler put his arm on Vince's shoulder and told him how much Penny liked him. Vince, the short, wide tough guy, cried openly. Because of this, Tyler would make damn sure Vince had a job for life.

* * *

Refreshed after his shower and a short nap, Tyler stepped off the elevator and noticed no one was at the nurses' station. When he turned the corner toward Penny's large, private room, he knew why. They were all in her room. He hoped something good had happened, but when he got to the door, he knew it was bad.

Brenda and her mother were holding each other off to the side. Dr. Meyers had his stethoscope over Penny's chest. He shook his head and said, "Again."

One of the other doctors called out a number, said the word *clear*, and placed the paddles on her bare chest. Her body arched as the current pulsed through it. He raised the paddles and stepped back.

Dr. Meyers quickly listened with his stethoscope. The doctor kept listening and moving the stethoscope from one position to another. After a while, he turned to the head nurse and said, "We have a weak pulse, but leave the crash cart. I want a nurse in here taking blood pressures and watching that monitor around the clock."

The nurse answered, "You got it, Dr. Meyers."

Dr. Meyers turned to Brenda and said, "Brenda, may I see the family in my office?"

Brenda and Martha insisted that Tyler join them.

Dr. Meyers began. "I've been treating patients with head injuries for more than twenty years. I don't have a crystal ball, so I can't be certain. However, my experience tells me something is happening. The swelling has eased, and I want to gradually take away the medicine we're using to induce her coma. I want to give her the chance to wake up. But I must warn you, I don't think she will."

"Is there anything else you can do?" Tyler asked.

"Not really, Mr. Harrison," Meyers responded. "Sooner or later, she has to make it on her own if she's going to."

"Doctor, how long will it be before we know if she can wake up and make it on her own?" Martha asked.

"Every case if different, but I should think within forty-eight hours."

Brenda took a deep breath. "I think we should do it, if it's okay with Mom and Tyler."

Martha agreed, and Tyler just nodded his head up and down. He might need to visit their chapel again. He promised himself he would remember to pray more often when he didn't want something.

*   *   *

Tyler looked at Penny and marveled at her beauty. In a hospital, no makeup, barely alive, and still awesome looking. He asked the doctor if there was any chance that Penny could hear or understand if he spoke to her.

Dr. Meyers smiled and simply said, "Maybe."

From that moment on, Tyler, Brenda, and Martha had taken turns talking to Penny.

At first, Tyler had felt kind of silly. It was pretty difficult to talk to someone who never answered, but he soon got used to it. It was like therapy, he guessed. He told her about the past and the present. He often talked about their future, but mostly, he told her how much he loved her and asked if she would please wake up. He couldn't stand to be out of the room for more than a minute.

It had been two and a half days since Dr. Meyers had stopped the medicine. It seemed longer, but it hadn't all been bad. Tyler, Martha, and Brenda had become quite close. They had managed to relax and have some fun in spite of the situation. Tyler had sent Liz to get some nail polish. She had returned with a dozen bottles, and Tyler painted each one of Penny's toes a different color. Everyone in the hospital had come to see that.

No one mentioned it, but they all knew the longer she stayed in a coma, the greater the chance that she would never wake up.

"Hey, Mr. H, how ya doin'?" Vince queried with his Brooklyn accent from the door.

"I'm okay," Tyler said. "Hey Vince, come here. I want to show you something." Tyler pulled the covers back so Vince could see Penny's feet. "What do you think?"

Vince laughed and said, "I took Liz to get that nail polish, but I didn't think you'd use 'em all." Vince looked up at Penny. "Miss Penny, you just got to wake up and see your toes. They look really good.

"Mr. H, Liz sent me to get you and bring you back for a quick shower. She said you were gonna stink up Miss Penny's room again."

"Maybe later, Vince," Tyler responded. "I need to be here."

"Tyler, you must get out of here," Martha ordered. "You need a little break. Please go with Vince. I promise to call you if something changes."

"Okay, but I won't be long," Tyler whined. He leaned over and kissed Penny on the forehead. "Love you, babe, and I'll smell really good when I get back."

In the elevator with Vince, Tyler almost decided to go back up to the room. Guilt was part of the reason, but not all. He had gone over and over it in his mind. Why had she come to the airport? Why had she driven across the field toward the runway? He would never know if she didn't wake up and tell him.

* * *

Tyler felt like an actor in a melodrama. He hated those afternoon soap operas, yet his life lately, if written into a script, could have been nominated for an Emmy. He was just a character now, forced to read lines and play a part he hated. Why had he lost control?

He knew the answer. He just didn't like it. He had lost control of his life and his relationship with Penny because of his pride. If Granddad Luke were there now, he would give Tyler a swift kick in the pants. What a mess he had made of things.

If there was a time machine for sale, he would buy it. Damn the cost! Tyler had gotten his precious feelings hurt, grabbed some paper, and left Penny an absurd letter. His stupid pride had caused him to get angry. He almost laughed out loud as he remembered what he'd written: "It's over! Our relationship could never work! Don't contact me! I don't want to be friends!"

He had never stopped loving Penny. That was impossible. He had just had a momentary lapse into shit-for-brains mode. Granddad's words haunted him: "Pride and Passion. They can be used for good or bad. You have a great capacity. Promise me you will always use them for good."

Tyler was ashamed now as he remembered the promise he had broken. If only he could go back, but no, it was too late. Nothing could change things now. Weary, he decided to take a little nap. His room adjoined Vince's, so he pushed the door between them open and asked Vince to wake him in an hour.

*   *   *

Tyler glanced at Martha and Brenda on the seat across from him. They were crying and looking out the window as the limo turned onto the campus of Winfield College. Penny's stepfather was in another car.

Vince steered the car through the campus and stopped in front of the most beautiful building there. Someone opened the door, and he waited for Brenda and Martha to emerge. When Tyler was outside, he straightened to his full height. He positioned himself between the two ladies, and they began to climb the steps. He looked up into the sun of a perfect mid-September day and saw the splendid steeple atop the Winfield College Chapel. It held no beauty for him that day.

The sanctuary seated more than one thousand people, and it was full. Tyler was aware that every eye was on him as they entered. It was difficult to breathe. The weight of the moment was pressing on his chest. He wanted so badly to be anywhere except there, but he had to do this. As he ushered the ladies down the center aisle, his eyes avoided the front of the chapel. He knew Penny was there, waiting.

While glancing from side to side, he was shocked to see so many people he knew. Family, friends, faculty, board of trustees, business associates, his employees, and the curious—they were all there. He tried to make eye contact with as many as possible.

They reached their reserved spaces on the front pew next to the aisle. Martha and Brenda went in first, while Tyler sat on the end. He looked up now into an enormous array of flowers. There were bunches of flowers everywhere. The entire front of the chapel, with the exception of the area around the pulpit, was obscured.

Finally, he looked at the casket. Brenda had told him what to expect. It sat low on a pedestal and was open for viewing. The casket was a rich ivory color with a light-pink lining. Penny's hair was styled the way she would have liked. She was a little thinner, but still strikingly attractive. As the minister began the funeral service, Tyler studied those features he had so loved—the prominent cheeks, the perfect nose, the full lips, and the chin and neckline that made her unique.

Around her neck was the locket that he had given her with her profile on the front. Placed between her long fingers over her chest was a single long-stemmed pink rosebud. Attached to the stem was a delicate white piece of ribbon with writing on it. Tyler had chosen it earlier. It simply said, "Love, Tyler." As he read the ribbon, he began to lose control. Brenda quickly held his hand and put her arm around him.

The funeral droned on with words and music. Tyler tried to listen but could only dwell on his own thoughts. Then the funeral director appeared and began to invite the closest friends and relatives to come forward for a final viewing. Tyler attempted to stand but never left the seat.

Memories of the wheelchair flooded him. He tried again—nothing. This was not physical. He knew his brain was shutting down from overload, and he felt like a fool. He had to get up and walk, but he couldn't. His heart was racing, and he felt faint. Tyler glanced at the casket and Penny. How do you say good-bye when you know it's forever? He needed help.

"Mr. H, Mr. H, you all right?" Vince asked.

Tyler felt Vince's hand on his shoulder. He tried to tell him he needed help, but the words were garbled.

"It's okay, Mr. H. I'm here. You was screaming."

Tyler didn't remember screaming. He turned and looked up at Vince, who was wearing a bright-yellow golf shirt.

"Vince, why in the hell would you wear that shirt to a funeral?"

Vince looked dumbfounded. "This ain't no funeral. Hey, Mr. H, you sure you're okay? I think maybe you was havin' one of them nightmares."

"Vince, how long did I sleep?"

Vince glanced at his watch. "Okay, Mr. H, don't get mad. I need to tell you what happened. When you laid down, I called Brenda, and she said you was worn out, so I was to let you sleep. So, I kept checking, and you was sleeping real good. Then, I heard you yelling. That's when I came and woke you up. You was asleep for about six hours."

"It's all right," Tyler assured him. "I needed the rest. You were right about the nightmare. I guess that's why I was yelling."

Vince smiled. "I'm just glad you're okay, 'cause you sounded like you was dying."

"I'm fine. As soon as I get dressed and splash on some aftershave, we'll head back to the hospital."

Tyler had his pants on and was deciding which shirt to wear when he heard the phone ring in Vince's room. He chose a green golf shirt with the Harrison logo and tugged it over his head. When he turned, Vince was standing in the doorway with a big grin on his face.

"Mr. H, you ready to go?" Vince asked.

"Almost, Vince."

"Good, 'cause Miss Penny is awake!"

Chapter 43

Going Home

The medical center was huge. Tyler and Vince experienced a severe case of euphoria as they tracked through the hospital. They were met with smiles and hugs at the nurses' station. Penny's room looked like a conference room. It seemed Tyler and Vince had been the last to receive the news. Her room was a large private suite at the end of the hall.

People began to separate when they saw Tyler. Finally, he glimpsed the bed but found it empty. What he saw next would always be unforgettable. Granddad Luke would have coined it a sight for sore eyes.

Penny was seated in a fabric chair. Her hair and makeup looked great, and she was wearing a gorgeous white and pink nightgown that wasn't hospital-issued. A tray of scrambled eggs and toast was resting in front of her.

She was attempting to answer questions from Dr. Meyers and stuff eggs and toast in at an eating-contest pace. Tyler knew she had only received a few cans of brown liquid food through a tube and a constant fluid drip for seven days and thought she looked more like a really hungry visitor than a patient.

Suddenly, she dropped the fork and began pushing the cart away. She reached for Dr. Meyers on one side and Brenda on the other. "Help me up," she demanded.

Dr. Meyers reached out to help and said, "Okay, Penny, but take it nice and slow."

Tyler knew this was one of those rare and special moments. It was confusion, happiness, unbounded love, and his faith being simultaneously mixed in a cauldron of irony. Every nerve ending that could sense pleasure was on overload. He started toward her, but she raised her hand, indicating he should wait. She began slowly to close the distance between them.

Although visibly weak, the determination was etched or her face. When she was but a whisper away, she stopped and gazed into Tyler's eyes. She began to smile. Penny reached out and let her hand linger on his face.

"I've loved you every day of my life since high school. We've been foolish and allowed events to separate us. For some reason I may never understand, we have another chance. I'm back, and we'll never be separated again. Do you hear me, Tyler? Never again!"

"Yes, Penny. I hear you. Never again."

*   *   *

Dr. Meyers insisted that she remain at the medical center for another five days. He explained how the brain was very adept at healing itself, especially when the patient was young. But there were no guarantees. He wanted her close for observation and some additional testing. Penny was not happy but relented. She even agreed to let Tyler go to Maryland and catch up on business. He did, however, promise to telephone many times each day.

Penny's mood was finally better. The past five days in the hospital had seemed a month. Tyler had kept his promise and called often, and now he was back with her. She was elated to be so miraculously on the mend, but she needed Tyler. They needed time together, and they would finally have it.

Tyler had been her manservant all morning. He had eaten breakfast with her, helped her pack, pushed her wheelchair down to the lobby, and put her in the Harrison limo. As he slid in behind her, he told Vince, "Get the hell out of here."

She turned and said, "I love this new limo. It's the first time I've seen it. There's so much more room in this one."

"You can thank Vince," Tyler said. "He picked it out."

"Hey, Vince," Penny ventured in her best New York accent, "you done good."

"Thanks, Miss Penny. I knew you would like it. It's real classy, like you. You still have all your toes painted a different color?"

Penny laughed and punched Tyler on the shoulder. "How did you know about that?" she asked.

Vince giggled and answered, "Mr. H showed me. He was real proud of them."

"I'm sure he was," she added.

With all of her attention focused on Tyler, she said, "So why exactly did you leave that nasty letter?"

Tyler pushed the button on the rear control panel that would close the privacy glass between them and Vince. As the divider slowly ascended, Tyler chuckled. "Vince, Miss Penny is about to say some bad words, and I know you have virgin ears."

Vince laughed loudly and replied, "Thanks, Mr. H."

"Why do you think I left a nasty letter?" Tyler questioned.

"Oh, no you don't. It's not up to me to explain your message," Penny replied.

"I've thought about it and regretted it many times. I know it caused the accident. I'd tried to be romantic in my attempts to win you back, but it wasn't working, and I guess it hurt my feelings."

"You mean your pride," she interrupted.

"Yes, damn it, my pride," he bristled.

"Thank you for being honest. We have to do this if we're going to be together. We're not in high school now, and we must stop playing games. We have to talk to each other and be honest when we disagree."

"I tried, Penny."

"I know you did, sweetheart. I was wrong. I've been guilty too. I know how much you love me, and I should've listened. The accident wasn't your fault. It was mine. When I got the message, I panicked and overreacted. I was afraid I'd lose you again."

"Why wouldn't you believe me, Penny? You know I don't love Geena, and I never did."

"Tyler, one of your most endearing qualities is your innocence. Most women who meet you want you. You're so friendly and sweet that you encourage them without even knowing it. Honestly, sometimes I'm just a jealous bitch."

"Okay, I can vouch for that," he said with a laugh.

"Stop it! Shame on you," she complained. "Really, sometimes I feel like I'm living a fantasy. I'm smart and not bad to look at, but I'm just a small-town girl. I guess it scares me sometimes. You can have or buy almost anything you want. It's just difficult to believe that you want me so badly. What happens if I can't live up to your expectations?"

Tyler placed his hand over hers and said, "You already have, babe. You're beautiful, smart, educated, sweet, and more special than you'll ever know. I have a real talent for ideas and making money, but I've never been good at philosophy. I won't attempt to define or explain love for anyone else. I only know you consume my thoughts. Everything in my life is better and brighter when I'm with you. Nothing I've ever done, or any success I've ever had, can compete with the joy I feel when we're together. I've never experienced that with another person. For me, that is pure love. You'll always be special to me."

Penny turned and gazed out the window for a little extra time to compose herself. "I'll never know how you do that. You always manage to touch me deeply. You're pretty special yourself, Mr. Harrison."

"Thank you, babe. We're so blessed, and you're right. We must always put our love for each other first and make certain that it endures."

Penny smiled warmly. "You've got a deal. Now, tell me about your plane."

Tyler smirked. "Oh, haven't you heard? Some crazy-ass woman crashed into it with her Corvette."

"Yes, I did hear about that," she said. "Was there much damage?"

"Depends on your definition of much. Two mechanics and a pilot flew in and did temporary repairs. Then they flew it to National Airport just outside Washington, DC, for the final repairs. Liz told me they finished and delivered it back to Stratford and put it in the hanger yesterday. We can use it whenever we want."

Penny hesitated and then asked, "Dare I ask how much it cost for all the repairs?"

"A little over seventy thousand."

"Wow! That much? I'm sorry I asked."

"Forget about it, Penny. I have you back. You're worth it, you know."

"I'm glad you think so, sweetheart. I don't think I'll ever get used to you having all that money. Oh, that reminds me. You never mentioned it. Is it okay if I keep the million dollars?"

Tyler gave her a confused look. "What million dollars?" he asked.

"You know. The million dollars I took when I left you."

"I'm not following you, babe. I don't understand."

"When I saw you with Geena at your penthouse, I ran. I went to the Washington Hilton that night. I was so angry and jealous that I only slept about an hour. The next morning, I took a cab to your bank and used that fancy credit card for a million-dollar cash advance. I asked for cash, but the nice manager gave me a cashier's check."

Tyler laughed so hard, he cried. Penny didn't see the humor until she realized why he was laughing. "Tyler, are you telling me that you didn't know I had taken the money?"

"Yes, babe. I swear. I guess Liz figured I was so upset when you wouldn't take my calls, she just never mentioned it. She did tell me you had cut up the card and sent it back, though."

"Holy crap, Tyler. That's almost sinful. You didn't even miss a million dollars."

"Well, I'm sure it was missed. We make a lot of money. That's why we established the foundation and give so much back. And the answer is yes. Of course you can keep the money."

Penny smiled and gave him a kiss. They snuggled and discussed plans for the next couple of weeks. The college had granted her as much leave time as she needed, and Tyler had promised to take her anywhere she wanted to go. She hadn't realized how difficult it was to decide where to go and what to do when the choices were endless. They were still finalizing plans when they realized the limo had stopped.

"We're here, Mr. H," Vince said over the speakers.

"Thanks, Vince," Tyler answered with his rear speaker button. He lowered the glass in the rear door on Penny's side.

When she looked out, she noticed they were parked on College Avenue in front of the old Eden West mansion. It appeared that it had become a construction project.

"Oh my! What's going on? Are they going to tear it down?" Penny asked.

"No, babe. You know the college owns it, but it's not on college property. President Fairchild and his wife only used a few rooms. The college couldn't afford to fix up the old place, so they've been trying to sell it for years. They finally found a buyer, and the Fairchilds have moved out. I'm sorry to tell you that you'll never get to attend another official college function there hosted by the Fairchilds."

She sighed and said, "I know it's silly, but I always felt like a princess when I dressed up and went to a party there. Do you know who bought it?"

Tyler frowned. "Yes, the decision was made at the trustees' meeting in late August, just before school started. It's supposed to be a secret until the end of the year. It was purchased by a rich, snobbish bitch who wants to live there."

"Do I know who she is?" Penny asked.

"Well, yes, I'm sure you've heard of her," Tyler replied.

"So, who is she?" Penny demanded.

"Babe, you have to promise to keep it quiet. I wouldn't want to compromise my seat on the Board of Trustees."

Penny leaned over so he could whisper. She loved gossip and secrets.

"I promise, Tyler. I won't tell anyone."

"Okay, if you promise," he said. "The buyer's name is Dr. Penny Kilmer."

"Who?" she muttered with an empty look.

"Dr. Penny Kilmer," he snickered.

She ventured, "But how … I mean … I didn't …"

Tyler just crossed his arms, sat back, and smirked.

"What did you do, Tyler Harrison?"

Tyler leaned forward, took her hands in his, and kissed her lightly. "I bought Eden West for us, but it will be in your name. I know how you've always loved going there, so after you sign a few papers, it will be all yours. Besides, we're going to need a place to live."

Penny kissed him quickly and then lingered for a longer kiss. "Does that mean what I think it does?"

He wrinkled his brow. "I don't know, babe. What do you think it means?"

"Well, I thought, maybe, it was a proposal."

"Oh, no. I'm sorry. I think we both just assume we'll get married and raise a family, but we need to spend some time together first. When I propose, it will be very special."

She smiled. "Really? How special?"

"Very special, babe. You know I'm a romantic devil."

"I know you're a devil, so don't wait too long," she mused.

"What's too long?" he asked.

"Well," she chuckled, "if some day you get a kick in the crotch, you'll know it's been too long."

"But I thought you loved my crotch."

"Oh, wow. You're right. Make that your shin."

Chapter 44

❧━━━◦◦❤◦◦━━━❧

Fear of the Future

*P*enny was soaking in her tub. She was exhausted. It was early January 1972, and her second semester at Winfield would begin tomorrow. The renovation of Eden West would be completed sometime in April. She and Tyler had spent the best month of her life together—Christmas shopping in Maryland with Tyler; the Christmas party at Vanguard for all Harrison employees, where the large bonus checks were given out; Christmas with the families in Stratford, where Tyler had given Grandma Ruth a new Lincoln; and skiing in Aspen, where she discovered that all homes on the mountain must be named with an official sign. Tyler had taken care of that before they arrived, and their chalet was named "Penny's Pleasure" with a very beautiful new sign. She giggled when she thought about the pleasure she had enjoyed there on a thick, soft, furry rug in front of a roaring fire.

No wonder she was tired. She had seen more, done more, and made love more in the past few months than most other women would in their whole lives. For New Year's Eve, Tyler had staged a grand opening of the new tennis shoe factory in Stratford, complete with fireworks. He had started a nationwide advertising campaign, which featured some of the country's most famous athletes.

The company already had more orders than they could fill. She wondered if there was anything Tyler Harrison couldn't do if he set his mind to it. He had even found her a dreamy new bathtub for Eden West. It was a huge double tub with water jets, and Tyler had promised to bathe with her often.

The end of the year also brought a new revelation. Penny had wracked her brain trying to figure out how and when her man would pop the question. She believed she finally had the answer. Tyler was now a man of the world, but she knew he was conservative and a bit old-fashioned. He would propose and marry her when he could take her to a proper home, and Eden West would soon be ready to welcome its new tenants. She could only imagine how grand her life would be living with Tyler in her mansion.

*   *   *

It was early April, and her ten-day spring break would begin the following week. Penny caught a glimpse of the gray sky through the leafless tree limbs and mused how this dreary day so perfectly fit her mood. She glanced now at the windshield wipers as they moved in perfect harmony without really seeing them. They were working to wipe away the cold spring rain. She was vaguely aware of Kate, who was beside her, driving the car.

"Penny, are you okay?" Kate asked.

"What?" Penny responded. "I'm sorry, Kate. Yes, I guess. I don't feel very well."

"I'm sorry. You didn't seem like yourself when I picked you up. Do you want me to take you back home?"

"No, no. I'm sure I'll be fine," she lied. "I skipped breakfast this morning. I'll have one of Grandma's homemade biscuits. They can cure anything."

"Good idea," Kate said. "Maybe I'll join you."

Kate steered the Buick onto the wide gravel driveway and parked next to Grandma's shiny, new Lincoln that Tyler had given her for Christmas. They filled their arms with enough cleaning supplies to do the whole farm and dashed toward the front porch through the cold rain. They were greeted with an open door and a smiling Ruth.

When Penny went through the living room, she couldn't help but notice Granddad Luke's empty recliner. She was glad she had come. If she missed him, she could only guess how Grandma must feel.

Grandma said, "My God, Kate, do you think you brought enough cleaning stuff?"

Kate said, "I'm pretty sure if we need it, I brought it."

"Grandma, do you have any of those wonderful homemade biscuits?" Penny asked.

"I always have biscuits, girl."

"I skipped breakfast," Penny ventured. "May I have one with some grape jelly?"

"You sure can, child. You sit down, and I'll get it."

"Since you're fixing, I'll take one too," Kate offered.

Ruth laughed. "All right, you two. One biscuit, and then we get to work."

"We promise, Grandma," Kate said.

Penny stared at the half-eaten biscuit. "Excuse me for a minute," she said before heading for the bathroom where she knew she would throw up.

When she returned to the kitchen table, Grandma said, "You look awful, child. Are you okay?"

Penny tried to smile. "Yes … well, no." Then she burst into tears.

"Sweetheart, it's okay," Grandma ventured. "What's wrong?"

Penny looked up through her tears and said, "I'm pregnant!"

A small pin hitting the floor would have sounded like a Japanese gong.

"My God, Penny. How did that happen?" Kate said.

Grandma quickly offered, "I guess they were getting it on, and she got knocked up."

When the spontaneous laughter subsided, Penny said, "Thank you, Grandma. I needed that."

Kate asked, "Are you sure, Penny?"

"Yes. The doctor confirmed it yesterday."

"But, Penny, you sweet child, why are you upset?" Grandma asked.

"Tyler doesn't know, and I'm scared."

"Why on earth would you be scared?" Grandma asked.

"Because I know Tyler. Everything in his life is planned. He's not obsessive-compulsive, but his life is very ordered, and that's the way he likes it. I wonder if I can sue the bastards that made those birth control pills. Everyone in America will soon be laughing at Tyler and me. If there is anything Tyler hates, it's someone laughing at him. Trust me, I know. You know how proud he is."

Kate thought for a moment and said, "Penny, I think he'll be pleased. You know he's crazy about you. Surely, after all the time you two have spent together, you must've talked about having children someday."

"Well, yes, we did, and that's why I'm scared. He's always said he wanted a family, and we shouldn't wait too long. But he also said he wanted to wait a few years, so we could spend those early years with just the two of us together."

Grandma said, "Penny, you must stop punishing yourself. This isn't your fault. Two people in love have to deal with life's little surprises when they come along. You need to tell him. You can't carry this burden alone."

"I know. You're right, Grandma. I'll tell him next weekend. He's coming home, so we can be together for spring break."

"Do you think you should wait that long?" Kate asked.

"No, but I don't have a choice. I won't see him until then, and I must tell him in person. I won't do it over the phone."

"Don't worry yourself now, child," Grandma offered. "I'm sure everything will be fine."

"I'm sure you're right, Grandma. Now enough about me. Let's get this place cleaned up."

They set about the spring cleaning, and somehow Penny managed to help them get it done without having another nausea attack.

Chapter 45

Penny's Birthday

Penny was awake now. Well, as awake as one could be after only one cup of coffee on a lazy Sunday morning. She was having trouble getting her head wrapped around being a mother. She had money and could do almost anything she wanted. Why not take a long weekend, slip up to New York, and get an abortion? There were always rumors in Stratford about others who had. Goose bumps appeared as a pang of guilt flowed through her. It had only been a momentary thought, and she scolded herself for having it. No matter what happened, she could never do such a thing.

Still, she couldn't help it. She was scared, and her mind raced. *How will Tyler react? My life is so perfect. No doubt it will change with the birth of my baby—no, our baby—but how?*

Penny was in no hurry to become an old fuddy-duddy. She was only thirty. *Oh my God!* Penny thought. With the pregnancy news, she had forgotten! *Today is my thirty-first birthday.* This one didn't seem too important, but reaching thirty last year had been a little depressing. It wouldn't be the first birthday she had celebrated without Tyler, but oh, how she wished he were with her.

No matter how hard she tried to push it away, the fear was still there. It was a physical fear. Although rare these days, some women died giving birth. But all women who gave birth suffered enormous stress to their bodies. She knew God had blessed—or damned, depending on one's point of view—women when He gave them female plumbing and decided in His great wisdom that they would be birthing the babies. If she could get her hands on the infamous Eve from the Garden of Eden, she might just kick her ass!

And then there was her body. She had to admit that she liked hers just the way it was, thank you very much. Sure, she would make a little change here or there, but overall, it was a great body, and she enjoyed being in it. Tyler Harrison certainly loved it. How would he welcome the changes, and exactly how much change would there be? Well, she had a pretty good idea. There would be a big belly, a bigger ass, probably bigger thighs, and for a while, bigger boobs. Then, after birth, she could look forward to needing to lose thirty or forty pounds, saggy skin, and stretch marks.

She needed more coffee. She was deep in thought about breast-feeding when the phone rang.

"Hey, babe," the voice on the other end said. "I'm crazy mad 'bout you!"

"Of course you are, sweetheart, but then, who wouldn't be?" she snickered.

"Well, that guy Milton seems quite happy with the big-breasted redhead since he dumped you."

"Shut up, Tyler. And I dumped him."

He changed the subject very quickly. "Hey, I almost forgot." He then broke into his best rendition of "Happy Birthday." But instead of using her name, he changed it to include all of her body parts that he loved.

"Wow, that was quite a song, crazy man."

"It was for a very special lady," Tyler noted. "I'm sorry I can't be there, babe."

"Me, too. I miss you."

"Did you get your present yet?"

"No."

"Well, that would be because it hasn't been delivered."

"You're so clever," Penny said.

"I know, but I can tell you this. It's wrapped in a large box with a big tag that says: open me first."

"Really? Sounds mysterious. What is it?" Penny asked.

"It's a secret," Tyler told her.

"Well, when will it be delivered?"

"That's a secret too."

She gave up. They talked about their plans for spring break, and then he had to go. She was wondering what the big present would be when the telephone rang again.

"Hello?"

"Happy Birthday, baby sister. I have a present for you," Brenda said.

"Is it from Tyler?"

"No, silly, it's from me."

"Oh," Penny said.

"I'll give it to you at lunch."

* * *

As Brenda and Penny began to enter the restaurant, they both stopped. Someone on the street was yelling for Ms. Kilmer to stop. Penny stepped back onto the sidewalk so she could see to the left and right. To her left on the sidewalk, about a hundred feet away, she saw their project manager for the renovation of Eden West waving his arms and running toward her.

"Slow down, Wayne, before you break a leg," Penny shouted.

Wayne slowed to a slow jog and caught his breath.

"What's wrong? Why are you running?" she asked.

He stopped and took a couple deep breaths. "Sorry to startle you, Ms. Kilmer. I'm afraid there's a problem with the granite countertops in the kitchen."

Penny noticed the confused look on Brenda's face and wondered if she had ever met Wayne.

"Wayne, this is my sister, Brenda. Brenda, this is Wayne Ross. Wayne is the project manager for the renovation at Eden West. He comes from the Cape Cod area of Massachusetts, and he is an expert at renovating large older homes."

"It's very nice to meet you, Brenda, but I think I've seen you before nosing around over at Eden West. Are all the ladies here in West Virginia this pretty?"

Brenda answered quickly. "There are many pretty ladies around here, but no, Penny and I are definitely the prettiest."

"Wayne, are you flirting with my sister?" Penny questioned.

Wayne glanced at his feet and sheepishly answered, "Maybe."

"How old are those boots you're wearing?" Penny asked.

"I'm not sure. Pretty old, I guess."

"I don't know if you know it or not, but Brenda owns Classic Shoes at the other end of Main Street."

"Really?" Wayne smiled. "Do you sell boots?"

"We sure do," Brenda answered.

"Good. I might just see you on Monday."

"Okay, enough about you two," Penny chuckled. "What's the problem with the countertops?"

"Well, there're five men who came down from Pittsburgh to install the countertops, and I made them wait. I don't think the color of the granite is what you ordered, and they're not very happy. Could you come up and take a quick look?"

"Brenda, do you mind?" Penny asked.

"No, that's fine. We can have lunch a little later. Come on. I'll drive you," Brenda offered.

"Okay, great. We'll meet you there, Wayne."

*   *   *

Brenda steered her car onto the new flagstone and stopped under the huge portico.

"Penny, I still can't believe you own this place, and you're going to live here with Tyler."

"I can't either. It's like a dream. Of course, the dream would be better if my special man would ever get around to proposing," Penny noted.

"What's he waiting for?" Brenda asked.

"Damned if I know. Come on, let's go look at some countertops."

Wayne had caught up with them. When they reached the large double front doors, he opened one and said, "After you, ladies."

Penny went in first and glanced down at the beautiful new polished marble foyer floor with its unique pattern and completely missed what was ahead of her.

"Surprise!"

Penny gasped, stepped backward, and then hung her head down with shock. With her head still down, she gave a weak wave. She recovered as the group began a loud, somewhat off-key version of "Happy Birthday."

Penny smiled and shook her finger at the group, as if to say, "Shame on you." She then turned so she could make eye contact with Brenda and Wayne. "You two need to know that both of you are now on my stinky list."

Brenda and Wayne grinned back and seemed quite pleased that they had been added to the list.

While the boisterous group continued to sing, Penny took a moment to scan the crowd. She saw many friends, college faculty, Harrison employees, her family, Tyler's family, and right square in the middle, singing her heart out, was Grandma Ruth.

As the singing and applause died down, Tyler's assistant, Liz, came forward and gave Penny a warm hug. "Happy birthday, Penny," she said.

"Was this your idea?" Penny asked.

"Oh, no! You're not going to blame this on me," Liz answered.

"Let me guess," Penny said. "Tyler Harrison, right?"

"Right," Liz said.

Penny glanced at the group now, searching for her man.

"I'm sorry, Penny," Liz said. "He's not here. I spoke with him this morning, and he's pissed. He had so much fun planning this for you, but he's in the middle of a new TV advertising campaign for Harrison Properties, and this was the only time the studio was available. I hope he doesn't kill someone out in California."

"He called me this morning and sang 'Happy Birthday' to me, but I was hoping …"

"No, I'm sorry, and I know he is too. But I know he's having a special gift delivered for you today. Now come on. There are a lot of people here who want to see you."

*　　*　　*

The party was well underway, and everyone wanted a tour of the newly remodeled Eden West. Penny had just finished the last tour. She had taken nine groups of ten people each on the grand tour. When she finished, Penny plopped down on the sofa between Liz and Grandma Ruth.

"You know," Penny said, "every time I go through this place, I find more things I love about it."

Liz answered, "It is amazing. Only Tyler could do all this in such a short amount of time and get it all so perfect."

Penny laughed. "You know, when Tyler and I dated in high school, I knew he was different and special, but I could never imagine all this. I pinch myself every day to make sure I'm not dreaming. I still can't believe he loves me so much. I'm just a small-town girl, and he could have almost any woman he wants. I don't think I'll every fully understand why he chose me."

"If you really want to know," Liz answered, "I'm sure I can tell you. He has only told me about a thousand times."

"Does he talk about me with you?"

"All the time, Penny. It's his favorite pastime. Penny said this, and Penny did that. He is consumed with you."

Penny smiled. "I hope he doesn't overdo it."

"No, he doesn't. He always does it in a cute way. I only wish my man loved me that much. You know, I've thought about him a lot. I don't think most other men have the capacity to love as deeply as Tyler loves you."

"I agree with you, Liz," Grandma added. "When Tyler is with me, he always babbles about you. I love hearing him, and I think it's sweet. It's so like him. Don't forget his family nickname—Pride and Passion. He is passionate about you and so very proud of you."

"Thank you, Grandma. I love that he shares that with you. Okay, Liz, so why did he choose me?"

"All right, I'll paraphrase, but these are like direct quotes. I can picture him grinning from ear to ear and saying, 'She is so intelligent and knows what she wants. She is so damn funny and always full of surprises. She's an awesome lover.'"

"Oh my God!" Penny gasped. "He told you that?"

"Yes, but he left out the details, even though I tried to get more information."

"Shame on you, Liz," Penny said.

"I know, right?" Liz giggled. "A woman can never get too much information about how to please her man, and evidently, you're quite good at it."

Penny blushed. "If you say so. What else?"

Liz continued, "He said he loves it when you two go somewhere, and although he has been on TV and everyone knows who he is, the people always stare at you. He said it's not just because you're beautiful, but because your beauty is classic and unique. He loves your drive and determination, and he's very proud of your accomplishments and the education degrees you've earned. He said he would never be happy with a weak woman. He likes your streak of independence and your pride. And finally, he said he loves your personality, because you're feisty, and you're a smart-ass."

"Wow! Thank you, Liz. That's quite a list. I guess he's told me all those things in one way or another, but I sort of thought he was just being romantic and sweet. It makes it more believable when it comes from someone else. I know how much he trusts you. I'll never tell him what you told me."

Liz smiled. "It's okay, Penny. I know he wouldn't mind."

"Excuse me, Penny," Brenda interrupted. "I'm sorry to break in, but you need to come see this."

Penny couldn't help but notice that everyone seemed to be making a mad dash for the front yard. As soon as she stepped outside under the portico, she wondered if a tornado was coming. She could hear a loud roar and feel a tremendous rush of wind. As she made her way, with Grandma right behind her, the sound began to come in waves. She could see other people, not under the portico, shielding their eyes and looking upward.

When she cleared the edge of the roof, she could see what all the fuss was about. There was a huge helicopter hovering above the treetops, and something was slowly being lowered from it.

Penny looked closely as a huge, square box wrapped in bright-red paper and topped with a large silver bow came down. The box was resting on a very large pallet attached to four cables, one on each corner. All four cables were attached to a big steel hook about twenty feet above. The pallet and its contents finally settled on the driveway.

From above, a booming male voice said through a megaphone, "Would someone please unhook the cables?"

Penny could see someone with a safety harness leaning out of the chopper and speaking into a mechanical megaphone. Wayne began waving his arms and moving toward the container. The helicopter guy had lowered the hook, and Wayne quickly released the four cables. He stepped back and waved his arms. The helicopter began to ascend at a much faster speed than it had descended.

When it was gone, Wayne said, "Hey, Penny, look at this." He was holding up a large piece of silver ribbon that said: "Open me first."

Liz stepped up and touched Penny's arm. "Well, you've got to admit it. The man ain't boring."

Penny laughed. "Oh, no! Passionate, somewhat pushy, often loud, more than a little strange, but never boring."

"Stop yakking and open your present," Grandma yelled.

"Will you help me, Grandma?"

"You betcha, girl. Come on," Grandma said.

Penny stepped forward slowly, trying to imagine what it might be. It was too small for a car and too large for an engagement ring. *Well*, she thought, *it might be a ring. Tyler had often wrapped a small package in a succession of larger boxes.*

"Hurry up, girl," Grandma said from behind.

"Okay, Grandma," Penny answered. She grabbed the large ribbon and yanked. The ribbon with the bow tore away, and she threw it on the driveway.

"Wayne, I may need some help with this lid," Penny observed.

They both grasped the lid and began to lift. When it flew upward so quickly, Penny wondered if the package had exploded. She screamed and fell backward, but Wayne caught her. Before she could catch her breath, she heard a very loud "Surprise!" coming from the package.

Tyler sprang up wearing a handsome dark business suit and a ridiculous happy birthday party hat. He quickly jumped over the edge of the box and landed on the ground in front of Penny. Before she could react, Tyler picked her up in his arms, spun her around and around, set her back down. "Happy birthday, babe."

Penny recovered quickly, wondered how high her skirt was while she was spinning, and hugged Tyler as if she would never let go.

"Tyler Harrison, you almost scared me to death! What would you have done if I would have fainted or had a heart attack?"

Tyler answered quickly, "I'm thinking mouth-to-mouth with booby massage."

"Oh my God, Tyler, you are so bad."

"Yes, but that's good, right?"

"That's very good, Mr. Harrison," Penny answered as she kissed him.

Their guests were yelling and applauding. Tyler broke away and bowed to the guests, and Penny did a superb curtsy.

"What are you grinning at, Tyler?" Penny asked.

"I just love looking at you."

Penny immediately saw herself standing in front of Tyler naked in about six or seven months. "I hope you'll always feel that way, Tyler."

"You know I will, babe. Now, come on. We have a party to go to."

*   *   *

The party was fabulous. Presents were opened, and cake was eaten. Nothing was pretentious. Penny watched and was amazed again at Tyler. He was always so relaxed and shared his time freely with everyone. It was no wonder he was successful and loved. Penny had always loved this old mansion and how she always felt like a princess while there. It was so like

Tyler to make sure it was perfect and give it to her. If she loved him one more ounce, she would burst.

Penny stopped daydreaming and asked for quiet. When the guests were silent, she said, "Please excuse Tyler and me. We have a couple of matters we must attend to. This won't take long, so please don't leave just yet. We'll be right back."

She led him to the master bedroom.

"Babe, this is the first time I've seen this room with furniture. You did a great job," Tyler said. "I love it."

"Thank you," Penny said as she led Tyler to one of the two love seats in the sitting area. "Sit down, Tyler. We need to talk."

Tyler sat as ordered, and asked, "About what?"

"Just hush. I'm getting to it."

Penny turned and began to walk around. When she had gathered her thoughts, she stopped in front of Tyler. "Tyler, I … I … need to tell … you something." She was beginning to cry.

Tyler sprang from the love seat and took her into his arms. "Sweetheart, it's okay. I'm here. You can tell me anything."

Penny stepped back and dried her eyes. "Okay, I've had my cry. Sit down."

He sat.

"Okay, Tyler, here it is. We're going to have a baby," she finally announced.

"What?" he asked.

"We're going to have a baby!"

"What do you mean?"

"I mean, I'm pregnant!"

"What the hell? How did this happen?"

"Well, according to Grandma Ruth, we were gettin' it on, and I got knocked up."

"Grandma already knows?"

"Yes," she said.

"Who else knows?"

"Your mother and the doctor."

In a confused and angry voice, Tyler said, "Damn it, what a mess! How pregnant are you?"

Penny couldn't help herself. She gave him the look. "One hundred percent!"

"I know that, Penny. I mean how long have you been pregnant?"

Penny couldn't help it. She had to smile. Mr. Hot Shot, Tyler Harrison, appeared to be in a mild state of shock. "Well, I checked the calendar for dates when we were together, and the doctor and I think about six weeks."

"Wow, six weeks."

"Yes, sweetheart."

"So, what do you think happened?"

"Well, I'm not certain, but—"

"What?" Tyler asked.

"Jesus, Tyler. Stop saying what. I guess the birth control pills are not foolproof."

"Are you sure you didn't miss one or two?"

"Yes, Tyler, I'm sure. And if you ask me if I'm sure this baby is yours, I'm going to kick you in the crotch."

"Okay. I'm not going to ask that."

"Are you okay, Tyler?" Penny asked.

Tyler did not look happy as he got up and walked across the room. "Jesus, Penny. I'm not ready for this. I don't know what to say. I don't need this now. I'm afraid this changes everything."

Penny's heart sank. *What the hell did that mean?* she wondered. It meant her greatest fear was on the mark. This was not planned. Tyler had not given his approval. His precious schedule would be altered, and the famous Tyler Harrison would be a laughing stock with his fat-ass, pregnant girlfriend. No way in hell would his pride allow this to happen.

"Tyler, turn around and look at me." When she saw his face, she almost felt sorry for him. He looked like he was in shock. "Do I own Eden West?" Penny asked.

He still looked confused, but he answered, "Yes."

"You're sure? Everything is legal, and I'm the sole owner?"

"Yes, of course I'm sure. Why would you ask me that now?"

She could literally taste the bile. The anger and disappointment was seething inside her. She forced herself to be in control. She had to do this. "I want you to leave. Get out of my house!"

"What?" he questioned.

"Stop saying that," she said. "Just go, Tyler."

"Why do you want me to leave?"

"Isn't that obvious? You haven't hugged me or kissed me. You said this changes everything. It's clear that you don't want this baby. I have a beautiful home, a great job, and more than $1 million dollars in the bank. I can raise this child alone, and I will."

"Wow, Penny, that was some speech," Tyler noted. "Now who's pride and anger is showing?"

He crossed the large bedroom so quickly, it scared her. He stopped inches away and put his hands on her shoulders. She braced herself. When she looked up, he was smiling. He took her face in his hands and kissed her eyes, her nose, and her lips.

"Dr. Kilmer, you're one hell of a woman," he said. "I love you more than life itself." He then kneeled in front of her and began to lightly rub, caress, and kiss her tummy. All she could do was run her fingers through his hair and cry.

Finally, he stood and said, "I'm sorry, babe. I guess I didn't take the news too well, but I couldn't be more pleased."

"Why did you say this changes everything?" she asked.

"Bad choice of words. I didn't think about how it sounded. Last week we had some very important meetings. I'm planning a huge expansion for our company. We're going to expand what we do into Canada and Europe. When you told me about the baby, I guess I sort of freaked out. The business side of my brain kicked into gear. I'll need to put some things on the back burner and restructure the company."

"Why would you need to do all that?" she asked.

"Because I have to be with you," he said.

"Tyler, the baby won't be here for seven and a half months."

"I know, but I'm going to be a daddy, and I don't intend to miss one minute. Besides, we have lots of things to do."

Penny nuzzled his neck and asked, "What kinds of things?"

"Well, lots of things. I need to meet the doctor, or maybe fly in another doctor. We need to find out about the proper diet and exercise for an expectant mother. We need to learn about the pros and cons of breast-feeding. I have to get us enrolled in Lamaze classes and decide where the baby will be born. Oh, and we need to choose possible names for a boy or girl.

"Then, we need to plan a nursery and build it. We need a perfect crib and lots of baby stuff. I guess we'll need a nanny, or maybe not. I'm not sure. You'll need lots of designer maternity clothes. You know, like bigger bras, and maybe some nursing bras, and comfortable shoes. I think maybe stuff for your tummy. You know, creams and lotions to help prevent stretch marks.

"I need to learn to give massages and proper back rubs. Pregnant women need lots of back and leg rubs. I have to get books on child-rearing, so we know what to expect and not make any mistakes. I think there's a good one by a Dr. Spock. Oh, and we need to decide whether we are going to use plastic or cloth diapers. They make many different kinds of strollers, so we need to learn about them. We're going to be very busy. We'll need a playpen too. Probably more than one.

"Oh my God! I forgot the most important thing. We need to talk to the doctor about sex. You know, like the safest positions and when to stop before the baby is born. We've got a lot to do."

It didn't seem right to laugh at the father of her child, but Penny did. She wasn't sure if he was finished or just pausing to reload. "That was some list you reeled off there, Harrison. Are you going to be one of those doting husbands and fathers?"

"Absolutely! Do you think I left out anything?" Tyler asked.

"That was very impressive, but yes, at least one very important thing," Penny noted.

"Okay, what's that?"

"Marriage."

"Of course. We can deal with that later. Come on now. We have guests waiting, and we've been up here too long."

"Not yet. After all this, I need to touch up my makeup and hair. Have Brenda bring up my purse."

"Okay, Mom. You've got it. I love you, babe." With that, Tyler was gone.

Penny smiled. What a man. How long would she have to observe Tyler Harrison being Tyler Harrison?

*　*　*

Penny and Tyler emerged from the bedroom and began walking toward the stairs. Her hair and makeup weren't great, but it was the best she could do with what she had in her purse. Penny suddenly stopped. "Sweetheart, do you want a boy or a girl?"

Tyler thought for a moment. "Well, I'd like ten fingers and ten toes. The sex isn't important. Besides, with you for a mother, I know whatever we have will be intelligent and very attractive."

Penny raised on her tiptoes and kissed Tyler. "Good answer, Harrison."

"Thank you, and after that little episode in the bedroom, remind me to never piss you off again."

Penny smiled. "I can do that." She absolutely felt regal as she descended the stairs with her man.

Then Tyler led her to the center of the huge living room. "Would everyone please gather around?" Tyler said. "I have a rather important announcement to make."

Penny immediately pulled Tyler closer and began to whisper in his ear. "What are you doing?"

"I'm going to burst if I don't tell everyone about the baby."

"Are you sure you want to do this now?"

Tyler kissed her on the cheek. "Yes, I'm sure. Why not?"

"I thought you might want to wait. Will this have a negative effect on your business?"

Tyler turned and grinned at the curious guests, as if asking for a little more patience. He leaned back toward Penny and whispered, "I'm going to be a daddy, and the most beautiful woman I have ever known is going

315

to have my baby. I don't think this will affect our business, and honestly, I don't give a damn."

"Okay, sweetheart, go for it," Penny agreed.

Tyler turned to the guests and smiled. "Sorry you all had to wait. It appears that I've been given permission to continue."

Penny smiled and gave Tyler a loving elbow to the ribs. Tyler took Penny's hand in his.

"Well, we have some news," Tyler began. "I'm going to be … well, I mean Penny is going … actually, we are … Okay. Let me start again. As you can see, I'm a little excited."

Penny was loving it—Tyler at a loss for words! He looked like a kid under the tree on Christmas morning.

Tyler continued. "I planned this party today to give Penny a special gift, and once again, she managed to beat me at my own game." Tyler's voice began to fail, and he paused. "This beautiful creature has just given me the best news I've ever received. We're going to have a baby!"

The guests cheered, and Grandma Ruth leaped from her chair and said, "Well, you took long enough, Tyler!"

Everyone wanted hugs and details. When the party was about to break up, Tyler asked for quiet one more time.

"In all the excitement today, I almost forgot. I did bring a gift for Penny." Tyler led Penny to one of the sofas. "You're wearing heels, and it's been a very long day for a mother-to-be. Sit down for a minute."

Penny gladly sat between Grandma and Brenda.

"Liz," Tyler asked, "do you have that box?"

Liz appeared through the guests, carrying a rather large cardboard box. She handed it to Tyler and stepped away.

"Thank you, Liz." Tyler peered into the box for a while. He pulled out a rather large gift-wrapped package. "No. This isn't it," he said and tossed it toward the foyer. He reached into the box, retrieved another wrapped package, and tossed it too. "No. That wasn't it either. Oh, here it is."

Tyler stepped forward and dropped on one knee in front of Penny. He set the cardboard box on the floor. He looked at Penny and smiled.

"Dr. Penny Kilmer—I just love saying that, by the way." When the laughter settled, he continued. "Penny, you know how much I love you. Everyone who knows me knows two Tylers. The good Tyler when we are together and the bad Tyler when we aren't. I'm asking you to make me the good Tyler for the rest of my life."

He reached into the box one last time and came out with a tiny, elegant, purple velvet box. He opened it and held it so she could see.

"Oh my God!" she said through her tears. "It matches the ring Grandma gave you."

Tyler smiled and leaned forward and kissed her. "Yes, it's a perfect match. Grandma's ring will be your wedding ring, and this will be your engagement ring. It is one of a kind, beautiful, and unique—just like the lady who will wear it."

"Tyler, it's perfect," Penny gasped. "I love it."

"Babe, I've been blessed and received many gifts, but you'll always be my greatest gift." He eased the ring onto her finger. "Will you honor me and be my wife?"

"Yes."

"A little louder, Penny," Brenda said.

"Yes!"

"One more thing," Tyler said. "A lot of people in this room know about the nickname my family gave me when I was younger. Penny, from this day forward, I promise that you'll always be the greatest source of my pride and passion."

arry Hall was born in Buckhannon, West Virginia. It's a small, sleepy town with a beautiful private college and an abundance of good people. His youth was spent with great parents, lots of sports, and many young friends. During his junior and senior years of high school, Harry attended Fishburne Military School in Virginia for a little polishing, and he graduated with honors.

After school and some college, he began an entrepreneurial career that continues to this day. Harry has been a land developer, residential and commercial building contractor, restaurant owner, and furniture business owner. One of his proudest accomplishments was returning to college in his late thirties and obtaining degrees in accounting, economics, education, and history.

Although semiretired and living in Florida, Harry has remained very active. His interests include flying private planes, riding his Harley, owning and managing a large business in Maryland, dabbling in other business interests, and traveling and playing golf with his wife, Peggy. Harry and his wife met in Florida and have been happily married for sixteen years. Harry credits her for inspiring him to finish *Pride and Passion* and for absolutely being the best thing ever in his life.

Author's Note

Many authors draw from their own life experiences when writing, as have I. Some of my wonderful and unusual experiences are loosely paralleled in this work of fiction. This novel has been in the making for more than fifteen years, but when the last paragraph was written, when the process was finished, I knew I would miss it.

I discovered that giving life to *Pride and Passion* has been a personal revelation. It has been the best and only therapy I've ever had. I'm convinced there is a better man inside me. If he ever emerges, I know I will welcome him with open arms.

Most of my pride and many of my passions can be found woven into these pages. During the writing and editing of *Pride and Passion*, I have often laughed and cried. It is my hope that my readers will do the same.